THE FRONTLINE FUGITIVES

NICK JACOBELLIS

BOOK I THE KHAKI COPS

The Frontline Fugitives Book I: The Khaki Cops

Copyright ©2016 by Nick Jacobellis

ISBN 978-0-9982956-0-2

Cover photographs by Alex Landeen of Landeen Photography

Book design by www.StoriesToTellBooks.com

E Mail: badgepublishing@gmail.com

Website: www.badgepublishing.com

CONTENTS

INTRODUCTION

he Frontline Fugitives is a plot driven historical fiction story about the search for two 18 year old fugitives, who join the U.S. Army to avoid arrest, after they rob a bank that results in the death of a New York City Police Officer. Their escape plan is both daring and ingenious. While being assisted by an aging retired gangster, the two fugitives change their appearance as best as possible and use fictitious identities to get through the Selective Service induction process. Once the two fugitives are inducted into the U.S. Army, the wanted men "blend in" with millions of troops and look forward to the day when they can live on foreign soil as free men when the war is over. Even if the two fugitives don't survive the war, dying in battle seems like a much better alternative than being arrested and convicted in a New York court for murder, bank robbery and other serious crimes.

The readers of The Frontline Fugitives Book I and Book II will follow the adventures of a fictional New York City based U.S. Army CID Task Force that is responsible to investigate black-market activities and conduct other criminal investigations during World War II. When government officials learn that the two fugitives joined the U.S. Army as a way to facilitate their escape, law enforcement officers from various agencies join forces with U.S. Army Investigators to pursue the fugitives identified as Ivan Larson and Francis Shorty Mc Ghee.

The hunt for the two fugitives is complicated by the fact that the wanted teenage felons have no prior criminal history. The investigators working this case are also unable to find any personal photographs of the two fugitives. Without photographs or fingerprints of the two subjects, the civilian and military investigators are unable to prevent the fugitives from being inducted into the U.S. Army.

The fact that the main witness in the case is a Negro Police Officer, also creates certain operational problems for the two primary law enforcement characters of this story. This is the case because it is no easy task for a Negro Police Officer (Patrolman Al Parker) and a white U.S. Army CID Agent (Major James Beauregard) to travel together in a segregated society while searching Army bases for two fugitives. Even more bizarre is how U.S. military personnel during World War II were segregated, despite the fact that white troops and African American soldiers were killed and wounded on the same battlefields without discrimination. The insanity of it all is mind-boggling, yet it happened.

Finding the two fugitives among the millions of men who are serving in the U.S. Army during World War II proves to be no easy task, especially when months pass and the members of the CID Task Force have to face the possibility that Ivan Larson and Shorty Mc Ghee could be serving overseas. This concern places tremendous pressure on the members of the U.S. Army CID Task Force as they race against time to locate the two fugitives.

The Frontline Fugitives Book I and Book II also lives up to the definition of good historical fiction by accurately describing what it was like to be a black market operator, a violent criminal, a fugitive, a police officer, a police detective, a police captain, a federal agent, a Provost Marshal, a military policeman, a U.S. Army CID Agent, an infantry soldier fighting in the jungles of Guadalcanal, a combat medic, a C47 pilot, a glider pilot, a U.S. Army Glider Infantryman and a U.S. Army Paratrooper during World War II. This includes characters from different ethnic backgrounds. Last but not least, this story also includes a number of named and unnamed characters who represent the forces of evil.

A NOTE FROM THE AUTHOR

I began writing *The Frontline Fugitives* Book I and Book II before the new Millennium. In between working on other projects, I finished Book I and Book II in the early summer of 2016. One of the reasons it took so long to complete Book I and Book II, is because I was determined to make *The Frontline Fugitives* as historically accurate as possible, while supporting a "believable" fictional plot and a cast of "believable" fictional characters.

In order to complete this process, I had to learn as much as I could about various subjects to include, life in New York City from the early 1900s to the 1940s, life in southern states during World War II, the history of the New York City Police Department and other law enforcement agencies during the early and mid 20th Century, the history of racism, segregation, ethnic rivalry and the assimilation of various ethnic groups in the United States, life in Nazi Germany before and during World War II, rationing and black market activities in the United States and in Europe during World War II, the Selective Service induction process during World War II, as well as information about basic training and life in the U.S. Army during World War II.

I also had to become familiar with The Punitive Expedition into Mexico in 1916, trench warfare and combat actions during World War 1, the duties of the military police, the U.S. Army's Provost Marshal's Office and the U.S. Army Criminal Investigations Division during World War II, U.S. Army glider training and various battles including, The Guadalcanal Campaign, The North African Campaign, The Invasion of Sicily, The Italian Campaign, The D Day Invasion of Normandy, France on June 6, 1944, Operation Market Garden – The Invasion of Holland in September of 1944 and The Battle of the Bulge in December of 1944.

One of my greatest sources of information for this book was my father, Benedict Jacobellis, a member of The Greatest Generation who was born and raised in New York City and served in the U.S. Army during World War II. As a boy growing up in the Flatbush section of Brooklyn, my father told me a seemingly endless number of stories about life in New York City before and during the war, as well as about life in the U.S. Army during World War II. These stories included information about rationing and black-market operations in New York City during the war years.

I also relied on my father-in-law, Louis Evangelista, a U.S. Army veteran who served as a member of the Allied Occupation Force in Germany, who at 88 years of age is able to remember details from the 1930s and 40s as if it was yesterday. In addition, I had several uncles and cousins who served in World War II.

While conducting research for this book, I also interviewed World War II veterans who served as U.S. Army Flight Officers and flew CG-4A Waco Gliders on a number of combat missions in the European Theater of Operation. Interviewing former U.S. Army glider pilots gave me a much greater insight into what it was like to fly an aircraft that had no engine in combat. Even some of the more personal tidbits of information that World War II veterans shared with me, helped to bring this historical fiction story to life.

Being an Italian American, who grew up in New York City in an era when different forms of ethnic rivalry and racism were prevalent, also enabled me to create certain characters from a historically accurate perspective. Some of the observations that I made while traveling and working in different parts of the country, also made it possible to develop a realistic fictional story line.

Over the years I also became familiar with various World War II era military and law enforcement firearms. This included field testing many of the law enforcement and military revolvers, pistols, rifles, carbines and submachine guns that are featured in The Frontline Fugitives. In addition, I became familiar with World War II era U.S. Army and German uniforms and equipment. I accomplished this by collecting military clothing and equipment, by attending one of the largest and most elaborately planned World War II reenactments and by visiting museums and other venues where antique military uniforms and equipment were displayed and sold.

Driving a World War II era Jeep around the U.S. Navy Base in Guantanamo Bay, Cuba, when I directed and participated in covert operations during our nation's Drug War, made it possible for me to experience what it was like to operate the most famous compact 4x4 vehicle of the 1940's. This is an important point because World War II era Jeeps are featured in a number of critical scenes in this series of books. Over the years, I also became familiar with other World War II era military, civilian and law enforcement vehicles.

I also became considerably more familiar with the capabilities of the twin engine DC3/C47 that was used to tow GC4A Waco Gliders during WWII, when my colleagues and I in the U.S. Customs Service used one of these amazing aircraft in one of our covert air operations during the Drug War. Learning how to fly and safely land a small single engine aircraft, with and without the engine operating, also made it possible for me to accurately depict certain flying scenes in this book series.

The fact that I survived the crash landing of a large twin engine (ex military) undercover aircraft, was a life changing event that had a significant impact on my ability to describe certain critical aviation scenes in Book I and Book II. During this in flight emergency I volunteered to serve as the co pilot and assisted the Contract Pilot in Command, even though at the time I had an expired student pilot's license and very limited flying experience. Serving as a co pilot during such a serious inflight emergency, also contributed to my ability to develop certain characters from a personal perspective.

My experience as a federal agent, uniformed police officer and New York (Manhattan) District Attorney's Office Investigator also enabled me to accurately develop the "police procedural" aspects of this story. I also relied heavily on my experience as a law enforcement officer who recruited and directed a number of reliable informants to develop characters such as Tony G., a colorful mobster who volunteers to assist military and civilian law enforcement officers investigate black market operations during World War II.

In order to make The Frontline Fugitives Book I and Book II as accurate as possible, I also included a number of footnotes to credit the research sources that provided the copyrighted information that was used to support aspects of the plot and aid in character development. *A list of general references sources and footnotes can be found at the end of the book.

I especially wish to thank Dr. Don Abbe, the Director of the Silent Wings Museum in Lubbock, Texas, for the assistance that he provided when I was putting the finishing touches to sections of this book that involve glider training and glider combat operations during World War II.

Two contacts in Belgium also assisted me when I put the finishing touches to the section of Book II that involves the GC-4A Waco glider resupply mission to a landing zone near the Village of Savy (a little over one mile northwest of Bastogne) on December 27, 1944. One particular photograph and one map that was provided by a contact from Belgium enabled me to complete a critical fiction aspect of this fugitive manhunt story, while making every effort to remain as true to actual terrain features as possible.

While every effort was made to make The Frontline Fugitives as realistic and historically accurate as possible, it is important to remember that this is a fiction story set in the 1940s when the world was at war. As a result, certain liberties had to be taken in order to combine fictional characters and a fictional plot with historically accurate events that occurred during the early and mid 20th Century.

*The names that were used in this book to identify different primary and secondary fictional characters were selected because the author liked the sound of these names. It is also important to remember that certain fictional characters included in this book are portrayed performing duties that were performed by real people who served with distinction in civilian life, in law enforcement positions, as well as in the U.S. Armed Forces during World War II. This includes enlisted men, non commissioned officers and commissioned officers who served in different training commands, support units and combat units. There is also no connection between any of the fictional characters in this book and anyone who lived in the past or is alive today. This includes individuals who served in the same or similar capacities as the fictional characters in this book.

*In order to be historically accurate this series of books uses the words Negro and colored to refer to African Americans because these words were commonly used in the early and mid 20th Century. Even though the "N Word" was used sparingly, this word was used in certain key scenes because it is historically accurate to do so. This book also includes other slang words and language that was commonly used in the early and mid 1900s.

This book series is dedicated to those who served in military and civilian positions and protected the United States and our allies during World War II. Clearly, the victory that was achieved during World War II, was made possible because decent law abiding human beings from different backgrounds banded together to fight the forces of evil.

Special thanks to my grandmother Fanny Budani for encouraging me to live my dreams in life and to my grandfather Nick Jacobellis for all that he taught me about life and my Italian heritage. Last but not least, I thank my wife for cheering me on and being incredibly supportive, while I completed this and other writing projects.

CHAPTER 1

PATRICK MURPHY JR. NEW YORK CITY COP TURNED JUNGLE FIGHTER

To the average American who lived and served during World War II, the Japanese were sneaky bastards who did not believe in the Marcus of Queens Berry rules when it came to fighting a war. In fact, the Japanese waged war under a code known as Bushido, a code that made it an honor to die for the Emperor of Japan and a disgrace to submit to capture. In contrast, most American soldiers would only fall on a live grenade to save a buddy and no one in his right mind ever rushed a Japanese machine gun nest for Franklin Delano Roosevelt. As far as most Americans were concerned, they fought because they were there and someone had to do it.

Despite the Hollywood image of American soldiers hitting the beach while patriotic music played in the background, the average American serviceman dreamed of the day when they could go home in one piece. Those who had no stomach for desertion, and preferred civilian life over being in the service, prayed for a "million dollar wound" that was serious enough to take them off the line but not disable them for life. The servicemen who were less fortunate were seriously disfigured, made blind, crippled and scarred for life in some way by their involvement in the war. The men who paid the ultimate sacrifice were laid to rest with other servicemen in a military cemetery on foreign soil. Sailors and some marines who were killed in action were buried at sea.

Unlike many young men of his day, Patrick Murphy Jr. was not obligated to serve in time of war. As a Patrolman with the New York City Police Department, Pat was exempt from military service because he was considered a member of an essential service at home. Regardless of how much his police career meant to him, enlisting in the U.S. Army on December 8, 1941 was above and beyond the call of duty and something that young Patrick did without hesitation.

Like many Americans, Patrick Murphy Jr. saw the sneak attack on Pearl Harbor as a violent assault on his virtuous nation. Pat also saw the German occupation of Europe as a sign of trying times to come. As a result, the youngest member of the Murphy clan decided to do more than sit out the war in the relative safety of his blue police uniform. Even though cops occasionally died in the line of duty back home, Patrick Murphy Jr. was a lot safer in the worst neighborhood in New York City than in any jungle in the Solomon Islands.

After serving as a patrolman for two years, Patrick enlisted in the Army with the hope of being sent into combat as soon as possible. Many of the men he left behind were older and had families. Others like his father served in World War I and already knew the horrors of war. The rest accepted their deferments and decided to remain behind to protect the city until he returned.

Despite his desire to fight the enemy, it took some doing for Pat to avoid the Army's plans to assign him to a military police unit. No matter how close some MPs could get to combat, Pat Murphy Jr. had no intention of giving up his police career so he could become a cop in the Army.

Once he made his way into a rifle squad, Pat was only a boat ride away from being deposited on a Japanese infested island in the Pacific. Although saving Australia from invasion was clearly a worthwhile cause, the ultimate objective was to turn the tide of the Japanese advance and achieve victory over the enemy.

As far as Pat and his fellow servicemen were concerned, the Allies had to turn the tide of the Japanese advance or risk losing the war in the Pacific. To prevent this from happening, the United States took the fight to the enemy in the Solomon Islands. This offensive began with the landing of U.S. Marines on Guadalcanal and Tulagi in August of 1942. In October of 1942, U.S. Army troops landed on Guadalcanal to help the U.S. Marines defeat the Japanese. As a result, Guadalcanal became the hell hole where Patrick Murphy Jr. would be tested in battle.

Making corporal happened back in the states after basic training. Due to his police background, Pat was light years ahead of many of the other recruits, including others like him who attended college for a period of time. This was the case because Patrolman Patrick Murphy Jr. knew how to follow orders and defend himself while using his hands and a firearm.

The Army's decision to promote Pat was a case of supply and demand. This happened when Pat's squad leader was killed in action and his company commander promoted him on the spot to sergeant. Due to the needs of the service, the business of waging war was a very callous and impersonal experience. One day you were alive and calling the shots and the next day someone was taking your place before the Graves Registration Unit threw the first shovel full of dirt on your face.

While armed with a Thompson Submachine Gun, a supply of spare magazines, a canteen, a razor sharp RH PAL 36 U.S. Army Combat Knife and his trusty police service revolver, Patrick Murphy Jr. followed his men on another patrol. As Pat's squad made its way deeper into the jungle, he wondered how the new replacements would perform, if the patrol encountered any of the enemy troops who were still offering resistance on Guadalcanal. Even though the new men seemed eager to get into action, no one really knew for sure how they would react when they came face to face with the harsh realities of war.

Jungle fighting was a nerve racking experience, one that was almost impossible to describe in words. In addition to the different sights and sounds, nothing on this earth could compete with its beauty, or the stench of death that was produced in the jungle. Jungle warfare was an especially new experience for soldiers who were born and raised in urban areas, small towns or on a farm. In fact, all the flag waving and patriotic slogans in the world didn't mean shit when you faced a group of fanatical Japanese soldiers in combat.

In addition to having to deal with the enemy, jungle fighters also had to operate in very challenging terrain, that included its fair share of snakes, bugs and vermin. With the monsoon rains came mosquitoes and malaria. The heat and the humidity was also intense enough to bring the toughest men to their knees, especially when troops experienced a shortage of purified drinking water.

Living with very little sleep in mud soaked fox holes and canvass tents, combined with the threat of being picked off by a sniper and enemy shelling, wore away at a man's body, mind, heart and soul like cancer. Troops who served in a forward area also had to cope with periods of waiting for things to happen. This included waiting for the enemy to attack, waiting for the word to move out and waiting for the mail from home to arrive. Having a bad case of the shits in the comfort of your own home was bad enough, but getting diarrhea and dysentery while living and fighting in the jungle was the definition of hell on earth.

At twenty five years of age, Patrick Murphy Jr. had seen enough carnage in his short time in combat to last several lifetimes. In the real world, home was a place with clean sheets, cold beer and three squares a day. On Guadalcanal, Pat Murphy Jr. lived in anything but civilized conditions, that included having to fight the Japanese in order to secure the island so it could be used as a base to project Allied power in the region.

Even though they didn't know it at the time, Pat and his men were one of the last rifle squads to engage the Japanese before Guadalcanal was officially declared secure. As usual, no one saw the Japanese sniper or knew where the shot was fired from that took the life of the man on point. Since Pat and the bulk of his patrol was comprised of combat veterans, his squad immediately reacted to the obvious presence of an enemy sniper by spraying the nearby tree tops with small arms fire.

After tapping his BAR gunner on the back, while he reloaded his automatic rifle, Pat gave his men the command to hold their fire. As soon as his men stopped shooting, the entire patrol braced for more contact with the enemy. By early 1943 Pat Murphy Jr. was a combat tested squad leader and his men knew it. It was even more amazing how the Irish American city policeman from Manhattan was at home in the jungle.

Immediately after spotting a flash of movement in front of their position, Pat directed his squad members to fan out and take cover along the edge of the tree line that ran parallel to a shallow jungle stream. A split second later all hell broke loose, as sixteen screaming and disheveled Japanese soldiers made their way across the shallow stream that separated one side of this jungle battlefield from the other.

The moment Pat spotted a hand-grenade coming his way he called out, "Grenade," as he threw the young rifleman on his right to the ground and covered him with his own body. As soon as the Japanese grenade exploded near the edge of the tree line, Pat qualified for his first Purple Heart when the back of his left shoulder was peppered with fragments of hot steel.

While his men raked the charging Japanese assault force with small arms fire, Pat did his best to ignore the pain as he helped the young G.I. up from the ground. As the battle raged on, Pat fired a short burst from his submachine gun at the sword wielding Japanese Lieutenant who was leading the charge on his side of the formation. When the mortally wounded enemy officer fell face down in the middle of the stream, Pat and the young rifleman, that he just saved from the grenade blast, continued firing and killed a pair of Japanese privates before they were able to reach their position.

When the bulk of the Japanese troops shifted their attack to the left side of his patrol's defensive position, Pat turned to the soldier who was reloading his Browning Automatic Rifle and slapped the top of his steel helmet to get his attention. While Private Pete Mackie from Philadelphia finished reloading his BAR from a kneeling position, he looked up as Pat motioned to the left and screamed, "Shift your fire!" All it took was one nod from Pat's BAR man to know that his order was received.

The Browning Automatic Rifle was an amazing weapon that was worth its weight in gold at times like this. While loaded with a twenty round metal box magazine, the gas operated 19.5 pound 1918A2 BAR could fire 350 or 550 rounds of .30-06 caliber ammunition a minute depending on the setting. As soon as Pete Mackie retracted the bolt to load the chamber, he had his BAR spitting out burst after burst of 30.06 caliber bullets at the enemy.

Being attacked by a screaming and fanatical enemy was a terrifying experience, especially for the newer men in a rifle squad. The closer the enemy got to your position the more scared you became. Even combat veterans were tempted to bang away as fast as possible to satisfy the desire to survive at all costs. Pat Murphy Jr. knew better and had no problem shooting his Thompson in short bursts, unless it was absolutely necessary to mow the enemy down gangster style. After two of his men dropped a pair of Japanese soldiers who almost made it to the tree line, Pat shot and killed another Japanese soldier who carried an American pistol in one hand and a machete in the other.

By now, Pat's entire squad was unleashing holy hell on the charging enemy with an assortment of infantry weapons. As the enemy soldiers fell like pins in a bowling alley, Pat spotted a Japanese sergeant strike the side of his helmet with a hand grenade to activate the fuse while he ran toward the BAR gunner's position.

While Pat screamed, "Pete, look out," Pat fired a short burst that stopped the Japanese sergeant dead in his tracks, just as the enemy soldier tossed his grenade toward the BAR man's position. As both men instinctively turned away from the blast, the grenade exploded just as Pat covered his BAR gunners body with his own. Once again, Pat Murphy Jr. absorbed the bulk of the shrapnel from the explosion but recovered quickly.

After throwing the last of their grenades, the remaining members of the Japanese assault force made their way across the stream and continued to attack the American patrol. While a pair of screaming enemy soldiers armed with bayonet tipped rifles charged their position, the 18 year old infantryman on Pat's right lost the tip of his right ear as he frantically tried to reload his M1 Garand. As Pat stepped in front of the wounded G.I., he killed the closest of the two enemy combatants with a long burst of fire.

Despite his combat experience, this was the first time that Pat found himself with an empty Thompson in hand when he needed to defend himself. As the veteran jungle fighter instinctively removed his steel helmet and threw it at his attacker, a bullet fired from the enemy soldier's Ariska rifle penetrated Pat's left shoulder. Once again Pat put his training to good use, as he stepped to the side and grabbed the enemy soldier's bayonet tipped rifle by the barrel. As soon as Pat slammed the Japanese private against the side of a tree, the G.I. with the wounded ear stepped forward and fired two rounds from his reloaded M1 Garand into the enemy soldier's chest.

After thanking the youngest member of his squad for coming to his rescue, Pat leaned against a tree and watched some of his men reload their rifles while others took care of the wounded. Between his time as a police officer and his experience as a jungle fighter, Pat Murphy Jr. had developed his instincts enough to suspect that this engagement wasn't over. As soon as Pat spotted two of his men step out into the open, to check the enemy casualties for intelligence information, the combat tested squad leader called out to his men. "Not yet, pull back!"

The second the two American G.I.s began to return to their previous positions, several rifle shots rang out that wounded one of the two soldiers before he made his way back to the cover of the tree line. Rather than attempt to retrieve and reload his Thompson, Pat drew his six shot Colt Official Police Model .38 Special revolver just as a second wave of enemy soldiers launched a follow-up attack.

While ignoring the potential threat to his own safety, Pat stepped out into the open and systemically began to shoot all five attacking enemy soldiers from a standing unsupported position. His performance was such an amazing spectacle that none of Pat's men opened fire. Instead, they stood by and watched their sergeant use his police service revolver to shoot and kill all five Japanese soldiers as if they were targets in a penny arcade.

For his actions that day Sergeant Patrick Murphy Jr. would receive the Silver Star in addition to a well earned Purple Heart. While four of his men sustained minor shrapnel and gunshot wounds, only one was killed in action. Of the entire attack force, only one wounded enemy soldier was brought back for interrogation.

As strange as it sounds, Sergeant Patrick Murphy Jr. was not all that happy to be helped out of the jungle and brought down to the beach for evacuation. Privately, Pat had to admit to himself that he was beginning to like being a leader of men in combat. In fact, in a strange sort of way, Pat felt just as cheated as he did lucky to be leaving Guadalcanal. Pat was also concerned that the U.S. Army would never let him return to combat and that his wounds might also be serious enough to prevent him from retuning to his duties as a Patrolman with the New York City Police Department.

After taking care of Patrick's multiple wounds, a U.S. Army doctor slipped a cigarette in between the young sergeant's lips while he waited to be evacuated down to the beach. When Pat asked if any of his wounds were bad enough to keep him from returning to his job as a police officer, the Army surgeon gently patted the side of his patient's right arm and said, "We'll know more once we get you on a hospital ship. In the meantime, try not to move and let the morphine do its job." The aid station doctor then turned to a nearby medic and said, "Sergeant Murphy is ready for his boat ride."

Nothing on the face of this earth could duplicate the effects of a shot of morphine. Within a matter of seconds Pat's eyes became filled with peace and tranquility as the pain of his multiple wounds began to fade away. As the Army Medic saw the patient's eyes begin to close, he pulled the burning cigarette from Sergeant Murphy's lips just as the liter bearers arrived by his cot.

As the wounded squad leader was transported down to the beach, Pat submitted to the pain medication and slipped off to sleep. Moments later Pat's dream was briefly interrupted by the sound of the ocean slapping up against the flat bow of the LCVP Higgins boat. While part of him desperately wanted to take one more look at Guadalcanal, the power of the morphine lured young Patrick back into a restful dreamlike state. Shortly after Pat went back to sleep, the landing craft that was made in New Orleans pulled up along side the hospital ship to unload its wounded passengers.

By the time Guadalcanal was declared secure in February of 1943, it became clear that the Americans and their Allies were determined to wipe the Japanese from the face of the earth, even if it meant that the U.S. had to take on two powerful enemies at the same time. Unfortunately, victory over the Axis Forces would take time to achieve.

CHAPTER 2

PATROLMAN AL PARKER

Because Al Parker was a 44 year old married police officer and World War 1 veteran he was exempt from military service during World War II. Even though he had his fill of army life in 1918, there were times when it disturbed Al that he was too old to serve. Al felt this way because like other Americans he had no love for the Japanese or the Nazi's. It was even harder for Al to watch Pat Murphy Jr. go off to war, then see his two sons enlist, while he stayed home to protect the City of New York.

The day that Al heard that young Patrick was wounded he went straight to the nearest church to pray for the young man he called his friend. Then the good news came and it was time to celebrate. Al's young protégé returned from the Pacific in one piece, even though a pair of Japanese grenades and a Jap rifle bullet sent Pat to several military hospitals before he was allowed to return home on leave.

Because the wounds that he sustained in battle were expected to cause young Patrick to lose a certain amount of mobility in his shoulder, the Army doctors disqualified him for combat duty. However, the same doctors certified him as being fit for stateside duty. After two surgical procedures, rehabilitation and some badly needed rest, Sergeant Patrick Murphy Jr. was ordered to assume the duties of a military policeman at Ft. Hamilton in Brooklyn.

As soon as Patrick heard that his combat days were over, he asked his father if he could pull a few strings and get him a medical discharge, as long as by doing so the police surgeon would declare him fit for duty as a patrolman with the department. After receiving this request from his youngest son, Police Captain Pat Murphy Sr. began the process of getting Patrick honorably medically discharged from the U.S. Army, so he could return to his previously held essential civil service position.

According to Selective Service Law, anyone on active duty was expected to serve for the duration of the war plus six months, unless a medical discharge was granted, or the person was court-marshaled. During World War II, medical

9

discharges were granted to military personnel who were permanently disabled and were unable to return to active duty. Servicemen who sustained less serious injuries or wounds who were unable to serve in combat, but were still able to serve, were assigned to non combat duties.

After a flurry of influential phone calls were made to the White House and the War Department, the decision was made to award Sergeant Patrick Murphy Jr. a medical discharge. The official reason for justifying this action was to return a decorated wounded soldier, who was unfit for combat, to his previous employment with a critical essential service at home.

After going through the formalities of being examined by a police surgeon, Patrick Murphy Jr. was certified fit for duty, even though the surgeon told him privately that his shoulder would probably give him trouble for the rest of his life. The day that Patrick "passed" his medical examination, his father welcomed him back into the police department at a party that went well into the early hours of the morning. Two days later Patrolman Patrick Murphy Jr. was back on patrol after qualifying with the same .38 Special Colt Official Police Model service revolver that he carried in combat on Guadalcanal.

Prior to the year 1911, the N.Y.P.D. also known as the P.D.N.Y. did not exist per say. Instead, New York City was comprised of various sections or neighborhoods that were broken up into five counties or boroughs, many of which had their own police force just like small towns do. New York City also had Negro police officers patrolling in Harlem as well as in Brooklyn long before the different agencies merged into one department.

Al Parker came on the job after the First World War, when the newly formed New York City Police Department hired white officers as well as a small number of colored men to serve as patrolmen. Even though the N.Y.P.D. established its own form of segregation, Al Parker knew that being a Negro cop in the 1920s, 30s and 40s was a tad better than being a Negro civilian. Like many of his friends, Al Parker was hoping that the atrocities that were being committed in the current conflict, would make people realize that it was wrong to treat another human being differently because of the color their skin, or because they had different religious beliefs.

While serving as a rookie cop, Al Parker was broken in by a veteran street cop who just happened to be Pat Murphy Jr's grandfather, a man who started his career with the Metropolitan Police and ended it as a Captain with the P.D.N.Y. As an "adopted" member of the Murphy clan, it only seemed right to have Al look after the youngest member of the Murphy family to re-join the department. With his grandfather now retired, his father recently promoted to Captain of Detectives and two of his older twin brothers and other relatives serving on the department, Pat Murphy Jr. was about as protected as any young cop on the job could be.

Because Al Parker was a U.S. Army veteran of W.W.I, it was easy for him to see that young Patrick was still coping with the horrors of jungle warfare whenever someone spoke of the war in his presence. As far as Al Parker was concerned, Pat Murphy Jr. may have been physically back in the states, but spiritually he never left Guadalcanal. All it took was a radio broadcast about the war, a newspaper headline or a car back firing for young Patrick to instantly transport himself back into the jungle. Just wondering who was killed, who was wounded and who was still alive in his old unit, was enough to make Pat chain smoke one cigarette after another in order to cope with a bad case of survivors guilt.

Even though Pat was grateful that his family had the political influence to get him discharged from the Army and returned to his police position, he wondered if being a cop would ever be the same after he used a variety of weapons to kill the enemy in combat. The more Pat wondered if he could make the transition from jungle fighter to policeman, the more he remembered the day when he used his service revolver to kill five Japanese soldiers. Even though Pat used the same police revolver on one occasion when he was a rookie cop, there was something about the last encounter that he had with the enemy that made Pat feel as if he was born to fight the forces of evil.

After completing his first week back on patrol, Pat Murphy Jr. did enough soul searching to resign himself to accept the fact that it was in his blood to serve as a member of the New York City Police Department. Once Pat realized that he never wanted to be a soldier until Pearl Harbor was attacked, he felt better about the idea of being back in the job that he wanted ever since he was a young boy.

In keeping with the request that was made by Pat Murphy Jr's father and his grandfather, Al Parker was assigned to the adjoining foot post that was patrolled by the youngest member of the Murphy clan to wear a police uniform. Just like other cops, Pat Murphy Jr. and Al Parker did their fair share of what was known as cooping. The trick to taking one of these unauthorized breaks, was to do so without getting caught by your sergeant. This day was no different.

The corner candy store that separated Al Parker's foot post from Pat's foot post was one of the best locations in the precinct for the local beat cops to use to take a break from their duties. Even though the back room was filled with magazines, newspapers and other merchandise, this location was dedicated as a safe haven where policemen could get away from the hustle and bustle of the city. Even in the summer months, this particular location was a comfortable place to relax, as long as the back door to the ally was kept open and a large fan worked overtime to cool the place off.

The owner of this corner store was a Jewish immigrant businessman known in the neighborhood as Cheap Charlie, a name that Mr. Federman did not deserve because he was a generous and hardworking man, especially as far as the police were concerned.

After seeing his young friend arrive, a smiling Al Parker held up a generous piece of Mrs. Federman's famous Applesauce Cake and said, "I'll bet you didn't get cake like this on Guadalcanal."

While Al sat on an empty wooden milk crate, a pissed off Patrolman Patrick Murphy Jr. stood in front of the fan to cool off and remarked, "I just had a run in with some up town asshole who tried to tell me I couldn't give him a ticket because he was a dollar a year man and was doing more for the war effort than I was.... Do you believe the crap that we have to put up with?"

"I hope you wrote his sanctimonious ass up," responded Al Parker, before he finished his piece of cake and washed it down with a sip of hot coffee.

The sight of Mrs. Federman entering the back room, while carrying a cup of coffee and a dish that contained a large slice of cake, brought Pat to meet the old woman halfway as she greeted him and said, "Here, Patrick. I made plenty so don't hesitate to ask for more."

When Pat graciously accepted the cup of free coffee and the slice of homemade cake, the young cop smiled and said, "Thank you, Mrs. Federman."

Once the kind old lady returned to the front of the store, Pat took a bite of the cake then sipped some coffee before he turned to Al and remarked, "I got my quota in for the month on that prick."

While Al removed a cigar from the open box that rested on a stack of news-papers, he looked at his young protege and said, "Good job. Now sit down and take a load off the floor."

After lighting the tip of his cigar with a wooden match, Al sat back against the wall and filled the back room with a cloud of light gray smoke. As the veteran patrolman looked at his young friend, he smiled as he held up the cigar box and remarked, "They're a little stale, but the price is right."

Even twenty months in the Army wasn't enough to make Pat forget what Al was really saying. Every cop knew that in police lingo the term "the price was right" "meant that the box of cigars were "on the arm" or free.

While Al extended his arm, he gave the box a jiggle before he lowered his hand and remarked, "Since when does a G.I. turn down free smokes?"

As Pat removed a Lucky Strike from the pack in his shirt pocket, the young cop seemed troubled as he shrugged his shoulders and said, "Come on, Al. You know I don't smoke stogies."

While Pat used his Zippo to light his cigarette, Al filled his hand with a mitt full of cigars from the open box and stuffed the stogies into Pat's police hat as he looked at his young friend and said, "No, but your grandfather does and so does your old man."

In an effort to raise the young cop's spirits, Al became philosophical as he sat back against the wall of the storeroom. "Your grandfather introduced me to the fine art of cigar smoking when I was assigned to be his driver."

After pausing for a second, Al continued. "I'll never forget my first night on patrol. It was cold as a witches tit." Al then got serious as he grabbed the left side of his chest and said, "Before we got into our car your grandfather grabbed my shield with his fist as he spoke with his heavy Irish brogue and said, "Alvin me boy, as long as you wear this badge you'll not be black or white, but blue and don't you ever forget that."

While Al tapped the ash from his cigar into a sand filled metal bucket, he continued as he looked directly at the smiling face of the young man who loved to hear stories about his family from one of the most famous Negro cops in the department. "One time your grandfather was out of cigars, so we had a drive into the neighboring precinct to find a store that was open at that hour. Don't you know it, but we walked right into a damn stick up."

As Al continued he leaned forward and slapped the top of Pat's left knee. "There I was, a rookie cop scared shitless about being off post, when this SOB started blazing away with a thirty two automatic." Then, in a much more serious tone, Al remarked, "We got our cigars that night all right."

Even though Pat Murphy Jr. heard this story before, he was never tired of hearing it again. As far as Pat Murphy Jr. was concerned, Al Parker was his favorite adopted uncle. After seeing Al pause while he puffed on his cigar, Pat spoke up and said, "You saved my grandfather's life that night."

While reacting as if what he did that night was no big deal, Al made a face and waved his right hand as he remarked, "I tripped that's all."

Pat had heard this story enough from his grandfather to know exactly what Al Parker did during that armed robbery in progress. Since Pat knew that Al was a humble man, he decided not to belabor the point about his heroic actions when Al was a rookie cop assigned to serve as his grandfather's driver.

After flicking the ash from his cigarette into the sand filled bucket, Pat chose his words carefully when he asked, "Does it bother you Al…I mean not getting promoted after all you did on this job?"

Patrolman Al Parker was one hell of a cop, a man who had survived two shootouts, including the time when he pushed Pat Murphy's grandfather aside and caught a bullet in the left shoulder during an armed robbery. The second shootout that Al survived took place when he was off duty and he observed two gunmen attempt to commit an armed robbery. When the smoke cleared one gunman was dead and the other was wounded.

When a white patrolman displayed such heroism it was common for the Police Commissioner to present the officer with a gold shield and an immediate promotion to the rank of Detective 3rd Grade. Being a Negro put Al behind the power curve so he graciously accepted another medal instead. Al also knew his limitations because he was not a good test taker. As a result, Al had little or no chance of ever scoring high enough on a civil service exam to get promoted to the rank of sergeant or lieutenant.

The fact that no test was required to be taken in order to get promoted to the rank of detective, meant that if Al wanted to advance in the department he had to make his way into the Detective Division. Becoming a 3rd Grade Detective also meant more to Al than making sergeant, because a detective's gold shield was awarded in recognition of an act of heroism and a cops ability to fight crime.

As far as Al Parker was concerned, nothing went with a good cigar better than a gold detective's shield, a new suit and a snub nose thirty eight caliber revolver. Unfortunately, even with the Murphy family serving as his "rabbi," the contract to promote Al Parker to the rank of 3rd Grade Detective could never be filled, not as long as there were others with more juice in the department who were white.

While speaking in a matter of fact tone of voice, Al remarked, "What can I tell ya."

As a persistent Pat Murphy Jr. leaned forward, he spoke as if he was more upset about his friend not being promoted than Al was. "I don't get it, Al. Forget about the two shootouts you were in, or all the felony collars you made, what about the fact that you speak fluent German. You'd think that detail you did in the Intelligence Division in the beginning of the war would have been more than enough for the PC to promote you."

Al appreciated young Patrick's kind words. Al also appreciated the strings that his father pulled for him to get him into that detail in the first place. Working in plainclothes on sensitive matters that related to the war effort seemed to be Al Parker's ticket into the Detective Division. As usual, Al did a magnificent job and worked his ass off to root out Nazi sympathizers in New York City. Unfortunately, Al's problem began when he refused to become the gofer for his superior, a man who didn't like having a Negro cop forced on his unit, even though he spoke German.

Al knew that he had to say something because his young friend's kind words deserved a response. After slowly crushing the remains of his cigar in a nearby ashtray, Al looked at Pat and said, "You know the story. Your old man did everything he could for me. I fucked it up, no one else."

Pat knew different and responded as respectfully as possible by saying, "That's not the way I heard it."

While continuing to look at his young friend, Al Parker remarked, "As much as I want'a gold shield I'll be dammed if I'm gonna let any boss on this job order me to wash his personal car once a week just to keep a detail that I earned because I speak German. Worse yet, that prick expected me to work miracles and keep every piece'a shit car in his family in running condition without going for spit."

After pausing for a split second, Al picked up where he left off and said, "You know me, Pat, I don't mind helping a fellow officer out but that son of a bitch, along with two of his relatives who are cops, dropped their cars off at my garage with a list of repairs that needed to be made as if I was their personal family mechanic. Everyone of those cheap bastards knows that I have a side business fixing cars and all they did was try and take advantage of me. I'm sorry but that's way too much ass kissing for me to do just to get a gold shield."

Once again Al paused for a split second before he continued. "You should'a seen the look on that boss's face when I told him that I wanted their pile of crappy cars removed from my private property 'cause I'm nobody's house nigger."

Like his father and grandfather Pat Murphy Jr. was a man before his time. Al Parker was a very close family friend and a first rate street cop who just happened to have a different color skin than the Murphys from County Cork. Even though there were some old tapes that played from time to time, the Murphys remembered their roots as poor Irish immigrants who were able to climb the social ladder as police officers in New York City.

From the moment that Alvin Parker joined the N.Y.P.D. the Murphy family let everyone know that Al risked his life and shed his blood without reservation to save the life of a young Army officer by the name of Patrick Murphy Sr. during World War I. Unfortunately, even though Al Parker's World War I heroics were well known in the department, he was still a Negro to some and a nigger to others.

The young patrolman knew by the way that Al reacted that he touched a nerve by taking this particular stroll down memory lane. Rather than push the issue any further, Pat spoke as he stood up and put on his dark blue police hat. "I'm sorry Al. I didn't mean to push the issue. I just hate to see you get screwed." Before Pat could go any further, Al was up on his feet and facing the young Irish cop.

After presenting a sincere smile, Al grabbed the young man on the side of his left arm and spoke in a very sincere tone of voice. "You know how much I worried when you were in combat on that hell hole of a Jap infested island?" As soon as Pat cracked a smile, Al continued. "You should'a seen your old man crying like a baby the day we found out that you were wounded. I've never seen a man cry like that before." Then, after pausing for a second, Al added in a more quiet tone, "Even I shed a tear or two."

After realizing what he just said, Al slapped Pat on the side of his arm as he transitioned to using a stern sounding tone of voice. "But don't let that get to your head. I'm under strict orders from your entire family to give you a good tongue lashing if I see you stepping outta line. Now get back on the job or else." Then, after a brief pause, Al added, "I'm not complaining mind you but between your father, your grandfather, those crazy brothers of yours and your other relatives who are cops calling at all hours to ask me how you're doing, being your honorary uncle is becoming a full time job."

When Mr. Federman entered the back room to say goodbye to the two patrolmen, Al spoke in German and said, "Once again you were a gracious host, Mr. Federman. Don't hesitate to call if you need anything."

After hearing Patrolman Murphy call out and say, "Take care, Mr. Federman. We'll stop by later to check on you and the Misses," Mr. Federman waved goodbye to the young war hero and said, "You and Al are always welcome, Patrick."

Charlie Federman appreciated the company of his two favorite local cops. For the price of a few cups of coffee, some of his wife's home made food, an occasional box of cigars and a carton or two of cigarettes, the man known as Cheap Charlie had all the police protection he could ever need. Being a German Jew made Mr. Federman appreciate the importance of having close ties with the police. In Nazi Germany the police were an extension of an evil state, while in America the police upheld the virtues of the Constitution and protected society from anarchy. In every respect, a good cop in America was worth the cost of a few considerations.

Luckily for Mr. Federman and his family, they were able to flee Germany before things became intolerable for Jews. Now that Mr. Federman was an American he would do anything for anyone who did all they could to keep the United States a nation where people were allowed to work hard and prosper. Even though prejudice still existed, the United States was a land of promise for all minorities and people on the bottom of the social ladder. In America the only way was up.

While it was true that Negroes, Jews and Italians couldn't get any lower on the social totem pole in New York City, it was possible to work hard and better their lives, even if it took twice the effort for some folks to succeed. Given the alternative, men like Charlie Federman and Al Parker did the best they could with what they had to work with. Besides, how could Charlie Federman pass up the chance to become friends with the only Negro policeman in New York City who spoke his native tongue.

CHAPTER 3

ARMED ROBBERY

As Ivan Larson flicked his cigarette butt into the gutter, he made sure not to make eye contact with any of the New Yorkers who were walking by the parked getaway car. Once the coast was clear, the soon to be eighteen year old hoodlum exited the stolen Oldsmobile and walked over to the doorway of a nearby apartment house.

While Ivan pulled a nylon stocking mask over his face, Terry Kelly waited behind the wheel of the getaway car. When Ivan was ready to make his move, he signaled Amos Washington to exit the back seat of the Oldsmobile. By the time Ivan entered the liquor store, his trusty Negro sidekick was following close behind.

The fact that old man Sweeny was hard of hearing became obvious, when Ivan Larson was able to sneak up behind the liquor store owner and knock him unconscious while he stocked his shelves with new inventory. As soon as Ivan eased the unconscious old man down to the floor, he instructed Amos to grab a case of liquor from the back room while he cleaned out the cash register.

While Amos headed for the storeroom, Ivan made his way behind the counter and quickly emptied the cash register. When Amos emerged from the back room carrying a case of scotch, Ivan grabbed Mr. Sweeny's licensed revolver and a box of ammunition from the ledge under the counter. With Amos following close behind, Ivan slipped the revolver and a box of ammunition in his pockets. After stopping by the front door to make sure it was safe to proceed, Ivan said, "Let's go," as he motioned Amos to follow him to the getaway car.

Once outside Amos quickly loaded the back seat of the getaway car with the stolen liquor, while Ivan walked around the front of the Oldsmobile and jumped into the front passenger seat. While Amos took a seat next to the case of scotch, Ivan closed the passenger door and said, "Nice and easy, Terry."

Even though they had access to an unlimited supply of black-market gasoline, Ivan instructed Terry to shut the engine off, to avoid raising suspicion when he parked the getaway car near the liquor store. After all, the average American would never sit in a parked car with the engine running when gasoline rationing was imposed to help the war effort. Less than two minutes after Terry started the engine and drove away from the scene of the crime, a customer walked into the liquor store and found old man Sweeny lying unconscious on the floor.

As soon as Ivan ripped off his stocking mask, he smiled from ear to ear as he held up a fistful of stolen money to show his partners in crime the fruits of their labor. After accepting a bottle of Dewars Scotch from Amos, the teenage criminal from the Hells Kitchen section of Manhattan removed the cork top and took a long drink of the burning liquor.

When Ivan asked Terry if he was thirsty, the young wheel man responded as he changed lanes. "I'll wait 'till we get back. Just save some for me."

"No problem. There's a bottle here with your name on it," remarked Ivan as he slapped the cork top back on the bottle.

After removing the stolen handgun from his pant's pocket, Ivan leaned over the front seat and passed old man Sweeny's nickel plated Hopkins and Allen Safety Model top break revolver to Amos. "This is for you, Amos. Compliments of old man Sweeny."

The fact that Amos was a Negro who could not complete an entire sentence without making a mess of his words, meant nothing to Ivan Larson because Amos was a hard working loyal son of a bitch. It was therefore Ivan's pleasure to relieve the unconscious Mr. Sweeny of his licensed revolver and give it to Amos.

Even though this particular revolver was chambered in the rather anemic .38 S&W caliber, the Hopkins & Allen was a medium grade handgun that was a popular choice for people who found the need to be armed with a concealable firearm. For someone like Mr. Sweeney, the Hopkins & Allen was a decent store keeper's gun and would serve as the perfect sidearm for a beginner like Amos Washington.

While Amos admired the nickel plated revolver, Ivan extended his left hand as he pointed his index finger at the revolver and said, "Here, let me show ya...press that lever to break it open just enough to see that the gun is loaded but don't open the cylinder all the way or you'll eject the bullets all over the place."

As slow as he was, Amos managed to follow Ivan's instructions and open the revolver enough to expose the bullets that were loaded in the cylinder. As Ivan continued he pointed to the bullets and said, "One bullet for each hole...got it?"

Because he stuttered Amos Washington was generally a young man of few words. After thinking about what Ivan said, Amos continued to admire the nickel plated revolver as he remarked, "Na..na..now.. wha...wha...what..da...da..do...I..I.. do, I..I..Ivan?"

After witnessing Ivan give Amos a handgun, Terry felt compelled to speak up."I can't believe you gave Amos of all people a loaded gun."

"Relax will, ya, responded Ivan who quickly added, "He's doing fine."

Once again Ivan turned to face Amos and said, "OK Amos, close it up and make sure you hear the cylinder lock in place."

After following Ivan's instructions, Amos slowly raised the revolver up a bit and looked down the sights as he remarked, "Ga..Ga..Gee...I..I...Ivan...I..I..I... ha..heard.. tha...tha...the...cla..cla..click...ju...ju..just la...la..la...like...yu...you.. sa...said."

Before turning around Ivan smiled then said, "OK, Amos put that gun away and don't touch it again until I tell you to. I also picked up a box of ammo for you. The next time Shorty works on one of our cars I'll let you practice shooting at garbage cans in the garage." As an excited Amos Washington slipped the revolver into his coat pocket he felt like a million bucks.

While Terry drove the stolen Oldsmobile back to their hideout, Amos felt a sense of pride that he never felt before. The revolver that rested in his pants pocket was without a doubt the greatest gift that anyone ever gave him. Up until now Amos was a man size teenager who did all the heavy lifting and ran errands for Ivan and the others. As far as Amos was concerned, even if he still ran errands and did all the heavy lifting the fact he was now armed meant that he was a full fledged member of Ivan's gang.

In the 1940s is was common practice and socially acceptable for policemen and other officials to receive gratuities from the general public for services rendered and ignoring minor infractions of the law. Store owners also rarely if ever complained when certain items of value mysteriously disappeared from a crime scene or after a fire was extinguished. Store owners also paid to keep police officers from giving their customers tickets when they double and triple parked in front of their stores. No pay off meant that the police would enforce the law to the letter of the law.

The police also knew which businesses in their precinct they should patronize to get the best deals and discounts.

Different types of gratuities and pay offs were also made so cops would not be as aggressive in enforcing the less serious "crimes" that society tolerated under the right circumstances. People who lived in the 1940s also had no problem with heavy handed cops running hoodlums off their beat, providing that they were only heavy handed with criminals and not with the good folks.

By the time Mr. Sweeny's son arrived at his father's store, two bottles of vermouth, three cases of Schlitz beer, one case of Rheingold beer and two bottles of Four Roses Whiskey went into the trunks of three police cars. Even old man Sweeny managed to receive medical treatment, while three patrolmen and one sergeant liberated the above mentioned items that would be listed in the police report as having been stolen by the armed robbers.

When the two detectives who responded to the robbery arrived at the scene of the crime, Detective Frank Angelone turned to his partner and rolled his eyes at the sight of so many empty shelves. After seeing Frank's reaction, a uniformed police sergeant by the name of O'Toole remarked, "Don't worry boys, there's a little something being brought up to squad compliments of the day tour."

Frank Angelone wasn't one to let such a promise go without a suitable response. "To tell you the truth, Sarge, I panic when I hear you use the word little."

While the barrel chested Irish American police sergeant put his arm around the nicely dressed Second Grade Detective, he smiled then remarked, "Have I ever let you down, Frankie?"

Without hesitating, Detective Angelone remarked, "There's always a first time, Sarge."

The moment his partner hung up the phone in the liquor store, Frank Angelone could tell he had something very interesting to say. As Detective Johnny Mc Donald walked around the counter, he spoke with a thick Irish brogue and said, "I've got good news and bad news, Frankie. What would you like to hear first?"

Frank Angelone and Johnny Mc Donald were the odd couple of police work in 1943. While most Irish cops were known to call the Italians dagos and waps, no one dared to utter such words in front of Detective Johnny Mc Donald about his partner. Their relationship began when they were rookie cops and they learned that they both served in the U.S. Army during World War I and fought in many of the same battles.

Their relationship was elevated to best friend status when Frank Angelone pushed Johnny Mc Donald out of the way, when a drunk with a switch blade knife tried to stab his Irish buddy during an off duty drinking spree. Twenty stitches later, Frank Angelone was hailed a hero in the saloon that was owned by Johnny's parents on the west side of Manhattan. Even the police department commended the two off duty patrolmen, for using bar stools instead of guns to disarm the knife wielding drunk in such a crowded environment.

The incident that further cemented their relationship occurred when both men met after going to court in lower Manhattan and they stumbled into an armed robbery of a jewelry store on Canal Street. After Johnny Mc Donald sustained a minor gunshot wound to his left leg during the shootout, Frank Angelone pursued the surviving gunman who made the fatal mistake of shooting his Irish American brother in blue. When backup finally arrived, off duty Patrolman Frank Angelone was found standing over the dead body of the armed robber in front of an apartment house on Mulberry Street. On the ground next to the gunman's body rested a .32 ACP caliber Remington Model 51 pistol and a sack of stolen jewelery and cash.

While being briefed by the responding officers, Frank learned that the other gunman was DOA at Bellevue Hospital and Johnny Mc Donald was being treated for the gunshot wound that grazed his left leg. As a result of this shootout, Frank Angelone and Johnny Mc Donald were promoted by the Police Commissioner to the rank of Third Grade Detective and assigned to the 19th Squad in Manhattan.

Johnny Mc Donald was known to drive his partner crazy by constantly asking him whether he wanted to hear the good news first or the bad. After eighteen years together, Frank Angelone gave up on trying to change his partner's lovable but obnoxious ways.

While Frank held up his hands and sounded as exasperated as usual, he looked at his partner and said, "Come on, Johnny. Give me a break with this good news bad news crap and tell me what's going on."

Without teasing his partner any further, Detective Mc Donald leaned closer to Frank Angelone and said, "The bad news is we're being transferred and have been ordered to report to Captain Murphy at the Chief of Detectives Office."

"Why, are we in trouble?" asked Frank.

After hearing his partner express concern about being called to the Chief's Office, Johnny Mc Donald put his right hand top of his partner's left shoulder and said, "Brace yourself, Frankie. We've been promoted to First Grade and assigned to work with the U.S. Army and a number of other agencies at the Provost Marshal's Office at 90 Church Street."

As happy as Frank Angelone was to hear that he and his partner were being promoted, he was not excited about the prospects of working with the U.S. Army. While ignoring the good news about their promotions, Detective Angelone remarked in his trademark pessimistic tone, "Just great, now we'll be chasing deserters all over hell and creation."

By 1943 standards Detectives Angelone and Mc Donald were considered honest cops who were well liked by the department brass. Because both men were members of an essential service, married with dependents and in their 40's they were exempt from the draft. The fact that Frank Angelone and Johnny Mc Donald were decorated World War I veterans, who were familiar with military service in time of war, also qualified them to represent the police department in the newly formed U.S. Army Provost Marshal's Office Task Force.

CHAPTER 4

JAMES BEAUREGARD

J ames Beauregard was an educated gentleman from the south who came from a long line of lawmen and military officers who served during the Civil War, in the Apache Wars, in the charge up San Juan Hill, in the Mexican Punitive Expedition, in World War I as well as during the gangster era. While Jim Beauregard's family were men of action and humble civil servants, his wife's family was one of the wealthiest in the State of Georgia.

Beatrice "Bea" Hamilton Beauregard was a beautiful southern belle who met the man she would marry when they were both students at the University of Georgia. As they would eventually admit to each other, their romance was a genuine case of love at first sight. Even when Jim told his future wife that he was joining the Atlanta Police Department, she never wavered or considered her options because Bea knew that it was meant to be for her and James Beauregard to be together.

Despite the class difference between them, none of that mattered once Bea's family got to know the man that their oldest daughter wanted to marry. This included Bea's mother who was incredibly happy about the marriage. It also didn't take very long for Bea's father to realize that James Beauregard was the son that he always wanted. From the moment that Jim asked Bea's father for permission to marry his daughter, Senator Clayton Hamilton began working behind the scenes to nudge his son-in-law's police career along. Jim's father, who served as a sergeant in the Atlanta Police Department, was also elated about the marriage and viewed Bea as the daughter that he never had.

Throughout their relationship together, Jim walked a fine line between wanting to be a self made man, while also not wanting to hurt his father-in-law's feelings. The problem that Jim had was that he really liked his colorful father-in-law. When Jim's father was killed in the line of duty, Senator Hamilton comforted his son-in-law and used his political connections to increase public support for the police, including when times were tough. Senator Hamilton was equally supportive of the Georgia National Guard, where Jim served as a commissioned officer after years of serving as an enlisted man. Even in the years when America was an isolationist nation, Senator Hamilton was a vocal supporter of the need to build the military capabilities of the United States.

When his father-in-law's best friend became Governor, Jim was offered the opportunity to retire from the Atlanta Police Department and become the Chief of the Georgia Highway Patrol. As a result of his father in law's political contacts, James Beauregard had a promising future as a police chief until the Japanese bombed Pearl Harbor.

Prior to December 7, 1941, the United States Army was filled with career officers who found it considerably more difficult to get promoted in the peacetime armed forces. The simple fact was, that career officers counted on the right opportunities to practice their trade and advance in rank. Since the war with the Axis Forces had all the trappings of a full scale conflagration, it was evident that the U.S. military would need millions of troops who would be led by a large number of commissioned officers.

As much as Jim Beauregard wanted to serve because it was the right thing to do, he also had other reasons for wanting to join the Army, instead of retiring so he could become the Chief of the Georgia Highway Patrol. Even though Jim loved being a policeman, he always wanted to lead men in battle. While being a cop fit that bill to some extent, nothing could take the place of being an officer in charge of troops who were serving in harms way in time of war.

Being born in 1897 made it possible for Jim to serve in the U.S. Army during the Punitive Expedition into Mexico. During this campaign, Jim served as a private under the command of General Blackjack Pershing and a young Lieutenant by the name of George S. Patton. Jim's front line service ended when he was sent to an Army hospital, after he sustained a minor wound during a skirmish with a small group of Mexican villa vistas.

When the U.S. entered World War I and the Georgia National Guard served in combat as part of the 42nd Rainbow Division, Jim was made a firearms instructor and later served as a military policeman. Despite his pleas for a combat assignment, Sergeant James Beauregard was kept stateside along with a young officer by the name of Dwight David Eisenhower.

When the First World War ended in November of 1918, Jim became the first Beauregard to attend the University of Georgia. After completing his first year of college, Jim was sworn in as a member of the Atlanta Police Department and was presented with the patrolman's badge that his father carried before he was promoted to the rank of sergeant. A week later the newly appointed policeman married Beatrice Bea Hamilton. One year later their son Peter was born. Then came their second son Michael.

As exciting as police work was, Jim still longed for another crack at Army life and joined the Georgia National Guard. After 20 years of combined active duty and National Guard service, Jim had no choice but to leave the state guard when the demands of his police career made it extremely difficult for him to meet both commitments. No one regretted this decision more than Jim Beauregard, when National Guard forces were federalized for national service in 1940 as the world seemed to be heading toward war.

When the Japanese bombed Pearl Harbor on December 7, 1941 Jim wanted nothing more than to be on his way to fight the enemy. Unfortunately, as a 44 year old married member of an essential service, James Beauregard was not high on Uncle Sam's list of eligible candidates for national service.

While Bea wanted Jim to remain home and serve as the Chief of the Georgia Highway Patrol, she knew that her husband would be miserable if he passed on the opportunity to serve the nation in time of war. Beatrice Beauregard also knew that both of their sons were anxious to enlist and were already talking to their father about how they should serve. While the thought of having her husband go off to war was bad enough, it would be considerably more difficult for a mother like Beatrice Beauregard to see their two sons enlist or get drafted.

The day that Jim decided not to retire and assume command of the state highway patrol, he met his father-in-law for lunch to let him know how much he appreciated everything he did for him and the two institutions that he loved the most next to his marriage. The fact that Jim had become as close to the aging Senator as a son could be to a father, made it even harder for him to tell the veteran politician that he decided to turn down the governor's appointment so he could join the Army.

After Jim made his case, the Senator realized that it was futile to try and convince his son-in-law to reconsider. When the old man went to reach for the check, Jim beat him to it as he remarked, "Please Pop, this is my treat."

As the old man stood up and said, "You win my boy," Jim helped his father-in-law put on his coat.

Just as they were getting ready to leave, the old man faced his son in law and said, "When I heard that my oldest daughter was madly in love with a policeman

I wasn't happy about it. I changed my mind the moment I finally got the chance to meet you. I hope you know Jim that you're like a son to me and because your like a son to me there isn't anything I won't do for you."

After pausing for a split second to think about the potential ramifications of his actions, his father in law continued and said, "I'll use every contact I have to get you a commission in the Army but you have to promise me son that you'll come back in one piece."

As soon as Jim said, "Thanks Pop," the veteran politician grabbed his son-in-law by the arm and escorted him to the exit.

By the time they reached the door the aging Senator remarked, "If your wife and her mother find out that I helped you get a commission that sends you off to war, I may have to enlist to get away from the women in our lives."

While Jim drove his father-in-law to the state office building, he had no idea that his two sons had also visited their grandfather to seek his advice and help. Even though Jim's sons spoke to their father about their intentions to enlist, both boys were also extremely close to their grandfather and would never make a major decision in life without seeking his council. With help from his grandfather, Jim's oldest son Peter enlisted in the U.S. Navy and received a commission. After completing his training, Ensign Peter Beauregard shipped off to war and served on a PT Boat. The day after Michael Beauregard graduated high school he enlisted and volunteered for U.S. Army airborne duty.

As much as the War Department needed combat troops and officers to lead men in battle, the U.S. Army also needed military policemen to keep everyone in line. Despite all of the flag waving that was going on, not every red blooded American wanted to do the right thing for God and Country, especially if it meant risking their life for someone else. The institution of wartime rationing regulations also created the perfect breading ground for black-market activities.

The more the War Department needed to support the Allied war effort, the more the civilian population did without. The needs of the armed forces also went beyond initiating a system of rationing and included eliminating access to certain products during the war years. This sacrifice was necessary to insure that the different branches of the Armed Forces had an ample supply of food, medical supplies, ammunition, weapons, vehicles, vessels, aircraft, tires, petroleum products, spare parts, parachutes, tents, packs, belts, holsters, steel helmets, rafts, different types of radios, clothing and uniforms for different conditions and duties, candy bars, cigarettes and other tobacco products etc....

Even though the United States was unprepared for a world war in December of 1941, once war was declared the American people supported the war effort in every way possible. In 1942 and 1943 the size of the Armed Forces grew in leaps and bounds as bases were built all over the United States to accommodate the millions of men who would serve in uniform for the duration of the war plus six months.

During World War II, U.S. troops were the best fed and best equipped soldiers in the world. Most went along with the program. The ones that didn't became targets of the Provost Marshal's Office and the military police. As a result of his education and law enforcement background, the recently commissioned Major James Beauregard was immediately sucked up into the ranks of the military police.

After a brief stint with the MPs, Jim was assigned to serve as the second in command of the Provost Marshal's Office in of all places but New York City. Even though Jim knew that serving as the lead investigator in this unit was an important assignment, he secretly longed for the day when he would be able to transfer to a combat command.

CHAPTER 5

BREAKING BARRIERS:
AL PARKER & THE MURPHY CLAN

Al Parker knew his foot post like the back of his hand. He knew who was religious and respectful and who to watch out for. Al was especially impressed by the way that the general public supported the war effort. Even when the enemy was achieving one victory after another, the average American was committed to doing their part to defeat the forces of evil. In fact, once the Japanese bombed Pearl Harbor, the average American believed that the world was now divided between good guys and bad guys, conquerors and liberators.

Al Parker took his job very seriously and always kept a sharp eye out for anyone who looked or acted suspicious. The rounding up of German agents, who landed on Amaganset Beach in Long Island in June of 1942, was a reminder to every God fearing American that the Germans were not beyond attacking the United States from within. Even with rationing and a heightened state of security, the average American had it pretty good compared to the people who lived in other parts of the war torn world. This was the case because nothing could compare to being bombed, occupied or enslaved by the Axis Forces.

After almost twenty three years on the job, Al Parker knew how to pass the time to keep his mind off the boredom of being a beat cop until all hell broke loose. In his favor, Al Parker could walk all day and then some without getting tired. Al developed this capability when he was a little boy and he walked the streets of Harlem, while helping his grandfather deliver fresh fruits and vegetables from a horse drawn cart. His education of about the realities of life continued in the winter months, when Al helped his grandfather deliver coal to homes and apartment houses in the area.

All it took was one winter of back breaking hard work, to turn a young Al Parker into the strongest kid in his class. At the time, Al had no idea that his grandfather was preparing him for the future. In addition to becoming as physically strong as an ox, Al Parker developed a very strong work ethic that would serve him well for the rest of his life. In addition, Al learned how to save his hard earned money, while also learning how to spend his hard earned money on the things that mattered the most in life.

When the Japanese captured the Philippines, all that Al could think about was the thousands of brave men who were forced to march at the end of a Jap bayonet to an overcrowded prison camp. Nazi Germany was also a savage enemy that was in the process of turning the world upside down and inside out. Even though life in the United States wasn't perfect, Al found it hard to complain whenever he thought about the freedom loving people who were trapped behind enemy lines.

The Parkers were a working class family with a strong faith and a family heritage of national service in time of war. Like most cops from his generation, Al even found a way to attend church services when he was on duty. Al Parker was also a loving husband and a father who was beaming with pride, now that his oldest son was training to serve as a fighter pilot and his youngest son was serving as a military policeman in the U.S. Army.

Compared to other Negroes, being a civil servant, and a policeman to boot, made Al top dog when it came to having a position of prestige and prominence in the Negro community. In fact, during the depression policemen were some of the richest men in America because they collected a steady salary, even if it was a modest one. This applied to all policemen, including Negro officers.

Trench warfare during World War I was without a doubt one of the most dangerous forms of combat that human beings have ever participated in. The long shrill of an officer's whistle sent waves of good men over the top and into their graves when enemy machine guns opened fire. The senseless slaughter of thousands of brave troops to gain what amounted to a few yards of mud, was no way for gallant men to die in the name of patriotism. When men ran out of conventional ways to maim and kill each other, poison gas was used with devastating effect.

In the middle of all this carnage, a young Negro U.S. Army Private by the name of Al Parker was assigned to serve in an intelligence unit. As far as Al Parker was concerned, the biggest mistake he made was letting the U.S. Army know that he spoke fluent German. The fact that Al had a knack for languages and learned to speak German, prevented him from serving as an infantryman in the 369th Infantry Regiment of the 93rd Division (Colored), also known as The Harlem Hellfighters.

Fortunately for Al Parker, he worked for a Negro U.S. Army Intelligence Officer who appreciated his desire to serve as close to the action as possible. Thanks to this Negro Army Officer, Al was allowed to take forays to forward areas to interrogate German soldiers who were taken prisoner and translate captured documents in a timely fashion. Even though Al didn't remain in a forward area for very long, his intelligence gathering trips enabled him to observe the sights and sounds of battle from a front line perspective.

Like many other Negro American soldiers who served in World War I, Al Parker believed that race relations would change for the better, if Negroes continued to prove their worth in battle. Even though not much changed after Negro troops fought with distinction in the Revolutionary War, in the Civil War, in the Indian Wars or during the Spanish American War, Al Parker eagerly volunteered to serve during World War I. As far as Al was concerned, World War I was another opportunity for men of color to distinguish themselves in combat so white folks would finally say, "Hey, those Negro soldiers are brave sons'a bitches. Let's treat them as equals."

Soldiers who did foolish things in combat either got in trouble, got killed or got a medal. After interrogating a captured wounded German soldier and examining the documents in his possession, Private Parker volunteered to remain at the front when enemy patrols started probing positions held by the American 369th and the French 4th Army.

During this enemy probing action, Private Parker effectively used his issued Colt 1911 pistol to help defend a section of the front line. After reloading his forty five caliber pistol and two spare magazines, Private Parker asked the Negro infantry troops to hold their fire, while he searched the dead Germans who fell in battle while trying to probe the Allied lines. When a Negro Sergeant tried to stop Al from venturing into no man's land, he told the non commissioned officer that the dead Germans might possess valuable intelligence information that could save Allied lives. As soon as Sergeant William T. Russell said, "OK, Parker, but you be careful and that's an order," Al belly crawled into the darkness and began to systematically search the enemy soldiers who fell in battle.

Immediately after Al recovered a 9mm Luger pistol and a map case from a dead German Lieutenant, he made his way back to his previous position and handed the map case to Sergeant Russell. "I found this map case on a German Officer, Sarge," whispered Al Parker, who quickly added, "I'll be back as soon as I search two more Heini enlisted men." Before the Negro Sergeant from the 369th could stop him from doing so, Al Parker was heading back into the kill zone that separated the Allied side of the battlefield from German held territory.

Just as Al Parker finished searching a dead German Corporal and he started to crawl back to the American lines, the enemy launched another probing action. This time, a German patrol attacked a French 4th Army unit that was holding a sector of the front line that was adjacent to the position held by the American 369th. After observing a contingent of Allied troops launch a successful counterattack and watching several men fall in the battle near the German lines, Al ignored the risks and went to the aid of the Allied casualties.

When Sergeant Russell spotted Private Parker heading toward German held territory on the French side of the front line, he turned to three of his men and said, "I need three volunteers to help me go after that crazy kid from intelligence." While pointing at the three American Negro soldiers, Sergeant Russell remarked, "You, you and you just volunteered. Let's go!"

After telling his corporal to take command, Sergeant Russell pointed toward the adjoining French 4th Army position and said, "We'll make our way to the French side of the line before we go running around on their side of the battlefield."

As the four man detail from the 369th snaked their way through their unit's defensive position, Al Parker was in the process of rescuing a wounded French soldier. Even though Al Parker only knew a few words in French, he could tell that the wounded French Private was desperately trying to tell him something important, when he pointed toward the German lines and whispered, "Americain blesse, Americain blesse." The second a star shell illuminated the night's sky over the battlefield, Al covered the wounded French soldier with his body.

After waiting for the flair to burn out, Al raised his body a bit and looked toward the German lines. Once Al saw that it was safe to move, he put his right index finger up to his lips as he looked at the French Private and whispered, "Quiet, mon ami."

Because Al could only take care of one man at a time, he dragged then carried the wounded soldier back to the closest French Army position. As soon as Al did so, the wounded soldier told an English speaking French Lieutenant that their American liaison officer was wounded and took cover in a bomb crater just beyond the position where he was found. After saying, "I'll be back, Lieutenant," Private Parker headed back into no man's land to go to the aid of the wounded U.S. Army Officer.

When an opportunity arose to do more than serve as a liaison officer, Lieutenant Patrick Murphy Sr. led the counter attack that forced the Germans to fall back to their lines. Despite the success of this combat action, Lt. Murphy sustained multiple wounds that made it impossible for him to return to the French lines without help. With no other options available, the Irish American U.S. Army Officer from New York City was forced to take cover near German held territory.

While moving as quietly as possible, Private Al Parker made his way deeper into no man's land. Whenever German flairs illuminated the night sky over the battlefield, Al stopped all movement and took cover by putting his face in the blood soaked mud. Before he moved on, Al Parker picked up a pair of wire cutters and two German hand-grenades from a dead enemy soldier.

After cutting his way through some barbed wire, Al Parker found the wounded American Army Officer in the bottom of a bomb crater with his pistol in hand. Once Al Parker made his way next to the Lieutenant, he whispered when he introduced himself. "Private Parker, Sir, 369th Intelligence. A wounded French soldier told me you might need some help."

While the U.S. Army Officer who was in obvious pain grabbed his badly wounded leg, he whispered as he leaned closer to Private Parker and said,

"Lieutenant Patrick Murphy, Liaison Officer to the French 4th Army. It's nice to meet you, Private. It looks like we're both a long way from home." After pausing again to grab his badly wounded leg, Lt. Murphy looked at the young Negro soldier who came to his rescue and whispered, "Thanks for stopping by, but I want you to head back to our lines. That's an order."

While ignoring the order, Al whispered, "As soon as I patch you up, Sir, we can head back together."

After placing a fresh bandage on the gunshot wound that creased the left side of the young officer's torso, Al used his pant's belt to apply a makeshift tourniquet to the Lieutenant's badly wounded leg.

While Al Parker finished rendering first aid to Lt. Murphy's wounds, Sergeant Russell and his three man detail were escorted through the French lines. After being introduced to the English speaking French Lieutenant, the decision was made to join forces to go to the aid of Private Parker and the wounded American Army Liaison Officer.

By the time Al Parker began to help Lt. Murphy out of the bomb crater, their attempt to return to Allied lines was cut short by the presence of a German patrol. During the initial exchange of gunfire Private Parker and Lt. Murphy were able to effectively use their pistols to repel the enemy attack.

When a German grenade was hurled their way, Al covered Lt. Murphy's body with his own, just before the grenade exploded on the edge of the far side of the bomb crater. Even though he sustained shrapnel wounds in his back and left arm, Al Parker continued to fight by Lt. Murphy's side to defend their position from being overrun. When the persistent German patrol launched a followup attack, Al used the Luger pistol and the two hand-grenades that he took from dead enemy troops to stall the German advance.

While Al Parker took advantage of the lull in the fighting to drag Lt. Murphy out of the bomb crater, the English speaking French Army Lieutenant, along with Sergeant Russell and a contingent of French troops and American Negro soldiers arrived to lend a hand. After motivating the survivors of the German patrol to return to their lines, the Allied rescue party brought Private Parker and Lt. Murphy back to the safety of the closest French defensive position.

While the two Americans were treated side by side, Lt. Murphy was intrigued to learn about the exploits of Private Parker from the French Lieutenant and U.S. Army Sergeant William Russell. This included hearing how the brave Negro soldier, who saved his life and the life of a French Private, was performing intelligence duties for the 369th in a nearby sector of the front when he went to their aid. As the French Lieutenant continued, he explained that once Sergeant Russell and his men spotted Private Parker going to the aid of Allied troops, they joined forces with French 4th Army soldiers to assist Private Parker in his rescue mission.

After serving for two days in a forward area, Al Parker earned a well deserved reputation as one hell of a soldier. Al's proudest moment was the day when he was awarded a Distinguish Service Cross and the French Croix de Guerre, even if these medals were presented with no fanfare in the all Negro section of an overcrowded army hospital. The French Army also decorated Sergeant Russell and his men as well.

When the French Army Officer completed the award ceremony and left the hospital, Al Parker's commanding officer handed him a letter from the U.S. Army Officer that he saved from being killed or captured. In this letter, Lieutenant Patrick Murphy Sr. stated that he was happy to hear that the U.S. Army accepted his recommendation that Private Parker was properly decorated for his heroic actions. In addition to thanking Al again for saving his life, Lt. Murphy extended an invitation for Al to look him up after the war.

After Al was discharged he went to work in his father's side business repairing expensive cars for influential white people, as well as for wealthy Negroes in Harlem.

When a local newspaper published a photograph of Patrick Murphy Sr. and described how the decorated U.S. Army Officer was now serving with the New York City Police Department, Al's father and his wife Mary encouraged him to contact the man that he saved during the war. Even though it took some doing, Al finally listened to his family members and contacted Pat Murphy Sr. at his home in Manhattan.

As soon as Al made the call, Patrolman Patrick Murphy Sr. invited Al and his wife Mary to dinner in his father's apartment on the upper east side of Manhattan. The rest is history. The Murphys were generous people who showered Al with a great deal of affection and gratitude. This included Pat Murphy Sr.'s beautiful wife Kathleen, who repeatedly told Al that he and his family were always welcomed in their home for saving the life of her husband and father of their three sons. Even Mary Parker was made to feel like part of the family, especially when she held the Murphy's youngest son Pat Jr. in her arms, while she enjoyed some private time with the women of the Murphy family.

After enjoying Sunday supper, the patriarch of the Murphy clan, Police Lieutenant Michael Murphy, sat with Al Parker and his son Patrick and sipped Irish whiskey while they did their best to recruit Al into the P.D.N.Y. Pat Murphy Sr.'s two brothers who were cops also came by to meet the brave former soldier from Harlem who saved young Patty from the Huns.

Al Parker was overwhelmed by the attention that he received from the Murphy family to repay him for saving Patrick's life. Even after Al repeatedly told the Murphy family that he really liked fixing cars, Pat and his relatives insisted that he give police work a try. When Lieutenant Murphy, who was about to get promoted to the rank of captain, told Al that he could continue fixing cars as a side business after he joined the department, Al began to see an opportunity that was hard to pass up.

After another glass of Irish whiskey, the thought of becoming a policeman began to appeal more and more to a young Al Parker. As far as Al was concerned, it was due to his brief experience in battle that earned him recognition in the white man's world. With so many Irish cops in his corner, Al figured that he would have the kind of protection that only white people with political connections had. After receiving the necessary support from his wife, Al Parker agreed to report to Police Headquarters at 240 Centre Street in Manhattan to be guided through the application process.

Al had to admit that it felt great to be treated like a white man. All it took was a whisper or a nod from the various members of the Murphy family who were on the job, to help Al pass each and every step of the recruitment process without a hitch.

Al knew he had the right connections, when a tough looking police sergeant patted him on the back when he was getting ready to begin the physical exam and remarked, "So, you're the Lad who saved my nephew Patty during the war."

Under the circumstances Al didn't know what to say. He simply wasn't used to such treatment, especially from white folks. Seeing Al act a bit shy brought the stern looking sergeant to crack a smile then whisper, "Come with me, Laddy. You passed your physical exam in France."

When Al was led away with two white applicants who had similar connections, he had to admit to himself that it felt great to be in a position of power. This experience made Al realize, that people who wielded tremendous influence and authority over others had no reason to voluntarily surrender or share control of the system, if doing so would limit any of their own power.

As a native New Yorker, Al also knew that other ethnic and religious groups felt a similar burden because people tended to judge the actions of the many by the actions of the few. Even though this was the case, Al never met a white man who wished that he was born black. This didn't mean that white folks didn't have problems and obstacles to overcome. Clearly, not all white people were privileged or born into money, fame or positions of prominence. The difference was obvious and quite evident by the fact that even a wealthy Negro could not go where a wealthy white man could go, nor could he do everything that a white man was able to do, unless it was in a segregated environment.

The pain and evil of prejudice and segregation could only be felt by someone who knew what it was like to be treated differently because of their race, religion, or heritage. Even though he didn't know it at the time, Al Parker was a pioneer, a trendsetter and a man who was making a difference for all people of color, despite the fact that the full impact of his contribution would not be felt for decades to come.

CHAPTER 6

THE ORPHAN BECOMES A CRIMINAL

After being left on the doorstep of a Catholic Church in Manhattan, the baby boy who was named after his prostitute mother's deceased father was left to be raised by an order of nuns. While a large number of Catholic nuns were motivated by the conviction of their faith, some nuns acted as if they lost sight of the fact that they served a loving God. The worst of the lot seemed to wear the black habit as if it was the uniform of a sadist. In fact, there was nothing Christ like about the abusive women who were quick to lash out in anger and deliver various forms of corporal punishment to the children who were placed in their care.

Despite the efforts that were made by one young nun to give Ivan the love that he deserved, a trio of nasty bitches in black used their hands, a long length of cord, a leather strap and a long wooden ruler to spank, slap, whip and beat young Ivan senseless on a regular basis. Clearly, Ivan Larson would have been better off if he was raised in a kennel at the ASPCA.

For as long as Ivan could remember, he dreamed of the day when he could escape living under a roof that was controlled by such abusive women. When Ivan finally decided to leave the hell hole that he called home, he decided to steal eighty two dollars in petty cash that he knew the Queen Bitch of Nuns kept in the orphanage office under lock and key. Ironically, the day that Ivan executed his escape plan, the nun who caught him in the act of stealing money was Sister Danielle O'Rourke.

If there was ever an angel who wore black it was Sister O'Rourke. To her, Ivan Larson was a young man who needed to be smothered in love, instead of being treated like a dangerous animal. Despite all that she did to help him, Sister O'Rourke knew that Ivan was terribly mistreated and lived for the day when he could escape the place that he called "the zoo."

As a child growing up in St. Mary's Orphanage, Ivan Larson was plagued with terrible nightmares. Between the lack of sleep and the mistreatment that he received on a regular basis, Ivan became a bully and used his strength to push the other kids around. Violence begot violence and being abused led to Ivan to abuse others with his fists. Only Sister O'Rourke seemed to be aware that Ivan was really crying out for help by his actions. As a result, turning him in was never an option. She loved him to much for that. Instead, Sister O'Rourke decided to help the teenager that she raised from a baby to escape the madness of the orphanage.

Without saying a word, Sister O'Rourke put her right index finger up to her lips, while she removed a set of keys from her pocket. After turning around, Sister O'Rourke used one of the keys to open the draw on the right side of the wooden cabinet that was positioned against the wall behind the desk. Inside was a large metal box.

After carefully removing the cash box from the drawer, Sister O'Rourke placed the box on top of the desk and opened the cover. Inside was several stacks of money and a ledger book. After removing one bundle of cash, she handed the money to Ivan then closed her hand over his without saying a word. By doing so, Sister O'Rourke was trying to make things up to young Ivan. After all, Sister O'Rourke knew that it would take money for a 15 year old boy to live on his own until he could find work.

As soon as the young nun stepped aside, Ivan knew that it was time to leave before they were both caught in the act of stealing from the orphanage. By this stage in his life, the beatings that Ivan received turned him into a tough kid, who was unable to feel unconditional love from anyone except Sister O'Rourke.

Even though it wasn't easy for him to display signs of affection, Ivan stepped closer to the young nun and gave her a generous hug. After taking a step back, Ivan turned and headed for the door. When Ivan reached the hallway, he faced the young nun who was wiping tears from her eyes. As Sister O'Rourke gripped the gold cross that she wore around her neck, she looked at her favorite orphan and whispered, "I'll pray for you, Ivan."

After stuffing the additional one hundred and fifty dollars into his coat pocket, Ivan pulled up the collar on his threadbare coat and said, "Thanks for everything, Sister. I'll never forget you." As soon as Ivan left the orphanage, he walked into a blinding snow storm. He was finally on his own.

One of the few personal feelings that Ivan ever discussed with his immediate circle of friends was how much he loathed anyone who wore a blue suit and sailed on ships. In fact, Ivan was quite frank about his absolute hatred for sailors. Ivan felt this way because the man who impregnated his prostitute mother was an American sailor who abandoned her when he learned that she was pregnant.

For several years, Ivan's prostitute mother would stop by St. Mary's and drop off a donation for the orphanage, as well as a gifts for her son. When Ivan got older, Sister O'Rourke told him about these acts of kindness, in order to make the young boy feel that he wasn't completely forgotten. These reports were always the same. Once a year on Christmas and on his birthday, his mother would visit the church that supported the orphanage to leave money and a gift for the boy that she requested be given the name Ivan Larson after her Norwegian father.

As a kid growing up in an abusive orphanage, Ivan had high hopes that his mother would come for him but she never did. Even when he got older, Ivan dreamed of the day when his mother would take him away from the place, that was more of prison than a home where children without parents should be raised.

According to an older prostitute that Ivan met after he left the orphanage, his mother desperately wanted the sailor to marry her and help her raise their son. Ivan's mother's heart was reportedly broken, when the sailor slapped her around and tossed a money clip on the bed when he walked out of her life. Rather than raise her son in a brothel, Ivan's mother decided to leave her new born baby on the doorstep of St. Mary's Church. While searching for his mother, Ivan also learned that she died from pneumonia two days before his thirteenth birthday. This explained why the donations and the annual gifts stopped coming the year that he officially became a teenager.

Once Ivan learned more about his mother and the fact that he wasn't the only boy at St. Mary's Orphanage who was born out of wedlock, he realized why some of the nuns behaved the way they did. After all, Ivan and the other orphans were bastards who were the result of a sinful one night stand.

Despite the overall support for the war, Ivan Larson knew that there were plenty of people who did not like living without various luxury items and other necessities of life. Once the federal government imposed rationing regulations and restricted the commercial sale of certain products, a portion of the population decided to do business with black market operators.

Ivan learned a lot about being a criminal in the time that he spent living with and working for Mad Mike Connely. If everything went as smoothly as Mike Connely predicted, he and Ivan would be well on their way to making one of their biggest scores yet. Their plan was simple. Over the past few months Mike Connely was loaning money to one of the customers at The Shamrock Bar who was a heavy drinker and a degenerate gambler. The reason Mike was so generous, was because the old man knew that Tommy Mulray drove trucks for a living that were often loaded with heavily rationed items. When the debt got big enough, Mulray would have two choices. Play ball and do as he was told, or go to the hospital or maybe even the morgue.

With Ivan serving as Mad Mike's debt collector, Mike enabled his young protege to establish a relationship with the man that they hoped to compromise. After collecting a pitiful sum of money from Mulray, Ivan made plans to collect the rest of the cash that the father of five owed Mike Connely.

As soon as Tommy Mulray entered the empty back room of The Shamrock Bar, Ivan motioned the truck driver over to the table where he was seated. While Mulray sat across from Ivan, he was visibly nervous when he removed a cigarette from the crumpled pack in his shirt pocket. After leaning forward to accept a light from Mad Mike's emissary, Tommy Mulray thanked Ivan for the light and apologized for being late. As usual Tommy Mulray was full of excuses.

Rather than listen to Mulray's sob story, Ivan raised his right hand and sounded as cold and calculated as possible when he remarked, "I'm here to collect a debt that you owe Mike. Do you have the money... yes or no?"

If anyone ever looked like they needed a drink it was Tommy Mulray. As Mulray slowly removed a handful of crumpled dollar bills from his pants pocket, he looked across the table as he spoke in a low tone of voice and said, "I'm sorry, Ivan. That's all I got."

After collecting the paltry sum of money, Ivan followed the plan that was devised by his mentor and placed the cash halfway between where he was sitting and where Mulray was seated. The second Ivan spotted the surprised look on Mulray's face, he knew that Mad Mike was right when he predicted how this pathetic loser would react. According to the famous gangster from the 1920s and 30s, Tommy Mulray would be eager to cooperate with their plan, once he knew that doing so would provide him with a way out of his outstanding debt. Mike also told Ivan that offering this loser a bonus for services rendered would further motivate Tommy Mulray to do as he was told.

As soon as Ivan saw the expression on Tommy Mulray's face, he slowly pushed the pile of money closer to the man that he was about to compromise. After continuing to see a look of bewilderment on his prey's face, Ivan decided to move things along and explain why he and his mentor were being so generous. "Go ahead, Tommy, pick it up," remarked Ivan, who quickly added, "According to Mike, you can keep your money and repay your entire debt in full, if you're willing to do us one favor. But it has to be a big favor."

The second Tommy Mulray went to pick up his money, Ivan proved that he was a well trained thug when he slammed his right hand over the small pile of cash. In addition to being a degenerate gambler, Tommy Mulray was a desperate man. As a result, Mulray decided to submit and appear interested to learn more about Mike Connely's proposal. While Tommy leaned forward and placed his arms on the table, Ivan lifted his hand off the pile of cash as he continued and said, "In addition to wiping the slate clean, Mike said we'll give you a piece of the action if you play ball."

Tommy Mulray proved that he was eager to cooperate when he swallowed hard and said, "What does Mike want me to do?"

While Ivan spoke he sealed the deal when he picked the money off the table and placed the cash in the truck driver's hand and said, "You drive trucks loaded with all kinds of rationed merchandize, including tires that can only be purchased by civilians once they receive written authorization from the Office of Price Administration. When you know you're hauling a load of new tires, I want you to tell me when and where we can meet. Make it near a diner where you can park your truck and go inside to get a cup of coffee on your way to your destination. When you exit the diner your truck will be hijacked at gunpoint by me. Once your turn over the keys all you have to do is walk away. My plan is to park the stolen car that I'll be driving as close to your truck as possible. If need be, I'll leave the damn thing in the middle of the street with the engine running. Doing so will help make your story sound legit when the cops show up."

After pausing to light a cigarette, Ivan continued. "Once I leave the area I want you to give me some time to get away before you call the police. When the cops arrive all you have to say is that some guy wearing a leather jacket, gloves and a stocking mask drove up in a burgundy colored Packard and hijacked your truck at gunpoint. You can also tell the cops that when you turned over the keys, the gunman told you to walk away and not look back."

While Ivan continued, he tapped the ash from the end of his cigarette into a nearby ashtray. "Remember, if the cops press you for a better description, all you have to say is that you have no idea what the hijacker looked like because he was wearing a stocking mask and gloves. If they ask you to describe the gun, you tell them that it was big and black. When they ask you who else knew that you were transporting a truckload of new tires, you act natural and identify everyone where you work who would know or could know about the cargo that you were carrying."

After placing his cigarette in between his lips, Ivan removed a wad of cash from his right hand pant's pocket and quickly counted out $70 dollars. As soon as Ivan removed the cigarette from in between his lips, he handed the money to Tommy Mulray and said, "This is from me to you to sweeten the deal."

While Tommy Mulray placed the unexpected bonus in his shirt pocket, Ivan could tell by the expression on the truck driver's face that he had his undivided attention. Handing such a pathetic loser a bonus, motivated Tommy Mulray to become a first class team player who enthusiastically repeated Ivan's instructions almost word for word.

As soon as Mulray finished speaking, Ivan pointed his right index finger at the truck driver and said, "I gave you that bonus because the cops and maybe even the feds are gonna go to work on you, once they hear that you lost a truck load of brand new tires. I'm telling you this because everyone knows that new tires are worth their weight in gold now that we're at war. As a result, you have to be prepared to be grilled by the cops, until they get tired of asking you questions. The good news is, as long as you stick to your story you won't have anything to worry about."

Just like Ivan expected Tommy Mulray seemed like a changed man when he remarked, "Don't worry. I'll play it just like you said."

After nodding his head as if he approved, Ivan remarked, "As long as you hold up your end, I'll personally deliver the bonus that Mike said that you'll get for making this deal happen."

When Tommy Mulray continued he sounded like a man was given a new lease on life. "You and Mike will have your tires as soon as I break in a new driver on Monday and Tuesday. On Wednesday and Thursday I make local runs but on Friday I'll be driving by myself. I can even ask for the Long Island run which is one of the biggest hauls we make. Best yet, this is a night run so it'll be dark when I turn over the keys." Ivan was even more impressed when the degenerate gambler added, "The Long Island run is also made with the newest truck in the fleet. That should bring you and Mike some extra dough if you decide to sell it. Heck, the parts alone on that truck are worth a pretty penny."

After hearing the young man he knew as Ivan Smith remark, "Now you're thinking," Tommy Mulray continued and said, "Unless things change...next Friday will be the day."

When Ivan asked where he wanted to make the exchange, Mulray considered the question for a second before he responded and said, "Why don't we meet at the Ft. Hamilton Diner. Stopping at a diner while making such a long run won't look suspicious, especially since I live on that side of Brooklyn and I know the best streets to take to get to Long Island. If I get out on time I should be able to get there between six thirty and seven. Once I park the truck I'll go inside the diner long enough to grab a cup of coffee and something to eat."

After hearing Ivan remark, "As soon as I see you leave the diner and head back to your truck, I'll drive up and make my move," Mulray responded and said, "Got it."

With their business concluded, Ivan poured two glasses of ice cold beer from the pitcher that was on the table and handed one of the glasses to Tommy Mulray. While Ivan lifted his glass and said, "Cheers," Tommy Mulray raised his glass and repeated the toast.

As the 1942 hit song, "A String Of Pearls," by Glenn Miller played in the background, Ivan finished his glass of beer before he stood up and said, "Why don't you stay and finish this pitcher of beer. And get yourself a sandwich."

After making a deal with the young man who called himself Ivan Smith, the truck driver from Brooklyn had a reason to relax. While Ivan walked around the table, he stopped and patted Mulray on the top of his right shoulder and said, "I'll call you at home next Thursday night to make sure we're still on for Friday."

As soon as Mulray responded and said, "I'll be waiting for your call," Ivan left the back room of the neighborhood bar on the west side of Manhattan that Mad Mike Connely owned, even though the license was in his cousin's name.

CHAPTER 7

NEW YORK CITY GOES TO WAR

During World War II the City of New York contributed to the war effort in many ways. Between marauding German U Boats that lurked off shore waiting to sink Allied merchant ships and naval vessels and the threat of sabotage by enemy agents, the city was on a war footing before Pearl Harbor was attacked. From the early days of the Lend Lease Act, merchant ships set sail to help America's future allies fight the Germans. When America became the Arsenal of Democracy, the Port of New York became the primary storage locker and departure point for massive amounts of cargo and personnel destined for the war against Germany.

In addition to the contribution that was made by significant numbers of New Yorkers who served in the armed forces and the defense industry, various ports in New York City and New Jersey formed the Port of New York. The Port of New York included several dozens shipyards and dry docks, a fleet of tug boats, enough dock space and protected anchorage to accommodate hundreds of vessels, including freighters, troop transports and combat naval vessels. The New York Port of Embarkation (NYPOE) also included staging areas that housed military personnel who were being shipped overseas as well as military stores and a massive transportation system that moved troops and the means to wage war to berthing areas in Port of New York. Once these vessels were loaded and made ready for sea, they set sail for various destinations in convoys that were protected by Allied naval vessels and U.S. Navy gun crews who served on board merchant ships.

The flagship of the Port of Embarkation was the Brooklyn Army Terminal. The Brooklyn Army Terminal was a massive storage facility, that included a railroad, as well as ample dock space to load merchant vessels. By the end of the war, several million troops along with tens of millions of tons of military equipment and supplies of all kind were shipped overseas through the Brooklyn Army Depot.[1] Unfortunately, many a ship's crew that departed the narrows of New York Harbor entered U Boat country with trepidation but went anyway.

James Beauregard was always called Jim and never Major, unless it was absolutely necessary to do so in order to satisfy some official protocol. Lieutenant Colonel Fred Richmond was a former infantry officer who became an FBI Agent after serving in World War I. While on military leave from the Bureau, Lt. Colonel Richmond put on his uniform again and agreed to serve as the Provost Marshal in New York City. Fred Richmond was the father of five girls and a devoted family man who never missed dinner at home unless duty called.

It was almost 1430 hours or 2:30 PM when Lt. Colonel Richmond pushed the squeaky door open a bit to check on his second in command before he left for the day. As soon as Major Jim Beauregard looked up and went to stand, Lt. Colonel Richmond waved his hand and said, "As you were, Jim. No need to get up on my account."

While Jim slowly sat back down in his chair, he immediately stamped out his cigarette and said, "Goodnight, Sir."

As soon as his commanding officer remarked, "Good luck tonight, Jim." Jim responded and said, "Thank you, Sir."

After checking his watch, Lt. Colonel Richmond continued as he stood in the open doorway to Jim's office. "After my meeting at the Police Commissioner's office I'll be heading home. Don't forget to call me later to let me know how things worked out and above all be careful."

As soon as Jim said, "Yes, Sir," Lt. Colonel Richmond tossed his second in command a casual salute as he stepped out of the office and closed the door.

Even though Jim enjoyed the investigative side of his duties, being away from home was not a very pleasant experience. Eating diner food and living in a cramped hotel room was also wearing thin on the veteran cop from Georgia. Jim changed his attitude when his eyes caught the front page of the newspaper that was folded on the right side of his desk. In the late summer of 1943 a world war was being waged on all fronts with the end still in doubt. Seeing the headlines made Jim feel ashamed that he complained about being stationed in New York City when chaos reigned supreme on planet earth.

While Jim lived on clean sheets and ate some of the best diner food in the world, there were millions of people living in war torn lands who would give anything to be in his shoes. Jim then thought of the Allied POWs who were rotting away in enemy prison camps and how every one of them would gladly trade places with him, if such an exchange could be arranged. After considering all that was going on in the world, the New York City skyline didn't look so bad to Major James Beauregard.

During the early years of World War II, the U.S. Army handled law enforcement matters through the Provost Marshal's Office and his staff of military policemen and investigators. This would change in January of 1944, when the U.S. Army established a more organized Criminal Investigations Division or CID under the Provost Marshal General's Office. Regardless of what the investigative component of the U.S. Army was called, the mission to solve crimes remained the same.

For various reasons, New York City was a busy place for the U.S. Army Provost Marshal's Office during World War II. Ever since the attack on Pearl Harbor, U.S. Army military policemen, U.S. Army Provost Marshal's Office Investigators, military intelligence personnel and civilian law enforcement officers from various agencies were kept busy protecting the nation in time of war. The duties they performed included pursuing deserters, criminals and enemy agents.

Being in the U.S. Army did not change the way that cops behaved just because the world was at war. Working stateside instead of overseas meant that Provost Marshal's Office Investigators could operate like police detectives and wear civilian attire when it was necessary to do so. Army investigators were also authorized to carry firearms.

When their issued .45 ACP caliber Model 1911s were secured in the office armory, some U.S. Army Investigators opted to carry a more concealable handgun, such as the Colt Model 1903 .32 ACP caliber pistol or the Colt Model 1908 .380 ACP caliber pistol. The Colt Model 1903 and Model 1908 were also issued to U.S. military general officers. A number of six shot Smith & Wesson Victory Model .38 Special revolvers with a four inch barrel and a rugged Parkerized finish were also issued to military personnel. Because of his duties, Jim Beauregard was one of the Army Investigators who opted to carry a more concealable Colt Model 1903 Pocket Auto Pistol at all times.

Even though Jim did not speak with a pronounced Southern drawl, his Georgia accent was different enough to motivate every cop and federal agent that he met in New York City to ask where he was from. Regardless, Jim was well received by the lawmen that he worked with because there was a fraternity between cops that transcended state lines.

In addition to a sarcastically irreverent and quick witted Italian American N.Y.P.D. Detective and his equally quick witted Irish American partner, the U.S. Army Provost Marshal's Office Task Force also included, a veteran FBI Agent, a U.S. Customs Agent who served as a CID Agent in World War 1 a U.S. Post Office Inspector who previously served as a Prohibition Agent, a Deputy U.S. Marshal, a New York State Police Investigator, a Naval Intelligence Officer, a 32 year old U.S. Army Investigator who served as a policeman in New Haven, Connecticut before the war, a retired police detective who was working for the U.S. Office of Price Administration and a pair of hard charging Jewish American Investigators from the New York District Attorney's Office.

Jim Beauregard knew that he and his New York City based colleagues had become friends when their work days were filled with plenty of joking around with no fear of insulting each other. Jim's standing among his fellow law enforcement officers was further bolstered by the fact that he gave up the chance to become the Chief of the Georgia Highway Patrol so he could serve as a cop in the Army.

One of the main advantages of working major cases with the FBI and the U.S. Army was money. Every city cop knew that if their informant could turn up something of interest to the feds, "the G" would pick up the tab. This included having federal authorities provide the money to pay certain investigative expenses and pay informants for services rendered.

Anthony Giordino or Tony G. was a first class wise guy who survived his entire career as a crook while only being convicted once for possession of stolen property. Because Tony G's father was French and his mother was Italian he was only able to serve as an associate member of the Mafia. Prior to the Japanese attack on Pearl Harbor, Tony G. was a well respected gangster who made money breaking the law. All that changed on December, 7, 1941, when Tony listened to the radio reports about the sneak attack on U.S. military facilities in Hawaii. Once the United States was compelled to go to war, Tony G. became determined to do whatever he could to help the war effort, even if it meant that he had to join forces with the police and the feds in order to do so.

While working for various government agencies, Tony G. developed an outstanding reputation as a provider of incredibly reliable intelligence information.

Tonight was no different. After Tony G. filed his initial report, a plan was put in motion to conduct a surveillance of the trucking company where one of his contacts worked as the shipping manager. The purpose of this surveillance was to follow the subject of their investigation once he departed to make his delivery.

As soon as Major Beauregard, Agent Dubrowsly, Detective Angelone and Detective Mc Donald met Tony G., they were taken to the fourth floor of the warehouse where they would establish their observation post. The plan that Tony G. put together, enabled the men from the Army Task Force to use an empty corner office to watch the front gate of the trucking company that was situated across the street.

After looking at his watch, Tony sat on the corner of the desk and said, "We're right on time. All we gotta do now is sit tight and wait for my guy, Sal to give us a call." While Major Beauregard used his Zippo to light a cigarette, Andy Dubrowsky puffed on his cigar, while Detective's Angelone and Mc Donald stood on both sides of the large open window to keep and eye on the trucking company.

After removing a cigarette from the pack that he carried in his pant's pocket and accepting a light from Major Beauregard, the man known as Tony G. began his briefing. "This is the deal. According to my buddy Sal, a driver by the name of Tommy Mulray is acting as if his luck has done a complete 360, which seems like a bit of a stretch because this truck driver couldn't pick a winner if his horse was the only nag in the race."

While the Major and his men grinned after hearing Tony's sarcastic description of the subject of their investigation, Tony G. kept a straight face as he continued and said, "When Sal called me about this guy I told him to play along and get back to me as soon as he knew more. Just like he promised, Mulray took Sal out for dinner and drinks after work yesterday. After they ate and they were having coffee, Mulray asked Sal if he could make the Long Island run. This is an important point for two reasons. First, Mulray has never been a team player. In fact, this loser has always given my guy Sal all kinds of excuses why he couldn't make the Long Island run in the past. Second, the Long Island run involves the largest delivery of tires that are shipped by truck at any one time to the civilian market. And, as you guys know, any truck load of tires in this day and age is worth a small fortune on the black market."

After hearing Detective Mc Donald comment, "The more we learn about this truck driver the more he sounds like he's worth tailing," Tony G. remarked, "You're right, Johnny, but there's more."

As soon as Major Beauregard spoke up and said, "Go ahead, Tony," Tony G. picked up where he left off. "Last night Mulray told Sal the reason he wanted to make the Long Island run is because he has a piece of ass on the side who lives near the Nassau County line and would like to use the company truck to swing by and see her on his way back to the city. Bear in mind that Tommy Mulray is a first class slob, who couldn't get laid in a whore house if he had a fist full of twenty dollar bills in each hand."

While Jim Beauregard and the others grinned after hearing Tony describe the subject of their investigation in a derogatory fashion, Tony went on to say, "This is a guy who up until yesterday has never had two nickles to rub together and is barely able to take care of his wife and five kids but he now claims to have money to spare and a girlfriend to boot. I'm sorry, but I don't buy it and neither does my buddy Sal."

After pausing for a split second to take a drag on his cigarette, Tony G. made eye contact with the Major and his men as he continued and said. "When Sal played his part and expressed his concern about getting fired for letting a driver use a company truck to take a detour for personal reasons, Mister Money Bags slipped Sal a ten spot to soften him up. Mulray then went on to say that his luck finally changed and that he won enough money lately to share his good fortune with the people that take care of him."

After pausing to stamp his cigarette out in the ashtray on the desk, Tony G. looked directly at Major Beauregard and said, "When Sal told me about this guy, I suggested that he let Mulray make the Long Island run so we could keep an eye on him and his truck load of tires. If by some miracle Tommy Mulray actually made a score and he's legit, we'll end up following him to the distribution center on Long Island. On the other hand, if this loser is up to no good, we'll be in a position to ruin his night."

Jim Beauregard agreed and was the first to react to Tony's plan. "You're right, Tony. We have nothing to lose and everything to gain by keeping an eye on this guy."

After having his plan validated by the number two man in the Provost Marshal's Office, Tony continued his briefing. "Now that Sal is on board, he agreed to keep me posted by calling the phone in this office when Mulray's truck is just about ready to go. Once Sal sees that we're in our cars, he'll wave Mulray on and leave the rest up to us."

After turning to face his favorite wartime helper, Detective Angelone remarked, "If this deal goes down it will be as good, if not better than the last caper you helped us with when we nailed that printer on 23rd street who was making counterfeit ration cards." When Agent Dubrowsky heard what Detective Angelone had to say, the veteran FBI Agent removed the cigar from the corner of his mouth and said, "Ange is right. If we can nail a ring of hoods hijacking a truck load of rationed tires we'll be knocking another home run outta the park."

Johnny Mc Donald agreed and added, "After hearing everything that Tony said about this guy, my gut tells me that Mr. Mulray is up to no good."

After taking one last drag on his cigarette, Jim Beauregard remarked, "Even though it's possible that Mulray's luck has changed, I'm still not sold on the idea that this guy can afford to buy his boss dinner and drinks, then bribe him with a ten dollar bill, while supporting a wife, five kids and a girlfriend."

While Jim put his cigarette butt out in the ashtray on the desk, he continued as he made eye contact with Andy, Tony G, and the two detectives. "Under the circumstances, we have no choice but to follow Mulray or risk waking up in the morning and finding out that we lost a large truckload of tires that are worth a small fortune on the black market."

"Then it's settled," remarked Detective Angelone who quickly added, "We're working late tonight."

The second the phone rang in the warehouse office, Tony G. remarked, "And the horses are at the gate," as he took the call. "Talk to me, Sal."

While Tony received an update from Sal, Detectives Angelone and Mc Donald continued to observe the trucking company where tons of rationed items were delivered to stores throughout the metropolitan area.

After thanking Sal for the heads up, Tony G. placed the phone back on the receiver, as he relayed what his contact at the trucking company had to say. "We better get into position, Major. Mulray's truck will be ready to roll in a few minutes. To delay him further Sal said he's gonna have Mulray drop him off by the front gate. When Sal sees that we're in our cars he'll cut Mulray lose."

Tony G. was no draft dodger and had a legitimate heart murmur that kept him from being inducted into the Army. While it's true that his one felony conviction was enough to initially keep him from being inducted into the military, later in the war provisions were made to draft men with criminal records, including men who were serving certain types of prison sentences.

From the moment that he was introduced to Jim Beauregard, Tony G. liked the police captain from Atlanta who was serving as the second in command of the U.S. Army Provost Marshal's Office in New York City. In peacetime, a guy like Tony G. would never give a cop the time of day, especially a fed. In fact, Tony went as far as telling his new associates in the Army Task Force, that once victory was achieved he would become a first class crook again.

Every Confidential Informant had a story but Tony G's was different. Even though he was a gangster and a crook, Tony loved his country and knew that life under the thumb of the Japanese or the Nazis would be horrible, even for criminals. What really motivated Tony G. was the memory of his older brother, who died at sea when his freighter was torpedoed by a German U boat and sank within sight of the U.S. coastline.

Once the Japanese attacked Pearl Harbor, Tony G decided to do all he could to help Uncle Sam. In the early part of the war, he helped root out German sympathizers along the waterfront. When his brother was killed, Tony became even more motivated to get involved in the war effort. Tony was able to do so because he knew first hand that the black market was flourishing and that anything not nailed down was being stolen and sold to anyone who had the money and the desire to circumvent the need to rely on ration books.

As Detective Mc Donald and his colorful partner positioned their unmarked police car to take the lead, Tony G. was invited to join Major Beauregard and Agent Dubrowsky in the unmarked U.S. Army sedan. Like most good street cops, James Beauregard had a few reliable informants of his own over the years. After turning around in the driver's seat, the Major pulled out a pack of Lucky Strikes and offered a smoke to Tony.

Tony G was a hardcore cigarette smoker who preferred Lucky Strikes over every other brand. Even though Camels would do in a pinch, Tony swore on a stack of Bibles that he would quit smoking before he would ever try another brand of cigarettes.

As Tony graciously accepted the cigarette and the light, he said, "Thanks Major," before he continued to keep an eye on the front gate of the trucking company.

Jim Beauregard knew everything the local cops knew about Tony G, including the part about his older brother. Now that they had worked a few successful investigations together, Jim got to know and like the man who had become the secret weapon of the U.S. Army Task Force. As a result, the Major wasn't being a tactful investigator who was playing up to the sympathy of an informant, when he turned sideways again in the driver's seat and said, "I'm sorry about your brother, Tony."

When Agent Dubrowsky repeated the same sentiment and Jim Beauregard saw the look of surprise on Tony's face, the Major remarked, "Frank told us what happened to your brother. He said your older brother was a real nice guy. Johnny liked a lot him as well."

After thanking the Major and Andy Dubrowsky for the kind words, Tony continued looking out the left rear passenger side window, while he imagined his brother drowning in the cold Atlantic after his freighter was sunk by a marauding U Boat. While Jim continued to observe the front gate of the trucking company, he expressed his gratitude for having such a street wise and well connected New Yorker providing valuable intelligence support to the Army Task Force. "You're a good man, Tony G. I don't know what we'd do without you."

CHAPTER 8

GOODING'S GARAGE AND THE BLACK MARKET

A t 17 ½ cents a gallon gasoline was rationed to limit unnecessary travel that was not essential to the war effort. During World War II, every civilian vehicle was required to display the appropriate decal on the front windshield that identified the driver's requirements and authorization level for purchasing fuel. People who were essential to the war effort and civil defense received certain considerations as far as the rationing of gas was concerned.

Gasoline ration decals that contained the letter A meant that the driver could purchase four gallons of gas per week in the early part of the war. This amount was reduced later on in the war. A fuel ration decal that displayed the letter B identified the owner of a motor vehicle operator as someone who was essential for the war effort. Any vehicle that displayed a B ration decal was authorized to purchase more fuel than the A ration decal. A fuel ration C decal was issued to essential government and civilian personnel who were critical to the war effort including mail delivery personnel, medical doctors, priests, ministers, rabbis, active duty armed forces personnel etc.... The T decal was a white letter on a dark blue background and identified the driver as having the ability to purchase unlimited fuel. It took until December of 1942 to implement nationwide gas rationing which in large measure was put into effect because of shortages in rubber.[2]

If you knew the right people, you could purchase what was known as black-market gasoline. During World War II, black market gasoline generally sold for .30 cents a gallon. The same went for obtaining new tires, certain meat products, cigarettes and other items that were difficult to impossible to obtain during the war. Unfortunately, the Japanese occupation of countries that hosted large rubber plantations caused a shortage of rubber in the United States.

Early in the war, attempts were made to re-groove worn out tires to get the most out of every tire on your car. Even the most heavily worn out tires were kept on the road by re-grooving. Thanks to American ingenuity, synthetic tires were created as a way to find a replacement for the tires that were traditionally made out of 100% rubber. Unfortunately, obtaining new tires was not as easy as it was before the war. This enabled anyone who had access to a supply of new tires, to fill orders for customers who were unable to comply with the rather strict Office of Price Administration regulations.

As soon as Ivan pulled the stolen Packard into the driveway, he honked the horn twice and waited for the young man with a pronounced limp to push the large wooden door open. With the gas tank sucking fumes, Ivan drove into the nondescript garage, while Curly Gooding closed the large door behind him.

Curly Gooding was a seriously disabled U.S. Army veteran who lost part of his leg and a chunk out of his skull, while engaging German armored vehicles with a bazooka in the Kassarine Pass. To their credit, the bazooka team of Private Gerard "Curly" Gooding and his loader were two of the Americans who did not turn tail and run, during the first ground combat action between the U.S. Army and the German Afrika Corps.

After knocking out an enemy armored car, the seriously wounded soldier from Parkside Avenue in Brooklyn and his loader were left for dead and ignored by the advancing German troops. Luckily, Private Gooding and his wounded loader were found by an American patrol that inspected the area after the battle. The fact that Curly and the Army Private who served as his loader were still alive, was considered a miracle by the Army doctors who treated the two seriously wounded G.I.s. For the disabling wounds that they sustained in combat and the heroism that these soldiers displayed in the Kassarine Pass, Curly Gooding and his loader were decorated while they recovered in their hospital beds.

After several operations and months in a military hospital, Curly was medically discharged with a steel plate in his head, a slightly shorter right leg and no hope of ever being completely normal again. Just like other Americans who served in combat during World War II, Curly Gooding came home a disabled veteran who could barely speak or walk right. His life was spent in his father's garage, where he sold black-market gasoline and other hard to get items to wealthy customers who had no desire to comply with rationing regulations.

While wearing a soiled pair of herringbone army fatigues and an oil stained field jacket, Curly wiped the grease off his hands with a shop towel as he approached the burgundy colored 1939 Packard Business Coupe. As the young man known as Ivan Smith got out of the car, he greeted the disabled veteran while he handed him a ten dollar bill and a bottle of prewar scotch. "The ten spot is for the gas and the bottle is for you, Curly. Whatever you do keep this away from your old man. He can drink his own booze."

While Curly tucked the bottle in his field jacket pocket and did his best to say thanks. "Tha tha thanks fa fa for tha tha ha ha hooch, Ivan."

After Ivan remarked, "What are friends for," he started to walk away then turned and said, "Do me a favor, Curly, and filler up."

While Curly stuttered again and said, "O O OK I Ivan," the disabled veteran backed away from the Packard as he grabbed the rubber hose from the top of the closest 55 gallon drum and went to work.

As Ivan walked away, he brushed a few cigarette ashes from his pants before he turned to Curly and said, "Is your old man in the office?" Curly had a hard time walking and chewing gum at the same time ever since the shell from a German tank ripped his body to shreds. Because he was slow to react, Curly kept pumping fuel with one hand, while he had to think about the question before he could respond. Instead of trying to stutter his way through a sentence, Curly simply pointed to the corner office in the garage where his father conducted his black-market activities.

While Ivan walked toward his office, Andy Gooding pushed his reclining chair away from his cluttered desk that was covered with a newspaper, a pile of old engine parts and a half eaten sandwich. After removing a Camel from the pack that he carried in his grease stained work shirt, Andy Gooding turned away from the fan that was circulating air in his office, while he used a wooden match to light his cigarette. As soon as Ivan entered the office, Andy Gooding took a drag on his Camel and exhaled a lungful of cigarette smoke before he remarked, "Where's my tires?"

Andy Gooding was more than just a good customer. As far as Ivan was concerned, Andy Gooding and his son Curly were good people.

While Ivan joined Mr. Gooding in a smoke, he responded and said, "Relax, you'll have 'em tonight, along with a truck in excellent condition that should bring us some extra dough."

As soon as Ivan looked through the office window to check on his car, Andy

Gooding spoke up and said, "Don't worry, he's a little slow but he knows what he's doing."

Even though Andy Gooding had a rough exterior, it troubled him to no end to see his youngest son come home from the war one notch better off than a vegetable. When Ivan asked if Curly was getting any better, Andy Gooding responded and said, "Unfortunately, my youngest son is fucked for the rest of his life thanks to the Third Reich."

Andy Gooding had a good reason to hate the war and the enemy. In addition to worrying about his two older sons who were fighting in the Pacific, Andy Gooding had to endure being notified that his youngest son was Missing in Action. Then came the telegram that said his youngest son was seriously wounded. Seeing Curly in a military hospital was sheer torment for Andy Gooding and the other members in his family. Despite his tough guy disposition, Andy Gooding was twice as grateful that his wife wasn't alive to see their youngest son have to live with such disabling injuries.

While Andy Gooding leaned back in his chair, he took a long drag on his Camel cigarette before he looked up at one of the youngest black-market operators in New York and said, "I'd like to get my hands on the Nazi son of a bitch who hurt my boy."

After taking another look at Curly while he gassed up the Packard, Ivan appeared lost in thought when he remarked, "Yea, me too."

While Andy Gooding leaned closer to his desk, he stamped his cigarette butt out in a metal ashtray before he looked up at Ivan and said, "Don't worry. With the way this war is going you'll get your chance to serve."

Ivan didn't need Andy Gooding to remind him that in a few days he would turn 18 years of age. Once this happened, Ivan would have to register for the Selective Service or face up to five years in federal prison and a fine of $10,000 if he failed to comply. No one was exempt and only the local draft board was authorized to classify a person as 1A eligible for duty or IV-F/4F ineligible.

Even though Ivan Larson was a crook who was actively involved in the black market, he considered himself to be a true patriot. Ivan also believed that he would make a good soldier when his time came to serve. In fact, the only reason Ivan didn't enlist when he turned 17, was because he wanted to bank roll enough cash to set himself up in a legitimate business after the war.

With only a short time to go before he had to register for military service, Ivan knew that it was only a matter of time before he would be off to basic training and on his way to war. Knowing that his days were numbered made Ivan consider his options.

Despite his involvement in criminal activity, Ivan was no different than other young men of his time. Many a night Ivan lay awake dreaming of the day when he would be called to fight. In order to help him to decide how he should serve, Ivan would see his favorite movies over and over again. As much as Ivan enjoyed movies like Sergeant York and The Fighting 69th, his favorite films were the military flying pictures. In fact, it was movies like The Flying Tigers, The Dawn Patrol, A Yank In The RAF, Desperate Journey, Eagle Squadron and Air Force that convinced Ivan that he was best suited to serve as a U.S. Army aviator.

As far as Ivan was concerned, being an Army pilot translated to being respected. Ivan also saw himself as an adventurer who was not afraid to do a job that was considered to be very dangerous by most people of sound mind. So, for various reasons, Ivan decided that when the day came that he had to serve his country, he would make every effort to do so as a U.S. Army aviator.

Sensing that the conversation was getting a little too private, Ivan immediately changed the subject and spoke as he stamped his cigarette out in the ashtray on Mr. Gooding's desk. "As soon as I get gassed up, I'll be meeting my tire contact. If everything goes according to plan, I should be back with a truck load of tires by eight o'clock tonight."

After hearing the good news, Mr. Gooding slapped the draw on the lower left side of his desk with open palm of his left hand. As soon as he pulled the desk draw open, Andy Gooding removed a half full pint bottle of prewar vintage Johnny Walker Red Scotch and said, "Good, 'cause I got two Wall Street big wigs, a bank president, a big shot lawyer from Lincoln Road and a half a dozen other patriotic Americans driving me crazy for new tires."

As soon as the veteran grease monkey removed the cork from the bottle, he poured two shots of scotch into two paper Dixie cups that he kept on the side of his desk for such occasions. After handing one of the paper cups to the young man that he knew as Ivan Smith, Andy Gooding slapped the cork back on top of the bottle before he picked up his shot of scotch and said, "Good luck tonight." As soon as both men finished their drink, Ivan checked his watch in preparation of getting on the road.

As soon as Curly came limping into the office, he was just about to stutter his way through a sentence and return his favorite customer's change, when Ivan smiled and said "Keep the change, Curly...I'll see you later, Mr. G."

When Ivan left the office so did Curly. Even though his limp slowed him down, Curly was able to catch up to Ivan as he did his best to thank him for the generous tip. While Curly stuttered and said," Tha tha thanks, Ivan," Ivan opened the door to the Packard and got in behind the wheel as if he was in a hurry to leave.

After calling out, "I'll see you later, Curly" Ivan started the engine and put the Packard in gear. By the time Ivan turned the stolen luxury car around, Curly was pushing the large wooden garage door open. While Curly stood by the open garage door, Ivan honked the horn as he drove down the driveway.

As soon as Curly started to push the garage door closed, a green colored 1941 Cadillac Sedan that belonged to a bank president arrived for his weekly tank full of black market gas. After seeing one of his father's best customers wave as he approached the driveway, Curly opened the door all the way and stood off to the side, as the banker from Ocean Parkway drove into Gooding's Garage to break the law.

CHAPTER 9

THE CLASH OF GOOD & EVIL

After taking a few puffs on his White Owl cigar, Al Parker took a sip of coffee and realized how much he had gotten used to drinking coffee with a dash of milk and no sugar. After removing a metal flask from his back pocket, Al turned to Pat Murphy Jr. and asked, "How 'bout a little coffee sport?"

Even though young Patrick was no longer considered a rookie by the police department, he had a tendency to go by the rules. As Pat covered his cup with his left hand, the youngest member of the Murphy family to serve as a city cop remarked, "Come on, Al, we're on duty."

Seeing Al shrug his shoulders was Pat's signal to relax. As soon as the young street cop removed his hand from the top of his cup, Al leaned over and quickly splashed two drops of Irish whiskey into Pat's coffee cup regardless of his previous objections. While Al laughed, Pat gave in and remarked, "What the hell," as he raised the cup to his mouth and took a generous sip.

As soon as Al finished screwing the top back on his flask, he spoke in a voice that was laced with friendly sarcasm as he said. "It's your grandfather's fault that I acquired a taste for Irish Whiskey. Your old man made a bad situation worse when he gave me a case of Irish whiskey the day I got sworn in." Seeing young Patrick crack a smile was all that Al was after. After taking a sip of his whiskey laced coffee, Al shook his head as he savored every drop and remarked, "Um, that's good."

While Pat sat quietly by the open back door of Mr. Federman's storage room, he seemed to be lost as he sipped his cup of coffee. After a solid thirty seconds of watching his young friend, Al was convinced that Pat was thinking about the men he left behind on Guadalcanal. In an effort to get young Patrick to open up, Al removed the cigar from the corner of his mouth before he spoke up and said, "I'll bet you didn't have hooch like this on Guadalcanal?"

The mere mention of the word Guadalcanal was enough to motivate Pat to come out of his trance and speak. "Some Navy Seabees whipped up a batch of jungle juice one night, but it was nothing like this," remarked the former combat veteran who now wore the uniform of a New York City Police Department Patrolman.

While Al tapped the ash from his cigar into a nearby metal ashtray, he looked directly at his young friend as he spoke in a soft tone of voice and said, "You're not back yet, are you? I mean all the way?"

Pat Murphy Jr. knew exactly what Al meant. Being in combat was unlike any other experience in life. Physically leaving a war zone and leaving a war zone was not the same thing. In every war since the beginning of time, combat veterans took the horrors of war back with them to civilian life. Veterans of World War II were no different.

After looking at two stacks of Life Magazines, that were piled up along the wall in the back of the storeroom, Pat paused long enough to collect his thoughts before he responded to Al's question. Just before he spoke, Pat put a Lucky Strike in between his lips and fired up his lighter. After exhaling a lungful of cigarette smoke, Pat looked at Al and said, "You know what it's like, Al. You were in combat."

Al Parker was a humble man and proved it when he remarked, "You can't count what I did as being in combat."

Immediately after hearing Al's response Pat objected in a very respectful but serious tone of voice. "I know what you did, Al. My whole family and every cop on this job knows what you did in the last war."

Pat Murphy Jr. was well aware that Al was decorated for saving his father's life, as well as the life of a wounded French solider. Whether it was Al's fate or his father's destiny, they became close friends as a result of a wartime experience. Pat Murphy Jr. also knew that Al could have performed his intelligence duties in the relative safety of a rear area headquarters. Instead, Al made every effort to perform his duties as a German speaking translator along the front line.

As far as Pat Murphy Jr. was concerned, it didn't matter whether Al Parker performed this heroic act because he wanted to prove something or because he was just plain brave. Al's actions on that frightful night in no mans land changed the lives of many people, including his own. In fact, if Al never ventured into no man's land there was an excellent chance that Pat's father might have been killed in action.

While disregarding his friend's attempt to make light of his war time heroics, young Patrick continued and said, "It doesn't matter whether you were in combat for one minute, one day, one month or one year. Once you've been exposed to war you become different from everyone else."

After hearing what Pat had to say, Al nodded his head in agreement and remarked, "I guess you're right."

Before he continued Pat took another drag on his cigarette then said, "I have to tell you, Al. As glad as I am to be home and back on the job, there are days when I miss being a squad leader."

As soon as Pat stood up, he faced the wall where Mr. Federman put up a poster that read Lose Lips Sink Ships. After taking another drag on his cigarette, Pat rubbed his bad shoulder while turned around and said, "I want'a write my buddies but I'm afraid to find out who got killed and who's still alive." While Al listened, Pat continued. "I know it sounds crazy, Al, but sometimes I wish I was still back in that God awful jungle fighting Japs."

After removing the cigar from its perch in between his teeth, Al looked up at his young friend and spoke in a fatherly tone of voice. "The main thing is that you're back and you're in one piece. I'm also sure your Army buddies are happy for you."

While raising the white porcelain coffee cup, Pat proposed a toast and said, "To the guys I left behind."

"Here, here" said Al, before he downed the rest of his whiskey laced coffee and grabbed his gun belt as he stood up.

After resting the empty cup on a nearby wooden crate, Al strapped on his gun belt while he looked at young Patrick and said, "It's time to get back on the job, Patrolman Murphy."

While Pat secured the back door that led to the alley, Al walked to the front of the store and told Mr. Federman that they would be back before midnight to make sure that he locked up without incident. Since Mr. Federman and his wife lived in an apartment above the candy store, the two cops didn't have to go far to make sure their favorite civilian safely made it home with the money that he earned after working another 16 day.

Once young Patrick joined Al by the counter, they waited for Mr. Federman to make change for a customer before the two cops said goodbye. As soon as they left the corner candy store, Pat faced Al and said, "After we make sure Mr. Federman gets home OK, you want'a grab a cold beer at Mc Donald's Bar? My old man said he'd meet us. He also said he owes you an Irish coffee for flushing the radiator in his Chevy to keep it from overheating."

"In that case, I'm go'in," remarked Al, who continued as he pointed his right index finger at the young cop. "Remember, you're in a different kind'a jungle now, so be careful."

Even though Pat was no longer a rookie, he proved that he appreciated Al's concern for his well being when he cracked a smile then said, "Yes, Sir." as he tossed his honorary uncle a casual salute.

As soon as Al remarked, "Make yourself useful and go give someone a ticket," Pat cracked another smile before turned around and headed in the opposite direction.

Ivan Larson had been a hoodlum long enough to know that it was in his best interest to get into position before Tommy Mulray arrived at the Ft. Hamilton Diner. He made the decision to do so, because Ivan had no reason to trust such a pathetic loser like Tommy Mulray.

After checking his watch, Ivan wasn't surprised to see his tire connection arrive a good twenty minutes late. Fortunately, Tommy Mulray was able to park his truck on the corner by the entrance to the diner.

While Ivan slumped down in the driver's seat of the stolen Packard, he continued watching Mulray exit his truck and walk inside. So far so good thought Ivan, as he continued observing the location where he intended to stage the hijacking.

Jim Beauregard and his team of veteran investigators decided to maintain a lose surveillance of Tommy Mulray in an effort to accomplish two objectives. One objective was to prevent a truck load of rationed tires from being stolen. They also wanted to arrest anyone involved in a truck hijacking, if Tommy Mulray failed to deliver the tires to the appropriate destination on Long Island.

As soon as Tony G. saw Tommy Mulray's direction of travel, he spoke like a typical fast talking New Yorker when he advised Jim Beauregard and Andy Dubrowsky not to make the next turn. "Excuse me, Major but we might want'a wait to see if Mulray continues driving through Brooklyn, or if he stops on the next block. I'd be especially interested to see if Mulray stops at the diner that's on the corner."

Without being asked to do so, Andy Dubrowsky volunteered to take a look around the corner to check on Mulray's current position. For a man his size Andy Dubrowsky moved fast and was in position on the corner in no time flat. The moment Andy glanced back and gave Jim Beauregard the thumbs up signal, the Major turned to Tony G. and said, "Sit tight, while I brief our favorite pair of detectives."

As soon as Jim opened the driver' door and exited the unmarked Army sedan, he motioned the two police detectives to hold their position. Jim then walked to the corner to meet with Andy.

"Tony was right again, Jim," said the veteran FBI Agent who quickly added, "By the time I got into position Mulray was just walking into the diner."

After taking a look for himself, Jim asked Andy to keep an eye on Mulray and his truck while he briefed Frank Angelone and Johnny Mc Donald.

As soon as Jim walked over to the unmarked police car, the Major crouched down by the open driver's side window and brought Detective's Angelone and Mc Donald up to date about the recent change of events. "Tony suggested that we wait to see if Mulray continued driving through Brooklyn, or if he stopped on the next street after he made the turn. As usual, Tony was right. Mulray parked his truck on the corner and went into the Ft. Hamilton Diner. Andy is keeping an eye on the truck as well as the entrance to the diner."

When Johnny Mc Donald heard what Jim Beauregard had to say, he leaned closer to his partner and said, "If you want, Jimmy, I'll move in on foot, while Frankie parks one block over."

Jim didn't have to think twice to know that Johnny's suggestion made perfect sense. While Jim looked directly at Detective Mc Donald, he approved the plan and wished him well. "OK, Johnny, but be careful."

Before he moved in on foot, Detective Mc Donald had one more point to make. "If you see me step outside and fix the brim on my hat standby to move in. If you see me draw my gun come running."

"You got, it, Johnny," responded Jim Beauregard who quickly added, "Don't forget to let Andy know what the plan is before you make your way to the diner."

"Will do," remarked Johnny Mc Donald as he grabbed the folded newspaper off the seat of the car, before he opened the door and stepped out onto the street.

While Detective Mc Donald walked to the corner to meet with Andy Dubrowsky, Jim looked at Frank Angelone and said, "You be careful too, Ange."

As soon as Frank Angelone remarked, "You too, Major," the veteran police detective went to drive away but had trouble getting the worn out transmission into gear.

"Lord help us," remarked Johnny Mc Donald as he looked back at his partner while he approached the corner where Andy Dubrowsky was standing.

Once Johnny Mc Donald was finished telling Andy Dubrowsky that he was moving in on foot, while his partner positioned himself one block over, the Irish American police detective added, "Providing of course that Frankie can get our car moving again."

By the time Johnny Mc Donald turned the corner, Frank Angelone had the unmarked police car in gear and was moving in the right direction. While Frank Angelone drove away, Jim cracked a smile and tossed the colorful police detective a casual salute before he returned to his car.

As soon as Jim got back behind the wheel of the unmarked Army sedan, he rubbed his hands together while he turned in his seat and said, "Once Frank and Johnny get into position Mulray and his truck will be boxed in."

After hearing Tony G. remark, "All we have to do now is sit tight and wait," Jim passed a pack of Lucky Strikes to Tony and said, "This is when the fun begins."

So far so good thought Ivan, while he waited for Mulray to leave the diner so they could execute the mock hijacking. Even when Ivan observed a well dressed man in his 40's walking toward the diner with a newspaper tucked under his arm, he had no reason to suspect that anything was out of the ordinary. However, just to be on the safe side, Ivan drew his Colt 1911 and racked the slide to load the chamber, before he applied the thumb safety and placed the .45 caliber pistol inside his waistband in a cross draw position.

While the Major sat in the driver's seat of the unmarked Army sedan and smoked a cigarette, Tony G. tapped the ash from his cigarette out of the open right rear passenger side window as he spoke up and said, "I gotta tell you, Major, my gut tells me that Mulray is up to something."

Immediately after Jim took another drag on his cigarette, he responded while he continued keeping an eye on Andy Dubrowsky. "Thank God for our side that gut of yours has always been on the money."

Tony G. had more to say and wasted no time in telling the Major what was on his mind. "The reason I think something's wrong is because we're only a few blocks away from where Mulray lives. If Mulray wanted to grab a cup of coffee or something to eat on his way to Long Island, why stop at a diner when he could go home? There's also better ways to get to Long Island from where he works and other places to stop along the way for a truck driver to take a break."

Even though Jim was from Georgia, he worked in New York City long enough to become familiar with different neighborhoods. As a result, Jim knew that the Bayridge section of Brooklyn was considered a nice area. Knowing this brought Jim to turn sideways in the driver's seat as he looked at Tony G. and said, "I'm curious, Tony. How can a loser like Tommy Mulray afford to live in such a nice neighborhood?"

As usual, Tony G. had an answer that made perfect sense. "According to my buddy Sal, the only reason Tommy Mulray can afford to live in a house in this section of Brooklyn, is because his mother left him the family home when she died. Otherwise, this loser and his family would be living in a one room dump."

As soon as Ivan spotted Tommy Mulray exit the Ft. Hamilton Diner, he put the Packard in gear and looked around before he drove down the block. The fact that it just rained, cooled things off enough to make the end of this late summer day considerably more bearable.

After stopping at the intersection, Ivan continued to scan the area while he let a passing car go by. All Ivan had to do to pull off the deal of the century, was pickup the keys from Tommy Mulray, park the stolen Packard and drive off with the truck. Once Ivan delivered the tires to Andy Gooding's garage, his end of this caper would be over.

After cruising through the intersection, Ivan couldn't believe his eyes when he saw his pathetic accomplice nervously smoking a cigarette, while he stood in the street as if he was waiting to meet someone. If anyone was paying attention, they would never believe that Tommy Mulray was hijacked, because any other driver would get back into his truck and drive away as soon as his break was over.

As soon as Ivan brought the Packard to a stop, he waited for Tommy Mulray to walk the rest of the way to make the exchange. When Detective Mc Donald observed Mulray step closer to the burgundy colored Packard, he left the diner and took a position out front. Just like he said would do, Johnny removed his black Stenson fedora from his head and fixed the brim to signal his fellow investigators to prepare to move in.

While Frank Angelone pulled the unmarked police sedan up to the corner with the headlights off, Andy Dubrowsky got back into the unmarked Army sedan and told Jim to make the turn and park down the street from the diner. After turning the corner, Jim drove down the block at a normal rate of speed and pulled into the first available parking space that faced the corner.

The moment Tommy Mulray handed the set of keys to Ivan, the sound of an approaching siren sent a lightening bolt of fear shooting through the young criminal's spine. As soon as Ivan drew his Colt 1911 pistol, he looked directly at Tommy Mulray and called out, "You set me up!"

The sight of Ivan with a forty five caliber pistol in hand caused Tommy Mulray to take a step back as he held up his hands and screamed, "I did not! Nothings changed! Take the damn truck!"

At the exact same time that Detective Mc Donald drew his Colt Detective Special and yelled, "Police! Stop in the name of the law," Ivan pointed his pistol at Tommy Mulray and fired two shots at close range into the truck driver's face. A split second later Ivan drove off at a high rate of speed, while Detective Mc Donald opened fire and riddled the back of the Packard with six bullets.

As far as Ivan Larson was concerned, Tommy Mulray was either a snitch trying to set him up, or his truck load of tires was being tailed by the police. Either way, Ivan believed that he had no choice but to eliminate the one person who was weak enough to implicate him and Mike Connely in the hijacking of a truck load of rationed tires. The fact that Ivan was in possession of two loaded handguns and a stolen car, paled in comparison to the trouble that he was in for committing murder. Ivan was also lucky to be alive, after a diner customer who turned out to be a cop opened fire as he drove off in the stolen Packard.

While Ivan sped away from the scene of the crime, an ambulance from a nearby hospital raced by the intersection. Regardless of whether the siren was on an ambulance or a police car, it was too late for Ivan to take back what he just did. Besides the fact that he lost the opportunity to pick up a truck load of brand new tires, Ivan was now a cold blooded killer who would become a wanted man if the police were able to identify him.

Just when Ivan thought that he was making a clean getaway, he spotted two cops in plainclothes exit their unmarked car with their guns drawn. Even though he was moving at a high rate of speed, Ivan knew that these cops had the potential to stop him dead in his tracks, if their bullets hit the mark while he drove by and fled the area.

While Detective Angelone struggled to get the worn out transmission in the unmarked police car to cooperate, he cursed out loud and said, "Come on you son of a bitch!"

After hearing Johnny Mc Donald call out, "He's getting away!" Detective Angelone muttered, "No shit!" while he continued trying to coax the worn out transmission into gear.

By the time Johnny Mc Donald reloaded his revolver and jumped into the passenger seat of the unmarked squad car, his partner managed to get the sedan moving again. Unfortunately, the unmarked police car stalled while turning the corner and had to be re-started again before the two detectives could give chase.

While the fast moving burgundy colored Packard approached their position, Jim Beauregard called out, "Get down, Tony," while he took cover behind the open driver's side door of the unmarked Army sedan.

Instead of standing out in the open, Andy Dubrowsky knelt behind the right front tire and aimed his revolver over the hood of the car. Rather than miss what was taking place, Tony G. ignored the Major's advice to take cover and looked over the top of the back seat to see what was going on.

While the stolen Packard raced down the street, Ivan held his pistol out of the open driver's side window and emptied the magazine at the plainclothes cop who was taking cover behind the open driver's side door of the tan colored Ford. At the same time that Jim Beauregard fired four rounds at the Packard, a string of .45 caliber bullets fired by Ivan Larson struck the Army sedan and grazed the Major on the left side of his forehead.

The second Jim Beauregard fell wounded on the ground, Tony G. jumped out of the back seat, picked up the Major's Colt pistol and emptied the magazine at the Packard, just as the gunman opened fire with his backup gun. While the Packard raced by the unmarked Army sedan, two of the six bullets fired from Ivan Larson's Colt revolver struck Tony G. in the chest at close range. As Tony G. fell mortally wounded next to Major Beauregard, FBI Agent Andy Dubrowsky stood up and emptied his revolver at the fleeing felon.

With the smoke from the shootout still hanging in the air, Frank Angelone and Johnny Mc Donald raced by the unmarked Army sedan with their siren blasting. Unfortunately, by the time the two detectives reached the corner, the Packard vanished from sight. While the sound of police sirens got louder, a number of bystanders left the diner and huddled around the dead body of the father of five who was killed by an unknown gunman.

As soon as Andy Dubrowsky holstered his revolver, he ran around the front of the shot up Army sedan and said, "Easy, Jim" while he helped the Army Investigator to get up on one knee.

While Jim Beauregard held his handkerchief against the large cut that ran across his scalp line, Andy Dubrowsky went to the aid of Tony G. just as a pair of police cars and an ambulance arrived on scene. When the mortally wounded informant looked up and said, "Do me a favor, Major and tell my mother that I died doing the right thing," Jim Beauregard did his best to sound enthusiastic when he remarked, "Hang on, Tony. You're gonna be OK. We're gonna get you to a hospital."

Under the circumstances, Tony knew better and decided to forgo the ride to the hospital so he could finish making his last request to his favorite Army officer. As Tony lifted his head off the ground, he patted the Major's arm and said, "It's too late, Major. My brother's here to take me the rest of the way."

Even though Jim Beauregard had seen other people die, they were usually people that he didn't know. This was different. The fact that Tony G. helped government agencies in time of war because he wanted to and not because he had to made him one of the "good guys."

As soon as Tony passed away, Jim Beauregard looked at Andy and said, "I never got a chance to tell him that we were putting him in for a full pardon."

After hearing Andy remark, "He knows now, Jim." the Major continued holding his blood soaked handkerchief over his head wound, while his partner helped him to stand up.

When an ambulance crewman arrived by the driver's side of the Army sedan with a stretcher, Andy Dubrowsky identified himself and said, "I'm with the FBI. Do me a favor and take our friend to the morgue and see to it that a doctor takes a look at my partner's head wound."

As soon as the ambulance driver responded and said, "Yes, Sir," Jim raised his right hand and remarked, "I'll be OK, Andy. I don't have to go to the hospital."

While Andy Dubrowsky instructed Jim that he could either go to the hospital in an ambulance or in a police car, a uniformed police sergeant and a patrolman walked over to the Army sedan and immediately took the two plainclothesmen for police detectives. As soon as the uniformed sergeant asked if Jim and Andy were from downtown, Andy Dubrowsky flashed his FBI credentials and said, "Andy Dubrowsky FBI. This is Major Beauregard from the U.S. Army Provost Marshal's Office. A bullet grazed the Major's head during a shootout with a truck hijacker. Can you do me a favor, Sarge and have someone take the Major to the hospital."

When Jim removed the blood soaked handkerchief from his head, the police sergeant leaned closer to examine the wound before he turned to the patrolman who was admiring the shot up Army sedan and said, "Tommy, I want you to take this Army Officer to the hospital. He's got a nasty grazing wound across the side of his head that needs attention."

As soon as the middle aged patrolman gently grabbed Jim Beauregard by the arm and said, "Easy does it, Major," Jim reluctantly remarked, "OK, I'll have a doctor patch me up."

While the Major was led away, Andy grinned then said, "That wasn't so hard. Was it?"

As soon as Andy Dubrowsky picked up the Major's empty pistol and stood back up, he pointed his left index finger toward the corner and began to brief the police sergeant about their case. "The recently deceased is a suspect in a hijacking case. The truck that's parked on the corner is filled with brand new tires that were supposed to be delivered to a distribution center on Long Island."

After pausing long enough to light a fresh cigar, Andy Dubrowsky asked the police sergeant if he could find out how Detective's Angelone and Mc Donald were doing in their pursuit of the killer who fled the scene in a burgundy colored two door Packard. "No problem," responded the fifty year old sergeant, who was exempt from military service because of his occupation, age and marital status.

While the sergeant walked over to a nearby lamp post and used the phone in the police call box to contact his precinct, Andy Dubrowsky called out, "I'll check on the dead truck driver and meet you inside the diner. The coffee's on the FBI, Sarge."

While Ivan drove away from the scene of the crime, he knew he had to dump the stolen Packard before he made his way into Manhattan. After nervously lighting a cigarette, Ivan began to justify his actions to himself. The more Ivan considered all that transpired, he convinced himself that he did exactly what he needed to do under the circumstances in order to survive. The good news was that no one except Mike Connely, the members of his own gang and Andy Gooding knew that he was meeting with his tire connection. This same gang of cohorts, along with Mr. Gooding's disabled youngest son, were also the only people who knew that Ivan was driving a burgundy colored two door 1939 Packard that night.

Now that the shipment of tires would never be delivered as planned, Ivan wondered if Andy Gooding would give him up to the police? In his favor, Ivan knew that Mr. Gooding was an ex con who hated cops with a passion. Andy Gooding also had no love for FDR and even less respect for OPA rationing regulations. Ivan also knew that Andy Gooding found it hard to be a law abiding patriotic American now that his youngest son was a seriously disabled combat veteran.

As the unofficial mayor and chief black-market operator of Parkside Avenue, Andy Gooding also had a reputation of being someone who could be trusted with a secret. After giving this matter some thought, Ivan had no reason to believe that the man he called Mr. G. would give him up, even if certain inducements were made by the police for people to come forward.

While Ivan did his best to avoid the main thoroughfares, he was glad that Curly Gooding filled the gas tank in the Packard before he went to meet Tommy Mulray. Even though the Packard was a fast car, Ivan knew that it was just a question of time before every police radio in Brooklyn bristled with reports about a burgundy colored Packard Coupe speeding away from a shootout at the Ft. Hamilton Diner. After considering his options, Ivan decided to continue driving and abandon the stolen car near the Brooklyn Bridge. Once Ivan crossed the East River and he made his way into Manhattan, he would be on more familiar turf.

After reaching the vicinity of the bridge, Ivan pulled over to the curb and used his handkerchief to wipe the Packard's interior and the door handle clean of his fingerprints. Rather than walk around with two empty handguns, Ivan decided to reload his .45 caliber Colt 1911 pistol and slip the empty revolver in his pants pocket. Once this was done, Ivan abandoned the stolen Packard and made his way across the Brooklyn Bridge. Fifteen minutes later, two patrolman from the Eight Four (84) Precinct found the stolen Packard abandoned on a city street near the bridge.

As soon as Ivan arrived in Manhattan, he looked around and remarked, "So far so good." Rather than walk down to the East River, Ivan decided to dispose of his firearms under more appropriate circumstances.

After his close call with the police, Ivan wanted nothing more than to make his way to Mike Connely's private warehouse office so he could meet with his mentor to explain what happened. After lighting a cigarette and taking a few drags, Ivan looked back at the Brooklyn side of the East River and regretted the day that he met Tommy Mulray.

As soon as they ended the pursuit of the Packard, Detectives Angelone and Mc Donald notified Mrs. Giordino that her son Tony died a hero's death and was being put in for a full pardon for his service to the nation in time of war. Once they spent some time with Tony G.'s mother, the two detectives were off to the Bronx to interview the owner of the stolen Packard.

After completing several interviews in the vicinity of the Ft. Hamilton Diner, Andy Dubrowsky was notified that two uniformed cops from the 84 (Eight Four) Precinct found the stolen getaway car abandoned within walking distance of the Brooklyn Bridge. As soon as Jim Beauregard was patched up, Andy Dubrowsky and his wounded partner were transported in a city police car to the 84 Precinct where the Packard was taken to be processed for evidence purposes. Arrangements were also made by the city police to recover the bullets that impacted the unmarked Army sedan. The Office of the Chief Medical Examiner would also be examining Tommy Mulray's body, as well as the body of Tony Giordino. An important part of this forensic examination included recovering any bullets that were lodged in their bodies.

While Detective Tim O'Donnell lifted a full hand print from the back of the Packard, Detective Marty Lane eased a third .32 caliber bullet from the driver's side door of the stolen getaway car. After watching Detective Lane carefully remove the bullet from the Packard, Andy Dubrowsky turned and faced Jim Beauregard and said, "It looks like you just missed hitting the driver with that pea shooter you carry."

While Jim took the ribbing like a good sport, he asked the detectives who were processing the stolen car for evidence if they recovered any fingerprints.

As Detective Lane placed the .32 ACP caliber bullet into a small envelope, Detective O'Donnell looked at the Army Investigator and said, "So far so good, Major. I pulled good prints from the trunk and the fender, as well as a partial from the gas cap. Whoever gassed this Packard up had a pair of greasy hands. The rest of the car is clean inside and out. All you have to do now, is pray that these prints are on file and you'll have a worthwhile lead to follow."

After hearing what his partner had to say, Detective Lane stood up and remarked, "Even the FBI won't have any trouble identifying these prints, Major."

Special Agent Andy Dubrowsky was a gentle giant of a man who looked more like a pro football player than a federal agent. The graduate of Annapolis was a former U.S. Marine who saw combat in World War I and earned a reputation for being a hard charging FBI Agent.

Even though he was considered an old timer by 1943 standards, Special Agent Dubrowsky was happy being a field agent and proved that point when he turned down several chances to become a supervisor. Andy Dubrowsky also knew from experience that local cops liked to needle FBI Agents, even if they had to do so with reverence, because Mr. Hoover was suspected of being able to hear criticisms from as far away as Washington D.C.

After accepting another evidence envelope from Detective O'Donnell, Andy turned to Jim and said, "If I lose any of this evidence I'll be lucky if I end up as a field agent in the ass end of Montana."

As promising as this evidence was, Jim knew that you could only use finger-prints to identify a subject if their prints were on file with a law enforcement agency. Unless the person who gassed up the stolen Packard was arrested, or had a government job that required that they be fingerprinted, this evidence would be useless.

After lighting his 40th cigarette for the day, Jim crumpled the empty pack up and tossed it into a nearby steel trash can while he stood next to the recovered stolen car. Even though Jim had one heck of a headache and should be resting in bed, his mind was still searching for ways that he and his colleagues would be able to develop credible leads to solve this case.

As soon as Jim considered their options, he turned toward Andy and said, "I got an idea how we can nail this son of a bitch."

Andy Dubrowsky responded while he accepted another evidence envelope from Detective O'Donnell. "What'a you have in mind?"

"Suppose we put a spin on this story," said Jim, "You know...leave out the part about Mulray acting suspicious and possibly being involved in a scheme to hijack a truck load of heavily rationed tires. Let's make him out to be a hard working father of five who was viciously gunned down by a truck hijacker."

Jim Beauregard didn't have to say another word to convince Andy Dubrowsky that he had an idea that was worth pursing. After nodding his head in agreement, Andy remarked, "You mean raise a little sympathy for the poor bastard."

Once again Jim sounded sure of himself when he responded and said, "It might come in handy if the fingerprints that were lifted from the stolen Packard lead us to someone who can identify the shooter."

"Sounds good to me," responded Andy, while he waited with his partner from the Provost Marshal's Office for the two detectives to complete one of the more tedious but important aspects of police work.

At 17 years of age Mike Connely enlisted in the United States Marine Corps in 1903 as a way to see the world and fight for his country. After serving in different locations during the period known as The Banana Wars, the young man who was called "Mad Mike" by his commanding officer decided to make a career in the Marines. Unfortunately, Mike's plans were cut short when he lost the bottom portion of his left leg below the knee, while fighting with the 3rd Battalion 5th Marines also known as 3/5 in the Battle of Belleau Wood during World War I.

After the war, Mike Connely decided to pursue his Plan B and become rich, even if he had to break the law in order to do so. Since he had no intention of becoming a salaried working stiff, Mike returned to the old neighborhood and rekindled his relationship with his childhood friends, many of whom were also veterans of World War I. In no time at all, Mike Connely was recruited into a local Irish gang that paid well and enabled its members to prosper.

Within a few years the man known as Mad Mike became a famous New York City gangster. Thanks to his service as a Marine, it was easy for Mike to advance in rank and run his own gang of Irish mobsters in the Hells Kitchen section of Manhattan. After spending three years in prison, Mad Mike decided to present more of a low profile and operate from behind the scenes. While using the money that he made smuggling and selling Caribbean Rum and Canadian Whiskey during Prohibition, Mike put up the cash to have two of his most trusted relatives open two bar restaurants and purchase a fleet of taxi cabs. During the depression Mad Mike also purchased several pieces of Manhattan real estate when it was possible to buy low.

In the 1930s Mike Connely was forced to slow down and manage his investments from a private warehouse office when he developed certain medical problems. Between his declining health and the realization that the old days were over, Mike became a recluse and spent considerably less time going to the two bars that his cousin Mickey Flynn ran for him. Mike also allowed his cousin Eddie Flynn to run the day to day operations of the taxi cab company that he purchased in the 1920s. Even though Mike had a long run as a successful criminal turned businessman, by 1943 the events of the past seemed like ancient history.

Life changed for Mad Mike when he ran into a fifteen year old runway from St. Mary's Orphanage by the name of Ivan Larson. At the time, Ivan was trying his hand at being a burglar. Little did Ivan know, that the apartment that he decided to ransack belonged to one of the most famous Irish mobsters who ever operated in New York City.

Even though Mike Connely was considerably older, young Ivan Larson was no match for the career criminal who also happened to be a highly decorated U.S. Marine combat veteran. The last thing that Ivan thought would happen, while he rummaged through the Manhattan apartment, was to get knocked on his ass from behind by an older man in declining health. While Ivan rubbed his sore buttocks and turned around, he saw Mike Connely standing over him with a pistol in one hand and a walking stick in the other. From that moment on the two became as close as father and son.

Although it wasn't anything like the old days, it didn't take long before Mike Connely had his one man gang pulling off jobs all over town. Ivan became the old man's legs and extended his rein of terror beyond the outskirts of the neighborhood into uncharted territory. Under Mike Connely's tutelage Ivan began to recruit a gang of his own. Terry Kelly was the first to pass muster with Mike Connely, then came a seventeen year old Italian American teenager from Mott Street.

When the soon to be 18 year old Antonio Ferini left Ivan's gang to go into business for himself, he ended up getting arrested for being in possession of stolen property in the Little Italy section of lower Manhattan. Instead of going to jail, the charges were dropped when the young man agreed to join the army. As Ivan would later find out, Antonio Ferini was killed in action while serving as a rifleman in New Guinea. When Amos Washington and Francis Shorty McGhee came along, Ivan had himself a tightly knit group that was loyal and eager to make money.

As strange as his lifestyle was, Ivan had a home of sorts to come back to every night. Even though they weren't related to each other by blood, they were one big happy family.

After arriving at the warehouse that Mike used as his private office and place of refuge, Ivan met his mentor in the back room to give him the bad news. As soon as a nervous looking Ivan Larson stood next to the roll top desk and said, "I'm sorry, Mike but this tire deal turned into a real mess," the old man put up his right hand to signal his young protege to stop talking.

"Before you go on I want you to take a seat," remarked Mike as he picked up a bottle of Glenlivet and poured a healthy shot of whiskey into an empty glass.

Luckily for Ivan, Mike Connely had been around long enough to know when a fellow crook was rattled after a deal didn't go as planned. As soon as Mike slid the glass closer to Ivan, he continued and said, "Drink this, light a cigarette and tell me everything that happened and don't leave anything out."

For the next few minutes Ivan gave Mike a detailed description of everything that transpired at the Ft. Hamilton Diner and why he took the action that he did. Ivan even back tracked a bit and told Mike about the stop that he made at

Andy Gooding's Garage. As soon as Ivan was finished, Mike spoke up and said, "It sounds like you were boxed in and had no choice. You also have to accept the fact that these things happen. Besides, Tommy Mulray was a useless piece of shit, so don't lose any sleep about the way things worked out. You did what you felt you had to do, so let it go."

As soon as Mike poured Ivan another shot of whiskey, the old man stood up and said, "First, I want you to give me the two guns that you used tonight. I'll make sure they're never found again."

Once Ivan placed the 1911 and the Colt revolver on the desk and said, "The forty five is loaded, Mike," the former Marine unloaded the pistol and placed the seven round magazine and the bullet from the chamber in his left front pant's pocket.

While Mike used his handkerchief to wipe both handguns down, he looked at Ivan and said, "I also want you to stay here tonight. Not that you'll need it, but there's another forty five in the desk. Also, don't call anyone and don't go for a walk...understand?"

After hearing Ivan respond and say, "Yes, Sir," Mike continued and said, "I'll have Terry and Shorty pick up Amos in the morning and bring him to the other warehouse. If I think its safe, I'll run you over there in the morning so you can stay with your buddies. Just remember...nobody is to know about this place. If you have to go on the run you come here. This warehouse office is our safe haven in this city. And don't worry if you have to leave town in a hurry. I always keep a few grand on hand in case of emergencies. If you have to stay away for a long period of time I can always sell some of my holdings. Either way, between what you have stashed away and what I can raise, you should have no problem making a fresh start someplace else."

While Ivan watched Mike put his suit jacket on, he felt a genuine sense of concern for the old man. Even though Ivan Larson was a tough kid, he was smart enough to know that Mike Connely cared for him a great deal. While Mike stood in front of his desk, he tucked the empty 1911 pistol inside his waistband before he picked up the empty Colt revolver and said, "I'll get the door. You stay outta sight and try to relax. I'll call you later before I hit the sack."

"I'm sorry for putting you through this, Mike," said Ivan as he stood up and faced the old man while he put his hat on.

As soon as Mike grabbed the Irish Shillelagh that he used as a cane, he looked at Ivan and sounded very supportive when he remarked, "This isn't just your mess, kid. This is our mess and I'm gonna do what I can to clean it up." While Ivan followed Mike into the garage area of the warehouse, the old man continued and said, "I know what you're going through. It stinks in plain English. Just remember, tomorrow's another day. Now do like I told you and stay put. There's enough food, coffee, booze and smokes stashed in this place to take care of ten men for a month."

Once Mike made his way over to his car, he opened the trunk on his Buick Roadmaster and placed Ivan's two handguns inside. After removing a blue steel Colt Model 1903 Pistol from an empty tool box, Mike slipped the .32 caliber automatic in his right side pant's pocket. Mike then placed Ivan's empty Colt revolver and the 1911 pistol inside the tool box and shut the trunk.

While Ivan stood in the open doorway to the living quarters of Mike's old hideout, the old man opened the garage doors to the warehouse. After returning to his car Mike looked at Ivan and said, "Remember what I told you."

Mike knew that Ivan got the message when his young protege limited his response to a simple, "Yes, Sir."

Once Mike got in behind the wheel, he started the engine, put the big Buick in reverse and slowly backed out of the warehouse. As tempted as Ivan was to close the wooden garage doors for Mike, he did as he was told and stood fast, while the old man secured the main exit to his hideout without help. A moment later, all Ivan heard was a car door close, as the man known as Mad Mike Connely drove away from his hideout on West 29th Street.

After hearing what Ivan had to say about the shootout at the Ft. Hamilton Diner, Mike decided to take immediate action to protect the young man who was like a son to him. In doing so, Mike would also be protecting himself.

As an experienced criminal, Mike Connely knew that the police would make every effort to identify and arrest the gunman who killed Tommy Mulray. Ivan was also in big trouble for getting into a shootout with the plainclothes cops who were present when Mulray was killed. The police and the feds would also be interested in pursuing everyone who was involved in a plan to hijack a truck load of heavily rationed tires in time of war.

In order to prevent Ivan from being identified and taken into custody, Mike needed to eliminate the only person who connected him and Ivan to Andy

Gooding. Even though there were others who knew certain aspects about their nefarious activities, John Miller was the person who introduced Ivan to Andy Gooding and that made him expendable. As a result, Mike knew that he had to act before the police revealed more information about this case to the general public.

With no time to waste, Mike called Miller from a pay phone to place another order for black market beef. Fortunately for Mike, the crooked meat supplier was known to work nights in his Manhattan warehouse that served as his illegal butcher shop. This made it possible for Mike to stop by and pay Miller for a side of butchered beef that Mike said a friend of his needed for his restaurant.

After meeting Miller in his warehouse office, Mike was convinced that he arrived in the so called nic of time, when the crooked butcher spoke highly of Ivan and asked when he and his buddies would be coming by to pick up Mike's order. As a result of this conversation, Mike was convinced that Miller was still unaware of the failed attempt by Ivan to hijack a truck load of tires that would be sold by Andy Gooding.

Mike was further convinced that Miller wasn't concerned about dealing with him or any of his associates, when the crooked butcher asked if one of Mike's taxi cabs could make some smaller deliveries to a few of his most trusted customers. Without hesitating Mike agreed to have his cousin Eddie Flynn handle these deliveries for his favorite war time meat supplier.

After offering Mike Connely a drink, the crooked butcher stood up and said, "This way, Mike and I'll show you what I have left in inventory before I receive my next shipment. Either way, it's all choice beef from a ranch out west."

While Mike continued to make small talk with the crooked butcher, he used his Irish Blackthorn Shillelagh as a cane, as he limped along to the left and a bit behind Miller. After walking around the back of Miller's delivery truck, the two men reached the large meat locker that the crooked butcher installed inside the warehouse.

As soon as Miller opened the heavy wooden door to the meat locker, Mike raised his Irish Shillelagh and smashed the crooked butcher in the back of his head. The fact that Miller worked alone made it possible for Mike to eliminate the crooked butcher without worrying about having to deal with witnesses.

After putting his leather gloves on, Mike dragged the body inside the meat locker and closed the door. Mike then used a shop towel that was hanging up in the meat locker to clean the top of his Shillelagh. As soon as Mike leaned his Irish walking stick against the wall of the meat locker, he drew the Colt Model 1903 pistol that he carried in his right side pants pocket. While Mike stood over the crooked butcher's body, he racked the slide to load the chamber before he shot Miller in the side of the head.

Once he placed the safety on, Mike slipped the Colt pistol back in his pants pocket, before he used his Shillelagh to brace himself as he knelt down to search the body. As soon as Mike picked up the empty shell casing and put it in the lapel pocket of his suit, he removed some papers and $800 dollars in cash from his victim's pockets and wallet. After leaning on his Shillelagh Mike stood up and brushed the sawdust from his suit pants.

After closing the door to the meat locker, Mike made his way into the warehouse bathroom, where he did a better job of cleaning any traces of blood from his Shillelagh. Mike then returned to the warehouse office to look for any records or information that connected him and Ivan to Miller's black market operation.

While continuing to wear a pair of leather gloves, Mike searched Miller's office and found what he was looking for. After placing a set of counterfeit meat stamps, a notebook containing customers names and addresses, a phone directory and a ledger book that contained a list of transactions in Miller's attache case, Mike picked up the shot glass that he drank from, as well as the cash that he left on the desk to pay for the beef that he ordered.

While using his Shillelagh as a cane, Mike limped out of the warehouse with Miller's attache case in his left hand. After walking to the corner and heading one block north, Mike Connely got into his black four door 1941 Buck Roadmaster sedan and drove away without being noticed.

Mike planned his moves well and waited until after he killed John Miller before he disposed of his Colt pocket pistol, the empty shell casing and the two firearms that Ivan used during the Ft. Hamilton Diner shootout. After driving uptown, Mike drove his Buick sedan to the middle of the George Washington Bridge before he stopped his car in the right hand lane.

Fortunately, the traffic was almost non existent when Mike raised the engine hood to give the impression that his vehicle broke down. While still wearing his leather gloves, Mike made sure that his actions were not being observed when he removed Ivan's handguns from the tool box in the trunk of the Buick. After walking over to the side of the bridge, Mike looked around again before he tossed all three handguns, the ammunition for the 1911 and the empty shell casing into the depths of the Hudson River.

As soon as Mike returned to his car, he closed the trunk and lowered the engine hood before he got back in his Roadmaster and drove to a diner in Ft. Lee, New Jersey to get something to eat. Later that night after Mike called Ivan, he burned the records that he removed from Miller's warehouse office in his apartment house incinerator. By the time the sun came up, Miller's empty attache case was throw away in a trash can.

CHAPTER 10

PURSUING THE SHOOTER

A fter hearing about the efforts that were being made by the police, to identify the gunman who killed Tommy Mulray and a civilian who was assisting the authorities investigate black market operations, Ivan decided to raise as much cash as possible in case he had to go on the lamb. Even though Ivan had immediate access to eleven hundred dollars of his own money, plus the cash that Mike said that he had available for emergencies, Ivan knew that he would need a lot more money than a few Gs to live life on the run. After all, even though several thousand dollars was a great deal of money in 1943, Ivan was a young man who was about to turn 18. As a result, Ivan would need a rather large sum of money to start a new life, without having to worry about working to make ends meet.

Ivan's other concern involved the war and how he could survive life on the run and not come under suspicion, unless he had a valid reason for not being in uniform. Ivan also felt bad about Mike selling some of his financial holdings just to raise the money for him to relocate. In addition, Ivan knew that it would be impossible for him to travel to any of the foreign safe havens where he would like to live now that the world was at war.

After another sleepless night, Ivan decided the best course of action for him to take was to rob a bank in Brooklyn that he considered robbing several months ago. The layout was perfect and offered him an opportunity to pick up a ton of cash, as long as he moved fast and overpowered the two elderly guards who were on duty inside the bank. Since Ivan needed help to pull this caper off, he wasted no time in recruiting the members of his gang to go along.

Even though Terry Kelly was three weeks away from joining the United States Coast Guard, the thought of leaving his mother with a few extra bucks, persuaded him to go along with Ivan's plan to rob the Lincoln Savings Bank in Brooklyn. Once Terry agreed to go along on the heist, Ivan turned to Amos Washington and said, "Well, Amos, how about you? Are you in or out?"

Because of his diminished capacity Amos Washington was not eligible for military service. As such, Amos was free to do as he pleased. In his case, the thought of being left out was frightening. Amos Washington felt this way because before he met Ivan Larson, he was a very lonely Negro teenager who was often made fun of and treated like the village idiot.

Even though he was a bit slow, Amos never questioned why a young white teenager was trying to push a brand new Pontiac that had a flat tire over to the curb in a pouring rain storm. After seeing the rather large Negro teenager standing on the sidewalk while he strained his back, Ivan asked Amos if he would like to make a few bucks by giving him a hand. Under the circumstances, Amos didn't know what to say because no white kid ever spoke to him before. When Ivan continued and said, "There's five bucks in it for you if you help me change this flat," Amos stepped forward and put his brute strength to work helping Ivan Larson. By the time Amos finished helping Ivan change the tire, he was a member of his gang.

In order to pull this robbery off, Ivan also asked Francis Shorty Mc Ghee to go along. According to Terry Kelly, Shorty was anxious to be more involved in their money making activities. Ivan had a good feeling about Shorty because Terry's buddy had an excellent reputation as a car thief who stole anything with wheels just to get the tires and a tank of gas. The fact that Shorty was never caught was even more impressive and qualified him as an excellent wheel man to drive the getaway car. Shorty was also an excellent mechanic who could fix anything that had moving parts.

According to Mrs. Mulray, her husband's best friend was a fellow truck driver by the name of David Axelrod. In fact, during the interview of Mrs. Mulray, the mother of five blamed David Axelrod for introducing her late husband to playing cards for money and gambling on horse races and boxing matches. The fact that Alexrod was an ex con didn't bother Mrs. Mulray but she was annoyed that Axelrod always seemed to win, while her husband always lost. When Detective Angelone asked if her husband recently had a change of luck, the widow wasted no time in saying, "I wish."

After picking up David Axelrod at his apartment house in the Bay Rridge section of Brooklyn, Detective Aneglone and his partner took the ex con to the 68 (Six Eight) Precinct for interrogation. As an ex con, Dave Axelrod was a definite subject of interest to the police and the feds, now that it was determined that he was involved in gambling activities and was a known associate of Tommy Mulray.

When Jim Beauregard witnessed the interrogation of Dave Axlerod, he had a flashback of his days as a cop in Atlanta. Even after five minutes of intense inter- rogation, their prisoner was sticking to his story that he knew nothing of Tommy Mulray's gambling habits or of his involvement in a truck hijacking scheme.

Seeing Detective Angelone pacing back and forth behind a seated Dave Axlerod, while he remarked, "So you don't know nothing uh?" was a clear indication that their prisoner was about to be motivated to cooperate.

As soon as Detective Angelone removed the rolled up newspaper from his back pocket, he smacked Axelrod on the back of his head with enough force to send the ex con flying out of his chair. While acting as a team, Detective Mc Donald helped their prisoner off the floor and put him back in his chair. The moment Johnny did so, Detective Angelone leaned closer to their prisoner and screamed, "Do you think we're playing games here? Your pal Tommy Mulray was shot in the fucking face at point blank range with a forty five caliber automatic over a truck load of tires. Unless you help us, Dave, you're going to jail for violating your parole. In fact, I'm gonna personally book your ass and see to it that you do time for being a first class prick."

Everyone in the room knew Axelrod was finally broken when he looked at Detective Angelone and said, "If I tell you what I know can I go home?"

After hearing Detective Angelone respond and say, "I give you my word, you'll be a free man the second you tell us the whole truth and nothing but the truth. I'll also let the DA know that you helped us out. That should put you in good graces with the City of New York."

When the ex con asked if he could have a smoke, Frank Angelone remarked, "Go ahead." As soon as their prisoner removed a cigarette from the pack that was on the table next to his other possessions, Detective Angelone remarked, "We're waiting, Dave."

After lighting the cigarette with the book of matches that were on the table, Dave Axelrod looked at Detective Angelone and said, "All I know is that Tommy owed some old guy a pile of cash. He never mentioned this guy's name but he did slip once when he was drunk and said that some punk named Ivan Smith was gonna put him in the hospital if he didn't pay his debt in full."

After pausing to take another drag on his cigarette, Axelrod looked around the room at his interrogators as he continued. "Two days ago Tommy was a different man. I never saw him happier. Not only did he have some cash in his pocket for the first time in I don't know how long, but he told me that he was a few days away from making some real dough. When I tried to press him for more information, he handed me the sawbuck that he owed me, cracked a smile and said, "Loose lips sink ships. Whatever he was involved in... he was keeping it a secret." After taking a drag on his cigarette Axelrod ended his statement by saying, "That's all I know."

When it came to identifying fingerprints, the FBI was the best in the business. Because every soldier, sailor, marine, coast guardsman, federal employee, defense worker and criminal was fingerprinted, it didn't take long for the ladies working in the file room in Washington D.C. to locate the print card that belonged to Private Gerard Gooding, a disabled U.S. Army soldier.

After checking with the War Department, FBI Headquarters called the New York Field Office and relayed an address in Brooklyn for the highly decorated disabled U.S. Army combat veteran whose fingerprints were found on the stolen Packard. As soon as Andy Dubrowsky received this information, the only FBI Agent assigned to the Provost Marshal's Task Force obtained a search warrant for Curly Gooding's home. After contacting the local precinct captain, Captain Pat Murphy Sr. also confirmed that Private Gooding's father was an ex con who owned a local garage and was suspected of being involved in different types of criminal activity. Once this information was passed to the Provost Marshal's Office, an additional search warrant was obtained for Gooding's Garage.

Thanks to the War Department records, Army Task Force investigators also knew a great deal about Andy Gooding's youngest son. Even though it was highly unlikely that a seriously disabled veteran like Private Gerard Gooding was the gunman who murdered Tommy Mulray, the fact that his fingerprints were found on the getaway car provided enough probable cause to pick him up for questioning. The decision to do so was made to motivate Private Gooding's father to cooperate with the investigation. Andy Gooding would be further convinced to cooperate with the authorities, if the raiding party located any incriminating evidence in his possession when the search warrants were executed.

While Jim Beauregard continued conducting the pre-raid briefing, he looked around the squad room and said, "It all fits. The stolen Packard the killer was driving was covered with fingerprints all around the gas tank. Since Private Gooding's greasy fingerprints were found on the getaway car, it seems logical to assume that the gunman who killed Tommy Mulray and Tony G. stopped at Gooding's Garage before he went to the Ft. Hamilton Diner. We also know that Gooding's Garage is a repair shop that doesn't sell gasoline, at least not legal gas."

After tapping the ash from his cigarette in a nearby ashtray, Jim continued and said. "As a result of all that we've been able to determine on such short notice, we have every reason to believe that Private Gooding is in no shape to do much more than limp around his father's garage after his run in with German armored vehicles in the Kassarine Pass."

As soon as the Major stopped speaking, Johnny Mc Donald remarked, "I'll bet the moment our shooter heard that ambulance siren he thought he was being set up."

While Major Beauregard stamped his cigarette out in a nearby ashtray, he agreed with Detective Mc Donald's assessment as did everyone else in the squad room.

Once Major Beauregard finished the briefing, Lt. Colonel Richmond walked up to the front of the room, while he addressed the roomful of lawmen in a fatherly tone of voice and said, "Before you head off to Brooklyn I ask each and every one of you to be careful. Even though we have a better idea of the type of people we're dealing with, we don't know everything so use caution when you carry out your duties" Then, after lighting his pipe with a wooden match, the Colonel ended the briefing by saying, "I'll be in the office if you need any assistance from my end. Good luck."

CHAPTER 11

THE RAID

The morning raid on Andy Gooding's garage went down with the precision of a trained commando operation. When the first marked police car pulled up to the wooden garage door, there was no coded honking of horns but the sound of an Irish cop pounding on the door with his fist and ordering the occupants to open up in the name of the law.

The second that Curly Gooding opened the door, a uniformed police sergeant stepped forward and grabbed the disabled veteran by the scruff of the neck and said, "Gerard Gooding you're under arrest."

War hero or not, Gerard "Curly" Gooding was handled a little on the rough side, when he was handcuffed and pushed up against the side of a police car under guard. Just as the raiding party expected, Andy Gooding went through the sea of cops like a hot knife through butter when he saw his disabled son in custody.

Even though he was being restrained by two rather large patrolmen, Andy Gooding continued to act like a bull in a china shop when he screamed, "Let the boy go, he's done nothing wrong." Then, in a more pleading tone that was laced with anger, Andy Gooding turned to the uniformed police captain and said, "My son's a fucking war hero...Look at him...that's the price he paid to serve our country. He doesn't deserve this for pumping black-market gas."

In order to turn up the pressure on Andy Gooding to cooperate, Detective Angelone stepped forward and grabbed the confused looking disabled veteran by the arm and said, "Let's go kid, you're under arrest for murder."

With two big cops still holding him back, Andy Gooding screamed, "Curly never hurt anyone except the fuck'in Krauts. He's innocent dammit!"

After seeing Andy Gooding react as anticipated, Jim Beauregard stepped forward and identified himself to the disabled veteran's father. "Mr. Gooding, my name is Major James Beauregard. I'm an Investigator with the U.S. Army Provost Marshal's Office in New York."

As soon as Jim Beauregard stopped speaking, Andy Gooding responded and said, "If you're from the Army then you should know about my boy. He got the Silver Star for what he did in the Kassarine Pass when everyone else ran the other way. Curly's no killer. He's a good kid.....he pumps gas for me, that's all. Please, Major, let my boy go and I'll tell you anything you want'a know."

After nodding his head ever so slightly, Major Beauregard addressed the patrolman who was standing guard over Curly Gooding. "Remove the handcuffs and put Private Gooding in my car under guard. We'll hold him until we hear what his father has to say."

The second Andy Gooding saw one of the patrolman remove the handcuffs that were placed on his son, he appeared grateful when he addressed Major Beauregard. "I'll tell you what you want to know. I know all about the shooting at the Ft. Hamilton Diner. I know the guy you're looking for, the one driving the Packard. His name's Ivan."

After turning to face his colleagues, Jim Beauregard spoke in a very official tone of voice when he said, "It seems that we have a lot to talk about with Mr. Gooding. Why don't we take this inside."

As usual, the entire operation was choreographed before the raid was executed. Local cops and federal agents were true professionals at orchestrating events to suit their needs. Even though it was not public information, law enforcement officers generally planned their moves with more precision than most people gave them credit for. After all, no cop or federal agent worth his salt would ever go after someone without knowing a great deal about the target of their investigation. This case was no different.

Ivan decided to pick up a newspaper from a nearby newsstand. When Ivan Larson spotted a patrolman on the corner, he decided to cross the street to avoid a possible confrontation. After stepping up on the sidewalk, Ivan tried not to make it seem obvious that he was concerned about the presence of a police car pulling over to the curb where the beat cop was standing.

As tempted as he was to start running, Ivan decided to casually walk into the corner candy store to pick up a newspaper. After paying the blind World War I veteran for the paper, Ivan casually looked across the street and was relieved to see the uniformed sergeant was only making a memo book entry in the patrolman's summons book and was not initiating a search of the area.

As soon as Ivan took a look at the front page, he did his best not to act shocked when he read the article about the attempted truck hijacking and the shootout at the Ft. Hamilton Diner. According to this front page article, Tommy Mulray was a well respected married father of five who was gunned down by a gun toting truck hijacker. Ivan was twice as pissed when he read how federal agents and city police detectives received a tip, that Mulray's truck load of tires was going to be hijacked on the way to a distribution center on Long Island.

Ivan also swallowed hard when the article mentioned that the gunman who killed Tommy Mulray was being pursued by a task force of investigators from various federal, state and local agencies who were assigned to the U.S. Army Provost Marshal's Office.

While Ivan tucked the newspaper under his arm and started walking back to his warehouse hideout, he thought to himself, "Just great, now I have the U.S. Army after me."

The members of the raiding party had high hopes that Andy Gooding would fully identify the gunman who killed Tommy Mulray, while also cooperating with investigators about black market activities in New York City. Unfortunately, once Andy Gooding saw that his son was off the hook and he had time to calm down, he decided that he wasn't about to make life easy for the authorities. The main reason why Andy Gooding had a change of heart, was because he felt protected by the fact that he did business with so many influential people.

After listening to Andy Gooding insist that he didn't know anything about a truck load of tires and that all he did was sell some gas to a kid driving a Packard who called himself Ivan Smith, Detective Mc Donald remarked, "If what you said is true then you should have no problem helping us find this kid."

While Andy Gooding remained silent, Jim Beauregard added, "While you're at it, you can also tell us who your other customers and suppliers are."

As soon as Andy Gooding folded his arms, he leaned back in his chair and said, "Telling you what little I know about Ivan Smith is one thing but there's no way I'm gonna tell you flatfoots who my suppliers and customers are. Besides, if you jokers knew who I do business with, you'd shut this thing down so fast your heads would spin."

Seeing the change in Andy Gooding's disposition made Frank Angelone's day. While Detective Angelone casually walked around the side of the desk, he looked at his partner and Jim Beauregard and said, "I think Mister Gooding is having a change of heart."

Without telegraphing his next move, Detective Angelone removed a telephone directory from the top of the cabinet that was positioned behind the desk and forcefully struck Andy Gooding across the back of his head. When Andy Gooding reacted by hunching his shoulders and covering his head with his hands, Frank Angelone yelled, "Resisting arrest are ya?"

While Andy Gooding turned away from the next assault, Detective Angelone used the telephone directory to beat the black market operator until the ex con fell off his chair and curled up in a ball on the floor. After tossing the telephone book aside, Detective Angelone knelt down, grabbed Andy Gooding by the hair and yanked his head all the way back, as he leaned closer to the black market operator's face and said, "Now you listen to me you piece'a shit. We have enough evidence on you to put your ass in jail for rest of the war and then some. As far as my colleagues and I are concerned, you're as guilty as the prick who pulled the trigger and killed Tommy Mulray. The fact that your buddy Ivan killed a friend of ours and wounded the Major also pisses us off to no end, so I suggest you show us some fucking respect and either start talking, or say goodbye to your son because we're taking him and you to jail!"

As soon as Detective Angelone forcefully let go of the prisoner's head and stood up, Andy Gooding relented and said, "OK, I'll talk but I want a deal for me and my boy."

Once again, Jim Beauregard was impressed. New York City cops were experts in the fine art of what would one day become known as enhanced interrogation. With his services no longer required, Frank Angelone looked at Jim Beauregard and nodded his head as he left the office.

While Detective Mc Donald helped Andy Gooding to get up off the floor and back in his chair, he patted the prisoner on the back as he said, "OK, Laddy, it's time to tell us what we want'a know."

Andy Gooding's situation got progressively worse when U.S. Army Lieutenant Don Lorenz entered the office and excused himself for interrupting before he filed his report to Major Beauregard. "I thought you should know, Sir. So far we found twenty five cartons of premium brand cigarettes, three full fifty five gallon drums of gasoline, several empty drums, hand pumps and one fifty five gallon drum of engine oil. We also found some crates and paperwork from the Brooklyn Army Depot that were placed next to a burn barrel out back. Andy Dubrowsky also found some paperwork and a pass to the Staten Island Fuel Depot in Mr. Gooding's car."

"Good work, Don," responded the Major who quickly added, "As soon as you and the others are finished with your search ask Agent Dubrowsky to join us in the office."

As a New Haven, Connecticut Police Officer who was now serving as an Army Investigator, Lt. Don Lorenz knew how to follow orders and wasted no time in saying, "Yes Sir," before he left the office.

While Lt. Lorenz returned to his duties, Jim Beauregard addressed Andy Gooding in a stern tone of voice. "Do you really think we believe that all you did was sell Ivan Smith some black market gasoline? You also have some hell of a nerve trying to act like a tough guy who isn't gonna cooperate. We haven't even searched your house yet and we have you and your son by the balls, so you better think twice about trying to bullshit us."

After pausing to light a cigarette, Jim changed his demeanor when he offered a Lucky Strike to a more docile Andy Gooding before he continued and said, "You said you'd cooperate if we gave you a deal. Let me tell you how this works. Unless you impress the hell out of me and my fellow investigators with some worthwhile information, you're gonna take the fall for your involvement in black market operations in time of war. The charges against you will include aiding a gunman who murdered two people while attempting to hijack a truck load of tires for the purpose of violating OPA regulations. The cigarettes and the petroleum products that we found in your garage will be more wood on the fire that gets you convicted. If that isn't enough, I know an IRS Agent who would love to make a case against you for tax evasion."

While Jim Beauregard stood over the front of Andy Gooding's desk, he took a drag on his Lucky Strike before he continued. "If you think I'm bluffing, you can take your chances with a jury of your peers. However, before doing so, I suggest you consider that the people who make up this jury will be pissed off to no end that you made a small fortune violating OPA regulations, while they followed the law and lived without unlimited access to various rationed products. On the other hand, if you decide to cooperate you have to come clean on everything. That includes identifying the people who supply you, as well as your black market customers. We also want'a know everything that you know about Ivan Smith." Then, after pausing to tap the ash from his cigarette into the ashtray on the desk, the Major looked directly at Andy Gooding and said, "Do I make myself clear?"

Under the circumstances, it didn't take a building to fall on Andy Gooding for the ex con to know that his goose was cooked. After taking a long drag on his cigarette Andy Gooding responded and said, "Everything you want'a know about my suppliers and my customers can be found in the ledger books that I have stashed in my house. These records include the date of every transaction, the type of car that we gassed up and the name of the customer, but I only listed the license plates of the cars that were driven by my more influential customers. I made the same entries when I sold cigarettes and whatever else I could get my hands on."

When Jim asked Andy Gooding if he kept detailed records of the vehicles that were driven by Ivan Smith, the black market operator shook his head from left to right before he responded. "Even though I did a lot of business with Ivan Smith, this kid wasn't someone I figured could deliver the kind of favors that bank presidents and other big shots could do for me. The only reason I kept any records on my regular customers, was to help me figure out what I sold and what I needed to order. I also figured it wouldn't hurt to have these records in my possession, in case I ever got nailed by the feds."

After pausing to take another drag on his cigarette, Andy Gooding sounded more like a team player when he said, "As far as this kid Ivan was concerned, I treated him like a good customer and limited my record keeping on him to include, his name, the date he made a purchase and what he purchased. I also loaned that kid my truck on several occasions so he could deliver fifty five gallon drums of gasoline to some cab company in the city."

As happy as Jim was that Andy Gooding was cooperating, he wanted to steer the conversation back to the night that Ivan Smith killed Tommy Mulray and Tony Giordino over a truck load of tires. In order to do so, Jim decided to direct Andy Gooding's attention to the night of the shootout at the Ft. Hamilton Diner. "Why don't we go back to the night you expected to receive a delivery of tires from Ivan Smith."

Once again Andy Gooding responded as if he was getting used to cooperating with the authorities. "As soon as we gassed Ivan up, he left to meet his tire contact. I didn't know who he was meeting or where this meeting was taking place. I also had no idea that Ivan carried a gun and never figured him for a killer. When Ivan never delivered any tires that night, I figured his contact never showed up or he was unable to deliver the goods. I changed my opinion of that kid when I read the morning paper and I listened to a radio broadcast about the shootout at the Ft. Hamilton Diner and how the gunman who got away was driving a stolen burgundy colored Packard."

As soon as Jim Beauregard made eye contact with Detective Mc Donald, the Irish American police detective picked up where the Major left off. "We'll need more than that to identify this Ivan character."

Without hesitating Mr. Gooding looked up at Major Beauregard and said, "I'm telling you, Major. This kid Ivan was a ghost. He called me. I never called him. I also have no idea where he hangs his hat. I can tell you that he's either 17 or 18 'cause we talked about him getting his chance to see this war up close like my son Curly did. The only reason I did business with him, was because he was recommended to me by the butcher that I buy my black market meat from."

When Major Beauregard said, "Tell us about this butcher," Andy Gooding responded without hesitation. "His name is John Miller. He operates out of a warehouse on the west side of Manhattan. I met Miller through the father of one of my customers, an old man by the name of Cooper. Earlier this year Mr. Cooper sold his grocery store on the west side of Manhattan after he had a heart attack. He moved to Brooklyn to live with his daughter in law and his grandchildren when his son shipped out again with the Merchant Marine. Since I knew his son before the war, I had no problem selling him or anyone else in his family gasoline whenever they needed some."

After pausing long enough to take one last drag on his cigarette, Andy Gooding exhaled a lungful of smoke before he continued and said, "Two weeks before he dropped dead Mr. Cooper stopped by to fill up his son's Chevy. While Curly was topping off the tank, the old man asked if I was interested in trading some gasoline for steaks. One thing led to another and Mr. Cooper told me about the butcher he did business with when he owned his grocery store in Manhattan. According to Mr. Copper, Miller was in businesses with another butcher by the name of Rudy Muller. Once rationing was imposed, Miller and his partner went their separate ways. That's when Miller went into business for himself selling black market beef."

As soon as Andy Gooding stamped his cigarette out in the ashtray on his desk, he went on to say, "That day Mr. Cooper put me in touch with Miller. Before I knew it, I was selling cases of steaks and even a few sides of beef to some of my customers. In addition to buying his meat, I fixed Miller's truck and kept him supplied with enough gasoline to make his deliveries."

Andy Gooding sounded like he was being completely honest when he continued describing his black market meat contact to Jim Beauregard and Johnny Mc Donald. "Miller is strictly business, no small talk. The only thing he ever told me of a personal nature, was that he came here from Holland in the early 30's. I also know that he buys a truck load of beef at a time from some ranch out west. I'm telling you, Major, this guy is so serious about his work, he actually built a meat locker inside his warehouse where he hangs and butchers whole sides of beef."

After pausing for a split second to catch his breath, Andy Gooding went on to say, "Miller supplies high quality beef to bars, restaurants, butcher shops and a select number of wealthy customers and he doesn't take ration coupons. He also doesn't sell one steak at a time. Just last week I picked up a completely butchered side of beef from Miller for some Wall Street big shots who want plenty of meat for the holidays. That one order alone involved over 200 pounds of premium grade beef. Trust me when I tell you, Major, John Miller is a big time operator when it comes to selling black market meat."

When Jim Beauregard asked their new informant when he last had contact with the crooked meat supplier, Andy Gooding continued to sound like he was telling the truth when he answered the Major's question. "The last time I saw Miller was when I picked up that 200 pound order last Thursday night. Miller normally works nights so I met him at 7PM. When I told him I needed another case of steaks and fifty pounds of ground beef, he said he'd be receiving another delivery by this Thursday or Friday night at the latest. If I couldn't wait, Miller said he'd be happy to sell me whatever I needed as long as he still had beef in his meat locker. Either way, he promised to get me what I needed as soon as his next delivery arrived from out west."

Based on what Andy Gooding said so far, it seemed logical that Jim and his fellow investigators would need to get John Miller to cooperate in order to learn more about the subject identified as Ivan Smith. In order to accomplish this,

Jim needed to know more. "What else can you tell us about Ivan Smith and his relationship with Miller?"

Without hesitating Andy Gooding looked up at the Major as he answered the question. "When Ivan told me he knew a Jew lawyer who was willing to pay top dollar for premium brand cigarettes all I wanted to know was how well he knew this guy. According to Ivan, this lawyer could be trusted because he was the mouthpiece for a client who ran two bars that bought black market beef from Miller. Ivan also said that him and one of his buddies never had any problems when they delivered Miller's black market meat to this lawyer's client."

As soon as Jim offered his new informant another cigarette and a light, Andy Gooding continued without being prodded to do so. "After I sold Ivan five cartons of Lucky Strikes and ten cartons of Camels, he showed up two weeks later with a wad of cash in hand and said this lawyer wanted to buy fifty cartons as soon as possible. This same lawyer also purchased several fifty five gallon drums of gasoline that I sold to Ivan."

When Jim asked if Ivan ever mentioned this lawyer's name, Andy Gooding said, "No, Sir, he didn't, but he did say this lawyer needed all the gas he could get his hands on, 'cause he drove a gas guzzling Oldsmobile, his wife had a gas guzzling Caddy and he also needed to keep his girlfriend's convertible Chevrolet on the road."

After pausing briefly Andy Gooding added, "I can also tell you that when Ivan showed up to pick up the fifty carton order he was driving a black 1937 Chevy Suburban with a dented left rear fender. This was the same vehicle that he used when he wasn't using my truck to make a delivery."

As soon as Jim asked where he obtained the black market cigarettes, Andy Gooding took another drag on his cigarette before he answered. "I have a contact who works in the Brooklyn Army Depot."

When Major Beauregard asked Andy Gooding how his contact managed to get his hands on such large quantities of cigarettes, Andy Gooding sounded like he wasn't all that happy about having to answer this particular question when he responded and said, "Sometimes a crate falls off the back of a truck. When that happened I get lucky."

Like it or not, Andy Gooding knew that he had to come clean or face being prosecuted to the fullest extent of the law. When the Major from the Army Provost Marshal's Office asked who his fuel contact was, Andy Gooding sounded just as reluctant to divulge these names when he responded and said. "About a month after gasoline rationing was imposed, I was approached by a guy I know who works at the fuel depot on Staten Island. When he asked if I was interested in buying fifty five gallon drums of gasoline and engine oil no questions asked and the price was right I said yes."

Over the years Jim interrogated enough suspects and prisoners to know that it wasn't easy for people to cooperate with the police. In order to show Andy Gooding that he understood the position that he was in, Jim tried to sound as understanding as possible when he said, "I know it's not easy to turn these people in but we need their names."

After hearing what the Major had to say, Andy Gooding opened his desk drawer and removed a small black notebook. While Andy Gooding handed the notebook to Jim Beauregard, he sounded as if he was submitting to the process of cooperating when he said, "My contact at the fuel depot is under G for gas. The name of my contact at the Brooklyn Army Depot is under D for depot."

After hearing what Andy Gooding had to say, Jim Beauregard turned to Johnny Mc Donald and said, "Let's button this up so we can preserve Mister Gooding's reputation as a black market operator. Thank the precinct captain for all of his help and have the uniformed cops return to their regular duties. We also need to make sure the press doesn't get wind of what we did here today. If anyone asks, we're looking for a stolen car that was used in the commission of a crime. Also, ask Lieutenant Lorenz to make arrangements to post a guard inside Mr. Gooding's warehouse until we identify all of his customers and suppliers. We also need to get those ledger books from Mr. Gooding's house without raising any eyebrows."

As soon as Johnny Mc Donald played along and said, "Yes, Sir," he left the Major alone in the office with Andy Gooding. After pulling a wooden chair away from the wall, Jim sat down across from his new informant and said, "If the U.S. Attorney and the DA agrees with my recommendation, you'll be working for us for as long as we need your help, so get used to the idea of having us around."

When Andy Dubrowsky walked into the office he handed Jim the inventory list from the search of Gooding's garage while he remarked, "We're ready for round two whenever you are, Major."

While Jim reviewed the list, he introduced Special Agent Andy Dubrowsky from the FBI to Mr. Gooding. As soon as Jim folded the list and put it in his suit jacket pocket, he looked at Andy Gooding and said, "OK, Mr. Gooding, let's take a ride over to your house so we finish our search and pick up those ledger books."

In the deal that was cut with the Chief Assistant U.S. Attorney for the Eastern District of New York, as well as the District Attorney's Office in Manhattan and Brooklyn, Mr. Gooding agreed to cooperate fully and pay a large fine for violating the Office of Price Administration Rationing Regulations. In addition, the contents of his garage would be seized and no charges would be filed against his youngest son.

As part of his plea agreement, Andy Gooding was required to provide a complete list of his customers, as well the names of his black market suppliers, to the Provost Marshal's Task Force. Mr. Gooding was also required to make himself available to assist federal and city authorities to identify the subject known as Ivan Smith. Last but not least, Mr. Gooding agreed to help government agents make a case against the butcher identified as John Miller. Failure to provide this assistance to the government would result in the immediate prosecution of Mr. Gooding for various violations of law.

By the fall and early winter of 1943 the United States and her allies were heavily engaged in a life and death struggle with the Axis Forces. Even though certain advances were made on the field of battle, the outcome of the war was still in doubt. Despite the seriousness of the situation, some refused to live without certain luxury items until the war was over. It was because of these acts of non compliance that the black-market flourished.

The fact that various influential New Yorkers purchased black market products from Andy Gooding was of great interest to the men working this case. Even though a percentage of these customers were regular folks and a few former government officials, Andy Gooding also did business with a rather impressive list of wealthy New Yorkers who wielded a great deal of influence in city, state and federal politics.

Clearly, anyone who had access to these ledger books would be in a position to give politically connected and influential citizens who violated OPA rationing regulations, an opportunity to cooperate on certain matters in lieu of having the general public find out about their indiscretions. After flipping through the ledger books that were recovered from Andy Gooding's home, Detective Angelone had a gleam in his eyes as he presented a devilish grin to the others and said, "We can trade off this information for some time to come, especially until the war's over."

Jim Beauregard couldn't help but grin at the antics of the New York City cops. Yankees or not, he had to admit that his northern cohorts were a colorful crew. After turning to Andy Dubrowsky, who also scored some big points with his boss in Washington, a man who was a master at trading favors on the federal level, Jim remarked, "Kind'a makes me homesick seeing all this underhanded treachery."

In order to remind the Major that he was now an honorary New Yorker, Johnny Mc Donald spoke up and said, "Don't worry, Jimmy. You're with us now."

That's right, Major," said Frank Angelone as he held open one of the ledger books and remarked, "You never know, Major, but the day could come when some of the big shots who did business with Andy Gooding will be more than happy to do you a favor, as long as you agree to remove their name from the pages of these ledger books."

The food at the Officer's Club at Ft. Hamilton was fast, hot, inexpensive and good tasting. After working all night, Jim Beauregard was so tired he felt as if he could use some help stirring his coffee. As Jim removed a cigarette from the half empty pack that he kept in his shirt pocket, his mouth tasted like the Russian Army walked across his tongue after encircling the Germans at Stalingrad.

While Jim held the Lucky Strike in his left hand, he seemed lost in thought while he used all the strength he could muster to raise the coffee cup to his lips. Even when Andy Dubrowsky remarked, "I don't know about you but I'm getting too old for these all nighters," Jim Beauregard didn't react and appeared to be in a pensive mood.

When Andy asked if Jim was alright, the Army Major who was serving as a Provost Marshal's Office Investigator came out of his trance and caught the FBI Agent completely off guard when he said, "Andy, I just submitted another request for a combat command."

As exhausted as he was, Andy Dubrowsky was so shocked after hearing what Jim had to say, he spoke just above a whisper when he responded and said, "Are you crazy?"

After lighting his cigarette, the Atlanta cop turned Army Investigator paused long enough to remove a tiny piece of tobacco from the tip of his tongue before he continued. "I didn't give up the chance to retire from the Atlanta Police Department and serve as the Chief of the Georgia Highway Patrol so I could become a cop in the Army. Sure enough, when I accepted my commission, the Army said they needed officers with my police background to serve in the MPs. Once the Army realized that I was a Captain of Detectives, I was transferred to command an investigative unit in the Provost Marshal's Office."

In an effort to interject some sanity into their exchange, Andy Dubrowsky remarked, "For once the Army made the right call."

As the former U.S. Marine and star football player at Annapolis sat back in his seat, Jim Beauregard took a drag on his cigarette before he leaned closer to the table and spoke in almost a pleading tone of voice. "I got'a get into this war, Andy. It's killing me that both of my sons are in combat units and all I'm doing is chasing crooks in New York City. How do you think that makes me feel as a father?"

Even though Andy Dubrowsky had three daughters, he knew what it was like to want to do more to help the war effort. Unfortunately, getting older meant that the younger men got to do the fighting. Unless you were a career soldier in the military, the older men were not being called up. If they were it was for a special purpose.

While Andy considered his friend's feelings, he spoke in a tone of voice that was laced with a tremendous amount of understanding. "I have three girls, Jim. The Good Lord never blessed me and my wife with sons and to tell you the truth I'm glad He didn't. After serving in France in 1918, I'm not sure I could handle watching my boys march off to war. Personally, I don't know how you and all of the other parents do it." After pausing for a split second to drink some coffee, Andy spoke from the heart when he continued and said, "Guys like us are doing what we do best to keep enemy agents out of the states and thieves from stealing the supplies that our troops need to win this war. If you were in some infantry unit there would be one less good cop taking care of this problem."

As Jim sat silent he still felt like shit. Even though he knew the importance of his current assignment, he felt cheated for not being allowed to lead men in battle. In an effort to explain himself further, Jim looked across the table at Andy and said, "All I ever wanted to be was a soldier and a policeman. Even though I saw some action when I served in Mexico with Pershing, I want'a do more. It's not just because my sons are fighting that I want a crack at combat. I know I can make a difference if they'd only give me a chance."

After pausing to stamp his cigarette out in an ashtray, Jim continued and said, "Just because I'm older doesn't mean I can't do something else besides being a cop. If they turn me down again they better send me home, 'cause chasing deserters and black-market operators in this town is not a mission that should be given to a southerner like me. In fact, I'm so determined to get overseas, I told Colonel Richmond I'd take a transfer to back to an MP unit if it would get me closer to the action." Instead of responding right away, Andy Dubrowsky removed a small notebook from his suit jacket pocket and spoke as he handed it to his buddy from the Provost Marshals Office. "My friend, you need one of these."

As soon as Jim examined the notebook that contained the names, addresses and phone numbers of a number of Andy Gooding's most prominent customers, he looked at Andy and said, "You think any of these characters would help me get a transfer to a front line unit?"

While appearing to be dead serious, Andy Dubrowsky remarked in a sarcastic tone, "They will as long as you take me and everyone else who has a copy of this list with you."

Even though Andy Dubrowsky was half joking when he suggested that Jim should use this list to secure a transfer to a combat command, it was good to see the Atlanta cop turned Army officer in better spirits. As soon as Jim handed the black notebook back to Andy, he raised his glass of water as if he was proposing a toast and said, "I said it before and I'll say it again. A gentleman from the south like me could pick up some very bad habits hanging around with you Yankees."

After both men smiled, Andy asked Jim to let him see the newspaper before they paid the check. As soon as Jim handed the veteran FBI Agent the morning paper, Andy examined the front page as he remarked, "Let's see what's going on in the world today."

The war news was both good and bad if you could believe the sensors. As soon as Andy looked across the table at Jim, he removed his eye glasses and said, "I don't know what's worse. Reading the newspaper before I eat or after I eat."

While Andy put his glasses back on, Jim leaned closer to the table to see which story caught his friend's attention. The article featured a riveting report about the missions that were being flown by the U.S. 8th Air Force over Germany.

While the solemn faced FBI man removed his glasses and said, "My brother's oldest son is a waist gunner on a B17 based in England. Every day we wonder if a telegram is gonna arrive to tell us that he's wounded, killed in action or in a German prison camp. His youngest son is in basic training and is destined to serve in the infantry. My oldest daughter was dating a boy who was killed in Sicily. He was a good kid. I still can't believe he's gone and neither can she." Then, after a brief split second pause, Andy handed the newspaper back to Jim and remarked, "I thought the last war was bad. This one's even worse."

CHAPTER 12

PREPARING TO GO ON THE RUN

Before leaving the warehouse that served as their base of operations, Ivan had everyone wash the getaway car, then wipe it down inside and out to remove any fingerprints from the vehicle. Ivan also had everyone clean and load their firearms while wearing gloves. This included paying special attention to the 1928 Model Thompson Submachine Gun and the assortment of 50 round drum and 20 round box or stick magazines that Ivan found in the warehouse/garage that served as his gang's hangout.

In order to prevent the police from obtaining their fingerprints, Ivan also insisted that everyone wear gloves during the robbery. Ivan also insisted that everyone wear a mask or a scarf of some kind, to prevent witnesses from being able to identify any of the members of the hold up team. In addition, Ivan reminded everyone not to slip and call each other by their real names. To keep things simple, Ivan suggested that they use numbers to refer to each other in case it became necessary to communicate during the robbery. As Ivan explained himself further, he instructed the members of his gang that they should call him Number 1, Terry Number 2, Amos Number 3 and Shorty would be Number 4.

So far, Ivan and his band of young thieves had eluded the police for almost three years. As long as they did everything that Mike Connely taught them to do, the cops would never be able to identify them or connect them to any of the crimes that they committed. Even the old cop who walked the beat in Mike Connely's west side neighborhood, was no match for them, although he did come close to stumbling on Ivan and his cohorts on a few occasions. After hearing that this cop had a heart attack and died after he was shot on duty, there was no one else from the local precinct who could identify Ivan or any of his buddies.

While driving in a stolen black 1940 60 Series Cadillac sedan, Ivan Larson along with Terry Kelly, Amos Washington and Francis Shorty Mc Ghee left their hideout in Manhattan, to conduct one last inspection of the area around the Lincoln Savings Bank before they executed the actual robbery. Under the circumstances, Ivan wasn't taking any chances and wanted everyone involved in the bank robbery to know exactly what was expected of them.

Instead of making cars during the war the Chrysler Corporation built 25,000 tanks. By February 10th, 1942 the last civilian automobile was driven off the assembly line in a Ford factory. The famous Willow Run complex in Michigan that was run by Ford Motor Company mass produced B24 liberators by the thousands.[3]

Since selling new cars was out of the question, due to the change over to mass produce military equipment, repairing automobiles became a big business. Car dealerships that once had showrooms that were filled with a revolving stock of brand new cars, were now bare because the entire car industry was devoted to making military equipment and munitions to wage war. As a result, the sales end of the industry stopped dead in its tracks and dealerships were turned into garages that spent their days fixing used cars.[4]

By 1943 Al Parker had a well earned reputation of being a master automobile mechanic. Al's capabilities as a talented mechanic were not developed overnight and took years to develop with the help of his father. Since Al's father didn't have the money to open up his own shop, he fixed cars on the side and worked his regular job with the Penn Central Railroad as a way to take better care of his family. As a result, when Al was growing up, he was raised under the hood of a car and spent all of his free time passing tools to his father and learning how to make vehicles of all kind run right. In the process, father and son bonded together and Al learned a valuable trade. Repairing vehicles for their customers also enabled Al and his father to drive all kinds of luxury cars that they could not afford to own.

Between the salary that he received for serving as a police officer and the extra money that he made fixing vehicles, Al Parker was able to provide a better life for his family. Because he had a very low overhead, Al was able to make repairs for a lot less money than the car dealerships and the private garages charged. Even more important was his reputation for doing excellent work. Civil servants like police officers and firefighters also counted on Al Parker to keep their family cars roadworthy. Al's side business became even more profitable when it became necessary during the war years to keep older vehicles in operational condition.

Eventually, Al had enough business to need more room to store vehicles and spare parts while he made the necessary repairs. When members of the Murphy family, including Pat Murphy Sr. and his three sons, moved to homes in the Flatbush section of Brooklyn, they encouraged Al to buy a garage in the same area that satisfied the needs of his expanding side business.

As soon as Al Parker found out that young Patrick was dating a girl who lived on Long Island and worked at the Grumman aircraft factory, he took on the responsibility of making his friend's 1936 Dodge Five Window Coupe roadworthy. After working in his spare time for two weeks, Al finally finished nursing the transmission on Pat's Dodge back to running condition.

Long Island was paradise in late 1943 and was comprised of small beach towns, fishing villages, the Grumman aircraft factory and potato farms. As far as young Patrick was concerned, all it took was one date with Mary Collins for him to feel as if he was shot in the ass by Cupid's arrow. Within six weeks of meeting the voluptuous red head, Pat Murphy Jr. was ready to ask Mary to marry him. Mary Collins obviously felt the same way, because she invited young Patrick into her bed to do what no other man ever did.

In addition to the fact that she was madly in love with Pat Murphy Jr., Mary Collins considered herself fortunate to have a handsome boyfriend, who completed his military service and had a secure civil service position with the police department. The fact that they didn't know each other very long, had no bearing on Pat's decision to ask Mary to marry him, providing of course that Al could fix his car in time for his big date.

After hounding his honorary uncle for several days, Al finally gave Pat the good news that his car was ready to make the trip to Long Island. With their last midnight tour of duty finished, Pat traveled with Al to his garage in Brooklyn to pick up his car. Once they took the repaired Dodge out for a test ride, Pat would be able to make the trek out to Long Island with confidence.

All the way to Brooklyn, Pat talked endlessly about the woman that he intended to make his wife. Even though Al was unable to get a word in edge wise, it was good to see his young friend in love with a decent girl after screwing his way from Brooklyn to Australia then back to Brooklyn.

While Al continued to drive to his garage, he enjoyed listening to his young friend talk about his future in such a positive way. As far as Al was concerned, every day that went by was one more day that Pat Murphy Jr. was away from the horrors of war. Even though his body would bear the scars of battle for the rest of his life, there was no reason for Pat or any other combat veteran to allow their wartime experiences to prevent them from enjoying the relative peace and tranquility of civilian life.

Between the support that he received from his family and friends, as well as the rewarding nature of his police career and the life that he wanted to make with Mary Collins, Pat Murphy Jr. was well on his way to becoming a well adjusted human being again.

While Al mumbled, "Time heals all wounds," Pat continued rambling on about Mary's ability to cook and how much they both wanted the same things in life.

While Shorty cruised the area around the Lincoln Savings Bank, Ivan turned sideways in the front passenger seat and made eye contact with the others and said, "Remember the plan. Keep your gloves on at all times and don't look anyone in the face until you put your mask on when you enter the bank. I'll take care of the guard on duty by the entrance, while Terry and Amos will take the other guard into the vault. As soon as he drops us off, Shorty will take a position across the street on Nostrand Avenue near the Church Avenue intersection so he can cover us if anything goes wrong. Once we leave the bank, we'll wait in between vehicles that are parked near the corner until Shorty pulls up and takes us to the other getaway car."

When Shorty approached the intersection of Nostrand Avenue and Church Avenue, Ivan pointed to parking spaces on the left and right side of Nostrand Avenue just before the intersection as he turned to Shorty and said, "Any place near this intersection will be a good place for you to park until we come out."

After seeing Shorty nod his head then remark, "Got it," Ivan continued as they proceeded through the intersection. "If everything goes according to plan the alarm won't go off until after we leave the bank. If for some reason the alarm goes off while we're still inside, this place will be crawling with cops in a matter of minutes. Should that happen, they'll never expect this intersection to be blocked by a getaway car, while the driver blasts away with a Tommy Gun."

While Ivan pointed to the right, he finished his tour of the area by saying, "That's the place where Shorty will pick us up. If the cops are on our tail I'll put the Tommy Gun to good use while Shorty does the driving."

After Ivan paused long enough to check his watch, he motioned Shorty to continue down Nostrand Avenue as he remarked, "After we check on the other getaway car that we have stashed behind Holy Cross Church, we can grab a smoke and wait for the bank to open."

As Shorty responded and said, "You got it," Terry spoke up and asked Ivan how big of a haul he figured they would be able to take from the bank. While Shorty made a right turn on Tilden Avenue, Ivan turned in his seat and said, "Enough dough to take care of us for some time to come."

When Al Parker dropped the keys to the Dodge Coupe in Pat Murphy Jr.'s hand, the young patrolman smiled like a kid who found a stack of presents under the Christmas tree with his name on it. Not only was his car running like a top, but Al also washed and waxed the otherwise dull blue coupe and brought it back to life.

The moment Pat reached into his right side pant's pocket, while he admired his car and said, "Gee, Al, she looks brand new," Al grabbed Pat's hand while it was still in his pocket and said, "I hope you're scratching you leg because I'd be offended if you tried to pay me."

After nodding his head up and down, the respectful young cop slowly removed his hand from his pocket. "I knew you wouldn't take any money," responded Pat, who quickly added, "So I got you a present instead. I know it's a little early but Happy Birthday, Al."

The package was neatly wrapped in colorful wrapping paper with a thin red ribbon holding it all together. As Al accepted the gift, he was speechless and started to get chocked up. While Al gained control of his emotions, he untied the ribbon and said, "You didn't have to do this you know."

As soon as Al carefully folded back the paper, his eyes opened wide when he removed the top of the presentation box and spotted the nicest bone handled pocket knife he had ever seen in his life. After carefully removing the pocket knife from the box, Al smiled from ear to ear as he pulled back the longer 3.5 inch blade, before he opened the smaller blade that was commonly called a California clip. As Al folded the smaller blade back into the handle, he looked at Pat and said, "I don't know what to say. This is one handsome looking pocket knife."

While Al continued to admire Pat's gift, he stared at the brand new bone handled knife and added, "I always wanted one of these." As soon as Al folded the larger blade closed, he looked at Pat while he slipped the knife in his pants pocket and said, "Let's take this baby out for a spin."

While Pat opened the driver's side door of his car, he sounded like a happy camper when he called out, "What do you say we go to Mc Donald's Bar for an early lunch? We can sit in the back room away from all the drunks and have some home made chow made by Johnny Mc Donald's mom. All I gotta do is hit the bank so I can cash my paycheck before we head back into the city."

After opening the front passenger door, Al looked over the top of the shinny blue Dodge as he remarked, "Lunch is on me or I'm not going."

Because Pat knew better than argue with Al Parker he agreed and said, "OK, Al. Lunch is on you but I'm buying the drinks."

As soon as Al responded and said, "Deal," Pat sat behind the wheel and smiled as he admired the condition of his well cared for car.

After turning to his right, Pat looked at his honorary uncle and said, "Thanks, Al. I mean it."

Even though Al was deeply moved by Pat's display of gratitude, he felt a bit uncomfortable belaboring the point. Rather than get all mushy in front of his young friend, Al pretended to get serious as pointed his left index finger at the dashboard of the Dodge Coupe and said, "Easy on the ignition when you start her up and don't flood it." Under the circumstances, Pat couldn't help but smile. Al Parker was a softy at heart and proved it by immediately changing the subject and trying to act like a bit of a hard ass.

While Pat remembered to start the car the way he was instructed, he glanced to his right to see if Al approved. Once he saw Al wink his left eye and grin, Pat gently slipped the transmission into reverse and applied just enough pressure on the accelerator pedal to slowly back out of Al's garage.

After putting the phone down Jim Beauregard rubbed his tired face before reaching for another Lucky Strike. As cooperative as Mr. Gooding had become, the teenage killer who went by the name Ivan Smith was still a mystery to the members of the U.S. Army Provost Marshal's Office Task Force.

With eight task force investigators assigned to further identify Ivan Smith and work with Andy Gooding to make a case against the crooked butcher, Jim asked Andy Dubrowsky and Deputy U.S. Marshal Kevin Kalb to help him locate a deserter. The reason this case was important, was because this deserter reportedly stole a loaded .45 caliber automatic from his drill sergeant before he went AWOL.

According to the case file that Jim Beauregard assembled to date, Christian S. Gatewood was one of those people who should have never been drafted. Simply put, Christian Gatewood refused to conform to any aspect of Army life. This included, complying with the rules that were originally put in place when the Continental Army was formed. These rules dictated that commissioned and non commissioned officers gave the orders and enlisted men did what they were told.

If a G.I. during World War II screwed up bad enough, he could count on receiving some form of punishment to help him to correct his errant behavior. In fact, it was standard operating procedure for the U.S. Army to use various forms of pain and suffering to motivate a soldier to learn a valuable lesson. Those who refused to conform faced different forms of disciplinary action. If the charges were serious enough, a person could be dishonorably discharged and even imprisoned.

Christian Gatewood was an artist by fantasy and a house painter by profession. He would have done well if the army had asked him to paint everything in sight in anything but a fresh coat of khaki green or olive drab. As fond as he was of painting, Gatewood did not work well under pressure and only painted when he was predisposed to do so. When all else failed, Gatewood's sergeant allowed the other troops under his command to take matters in their own hands. Turning a blind eye to this type of peer pressure, was done to help motivate the Sad Sack in his unit to get his shit together. When Gatewood failed to conform, his fellow soldiers gave him a blanket party after lights out. Although the Army was risking a visit by the Inspector General, the powers to be decided to break Gatewood at all cost.

To his credit, Christian Gatewood refused to talk about how he received his injuries. Instead, he stopped bathing. This brought on more harassment and resulted in his fellow soldiers dragging him into the head (aka bathroom) to give him what was known as a G.I. shower. After receiving this form of harsh treatment, Gatewood was thrown outside into the mud and left to shiver in the cold rain.

Even after his G.I. shower and mud bath in the freezing rain, Gatewood refused to say who was responsible for his mistreatment, when an inquiry was made by an Army Captain who noticed the bruises on his face, neck and hands. Instead, Gatewood accepted more company punishment without any complaint and continued to spend time peeling potatoes, cleaning latrines, picking up garbage and walking guard duty.

The day he decided to go AWOL Gatewood stole his sergeant's prize possession, a loaded Remington Model 1911 .45 ACP pistol with nicely worn pair of ivory grips that the non commissioned officer carried while fighting in North Africa. As far as Christian Gatewood was concerned, his sergeant represented everything that was wrong with the United States Army, because he cherished his issued .45 caliber pistol more than he seemed to care about the recruits who did not respond well to being mistreated.

In order to pay his sergeant back, Gatewood decided to toss the pistol into Sheepshead Bay and send him a hand written letter that explained what he did and why he did it. If that didn't give the old war horse a heart attack nothing would. With the stolen pistol in his possession, Christian Gatewood left Ft. Dix in the back of a delivery truck and became a deserter.

CHAPTER 13

THE LINCOLN SAVINGS BANK

W hile Shorty Mc Ghee drove the stolen black four door 1940 Cadillac 60 Special down Church Avenue, Ivan turned sideways in the front passenger seat and spoke as he made eye contact with Amos and Terry. "You boys ready?"

Terry Kelly was an accomplished crook by now, even if he had never robbed a bank before. As soon as Terry racked the slide on his Colt Model 1908 Pocket Auto Pistol and applied the safety, he looked directly at Ivan and said, "I'm ready when you are Number 1."

Just as Ivan expected Amos Washington was a mixed bag of feelings as he sat in the back seat behind Shorty Mc Ghee. While part of him was proud to be accepted by this gang of white hoodlums, the other part of him was petrified about the prospects of robbing a bank. With his face covered with sweat, Amos nodded his head before he spoke up and said, "I'm I'm ra ra ready ta ta too I I Ivan. I I mean Na Na Number 1."

Ivan knew that he was taking a chance bringing a retarded colored kid along on a bank heist but he had no choice. Even though Amos was handicapped, he was strong as an ox and incredibly loyal. As a result, Ivan and the others agreed that Amos should be responsible to carry the heavy sacks of money out of the bank, while everyone else did the shooting in the event that something went wrong.

For all of his shortcomings, Ivan felt a sense of compassion for his trusted Negro sidekick. To reassure Amos that his presence was needed Ivan remarked, "We can't do this without you, Amos. Are you OK?"

While feeling invigorated by the fact that he was needed, Amos removed his nickel plated revolver from his pants pocket as he responded in a more confident tone of voice and said, "A a I'm O O OK Na Na Number 1."

After telling Amos to put his gun away until it was needed, Ivan Larson drew his Colt 1911 .45 caliber automatic and racked the slide to load the chamber before he applied the safety and tucked the full size pistol back into his waistband.

By the time Shorty was pulling up in front of the bank, Ivan was filling his jacket pockets with several spare seven round pistol magazines in case the robbery failed to work out as planned.

As soon as Ivan started to open the door of the getaway car, he stopped long enough to look back at Shorty and say, "I gave you that Tommy Gun for a reason. Don't be afraid to use it if you have to."

While Shorty gripped the steering wheel with gloved hands, he spoke with confidence as he responded and said, "Don't worry Number 1. I'll be here to pick you guys up when you come out."

With nothing else to say Ivan looked at the pensive faces of his fellow crooks and said, "Let's go," before he stepped all the way out of the car and stood on the sidewalk by the Church Avenue entrance of the bank.

Just before Ivan stepped inside the Lincoln Savings Bank he slipped on his stocking mask. The moment Ivan entered the bank, he approached the elderly bank guard who was on duty by the entrance and stuck his pistol in the old man's stomach as he whispered, "Don't move, Pop, or I'll start shooting."

Once Terry Kelly and Amos Washington entered the bank, Ivan relieved the bank guard of his six shot Colt Official Police revolver and tucked it into his waistband while he called out, "This is a stickup! If I hear an alarm I'll start shooting."

While Ivan called out, "Everybody down," Terry Kelly disarmed the second bank guard and led him into the vault with Amos Washington following close behind. As everyone in the bank complied, Ivan continued to stand by the entrance so he could grab any additional customers who entered the bank. The first to do so was an elderly medical doctor, who did as he was told when Ivan Larson stuck his forty five caliber pistol in the man's chest and suggested that he take a position on the floor by a nearby desk.

After stopping his car next to an available parking space on Church Avenue, Pat Murphy Jr. struggled with the gear shifter as he tried to find reverse. Just as Al said, "Nurse that tranny, Pat and she'll last you forever," Pat found the right gear and backed his car into a parking spot that was down the block from the Lincoln Savings Bank. As soon as Pat partially opened the driver's side door of his car, he looked to his right and said, "I'll be back in a minute, Al."

Al Parker responded as he removed his new bone handled folding knife from his pant's pocket. "Don't worry about me. I'll just sit here and play with my new knife while you take care of business."

After Pat looked to see if any vehicles were coming, he opened the driver's side door all the way. As Pat stepped out of the vehicle, he joked around with his honorary uncle. "Don't cut yourself, Al and please don't get blood all over my seats."

As Al turned to his left and remarked, "Will you get going, I'm hungry," Pat closed the door and walked around the front of the vehicle as he made his way to the sidewalk.

By now Al had played with his new knife long enough. While Al slipped the knife in his left side back pocket, he quickly rolled down the passenger side window and called out, "And don't make time with any of them pretty bank tellers 'cause you're almost a married man."

After hearing what Al had to say, Pat looked back, cracked a smile and waved his left hand as he continued to walk toward the bank.

After walking almost all the way to the corner, Pat stopped and stood off to the side to let other pedestrians pass by. While Pat stood near the entrance to the bank, a wave of sadness fell over him like a warm blanket as he remembered his last patrol on Guadalcanal. Before Pat knew it, he was reliving the day when a determined group of Japanese soldiers attacked him and his men across a shallow stream in the jungle. Even though Pat survived a number of other combat actions, his last encounter with the enemy was the one that affected him the most. In an effort to shake off his wartime flashback, Pat decided to smoke a cigarette to calm his nerves before he entered the bank.

Once he made his way into the vault, Terry Kelly ordered the disarmed bank guard to stand in the corner, while he and Amos filled two large sacks full of cash. As soon as the bags were filled, Terry ordered the guard to lead the way to the front of the bank. The moment they entered the customer service area, a well dressed woman entered the bank and began screaming before Ivan could stop her from doing so. A split second later the bank manager pressed the alarm button.

The moment Ivan yelled, "Lets go!" off duty Patrolman Pat Murphy Jr. entered the bank with his Colt Detective Special revolver in hand and yelled, "Stop Police!" as he confronted the armed robbers.

The first to shoot was Ivan Larson. Even though Pat was hit in his right side, he pulled the trigger twice and killed Terry Kelly, while the 17 year armed robber held a Colt pistol in his right hand. While Terry Kelly collapsed on the marble floor of the bank, Ivan went berserk and emptied the remaining five rounds from his forty five into the young cop who was blocking their escape.

The second Al Parker heard the bank alarm sounding and shots being fired, he looked up just in time to see Pat Murphy Jr. stumble out of the bank and collapse on the sidewalk. As shocked as he was by what he just observed, Al quickly exited Pat's car with his off duty revolver in his right hand and his silver Patrolman's shield in his left. While Al ran toward the bank, he held his short barreled revolver by his right side and his patrolman's shield up high for all to see, as he identified himself as a police officer and pushed his way through the crowd of panic stricken pedestrians.

With no time to morn his friend, Ivan quickly reloaded his pistol. As soon as his Colt 1911 was reloaded, Ivan retrieved the sack of cash that was on the floor next to Terry's body and yelled, "Let's go, Number 3."

While Ivan pushed Amos out of the bank, he spoke in a raised voice so he could be heard over the noisy alarm. "No matter what happens don't stop until you get in between the cars that are parked out front!"

After taking one last look at the lifeless body of his dead friend, Ivan Larson left the bank with his pistol in one hand and the sack of stolen money in the other.

The moment Al Parker saw the two armed robbers emerge from the bank carrying two sacks of cash, he took cover behind a parked delivery truck and yelled, "Stop Police!" before he aimed and fired twice. When one of Al Parker's .38 Special bullets wounded Amos Washington in his left leg, the man size Negro teenager limped the rest of the way to a position of cover in between two parked cars, while Ivan used his pistol to keep the Negro cop pinned down.

Between the bank alarm going off, the presence of a Negro cop in plainclothes trying to prevent their escape and the sound of sirens getting closer, the last thing that Ivan Larson needed was a uniformed traffic cop running his way with his service revolver in hand. Rather than wait for the traffic cop to get any closer, Ivan quickly reloaded his pistol before he leaned over Amos Washington's left shoulder and fired one well aimed shot at the traffic patrolman. The second the traffic cop fell wounded on the sidewalk, Ivan continued firing at other targets of opportunity.

After firing four shots in rapid fire succession at the bank robber who was armed with the .45 caliber pistol, Al Parker left his position of cover and went to the aid of the wounded traffic cop. Even though Ivan Larson wasn't hit, the sound of bullets striking a nearby car fender forced him to duck down and take cover. This enabled Al Parker to drag Traffic Patrolman Thomas Garfield to a position of safety in between the parked delivery truck and a parked car.

After pausing to catch his breath, Al handed the wounded cop a clean handkerchief and said, "I'm Patrolman Parker. You'll be OK. Just put some pressure on that wound in your shoulder." While Al moved closer to the back of the delivery truck, he quickly reloaded his off duty revolver with six rounds of spare ammunition that he carried in his right side pant's pocket.

As soon as Al peered around the right rear fender of the delivery truck, he saw an opportunity to take another shot at the gunman he wounded earlier, who wasn't fully concealed behind the cover of a parked car. While taking careful aim at the partially exposed target, Al cocked the hammer on his Smith & Wesson M&P revolver and fired one shot that struck the larger of the two bank robbers just below his left buttocks.

As soon as Amos Washington screamed in pain and called out that he was shot again, Ivan stopped firing his pistol and checked on his friend's condition. After examining the wound Ivan leaned closer to Amos and said, "Hang on Number 3. We'll be outta here soon."

As bullets wizzed overhead and blew out nearby car windows, Ivan Larson remained crouched down in between the two parked cars, while he continued trading shots with the small army of police officers who responded to the robbery. This included keeping an eye on the Negro cop who was still behind the delivery van that was parked several vehicles away from his current position.

If Ivan was grateful for one thing, it was making the decision to include Francis Shorty Mc Ghee on this caper. Shorty Mc Ghee proved to be a worthwhile member of Ivan's gang, when he blocked traffic at the intersection of Church Avenue and Nostrand Avenue with the getaway car and he used old man Connely's Tommy Gun to put two responding police cars out of action. Even the police officers who had Ivan and Amos pinned down, were unable to advance on their position, as long as Shorty kept spraying both sides of the street with burst after burst of .45 ACP caliber ammunition.

As soon as Al Parker fired five more rounds at the bank robbers, he knelt down behind the delivery truck and ejected the empty cases on the ground. While Al reloaded his six shot Smith & Wesson M&P revolver, he periodically looked around the back of the truck to keep an eye on the pinned down bank robbers.

The moment Al stood up in a slight crouch, Patrolman Garfield called out, "Stay down. They have a machine gun."

As Al took another quick peek around the right side of the delivery truck toward the corner, he felt the pit of his stomach tighten in knots when it appeared that young Patrick wasn't moving. After turning to face the old traffic cop, Al sounded as determined as ever when he called out and said, "I gotta try and stop those bastards! They shot an off duty cop friend of mine who walked into the stickup!"

By the time the wounded traffic cop wished Al good luck, the driver of the getaway car jumped into the vehicle and drove the bullet ridden Cadillac to the corner of Nostrand Avenue near the entrance of the bank. While the getaway car traveled the short distance to the corner, Ivan laid down covering fire with his pistol. Once Shorty put the car in reverse, he backed up so he could extract his two accomplices from harms way.

When the getaway car came to a screeching stop, Ivan Larson continued to lay down covering fire with his pistol, while Shorty finished reloading the Tommy

Gun with a fifty round drum of ammunition. While Ivan reloaded his pistol, he screamed, "3's hit. Cover me!"

While Shorty stepped out of the getaway car and opened fire to cover the extraction, Ivan Larson traded shots with the Negro cop who was making his way toward the corner. When several bullets fired by Ivan Larson came within inches of hitting his target, Al Parker dove for the sidewalk and gave the gunman the impression that he was hit.

Even though Al was out of ammunition, he had no intention of giving up his pursuit of the bank robbers who gunned down his friend. While Ivan Larson tossed the two sacks of cash through the open front passenger side window of the Cadillac, Al Parker made his move.

As soon as Al Parker got off the ground, he slipped his empty revolver in his back pocket and ran in a slight crouch to the location in between the two parked cars where the shot up Cadillac was parked. While Shorty continued firing at the police from the driver's side of the car, Ivan was just finished helping Amos into the back seat when someone grabbed him from behind. The moment Ivan was forcibly ripped out of the getaway car, he dropped his .45 caliber pistol on the floor of the stolen Cadillac.

As soon as Al Parker slammed the fairly tall and thin bank robber up against the side of the getaway car and screamed, "You're under arrest you son of bitch," he removed the stolen bank guard's revolver from the gunman's waistband with his right hand, while he used his left hand to forcibly remove the stocking mask off Ivan Larson's head. The moment a shocked Al Parker looked at Ivan Larson's face and screamed, "You're just a fucking kid," Amos Washington leaned out of the open right rear door of the getaway car and fired one round from his revolver at the off duty Negro cop.

The second Al Parker flinched after being shot, Ivan Larson punched the Negro Policeman in his wounded right arm with enough force to send him reeling backwards in searing pain. When Ivan screamed, "Let's go," he jumped into the back seat and closed the door while Shorty sprayed the area one last time. Once Shorty passed the submachine gun to Ivan, he jumped in behind the steering wheel and drove off at a high rate of speed.

Despite the pain that he was in, Al Parker checked to see if the revolver that he took from the teenage bank robber was loaded. While the getaway car made a sharp right turn on Nostrand Avenue and raced by a shot up police car, a pissed off

Al Parker stood up and ran toward the corner. Even though he was right handed, Al used his weak hand to fire all six shots at the fleeing felons but failed to inflict any damage on the Cadillac or its occupants. When six cops in three police cars tried to give chase, Ivan Larson put the Thompson Submachine Gun to good use and ended the pursuit.

While Al Parker stood next to a uniformed police sergeant, the medical doctor who was a customer in the bank during the robbery, knelt over Pat Murphy Jr's body and listened for signs of life. After removing his stethoscope from his ears, the doctor slowly stood up and addressed Al Parker and the police sergeant. "I'm sorry. There's nothing I can do for your friend."

Besides being wounded, Al was in shock after hearing a doctor confirm what he already knew. It was almost as if Al didn't believe his own eyes, when he saw Patrick Murphy Jr. lying on the sidewalk with his lifeless body riddled with multiple gunshot wounds.

As soon as Al turned to face the uniformed police sergeant, who gripped him by his good arm to keep him steady, he sounded as if he was in a state of complete denial when he said, "Pat can't be dead. He's a war hero. He didn't survive Guadalcanal just to come home and get killed in a bank robbery."

As the old Irish police sergeant gently patted Al on the back, he spoke in a soft tone of voice and said, "Come on, Laddy. We need to get you to a hospital."

While Al was led away, he looked back as Pat Murphy Jr. was lifted off the ground and placed on a stretcher. Once again the veteran police sergeant spoke with a soft Irish brogue as he escorted Al to a nearby ambulance and said, "Rest assure, Patrolman Murphy is in a better place."

CHAPTER 14

AMOS WASHINGTON SURPRISES EVERYONE

When it came to planning criminal activity, Ivan Larson covered every detail as if he was a general developing an operational plan for a military operation. Because he had such attention to detail, Ivan knew that one of the most critical parts of the robbery was when he and his fellow robbers fled the scene of the crime and they needed to change cars.

One of the reasons why Ivan elected to rob the Lincoln Savings Bank, was because he and Terry found a house near Holy Cross Church that was perfect for their escape plan. In addition to its location and the length of its driveway, this home was owned by an elderly woman who was more than happy to rent her garage, as well as a parking space in her back yard, to the two young men because she had no car.

Because of the impact of the war on the home front, the old lady believed the two young men when they said they needed a place to park their car and their father's car due to gasoline and tire rationing. Even though Ivan had to pay to rent this garage for several months, doing so enabled him and his gang to have access to a suitable location to change cars in order to facilitate their escape into Manhattan.

After hiding the shot up getaway car inside the rented garage on a side street near the church, Ivan Larson and Francis Shorty Mc Ghee helped Amos Washington into the back of a tan over brown colored 1938 Ford Sedan Delivery vehicle. By moving as quickly as they did, the three bank robbers were able to flee the Flatbush section of Brooklyn, before the police were able to set up road blocks in the immediate area.

After stopping once to check on Amos, Ivan tried to bolster his colored sidekick's morale by saying, "After we get you patched up, we'll get something to eat and head south."

Amos Washington might have been dumb but he wasn't stupid. He knew he was hurt bad enough to need a doctor, as well as time to recuperate before he would be healthy enough to travel. While lying on his side in the cargo compartment of the second getaway vehicle, Amos grimaced in pain while he held his bloody leg and looked up at Ivan and said, "A a all a a I'm ga ga gonna da da do is sa sa slow you da da down, I I Ivan."

As troubling as it was to see Amos suffering from two gunshot wounds, being hunted by the police and the feds made a bad situation a lot worse. Ivan also knew that driving all the way to Mexico with a wounded colored teenager would not be an easy task.

Hearing Shorty ask him for the third time, "What are we gonna do now?" was beginning to drive Ivan to his breaking point.

While Ivan turned in his seat, he lashed out at Shorty and yelled, "Would you shut up for a minute and let me think!"

With no other worthwhile options to consider, Ivan Larson made a command decision to take Amos to his Uncle Dwayne. Ivan hoped that Dwayne Washington would use Amos's cut of the money to get his nephew medical attention from a colored doctor in Harlem who had no love for the police. As soon as Amos was fit to travel, his uncle could take him down south where Amos could hide out with relatives. On the surface Ivan's plan made perfect sense. Even Amos liked the idea of going back home to South Carolina to live with family members.

After hearing Shorty Mc Ghee remark, "Now that you did what you could for Amos what about us? How the hell are we supposed to escape and live happily ever after?"

Ivan Larson was at a complete loss for words after coming down from a massive adrenaline rush. While Shorty continued driving to Harlem, Ivan nervously tapped his right foot on the floor board of the Ford as he said, "We have to listen to the radio to get an idea what the cops are doing."

After hearing Ivan's last remark, Shorty lost it and screamed, "I'll tell you what the cops are doing and I don't have to listen to the radio to find out. The cops are tearing this city apart looking for us."

Ivan might have been a bit unsure of himself but he was still in charge and proved it when he grabbed Shorty's right arm and said, "You gotta problem with the way I do business?"

Even though Shorty was a good wheel man, who proved to be a quick study when it came to handling a submachine gun, he was a follower and not a leader. In an effort to write off his outburst as a reaction to things not working out, Shorty tried to diffuse the situation by saying, "It's not your fault that some off duty cop walked into the bank and some off duty colored cop was outside when we hit the place."

As soon as Ivan let go of Shorty's arm, he sat back in his seat while Shorty pulled a fresh pack of cigarettes from his jacket pocket and offered one to Ivan. "Smoke?" While Ivan accepted the cigarette he turned to his left and said, "Thanks."

After lighting the cigarette, Ivan seemed more relaxed as he turned to Shorty and said, "What the hell are we gonna do?"

Shorty was also at a loss for words and had no idea what move they should make next. Then, out of the back of the vehicle, a friendly voice was heard saying, "U u ca ca could ja ja join tha tha Army."

While Ivan quickly turned around and looked at his wounded friend, Shorty remarked, "He's delirious."

For various reasons Ivan was very protective of his Negro sidekick. After hearing Shorty's comment, Ivan looked at his wheel man and remarked, "Be nice will ya. Amos saved my life back there and he probably saved yours as well when that colored cop grabbed me from behind."

While Shorty kept quiet and continued driving, Ivan did his best to cheer up the only colored member of his gang. "Hang on, Amos. We're almost there."

As lightheaded as Amos was from the loss of blood and the shock of being wounded, he was determined to get Ivan and Shorty to take his suggestion seriously. After pulling himself closer to the front passenger seat, Amos asked Ivan if he heard what he said?

When Ivan responded and said, "Yes, Amos, I heard you," Shorty proved that his nerves were unraveling at the seams when he glanced back and blurted out, "I'm not joining the fucking Army just to get away from the police."

While Ivan sat sideways in his seat, he smacked Shorty on the side of the right arm as he yelled, "Would you let the man speak."

Without waiting for a response, Ivan looked in cargo compartment of the stolen delivery vehicle and encouraged Amos to continue. "Go ahead, Amos, finish what you were saying."

Ivan could tell by the presence of the blood soaked rags that served as a make-shift bandage that Amos was in bad shape. While Amos continued to lay on his side in the back of the vehicle, he spoke in a slow but understandable tone of voice that was laced with a southern accent. "The the ca ca cops a a ain't na na never ga ga gonna la la look fa fa for yu a a and Sha Sha Shorty in tha tha ar ar Army." Then, after pausing briefly, Amos composed his thoughts as he continued and said, "E ee even if they they da da did, tha tha they wu wu would na na never fa fa find you. Ba ba besides, you're ga ga gonna ha ha have ta ta go sa sooner or or la la later."

The second that Shorty started to make another derogatory comment Ivan cut him off and said, "He's right. If we join the Army they'll put us on a train and send us to some base for training."

Under the circumstances Shorty couldn't believe what he was hearing. After hearing Shorty remark, "The both of you are crazy," Amos spoke up again and said, "Ba ba besides ga ga getting a a away yu yu you'd be be da doing a a good tha thing by by sa sa serving a a our ca ca country."

By now Shorty was shaking his head almost non stop and muttering, "I ain't joining the fucking army just to escape and that's that."

As Ivan turned all the way around and faced forward in the front passenger seat, he had to admit that what initially sounded like a crazy idea was a plan that warranted further consideration. The thought of making a fresh start appealed to him, especially now that he was on the run. Even though Ivan had no use for the police, he hated the Nazis and the Japs. The more Ivan considered the suggestion that was made by his handicapped Negro friend, the more Ivan liked the idea and wondered if the Army would make him a pilot.

While Shorty continued to drive uptown, Ivan took a moment to daydream about becoming a genuine war hero, who was able to make a new life overseas when the war was over. Unfortunately, the reality of the situation became painfully obvious when Ivan heard Shorty arguing with Amos about the merits of his plan.

The moment Ivan raised his voice and said, "That's enough," the arguing stopped. Once again Ivan took command. While facing Shorty, Ivan continued to endorse the plan that Amos just proposed. "Amos is right. We have clean records which means we've never been fingerprinted or photographed by the police. In addition to the fact that I don't have any family pictures for the cops to find, you told me that your no good stepfather ripped up and threw out every picture of you that your mother ever had when he tossed your ass out into the street. That means that if we use different names when we enlist, we should have no problem getting lost in an army that's filled with guys that look a lot like us."

As Shorty turned the car down the street where Dwayne Washington lived, he glanced over to Ivan and responded in a calm tone of voice. "You're going through with this?"

After nodding his head in agreement, Ivan remarked, "I always wanted to be a pilot. Pilots get respect."

"What happens if we get killed," asked Shorty.

Without hesitating, Ivan responded in the frankest of terms and said, "I'd rather die fighting the Japs or the Germans than get fried in the electric chair for killing a cop or that pathetic loser Tommy Mulray."

After hearing what Ivan had to say, Shorty had to admit that they might be better off hiding out in the Army than risk getting picked up while trying to live on the run as civilians. As soon as Shorty stopped the vehicle so he could parallel park, he looked at Ivan and said, "If we can't come up with a better way outta this mess I'll join up with you."

As much as Shorty hated to admit it, Ivan and Amos were both right. There were millions of young men serving in uniform. It was also no government secret that a large number of servicemen never saw actual combat. Even though this plan had merit, both Shorty and Ivan had a number of questions and concerns about the best way to proceed. In addition to the issue of how to stash the money they stole, they also had to be concerned about the possibility of being sent to different units or different theaters of operation. After all, one of them could end up stateside, while the other could get shipped overseas.

Shorty proved that this was something that he was concerned about when he remarked, "I hate to be the bearer of bad news but if we go through with this plan, I could end up in the Pacific fighting Japs and you could end up in Europe fighting Krauts. Then what?"

While Shorty finished parking the Ford, Amos wasted no time in providing his friends with more advice from the back of the vehicle. "If if you you ba ba both ja ja join tha tha Air Air Ca Ca Corps yu yu you'll ha have a a ba ba better cha cha chance of be be being ta ta together."

After putting the gear shifter in neutral and pulling on the emergency brake lever, Shorty sat sideways as he looked at Amos and said, "For a guy who never made it past the third grade you have some imagination."

While Amos thanked Shorty for the compliment, Ivan removed a bundle of cash from the money sack and counted out $500 dollars. It was time to part company. Amos knew that he could never go where Ivan and Shorty were going. Even if they decided not to enlist, they would be long gone before Amos recovered from his gunshot wounds.

When Ivan handed Amos his cut of the money, he did his best to sound as up beat as possible. "This ought'a be enough to get you a fresh start in South Carolina."

Amos Washington had never seen so much money before in his life. As soon as Amos stuffed the $500 dollars in his suit jacket pocket, he thanked Ivan for the money and said goodbye to Shorty.

"Hold on, Amos and I'll help you get out," said Ivan as he exited the vehicle and walked around back to open the door.

While Shorty kept the motor running and nervously looked around, Ivan helped Amos exit the back of the delivery vehicle. As Amos balanced himself on one foot, he looked at Ivan and said, "U an an and Sha Sha Shorty ba ba better ga ga go Na Na Number Wa Wa One."

Seeing Amos in pain made saying goodbye harder than he expected. To soothe his guilty conscience, Ivan reached into pocket, pulled out a wad of cash and peeled off another $200 dollars. As Ivan tucked the money into Amos's shirt pocket, he smiled then said, "I'll save the rest for you until we meet again after the war." Amos was overwhelmed. No one had ever shown him the kind of respect and friendship that his good buddy Ivan did. "Tha tha thanks I I Ivan."

Deep down inside Ivan felt like crap for leaving his most faithful companion besides Terry Kelly behind. "I'm the one who should be thanking you, Amos. You saved my life and I'll never forget it." said Ivan as he shook hands with his Negro friend.

After hearing Shorty say, "We better go. We stick out like sore thumbs in this neighborhood," Ivan closed the door to the rear compartment and got back into the passenger seat.

While Ivan looked to his right, Amos sounded as sincere as ever when he looked back and said, "A a I'll be be pra pra praying fa fa for u u you an an Sha Sha Shorty, I I Ivan."

As soon as Shorty put the Ford in gear, Ivan remarked, "We're gonna need it where we're going." After taking one last look at his trusted Negro companion, a somber looking Ivan Larson looked straight ahead and said, "Let's go."

While Ivan and Shorty drove away, Amos limped into his Uncle's ground floor apartment. When Shorty went to speak he decided against doing so when he spotted the sad look on Ivan's face. This was a side of Ivan Larson that was never displayed in public and served to remind Shorty that his partner in crime was human after all.

When Ivan finally spoke he was all business as he turned to Shorty and said, "Head downtown. As soon as we transfer the cash to the Chevy, I'll take you to another warehouse that only me and Mike know about. Even Terry didn't know about this place."

After pausing long enough to offer his partner in crime a cigarette, Ivan pulled one out of the pack for himself as he continued. "Now that we're on the run together we can lay low in this place until we make our next move."

As soon as Ivan leaned to his left and offered Shorty a light, he sat back and placed the flame from his Ronson lighter near the tip of his Camel cigarette while Shorty exhaled and said, "What a day."

"You said it," responded Ivan before he took another drag on his cigarette, while Shorty continued driving the Ford downtown.

After remaining silent for the length of an entire city block, Ivan decided to share what he was thinking about with Shorty. "Even though we have enough cash to make a fresh start in Mexico, we still have to get there. Since neither one of us has ever been outta New York, we have no idea what it would be like to make our way south of the border. The fact that there's a war on won't make this trip any easier, especially if we get stopped by MPs who are looking for AWOL G.I.s and sailors. If that happens what are we supposed to tell 'em. Sorry, we never registered for the Selective Service because we're wanted by the police."

As soon as Ivan paused to take another drag on his cigarette, he continued and said, "The more I think about it the more Amos is right. In addition to the fact that we can get lost in an Army that's filled with millions of soldiers, Uncle Sam will take care of getting us out of New York."

Even though Shorty preferred to wake up and find himself living in a place where a gringo with money was treated like a king, he had to admit that Ivan raised some valid concerns. While Ivan sat with his right arm resting on the open passenger side window, Shorty responded as he tossed his cigarette butt out of the open driver's side window. "You're right. The war complicates everything."

When Shorty changed lanes, Ivan crushed his cigarette butt into the car's ashtray before he remarked, "Once we change cars again, I call Mike and ask him to meet us. If anyone can help us he can."

After inspecting his nephew's gunshot wounds, Dwayne Washington wasted no time in taking Amos to Doctor Anton Carter, a well known member of the community in Harlem who postponed his plans to retire when the Japanese attacked Pearl Harbor. While Dr. Carter removed two .38 Special caliber bullets from Amos Washington's left leg and lower buttocks, he wondered if his patient was involved in the bank robbery that occurred earlier that day in Brooklyn. After all, Negro teenagers in Harlem didn't usually show up for treatment with a nervous relative and two gunshot wounds within hours of a bank being robbed. Dr. Carter became even more suspicious of his patient's wounds because radio reports stated that an off duty patrolman by the name of Al Parker was wounded during the Brooklyn bank robbery.

The fact that the radio reported that Patrolman Parker performed heroically during the bank robbery, that claimed the life of off duty Patrolman Patrick Murphy Jr, didn't surprise Dr. Carter. As a prominent resident of Harlem, Dr. Carter knew the Parker family quite well. Not only did he know Patrolman Parker from the neighborhood, but Dr. Carter had two of his cars maintained by Al Parker and his father. As a result, Dr. Carter was determined to convince his patient's legal guardian to let him contact the one police officer who would bring his nephew in alive to face trial.

While Dwayne paced back and forth in the doctor's waiting room, he died a thousand deaths while he worried about his nephew. By all accounts, Dwayne Washington was a hard working man who promised his dying brother that he would take care of his only son. Between working for the New York City subway system by night and working a side job during the day, Dwayne Washington did not have much time to watch over Amos. Like it or not, things had gone too far. Even though it was a bitter pill to swallow, Dwayne knew that he had to turn Amos in or help him escape.

On one hand Dwayne had enough money to get his nephew to South Carolina so he could hide out in the back woods with relatives. Dwayne also knew that a great deal depended on whether Dr. Carter would call the police, to report that he just removed two .38 Special bullets from a Negro teenager.

Despite his personal feelings, Dr. Carter had an obligation to care for the sick regardless of their standing with the law. He also knew that doctors were required to report all gunshot wounds to the police. Furthermore, Dr. Carter was now a witness since Dwayne was unable to provide a logical explanation of how his nephew was wounded, other than to say that his nephew was shot by some white boys because he was on the slow side and was always being made fun of.

While Amos slept after being sedated, Dr. Carter covered the young man with a blanket before he went into his office. As soon as he walked inside, he found his patient's uncle pacing back and forth, while nervously puffing on an inexpensive cigar. Dwayne needed no invitation to speak and stopped pacing when he asked the Doctor how his nephew was doing.

As Dr. Carter stood behind his desk, he spoke as he opened the top draw. "He'll be fine. He's sleeping now."

After ignoring the Harrington Richardson revolver that rested comfortably under some papers in his top desk drawer, Dr. Carter smiled and remarked, "There it is," as he retrieved a small key that opened the liquor cabinet.

While Dr. Carter slowly closed the draw and turned around to open the liquor cabinet, a nervous sounding Dwayne Washington approached the desk and spoke in a curious tone. "I gotta ask you, Doc. Are you gonna report this to the police?"

After removing a bottle of bourbon, Dr. Carter poured two healthy shots into a pair of sparkling clean glasses. As Doctor Carter presented Dwayne with a glass of bourbon, he spoke in a calm and friendly tone of voice. "Won't you join me?" As soon as Dwayne accepted the glass and took a sip, Dr. Carter continued and said, "Tell me about your nephew?"

After sipping a more expensive brand of liquor than he was used to drinking, Dwayne Washington began to describe in detail how his brother died and left his only son to his care and custody. Clearly, Dwayne Washington was genuinely guilt ridden for not doing a better job of raising his nephew. Then, he slipped and used his nephew's first name. To make matters worse, Dwayne realized that he had his nephew's revolver in his pants pocket, a handgun that he was prohibited to possess in New York City without a license. Rather than make a bad situation worse, Dwayne slowly removed his nephew's revolver from his pant's pocket and set it on top of the doctor's desk.

Realizing the turmoil that his patient's uncle was in, motivated the kind old doctor to come around his desk and pat Dwayne on the back as he remarked in a reassuring tone, "Tell me what's wrong. Maybe I can help."

Without hesitation Dwayne looked at the concerned physician and said, "My nephew got involved with a gang'a white boys. I knew they were up to no good but I looked the other way 'cause they accepted Amos."

When Dr. Carter remarked, "Don't be too hard on yourself. I'm sure you did what you thought was best for your nephew," Dwayne continued and said, "I never saw the boy happier. They drove around in big fancy cars and always had plenty of money. Heck those white boys took better care of Amos than I did."

As soon as Dwayne placed the glass of bourbon on the edge of the doctor's desk, he continued and said, "I had no idea that Amos and those white boys were gonna rob that bank in Brooklyn."

While Dwayne looked directly at Dr. Carter, he spoke in a pleading tone of voice as he continued. "You gotta believe me, Doc. Amos is a good boy. He ain't well. He just got mixed up with the wrong crowd. Them white boys was doing all the thinking."

After pausing long enough to take a sip of his drink, Dr. Carter invited Dwayne to have a seat before he walked around his desk and said, "If the police move in to arrest Amos and he fails to respond appropriately, the police will have no choice but to use their guns. Remember, the police don't know anything about Amos."

Even though Dwayne was not an educated man, he was smart enough to know that Doc Carter was 100% correct. At this point in their conversation Dwayne was open to any advice that the good doctor had to offer.

While Mr. Washington buried his face in his hands and repeated over and over again how Amos wasn't normal like other boys, Doctor Carter proved he had a terrific bedside manner when he said that he would be happy to speak to the District Attorney and the Judge about his nephew's limitations.

Under the circumstances, Dwayne could not ask for a better deal. As soon as Dwayne thanked the Doctor for all of his help, Doc Carter reached for the phone on his desk and said, "I know a policeman who can help."

CHAPTER 15

ARRESTING A DESERTER

After checking his notebook, Jim looked up and said, "That's it on the corner."

As soon as Andy Dubrowsky shut off the ignition of the FBI car, he slipped the car keys into his suit jacket pocket as he opened the driver's side door and said, "I wonder if he's home?"

While Jim Beauregard opened the passenger side door and stepped out onto the sidewalk, he sounded exhausted when he remarked, "To tell you the truth, Andy, I hope this kid is hiding out someplace else, because I'm in no mood to chase after a deserter if he takes off on foot, especially if he's carrying a stolen forty five."

After hearing Andy remark, "You ready?" it was back to the business at hand. Like most police partnerships, it wasn't uncommon for one cop to bitch and moan and have his partner bring him back to reality.

As soon as Jim perked up and said, "I'm ready...I'm just moving slow."

Jim and Andy got out of the FBI car just as Deputy U.S. Marshal Kevin Kalb arrived on scene and parked nearby.

"Sorry, I'm late, Major," remarked the only federal marshal assigned to the Provost Marshal's Office Task Force.

"No problem, Kevin," responded Jim who quickly added, "You're just in time to help us canvass the neighborhood. Why don't take the other side of the street and we'll meet in front of 609 Rogers Avenue."

As soon as the twenty one year veteran of the U.S. Marshal's Service, who served as a tank crewman in the 304th Tank Brigade under George Patton in World War I, called, out, "Got it," Jim and Andy began canvassing their side of the street.

Within a few minutes of showing Christian Gatewood's photograph around the neighborhood, Andy Dubrowsky and Jim Beauregard were convinced they had their deserter located. Kevin Kalb confirmed their findings, when he told Jim and Andy that the local grocer thought Gatewood was medically discharged from the army after being injured in training. While Kevin finished filing his canvassing report, he looked directly at Jim Beauregard and said, "He also said Gatewood just bought groceries for his aunt and offered to deliver bread and milk to an old man who lives across the street on his way home."

"Good work, Kevin," remarked Jim who continued while he pointed to the FBI car that was parked nearby, "Let's open the hood on Andy's car and make it look like we have engine trouble while we wait for Gatewood to show up."

After huddling around the open engine hood for a solid minute, Andy Dubrowsky spotted Gatewood coming their way while carrying a box of groceries. "Don't look now, but here he comes."

As soon as Jim agreed and said, "That's him," he looked at Andy and Kevin and added, "If this kid runs on us I hope that beat cop can cut him off at the pass."

After hearing what Jim had to say, Andy Dubrowsky proved that he had a good sense of humor when he remarked, "Cut him off at the pass. I like that. I guess that means me and Kevin are working with Hopalong Cassidy."

The moment Jim cracked a smile, Kevin Kalb remarked, "He got you that time, Major."

"What can I tell you, I like westerns," responded Jim, who quickly added, "OK, guys, here we go."

In anticipation of arresting an AWOL soldier who stole a .45 caliber pistol, the three representatives of the federal government instinctively unbuttoned their suit jackets in preparation of having to draw their sidearms. While Christian Gatewood continued walking toward his aunt's apartment house, Andy Dubrowsky and Kevin Kalb casually walked into the street to execute a flanking maneuver, while Major Beauregard drew his Army issued Colt Model 1903 Pistol and called out, "Military Police you're under arrest!"

In addition to facing an Army Investigator, Gatewood also had two lawmen in plainclothes armed with very large revolvers screaming "FBI!...Federal Marshal!" while they took cover behind the car that was parked in front of his aunt's apartment building.

Even though Christian Gatewood was a non conformist, he reacted appropriately by dropping the box of groceries and holding up his hands as he called out, "Don't shoot. I give up."

As the cop who was on a foot post one block away responded with his revolver in hand, Andy Dubrowsky, Keven Kalb and Jim Beauregard slowly moved in while Private Gatewood continued to hold his hands in the air. After holstering his pistol, Jim Beauregard patted Gatewood down, while Andy Dubrowsky and Kevin Kalb stood off to the side and covered the prisoner with their revolvers.

When the uniformed patrolman arrived on scene, Major Beauregard did the honors and called out, "U.S. Army…Provost Marshal's Office….we're arresting a deserter." Without hesitating, the veteran patrolman holstered his revolver and went to work holding back the small crowd of onlookers, who were beginning to assemble in front of 609 Rogers Avenue.

As soon as the Major handcuffed his prisoner, he leaned closer to Christian Gatewood and said, "My name is Major James Beauregard and I only have one question for you. Where's the forty five?"

After presenting a sinister grin, the deserter seemed proud of the fact that he destroyed his sergeant's personalized sidearm when he said, "I tossed it in Sheepshead Bay, Sir and I hope you tell Sergeant Hargrove that I did so."

Under the circumstances, Jim Beauregard had no way of knowing if Christian Gatewood was telling the truth or not. Since Gatewood wasn't carrying the stolen pistol at the time of his arrest, Jim Beauregard decided to ask Mrs. Cynthia Gatewood for permission to search her apartment.

Losing one son in the Battle of the Coral Sea, while her other son was a Prisoner of War in the Philippines motivated Mrs. Cynthia Gatewood to welcome her AWOL nephew into her home. Despite all of the flag waving that was taking place after December 7, 1941, Mrs. Gatewood didn't care that her nephew was Absent Without Leave. All she wanted was to see young Christian remain alive and in one piece. The fact that her husband was lost at sea, when his merchant vessel was sunk in route to Murmansk, further embittered the widow about the war.

Once Jim Beauregard explained the seriousness of the situation, Mrs. Gatewood gave him permission to search her apartment. All she asked for in return was to speak to her nephew before he was taken away.

While Andy Dubrowsky and Kevin Kalb placed the handcuffed prisoner in the back seat of the FBI car, Jim Beauregard faced Mrs. Gatewood and said."Of course, Ma'am."

After removing a set of keys from her pocket, Cynthia Gatewood said, "This way, Major," as she began walking into her apartment building. As soon as Jim began to follow the Gold Star Mother up the stairs, he told Andy and Kevin that he would be right back.

While Jim searched the room where Christian Gatewood lived after going AWOL, Andy Dubrowsky passed the time by having a conversation with the uniformed patrolman.

When Gatweood spoke up and said, "Excuse me, Sir, but I was telling the truth when I told the Major that I dropped my sergeant's pistol in Sheepshead Bay," Kevin Kalb remarked, "The Major is doing his job, son."

A few minutes later Jim Beauregard left the apartment house carrying an Army uniform. Following close behind was Mrs. Gatewood. While Mrs. Gatewood was allowed to say goodbye to her nephew, Jim met with Andy and Kevin off to the side to have a private chat about the missing pistol. "It wasn't in the apartment," remarked, Jim Beauregard who quickly added, "I think this kid is telling the truth about tossing his sergeant's forty five in Sheepshead Bay."

"He certainly seems proud of what he did," responded Kevin Kalb.

After checking his watch Andy faced Jim. "By time we turn Gatewood over to the MPs, it'll be time for us to grab something to eat. Come on, Hopalong, dinner's on me."

When Andy invited Kevin Kalb to join them for supper, the 46 year old federal marshal remarked, "I gotta take a rain check on dinner, Andy. My family's getting together tonight before our youngest son goes off to basic training."

After thanking Kevin for giving them a hand, Jim and Andy drove off to lodge their prisoner with the military police at Ft. Hamilton. As Jim Beauregard would later find out, Christian Gatewood's future was decided when he refused an offer to show Navy divers where he dropped his sergeant's pistol in Sheepshead Bay. While serving time in the stockade for the theft of government property and the destruction of government property, Christian Gatewood was dishonorably discharged from the United States Army.

CHAPTER 16

THE FIRST BREAK IN THE CASE

P olice department policy dictated that sworn personnel who were personally involved in a particular incident, were prohibited from participating in any aspect of that case except as a witness. Al Parker knew that he was breaking department policy when he decided to arrest Amos Washington on his own, instead of alerting the detective who was officially handling the case.

As far as Al was concerned, he felt an obligation to avenge the death of his young friend, even if by doing so he pissed off everyone from the lead detective on the case to the Police Commissioner. What troubled Al the most, was that he spent so much time grooming young Patrick to do the right thing and here he was taking action on his own in violation of the rules and procedures of the P.D.N.Y. After a great deal of soul searching, Al pulled the steering wheel of his personal car sharply to the right when he spotted a police call box on the next corner.

For decades police officers communicated with their precinct and headquarters by using special phones known as a "call box." These dedicated police telephones were concealed in a locked metal "call box" that was secured to a wooden telephone pole/street light pole or on the side of buildings. In order to use one of these special police telephones, every cop was issued a call box key and was authorized to use this communication device whenever it was necessary to contact his command.

After using his call box key to unlock the metal cover on the call box, Al identified himself and asked the police operator to connect him to Captain Patrick Murphy Sr. The call went through immediately. After hearing the familiar voice of Pat Murphy Sr. answer the phone, Al spoke up and said, "I'm sorry to bother you, Captain but it's important."

Captain Patrick Murphy Sr. never forgot the day that he caught a burst of German machine gun fire and fell face down on a battlefield in Europe during World War I. Because he was badly wounded, the young Army officer had no way of getting back to the Allied lines without help. Once the shooting stopped, an eerie silence fell over the area known as "no man's land." He also knew that he was relatively close to the German lines, because he could hear the voices of German soldiers who were located in a nearby defensive position.

Even though he was no stranger to the dangers of being in combat, it took every ounce of courage that the young Army Officer possessed not to panic when he realized just how bad his situation was. To keep from being spotted, Lt. Murphy slid into a nearby bomb crater and did his best to remain as quiet as possible. His situation was complicated by the fact that he was surrounded by a sea of barbed wire, muddy shell holes and open terrain.

Immediately after another German star shell burned out, the young Army Officer thought he heard the sound of someone cutting his way through barbed wire from the direction of the French lines. A few seconds later, an American Negro soldier crawled through the entanglements and slid into the bomb crater with a pistol in hand. The fact that the young American soldier who came to his rescue was a Negro made no difference to the Irish American Army Officer.

While Police Captain Pat Murphy Sr. remembered what happened that night, his thoughts were filled with vivid images of a young Al Parker tending to his wounds and ignoring his order to return to the Allied lines. Instead, Al Parker began to help him out of the bomb crater just as they heard the sound of clanging battle gear and soldiers whispering in German. The young Army Officer was even more impressed when Private Parker quietly translated everything that the Germans just said. Clearly, being rescued by a Negro Private from the "all colored" 93rd Division, who served in an intelligence unit and spoke fluent German, was something that the Irish American Army Officer would never forget. The second the enemy troops appeared out of the darkness, the two Americans opened fire.

As Captain Murphy continued to be overwhelmed by the flashback of what happened that night, he remembered a young Al Parker fighting by his side to repel the enemy attack. Even when Al was wounded by grenade fragments, he never wavered and continued to put his 1911 .45 caliber pistol, a captured German Luger and two German grenades to good use.

While taking advantage of a lull in the fighting, Al began dragging the wounded Army Officer out of the bomb crater, just as a group of French 4th Army troops and American Negro soldiers from Al's unit made their way to their position. After providing enough supporting fire to prevent the enemy patrol from launching a counter attack, the combined French and American rescue party helped Pat Murphy Sr. and Al Parker back to the safety of the Allied lines. As a result of this incident, U.S. Army Lieutenant Pat Murphy Sr. and U.S. Army Private First Class Alvin Parker became close personal friends.

As soon as Captain Patrick Murphy Sr. came back to reality, he heard Al Parker's voice on the other end calling out, "Captain, are you there?"

"Yes, Al, I'm here." responded the police captain who quickly asked how Al was feeling after being wounded during the bank robbery.

After telling Captain Murphy that he was OK, Al explained the reason for the call. Under the circumstances, Pat Murphy Sr. thanked Al for calling him when he decided to break the rules and go after one of the bank robbers without bringing in the detective handling the case. Before he hung up the phone, Captain Murphy told Al to wait for him outside Dr. Carter's office and not breathe a word of this break in the case to anyone else.

That afternoon Captain Patrick Murphy Sr. and Patrolman Al Parker were featured on the front page of the evening newspaper as they escorted their wounded prisoner into police headquarters. Even though the detective who was assigned to take the lead on the case was pissed off to no end, he was forced to keep his opinion to himself because Al Parker was smart enough to bring the slain cop's father with him when he violated department policy.

The fact that Captain Murphy violated the same policy was also overlooked for obvious reasons. In fact, under the circumstances Captain Murphy publicly praised Al Parker for being so well respected by the community in Harlem, that he was the only officer in the entire police department to receive the tip that led to the arrest of one of the bank robbers. As he ended his briefing to a sea of reporters, Captain Pat Murphy Sr. made a sincere plea to the residents of New York City to help the police identify the two remaining gunmen who were still at large.

After lodging their prisoner with the military police at Ft. Hamilton, Jim Beauregard and Andy Dubrowsky received an urgent message to call Detective Frank Angelone or Detective Johnny Mc Donald at the Chief of Detectives Office. Even though the telephone conversation that Jim had with Frank Angelone wasn't all that long, it was a very informative briefing that explained why Jim and Andy needed to respond to police headquarters as soon as possible.

While Andy exceeded the posted 35 mile an hour speed limit, Jim tossed his cigarette butt out the window as he continued to brief the lead case agent from the FBI on his discussion with Detective Angelone. "Frank said we need to have a chat with a colored kid who was just brought into police headquarters for being involved in a bank robbery in Brooklyn. This kid's not talking but his uncle is. According to Frank, the kid's uncle agreed to cooperate in return for leniency for his nephew. It seems this colored kid is on the slow side and was involved with a gang of young white boys who were up to no good. The ring leader of this gang is a kid by the name of Ivan Larson. The colored kid's uncle also said that the 17 year old bank robber who was killed during the holdup gave him the address of Gooding's Garage so he could buy black market gasoline. Although it hasn't been confirmed for sure, it looks like Ivan Larson used the name Ivan Smith when he dealt with Andy Gooding."

When Jim paused for a split second Andy spoke up and said, "This sounds like the break we've been waiting for."

Jim agreed and added his own thoughts to the conversation. "I'll bet Larson was trying to get his hands on a pile of cash before he went on the lamb after killing Tommy Mulray. It's just a damn shame that an off duty cop walked into that bank while it was being robbed."

While the FBI car made its way across the Brooklyn Bridge, Jim continued filling Andy in. "It gets better. According to Frank, the off duty colored cop who was involved in the shootout at the Lincoln Savings Bank got a good look at one of the robbers before he was shot in the arm. Based on what Frank said, this Negro Patrolman is one hell of a cop. Both Frank Angelone and Johnny Mc Donald have known this colored cop for years. Apparently, they're all close friends with the family of the young cop who was killed." After pausing briefly, Jim added, "In fact, the dead cop's father is our point of contact in the Chief of Detectives Office."

Hearing that a cop was killed was bad enough but hearing that he knew the slain officer's father brought a shocked Andy Dubrowsky to say, "Captain Murphy's youngest son was the cop who was killed in that bank robbery?"

As soon as Jim responded and said, "That's correct," Andy glanced back and forth while he continued telling Jim about the Murphy family. "I've known Pat Murphy Senior ever since he was a Lieutenant of Detectives. The police department is filled with members of the Murphy family. They're good people."

After pausing for a split second, Andy continued and said, "Captain Murphy's two oldest sons are also cops. His youngest son Pat Junior was a uniformed patrolman before the war. He enlisted after Pearl Harbor and served on Guadalcanal. After Pat Murphy Jr. was wounded, he was reassigned to stateside duties as a military policeman at Ft. Hamilton. Based on what I heard, the Murphy family pulled some strings and got the young cop medically discharged from the Army, so he could return to his duties with the police department."

After hearing what Andy had to say, Jim remarked, "There is something really wrong with this world when a guy can survive combat on Guadalcanal, only to come home and get killed while trying to stop a bank robbery in Brooklyn."

While Andy continued driving, he spoke as he glanced back and forth at his partner from the Provost Marshal's Office. "Trust me when I tell you, Jim. The Murphy family and every other cop in New York are gonna turn this town upside down and inside out to locate everyone who was involved in this bank robbery."

Immediately after Jim removed another Lucky Strike cigarette from the pack that he carried in his pants pocket, he used his Zippo to light his cigarette. After pausing long enough to take another drag on his cigarette, Jim looked at Andy and said, "If Ivan Larson and Ivan Smith are the same person, someone with a badge has to stop this kid before he hurts someone else."

"I agree," responded Andy Dubrowsky who quickly added, "But before that can happen someone has to get the kid they have in custody to talk."

After taking another drag on his cigarette, Jim turned toward Andy and said, "Hopefully, we can help."

While the FBI car drove into lower Manhattan, Andy Dubrowsky spoke as he looked straight ahead. "Next stop police headquarters."

CHAPTER 17

MAD MIKE CONNELY COMES TO THE RESCUE

With the police clamoring to identify the killer of Patrolman Murphy, Ivan Larson knew that he had to leave New York as soon as possible. Once Shorty Mc Ghee parked the car inside their new hideout, Ivan told his wheel man to stay put while he went to speak to Mike.

As Ivan approached the section of the warehouse that was turned into an office and living quarters, he called out, "It's me, Mike."

While Mike Connely was waiting for Ivan to arrive, he sat at a roll top desk and sipped a glass of Irish Whiskey. As soon as Ivan heard Mike respond and say, "I'm in the back," he made his way through the warehouse to the area that was turned into fairly comfortable hideout.

Long before Ivan and Shorty arrived, Mike knew that his young protege and his sidekick were in very serious trouble. Mike learned about the robbery when he heard a news broadcast over the radio that reported that a gunman identified as Terrance Kelly was killed during the holdup. The fact that an off duty cop was shot and killed by one of the gunmen who fled the scene made a bad situation worse.

While standing next to the roll top desk, Ivan waited for Mike to shut off the radio before he spoke up and said, "I screwed up, Mike. This is worse than what happened at the Ft. Hamilton Diner. In fact, it's so bad I have to leave town right away."

Rather than get upset, old man Connely limited his remarks to saying, "I know. I heard about it over the radio. It's a real mess." Then, after pausing for a split second, Mike added, "I already heard what the police are saying about the robbery. Now I want'a hear your side of the story and give it to me straight."

Ivan was scared and Mike knew it. As soon as Mike pointed to the chair that was next to the desk, Ivan sat down and began to fill his mentor in on what happened. "After I killed Tommy Mulray I decided to rob that bank in Brooklyn that me and Terry considered hitting a few months ago. The layout was the same as before. Nothing changed. Even the two old bank guards still worked there. Just like we originally planned, we went in before the bank got crowded with customers."

After pausing for a split second to catch his breath, Ivan looked directly at Mike as he continued. "I know you told me to lay low. I just figured it wouldn't hurt to put my hands on some extra cash in case I had to go on the run. I'm sorry, Mike, but I didn't want you to have to sell any of your property just to bail me out."

Immediately after Ivan removed a cigarette from the pack in his pocket, Mike handed the young man a box of matches and said, "Go on."

As soon as Ivan used a wooden match to light his cigarette, he handed the box of matches back to Mike as he continued. "We had two sacks of cash in hand and were getting ready to leave the bank when this young cop in plainclothes came through the front door and started blasting. It all happened so fast. He killed Terry and I shot him. Once we got outside all hell broke loose and Amos got hit twice. Just as we were getting ready to leave, a colored cop grabbed me from behind, ripped off my mask and got a good look at my face. If Amos didn't shoot that cop in the arm I'd be in jail right now."

After taking a drag on his cigarette, Ivan continued and said, "Once Shorty picked us up, I used your old Tommy Gun to put the cop cars that were chasing us outta commission. As soon as we dumped the Caddy, we used the Ford to drive into the city. After we took Amos to his uncle's house, me and Shorty drove the Ford downtown and transferred the cash to the Chevy before we came here."

Initially, Mike limited his response to saying, "What a mess," Then, after pausing briefly, Mike continued and said, "Whether you didn't mean it to happen or not, killing a cop, especially a war hero who comes from a cop family, means you're gonna have to get far away from this city. You also have to expect that someone will always be looking for you. That means you'll always have to be prepared to go on the run."

After pouring Ivan a drink, Mike continued while Ivan took two back to back sips of Irish Whiskey. "Do you have a plan?"

"Yes, but I haven't worked all the details out yet," responded Ivan as he put the glass on the corner of the desk.

The old man seemed revitalized by the sense of being needed by a fellow criminal who for all general purposes was his unofficially adopted son. While speaking in a matter of fact tone of voice, the man who was once a well known gangster continued giving Ivan some sound advice. "The first thing you need to do it change the way you look. Get a hair cut and shave that crap off your face."

As Ivan gently touched the corners of his mustache, the old man continued, "You also need a new name and a new background to go with it."

"I know," said Ivan.

As soon as Mike leaned over, he opened the bottom right side drawer of the desk and removed an old cigar box. While Mike placed the box on the desk, he looked at Ivan and said, "I have something in here that can help."

After opening the box to expose its contents, Mike Connely smiled from ear to ear as he spotted his most cherished possessions. Only another U.S. Marine could truly know the pride that a Marine had for his Honorable Discharge and the Navy Cross.

As the old man held up the medal, he looked at Ivan and said, "I've never said this to anyone, Ivan, but I wish I could do it all over again. If I hadn't lost the bottom half of my leg, I would'a stayed in the Corps instead of becoming a fucking gangster."

After placing his cherished medal on the top of the desk, Mike looked at Ivan as he continued and said, "I steered you wrong, son, and for that I'm sorry."

Ivan wasn't used to old man being a softy. Besides, as far as Ivan was concerned, it was too late for Mike to regret turning his young protege into a seasoned criminal. The second that Ivan remarked, "I ain't complaining," Mike Connely grabbed Ivan by the arm and said, "You listen to me tough guy. Being a gangster is great when you have a big wad of cash in your pocket and a pair of blondes hanging on each arm, but all that changes when the cops are hunting you down with a vengeance."

After letting go of Ivan's arm, Mike changed his tune and spoke in a more composed tone of voice. "I'm gonna help you get a fresh start, but you gotta promise me you'll go straight and make something of yourself, providing the fucking cops don't gun you down first, or put you on death row for killing one of their own!"

While Ivan rubbed his sore arm where Mike Connely grabbed him, he had no choice but to admit that the old man was right. Ivan's days of being a hoodlum were over. Being a thief and selling black-market merchandise was bad enough, but killing Tommy Mulray, Tony Giordino and a police officer made Ivan Larson a first class criminal who would be pursued at all cost. It was almost as if by the time Ivan realized that his life was out of control, it was too late to do anything to stop things from getting progressively worse.

While Ivan sat in a chair next to the desk, he surrendered his pride and said, "I promise, Mike," as if he truly meant it.

"That's good," remarked the old man as he continued going though the old cigar box until he came to the paper he was looking for.

As soon as Mike Connely handed Ivan an old birth certificate, his voice was laced with a bit of sadness when he said, "This belonged to my youngest sister's only son." Immediately after Ivan read the name, "Daniel Gannon" out loud, Mike continued the conversation where he left off. "Danny died the year after he was born, which makes him your age." After pausing for a split second, Mike added, "My sister Ann and her husband blamed themselves for the baby's death. They were never the same after that. Six months later they died in a car accident. According to the police, they were both drunk at the time."

As Ivan slipped the birth certificate into his jacket pocket, he smiled a bit then said, "Using Daniel and Danny as my first name suits me fine because the name of the nun who was real nice to me in the orphanage was Sister Danielle O'Rourke."

After hearing what Ivan just said, old man Connely remarked, "All the more reason to use it then."

Now that Ivan had a new birth certificate, he would have a much easier time executing his rather unorthodox escape plan. Rather than keep his plan a secret, Ivan wasted no time in telling Mike what he and Shorty were planning to do, to get as far away from New York as possible. "Shorty and I are thinking about joining the Army to get away. We figure the cops will never look for us in the service and even if they do they'll never find us mixed in with millions of other guys."

At first Mike Connely was speechless. He figured Ivan to be more of a hot head who was destined to shoot it out with the police rather than be taken into custody. After pausing long enough to compose his thoughts, the old man couldn't help but ask, "Why not try for Mexico or South America? A guy could live pretty good on the money that I plan to give you, plus the dough that you took from that bank."

When Ivan responded he proved to Mike that he considered all of his options, as far as his escape plan was concerned. "I thought about going to Mexico. And you're right. Me and Shorty have enough cash to live like kings south of the border. My concern is that making our way to Mexico or South America won't be easy during a world war."

As Ivan continued he spoke in a confident tone of voice. "I could be wrong but I think we'd be better off in Europe. Even if we end up in the Pacific, me and

Shorty can live real good in the Philippines once the war's over. The way we see it, any country that we liberate and save from the Japs or the Germans should be real friendly to any Americans who served in the U.S. Army."

Under the circumstances, old man Connely was very impressed. He was also glad that Ivan confided in him. Having served in the Marines, Mike Connely knew the drill. He also knew how the MPs would try to find Ivan and Shorty. "Excellent plan," remarked Mike who quickly added, "I'm also glad you told me your plan because I can help."

Ivan didn't have to speak to show that he was a bit bewildered by the old man's last remark. Rather than dilly dally with a long drawn out explanation, the old man cut to the chase and said, "I can see you're puzzled by what I said. Don't worry, just trust me. I know what I'm doing. If you and Shorty want'a stick out like sore thumbs you'll go into the service and never receive any mail."

The old man's wisdom was overpowering. "You're right. I didn't think of that," said Ivan.

After pausing to light a cigar, Mike continued explaining the importance of developing a new identity that would be reinforced by receiving mail from home. "Once the cops learn more about you and I expect they will, they'll be looking for an orphan and his teenage partner in crime who was thrown out of his home by a drunken stepfather. As soon as you let me know your unit and where you're stationed, I'll send you letters and the kind of crap that soldiers are always getting in the mail from home."

When Ivan said, "What about Shorty," Mike Connely responded and said, "I'll do the same for him as well. Just remember, from now on you boys are cousins who are as close as brothers. Your mom took Shorty in when his mother died when he was born. When your mom got sick and passed away a few years later you and Shorty came to live with your Uncle Mike. You moved in with me because your fathers were away a lot because they were merchant seamen. Just before the war they took jobs on a construction contract in the Pacific. You haven't heard from them since the Japs went on the warpath. When people hear this sob story they'll feel sorry for you boys and won't ask any more questions about your past."

Despite his failing health, Mike Connely seemed revitalized by the discussion that he was having with Ivan. As the old man continued, he looked directly at Ivan and said, "Remember, if anyone asks you a personal question that you can't answer, you need to act like the topic of your family situation is too upsetting to talk about and behave like a typical pissed off American who hates the Japs and the Germans for starting this war."

While Mike closed the cigar box he continued and said, "I'll fix Shorty up with a new identity as well. I can also help you get through the induction process but I'll explain more about that in the morning. In the meantime, I suggest that you and Shorty let me hold onto the bulk of your cash, minus a grand or two that you should have on hand at all times in case you have to go on the lam. Should that happen, I want you to get to a phone and call me. I also want you and Shorty to take some cash with you when you ship out. Whether you stash some cash in a bank or under a rock, you need to be able to pay for food, transportation and a safe place to stay, until I can make arrangements to get you the rest of your money. Remember, you won't last thirty seconds if you have to go on the run without money."

As soon as Ivan thanked Mike for all of his help, the old man continued and said, "I also suggest that you and Shorty consider going to Ireland when this war is over. I have family members in the old country who will take good care of you boys. I also want you to know that after I take care of Mickey and Eddie Flynn, I'm leaving everything else that I own to you. I'll also put a little something in the pile for Shorty as well."

While Ivan remained seated by Mike's side, the old man finished explaining how he intended to help him and Shorty establish a new life after the war. "Once you get into the Army I'll have my Jew lawyer start selling my holdings. I'll give this cash, as well as the rest of the money that you took from the bank, to my cousin Mickey. Once you make your way to Ireland, I want you to visit my sister Kathy and her family. Her husband Dennis owns a pub that I helped him buy. He's a good man. Between Dennis and my sister you boys will be well cared for. If he survives the war, you can also count on Mickey's youngest brother Brian to help you boys get settled. As soon as you tell my sister and her husband who you are, and that you need to get a message to Mickey and Eddie in New York, they'll take care of the rest."

Listening to Mike made Ivan realize that it would take a lot more than joining the army to execute a successful escape. After telling Mike that he understood his instructions, Mike continued and said, "Before you ship out I'll give you and Shorty the names and addresses of my closest family members in Ireland. In addition, I'll give you instructions how you can contact Mickey and Eddie if you're unable to make your way to Ireland. In the meantime, you and Shorty need to stay put in this warehouse until I make arrangements to move you boys to another location."

"Don't worry, Mike, we'll stay put," responded Ivan.

Seeing Mike stand up was Ivan's cue to get up as well. While old man Connely leaned on his Irish Shillelagh he looked at Ivan and said, "I'll bring you and Shorty some clean clothes later on today. In the meantime, I want you boys to wipe that car down and stay put. Once you're gone, I'll clean the place up so the cops won't find any trace of your existence."

After re-lighting his cigar Mike added, "Before I leave I want'a tell Shorty what the plan is." Without saying a word, a more docile Ivan Larson followed Mike into the warehouse, where Shorty Mc Ghee was found smoking a cigarette, while he paced back and forth in between the Chevrolet getaway car and Mike's Buick.

CHAPTER 18

THE INTERROGATION OF
AMOS WASHINGTON

While Andy Dubrowsky parked the FBI car on Centre Street, Frank Angelone and Johnny Mc Donald left police headquarters in an obvious hurry and walked over to meet Jim Beauregard and the lead FBI Agent assigned to the U.S. Army Task Force.

As the two detectives approached the FBI car, Detective Angelone called out and said, "You and Andy better get up stairs, Major. They're gonna start working again on the colored kid who shot Patrolman Parker during the bank robbery that cost the life of Patrolman Murphy."

As soon as Andy Dubrowsky asked where they were headed, Johnny Mc Donald responded and said, "When Captain Murphy heard we were driving an unmarked car with a bad tranny he got us a car that runs right. Right now we're on our way over to help canvass the neighborhood around the Lincoln Savings Bank. After that we're gonna visit Andy Gooding to see what he remembers about meeting this colored kid's uncle. We also plan on having Mr. Gooding place an order for more beef from his crooked butcher. While we're doing this, Joe Coppola, Sal Jacobi, Don Lorenz and Jimmy Scott are taking turns sitting on Miller's warehouse."

While Frank Angelone unlocked the passenger side door for his partner, Johnny Mc Donald wished Jim and Andy good luck before he got into their newly assigned vehicle.

"We'll see you back at the office," responded Jim.

While the two detectives drove away, Jim Beauregard and Andy Dubrowsky walked at a quick pace to the entrance of police headquarters.

While Shorty stood guard with the Thompson Submachine Gun, Ivan went to work with a shaving razor and a pair of scissors to change the way he looked. By the time he was finished, the bathroom in the dingy warehouse was covered with hair. After Ivan finished, he traded places with Shorty and kept a sharp eye out for the police. While Shorty shaved his head, Ivan smoked a cigarette and remarked, "So far so good."

Initially, the interrogation of Amos Washington did not go well. Nothing bothered the police more than not being able to break a suspect in the interrogation room. It also frustrated the police to no end that they were dealing with a moron. Even Jim Beauregard and Andy Dubrowsky knew that this kid would be a tough nut to crack.

While a uniform patrolman stood guard over Amos Washington in the interrogation room, Captain Murphy approached Major Beauregard and Agent Dubrowsky and asked how the questioning of Amos Washington was proceeding. After shaking his head, Jim Beauregard said, "Not good, Captain. When we asked him if he knew anyone by the name if Ivan Smith or Ivan Larson, he lowered his head and kept his mouth shut."

After hearing what Jim had to say, Andy Dubrowsky remarked, "This kid definitely knows something but so far he's not talk'in."

"He's a loyal son of bitch. I'll give him that much," added Jim.

The news was disappointing. Being a Captain of Police was a tremendous responsibility but being the father of a slain patrolman was a burden that no one in law enforcement ever wanted to bear. Seeing a despondent look consume Captain Murphy's face brought Jim Beauregard to sound confident when he spoke up and said, "Don't worry, Captain, we'll break him."

Just as Captain Murphy nodded his head, Detective Johnny Tramane made the mistake of speaking loud enough to be heard when he remarked, "Maybe we should let Patrolman Parker talk to this kid. He speaks nigger."

As soon as Detective Tramane begin to snicker, his partner stepped aside the moment he spotted the grieving father of the slain patrolman charge across the squad room.

The second Captain Murphy grabbed the young detective from behind and pinned him up against the wall, the expression on Tramane's face changed to sheer terror when Pat Murphy Sr. spoke in a sneering tone of voice and said. "While you were prancing around all decked out in your new suit and sporting your gold shield, Patrolman Parker was calling me to assist him in arresting one of the suspects in your case."

After hearing the young detective begin to choke, Major Beauregard stepped closer to Captain Murphy and said, "He's not worth it, Captain." Even though the Major was right, Captain Murphy decided to squeeze Tramane's throat one more time before he shoved the smart mouth aside.

While the police captain looked around the room, several of the men present put their heads down to avoid making eye contact with Patrick Murphy Sr. as the pissed off superior officer continued. "The next man I hear make a derogatory remark about Patrolman Parker will answer to me! That man saved my life in the last war, he saved my father's life when he was a rookie cop and to top it off Patrolman Parker was wounded trying to go to the aide of my youngest son during that bank robbery in Brooklyn!" After pausing for a split second, the Captain added, "If Al Parker didn't shoot the half-wit in the interrogation room none of us would be here right now."

As Captain Murphy started to storm out of the squad room, he stopped in mid stride and turned to face Detective Lieutenant Steve Doorman and barked, "Lieutenant, I want Detective Tramane transferred to the ass end of Staten Island forthwith. Let's see how Mr. Smart Ass likes living next to fucking New Jersey."

After pausing to regain his composure, a more cordial Captain Murphy turned to the visitor from the Army Provost Marshal's Office and said, "You'll have to excuse me, Major, but I'm having an exceptionally bad day."

Jim Beauregard could not imagine the private hell that Captain Murphy was going through after losing his youngest son in the line of duty. Even though the Provost Marshal's Office had plenty of cases to work, the cop in Jim Beauregard wanted to be actively involved in the manhunt to locate and arrest Ivan Larson and his bank robbing partner in crime.

When Jim stepped closer to the father of the slain patrolman, he looked into Captain Murphy's bloodshot eyes and said, "With your permission, Captain, my men and I would like to help."

After rubbing the corners of his mouth while he considered the request, the veteran police captain nodded his head in agreement then remarked, "I'll do one better than that."

As Captain Murphy turned to Lt. Doorman, he spoke in a businesslike tone of voice and said, "Lieutenant, from now on Major Beauregard and his men will assume command of this investigation. Detectives Mc Donald and Angelone will serve as the lead investigators from this department. I also want Patrolman Parker detailed to the Provost Marshal's Office to assist in this investigation because he can identify one of the gunmen."

Without hesitation, Lt. Steve Doorman nodded his head like a good team player and said, "Yes, Sir."

After opening the door, Captain Murphy looked back at Major Beauregard and said, "If there's anything you need from the police department don't hesitate to call me at any hour of the day or night."

As soon as Jim Beauregard said, "Thank you, Captain," Pat Murphy Sr. left the Chief of Detectives office to finish planning a funeral for his youngest son.

After losing a member of the department, everyone was under pressure to produce results as soon as possible. As a result, this was no time to be parochial. With Major Beauregard and Andy Dubrowsky standing nearby, Lt. Doorman reacted harshly to being embarrassed by one of his loud mouthed detectives.

As Lieutenant Doorman faced the roomful of detectives he called out, "Tramane, in my office! The rest of you get back to work or get back in the bag!"

There wasn't a detective on the job who had to be threatened twice with being re-assigned back to uniform patrol duty, as the term "back in the bag" implied. Within seconds the crowd of detectives scattered into the wind. Those who had an excuse left the squad room immediately, while everyone else buried themselves in their work.

The last thing that Al Parker expected when he entered the Chief of Detectives Office was to have Lt. Doorman call out in a friendly voice and say, "Hey, Al, you got a minute?"

As Patrolman Parker walked over to the Lieutenant, he couldn't help but notice how the detectives in the squad room were trying to look busy, while at the same time they were all trying observe what was going on between their boss and the Negro cop from Harlem. It was almost childish to see grown men with badges and guns behave in such a fashion. With his head held high, Al walked over to where Lieutenant Doorman was standing with two strangers who looked like feds.

Steve Doorman was no fool. Besides the fact that he had tremendous respect for Captain Murphy, Lieutenant Doorman also liked Al Parker. One reason for this was because Al Parker was largely responsible for Steve Doorman being promoted from Third Grade Detective to Second. This happened when Patrolman Parker spotted a man walking to a parked car who appeared to be packing a handgun under his jacket. After confronting the man and tackling him when he tried to run, Al recovered a loaded revolver and an envelope containing a ransom note.

Knowing that the detectives downtown were investigating the kidnapping of a teenager, Al wasted no time in phoning a young detective by the name of Steve Doorman to tell him what he found on his prisoner. Even though they were not friends in the traditional sense, Al Parker liked Steve Doorman because he always treated him with respect. While the two cops worked in the same command, they developed a friendly professional relationship, with Al sharing several of his arrests with the young detective, who was stuck working in Harlem just like Al but for different reasons.

As it turned out, Al Parker arrested the driver of the getaway car that was used to kidnap the son of a very wealthy businessman from Manhattan. Rather than call in the big guns from headquarters, Detective Doorman was given the green light by his supervisor, a Detective Sergeant by the name of Pat Murphy Sr., to break the suspect and solve the case before the boys from downtown showed up to take the lions share of the credit.

To his credit, Detective Doorman worked fast and was able to convince the prisoner to cooperate and give up his two accomplices, as well as the location where the victim could be found before he was harmed. Immediately after the other kidnappers were arrested and the victim was saved, Detective Doorman was promoted to Second Grade Detective, Sergeant Pat Murphy Sr. was transferred to police headquarters and Patrolman Al Parker remained in Harlem.

After introducing Al Parker to Major Beauregard and Andy Dubrowsky, Lt. Doorman said, "Captain Murphy has assigned this case to the U.S. Army Provost Marshal's Office Task Force at 90 Church Street. Detectives Angelone and Mc Donald are representing our department. The Captain also wants you detailed to this unit to provide assistance because you're the only cop who can identify one of the robbers."

Since he was aware of the importance of this case, Steve Doorman pointed to the interrogation room as he continued and said, "It's your collar, Al. Why don't you take a crack at this kid and see if you can get him to give up his friends."

After Al Parker responded and said, "I'd be glad to, Lieutenant," Steve Doorman was happy to see that things were back on track. Even Jim Beauregard and Andy Dubrowsky thought it made sense to have a Negro policeman talk to a colored prisoner, especially since Amos Washington was the bank robber who shot Al Parker in the arm.

As far as Al was concerned, being given the chance to interrogate Amos Washington was the break of a lifetime, because it allowed him to remain active in the manhunt for the teenage bank robber who gunned down Pat Murphy Jr. While Al ignored the throbbing pain in his right arm, he turned to the Major from the Provost Marshal's Office and said, "I'm ready when you are, Major."

While Lt. Doorman walked toward his office, he glanced back and remarked, "If the three of you can't break this kid there's no hope." Then, in a tone that only a frustrated police lieutenant would use when he was under pressure to turn in some positive results, Lt. Doorman added, "Good luck."

Before they entered the interrogation room, Major Beauregard briefed Patrolman Parker about the information that was developed to date about the suspect identified as Ivan Smith aka Ivan Larson. Jim Beauregard's comments included a physical description of Ivan Smith that was provided by Andy Gooding.

After hearing what the Army Major had to say, Al Parker remarked, "That sounds like the gunman I ripped out of the getaway car before I was shot by Amos Washington."

With nothing else to discuss, Jim Beauregard opened the door to the interrogation room and said, "Like Lieutenant Doorman said, it's your collar."

Amos Washington's disposition changed for the better the moment he spotted Patrolman Parker enter the room. Amos also felt incredibly important when Agent Dubrowsky and Major Beauregard returned to speak to him again. After all, it wasn't every day that a kid like Amos was interrogated twice in the same day by one of Mr. Hoover's G Men and a high ranking U.S. Army officer.

Even though Amos was handicapped, he was smart enough to know that he took part in a bank robbery that resulted in the death of one police officer and the wounding of others. When Al Parker pointed to his wounded arm and he reminded his prisoner that he was the one who shot him, Amos bowed his head in shame. Despite the fact that Amos was a teenager, Al Parker knew that he was dealing with a child. In a way, Al felt bad for Amos but not as bad as he felt for the Murphy family or himself. Al also knew that he had a job to do, one that involved playing hardball with his prisoner in order to get him to cooperate.

After hearing Al Parker remark, "I'll bet those white boys you ran with treated you real good didn't they?" After nodding his head in agreement, Amos responded and said, "They they sha sha sure da did." While maintaining a friendly and supportive tone of voice Al continued with his line of questioning. "And I'll bet they gave you the gun that you shot me with?"

Once again Amos proved that Al was right on the money when he acted genuinely surprised and said, "How how how da da did yu yu kna know tha tha that aw aw Officer Pa Pa Parker?"

Al then reminded his prisoner that he wasn't in the mood to be lied to because his arm hurt like hell and he couldn't go home to rest until Amos cooperated.

As Al adjusted the sling on his arm, Amos bowed his head before he looked up and said, "A a I'm sa sa sorry aw aw Officer Pa Pa Parker. I I da da didn't ma ma mean ta ta hurt you."

While raising his voice an octave, Al yelled, "You didn't mean to hurt me. What kind of foolishness is that? What do you think happens when you shoot someone? Do you think this is a kid's game we're playing here, or do you think shooting me doesn't count because I'm colored like you? Then, as Al raised his voice another octave, he yelled, "Answer me, boy!"

Both Major Beauregard and Special Agent Andy Dubrowsky were very impressed by Al Parker's performance. Seeing Amos break down and cover his face with his handcuffed hands was a promising sign that the worm had turned.

As Al leaned over, he patted Amos on the back, while he spoke in a much softer tone and said, "Your Uncle Dwayne said you tried to enlist in every branch of the service but they wouldn't take you."

Al knew he struck a chord when a teary eyed Amos Washington looked up and said, "Ya ya yes Sa Sa Sir I I da did."

Call it a gut instinct or good police work but Al Parker knew exactly what he needed to do to get his prisoner to fully cooperate. After looking at Major Beauregard then back at Amos, Al spoke in a very friendly tone of voice as he continued. "Tell me, Amos. How would you like to get a commendation from Major Beauregard for helping the United States Army with an official investigation?"

Everyone in the room knew that Al Parker hit one out of the park, when Amos sat up straight in his seat and enthusiastically responded to the question. "U..u...you ma ma mean tha that aw aw Officer Pa Pa Parker, a a ra real ca ca commendation fra fra from tha tha Army?

After seeing his cue, Major Beauregard leaned on the table while he looked directly at Amos and said, "That's right, Amos. If you help us I'll personally write the judge on government stationary and tell him that you were responsible for assisting the United States Army with a major investigation."

Even though it didn't sound like he was going to receive a medal, Amos was still impressed that the Army would do such a thing for him. While seeing Amos working hard to process everything that was just said, Al Parker remarked, "This is your chance to serve our country, Amos."

As tempting as this offer was, Amos still had second thoughts about giving up Ivan and Shorty. The second Al spotted the change come over the prisoner's face he spoke up and said, "Your family will be real proud of you if you got a commendation from the army in time of war."

For someone with an obvious disability Amos sounded very articulate when he responded to Al Parker's statement and said, "I I da ga give a a anything ta ta get a a ra real ca ca commendation fra fra from the Army, I I ja just da da don't fa fa feel ra right sa sa saying anything a about ma my friends."

Again, Al Parker acted like a Dutch Uncle when he continued and said, "I know it isn't easy but you're the only one who can help us find your buddy Ivan before he hurts someone else."

With all the innocence of a child Amos Washington responded and said, "Da da don't wa wa worry aw aw Officer Pa Parker, a a a Ivan a a a ain't gonna da da do na nothing ba ba bad a a any ma ma more ba ba because I I Ivan is is ga ga gonna ja ja join the the Army an and ba ba be a a hero."

Needless to say, everyone in the room except Amos Washington was shocked by what their prisoner had to say. Before Al Parker could respond Major Beauregard leaned on the table again and looked directly at Amos and said, "How do you know that, Amos?"

Once again Amos spoke in a very sincere tone, one that was filled with pride. "Wa wa when I I Ivan fa fa figured it wa was ba ba best that that he he ta ta take ma me ta to my my a a uncle, Sha Sha Sorty ggg got ma ma mad ca ca cause tha tha they da da didn't ha ha have na na no pla pla plan ta ta ga ga get aaa out'a ttt town wa wa without ba ba being aaa rested. Tha tha that's wa wa when I I spa spoke aa up and sa sa said why why da da don't you you ja ja join the the army. The the po..lice aa ain't na na never ga ga gonna fa fa find yu you in in no ar..mee." Then, after pausing for a split second, Amos added, "I I Ivan, he he a a agreed wa wa with ma me an and sa sa said it wa was a a ga good a a idea."

While Jim Beauregard and Andy Dubrowsky looked at each other, a dumb-founded Al Parker remarked, "It was your idea?"

Amos showed how proud he was by shaking his head up and down then saying, "Ya ya yes, Sa Sir, aw aw Officer Pa Pa Parker, an and it it wa was a a ga ga good one ta too."

After considering the odds of locating two wanted teenagers in the U.S. Army, Andy Dubrowsky remarked, "I can't even begin to figure out the odds of us being able to find two fugitives who are hiding out in the U.S. Army in time of war. Even with Patrolman Parker and every other available witness in this case helping to identify Ivan Larson and his sub machine gun toting sidekick, we'll probably be fighting the next war before we get our first lead in this case. Just checking photos of new recruits from New York City alone will take time to complete."

Even though he knew that Andy was right, Jim Beauregard decided to remain as positive as possible as he opened a bottle of soda pop and handed it to Amos as he said, "Tell me, Amos. If Ivan did manage to get inducted into the Army do you have any idea what he would like to do. What I mean is, would he like to drive a tank, serve as a paratrooper or be in the infantry?"

After taking a sip of the room temperature soda pop, Amos answered the Major while Jim Beauregard lit a cigarette and Al Parker fired up a White Owl cigar. "Wa wa when Ta Ta Terry sss said he he wa wa was gonna in in enlist in in the the ca ca coast guard he he a a asked I I Ivan if he he wa wa wanted ta ta ja join aa up wa wa with him. I I Ivan sa sa said no no no offense Ta Ta Terry ba ba but he he ha hated sa sa sailors ca ca cause his da da daddy wa wa was wa one and he he ain't na na never ca ca come aa round wa wa once."

After taking another sip of his soda, Amos continued as he looked up at Major Beauregard and said, "Na na no Sa Sa Sir Ma Ma Major, I I Ivan sa sa said he he wanted ta ta be be be a pa pa pilot ca ca cause a a Army pa pa pilots ga ga get re spect."

The moment Amos finished speaking Andy Dubrowsky stepped forward and asked, "What about Shorty, Amos? Did he want to be a pilot too?"

As Amos put the soda bottle on the table in the interrogation room, he looked up at the FBI Agent and said, "Sha Sha Shorty sa sa said he'd ga ga go wa wa where I I Ivan da did."

From that point on Amos Washington was like a river of information and didn't shut up for ten minutes. Not only did they have their confession but they confirmed that the ring leader of this band of teenage crooks was Ivan Larson, an orphan who operated out of several locations, including a garage that was located somewhere on the west side of Manhattan. Unfortunately, Amos was unable to remember where this garage was located. Amos also had no idea what Shorty's real name was but he did say that Shorty would make a good soldier because he knew how to use a Tommy Gun. Amos also said that it was Ivan who shot the policeman who entered the bank during the robbery after that policeman shot Terry.

When Amos was pressed for more information he remembered that the house they used to change getaway cars was pretty close to the back of a church. Amos also said that he ate lots of steaks when he hung out with Ivan and the other members of his gang because Ivan had a friend who was a butcher. According to Amos, he helped Ivan and Terry deliver big pieces of meat the size of "a half a cow" to two restaurants late at night. When Amos was pressed to remember where the beef came from or where the deliveries were made he couldn't remember.

As slow as he was, Amos Washington was very well versed about the war. When it came to the war news, Amos knew who did what, where, when and how. Just because he could barely read did not mean he was void of any ability to retain information. For some reason there was a crevice in his damaged brain that was a magnet for any news about the combat exploits of the Allied Forces in every theater of operation.

Based on what Amos had to say, Major Beauregard and the others believed that if Ivan Larson had his way he would make every effort to get inducted into the U.S. Army Air Forces. Major Beauregard also knew that even though the U.S. Army sent plenty of troops to other theaters of operation, Ivan Larson and Shorty Mc Ghee had a pretty good chance of making their way to Europe in 1944, because of the expected buildup for the invasion of France.

An Irish funeral in 1943 is best described as a party with tears. While Al Parker sat sipping a glass of Irish whiskey, his loving wife Mary sat on his right and gently caressed his wounded arm, while his father sat on his left. When Mary asked why Al removed the sling from his wounded arm, Al responded and said, "As long as I wear a sling, they'll stick me behind a desk and force me to remain on light duty." After seeing the look of concern on his wife's face, Al remarked, "I promise I'll put it back on when no one's around."

The sight of Pat Murphy Sr. coming his way filled Al's mind with a collage of memories of days gone by. As soon as the old Irish cop warmly thanked Mary Parker and Al's father for coming to the funeral, he turned and faced his old friend. After losing his wife several years ago, Pat Murphy Sr. never expected to experience another loss of this magnitude. Even when his youngest son went off to war, he always believed that Patrick would eventually come home and have a successful career in the police department.

As soon as Pat Murphy Sr. faced his old friend, he remembered the day when he first met Al Parker on a battlefield in Europe during the last war. The moment Pat Murphy Sr. heard Al say, "I'm sorry, Captain. I should'a went with Patrick into that bank," the father of the slain patrolman said, "You listen to me, Al. I won't let you blame yourself for what happened. It's not your fault. Patrick walked into an armed robbery in progress. It happens."

While both men did their best to maintain their composure, Pat Murphy Sr. smiled a bit then said, "I know I told you this before but when Patrick was a little boy he loved it when he helped his Uncle Al work on all kinds of cars and trucks." As the Captain continued, he seemed to enjoy taking this stroll down memory lane. "I can't tell you the number of times I'd be driving around with Patrick and he would point to different vehicles on the road and say. "Look Dad, that's a 1932 Ford Vicky, that's a 1933 Pontiac Five Door Coupe, that's a 1931 Chevrolet Sedan, that's a 1929 Dodge Brother's Truck, that's a 1934 GMC truck....I helped Uncle Al fix everyone of those cars and trucks." Then, after pausing for a split second, the Captain pointed to his heart and said, "Patrick will always be with us, Al."

While tears streamed down Al's face, Captain Murphy gently patted his old friend on the side of his wounded arm as he looked at Mary Parker and said, "I'd order Al to put that sling back on his arm, Mary, but in all the years we've known each other your husband has never followed one of my orders, but I know he'll listen to you." Seeing Al crack a smile as he wiped the tears from his face, was all the Captain was after as he walked by Al and his wife to visit with other mourners.

Later that night, Al's father found his son sitting by himself while he sipped a glass of Irish whiskey. After hearing his father ask if he was alright, Al continued to look straight ahead when he remarked, "No, Pop, I'm not."

While his elderly father patted his son on his knee, Al took a sip from his glass of Irish whiskey before he turned to face his dad and said, "Don't say anything about this to Mary, Pop, but I'm gonna find the bastard who killed young Patrick if I have to enlist in the Army again to do so."

CHAPTER 19

MAD MIKE COMES TO THE RESCUE AGAIN

O n December 7, 1941 anyone already in the military, including those who were about to finish their one year commitment, was retained for what was called the duration of the war plus six months. Literally, overnight, the Selective Service Boards, otherwise known as Draft Boards, began assembling lists of American males between the ages of 18 and 64. Before the war would end some 20 million men were evaluated and classified with 11 million actually being inducted into the armed forces. One major change in the Selective Service System involved being less liberal with handing out deferments. This was the case because the armed forces needed men to support the demands of the war effort. As a result, men who were not accepted for national military service in the early years of the war were classified fit for duty in 1943 and 1944. Previous restrictions on drafting older men, men who were fathers and convicted felons were also eventually lifted. Even men who were serving prison sentences were paroled if they were otherwise fit for military service.[5]

The U.S. Navy and the Army Air Forces did everything possible to recruit and hand pick the cream of the crop to serve as sailors or aviators. Even the U.S. Marine Corps did everything possible to select the best candidates from the Selective Service process. As a result, there was often shortages of young healthy males who could be turned into ordinary trigger pullers in the less glamorous but essential foot slogging U.S. Army infantry. This also meant that many of the men who wanted to serve as a combat aviator would not have their dreams come true for the simple reason of supply and demand. The most important test a man had to pass besides his medical examination and background check was the Army General Classification Test. Draftees or inductees were given forty minutes to complete a 150 question intelligence and general knowledge test that would go a long way in deciding their fate in the military. A numerical rating was assigned to each test that put a draftee or inductee into one of five categories.[6]

Killing a New York City cop who turned out to be a war hero and the son of a police captain made the crime of bank robbery seem like a misdemeanor. With every police officer and scores of FBI Agents in New York City looking for Ivan Larson and a John Doe who went by the nickname of Shorty, the two fugitives had no choice but to get out of town as soon as possible. Fortunately for the two fugitives, Mike Connely was providing the assistance that Ivan and Shorty needed to dramatically increase their chances of facilitating their escape.

While Ivan slept on a well worn red leather couch, Shorty sat at the roll top desk in the warehouse office smoking a cigarette and sipping a hot cup of coffee. As soon as Ivan smelled the aroma of freshly brewed coffee, he rolled over on his side and pulled a Camel cigarette from the crumpled pack in his shirt pocket as he remarked, "Don't tell me you made coffee?"

Shorty responded while he held up his coffee cup. "Wake up sleeping beauty. The old man's here with some news."

Rather that take them to Jersey City on an empty stomach, Mike Connely decided to send his boys off to war with a decent meal under their belts. After making sure that he wasn't followed, Mike brought six eggs, a loaf of bread, a can of Spam, a can of coffee and a bottle of milk over to the warehouse where Ivan and Shorty were hiding out.

While Ivan placed the flame from his Ronson lighter to the tip of his Camel, he could smell the distinctive aroma of Spam being cooked with his morning breakfast. Ivan was moving slowly, and was still groggy after a lousy night of broken sleep, when he entered the area of the warehouse designated as the kitchen. As soon as Shorty handed Ivan a cup of freshly brewed coffee, Mike Connely sounded like an old Marine when he called out, "Rise and shine. I got something to tell you and it ain't good."

"What's up?" asked Ivan, as he sat in a nearby chair and smoked his cigarette while he waited for Mike to fill him in. While Ivan sipped his morning coffee and Mike Connely flipped slices of spam in a frying pan, Shorty stood nearby and nervously smoked a cigarette.

As soon as Mike removed the cigar from its perch between his yellow stained teeth, he looked at Ivan and said, "The cops know your name. If you ask me that halfwit nigger friend of yours gave you up."

As soon as Shorty Mc Ghee took a quick drag on his cigarette, he spoke up and said, "Mike's right. I heard it on the news before Mike got here with our breakfast. The radio also said that Amos was arrested by that colored cop that he shot in the arm." While a frustrated Shorty Mc Ghee forcefully stamped his cigarette out in a nearby astray, he continued and said, "That's what we get for taking that dumb prick to his uncle so he could get patched up by a colored doctor in Harlem. Worse yet, that doctor also ended up knowing the colored cop who got a look at your face before Amos shot him in the arm. Talk about a stream of bad luck."

Even though Ivan knew that Amos would crack under interrogation, he didn't have the heart to kill his friend to prevent him from being duped into cooperating with the police. As far as Ivan was concerned, killing Tommy Mulray and the off duty cop during the robbery was something that had to be done, but eliminating a loyal son of a bitch like Amos Washington was too distasteful to consider. Ivan also never figured that Amos would end up getting treated by a doctor in Harlem, who knew the same colored cop who responded to the bank heist in Brooklyn.

After rubbing his face with both hands, Ivan looked at Shorty before he turned to face Mad Mike and said, "I'll bet anything that Amos was tricked into cooperating with the police."

While Mike Connely flipped the eggs over in the skillet, he spoke with his back to Ivan and said, "It doesn't matter who gave you up or why. You should also count your blessings that you listened to me and you never took that dumb fuck Amos to this place."

Ivan didn't care whether Shorty Mc Ghee was kissing the old man's ass, or having an original thought when his partner in crime spoke up and said, "Mike's right. All they have is a name and only one cop got a look at your face and that was before you changed the way you look."

Even though Ivan wanted to ask Shorty how he was going to feel when the cops eventually figured out who he was, he limited his response to a simple, "I guess you're right. It could be worse."

While Mike continued he filled three plates with eggs, slices of grilled Spam and slices of freshly made bread. "As far as I'm concerned nothing's changed. The fact that you boys have never been arrested means you've never been fingerprinted or photographed. That means that it will be difficult to impossible for the cops to find you boys once you get through the induction process." After Mike placed the food on the table, he finished his remarks by saying, "Now you boys know why I insisted that you always work smart."

While Ivan stamped his cigarette butt out in a nearby ashtray, Mike took a sip from his coffee cup before he looked at Ivan and continued. "I also have to tell you that according to one of Mickey Flynn's contacts in the police department, Andy Gooding is cooperating with the cops and the feds. That means that even with a clean shave and a haircut, you have to be concerned that there are people like Andy Gooding, his disabled veteran for a son, your pal Amos and that colored cop from the bank robbery who can identify you." Mike then looked at Shorty and said, "You're in a little better shape as far as witness who can identify you are concerned, but not by much."

After hearing Mike's last remark, Ivan decided to avoid discussing the fact that someone did him a favor by killing John Miller. Instead, Ivan appeared genuinely surprised when he expressed his opinion about Andy Gooding cooperating with the police and the feds. "Of all the people we dealt with I figured Andy Gooding would be the last person who would ever turn stool pigeon."

"You guessed wrong," responded Mike, who quickly added, "Learn from it and move on 'cause you and Shorty are starting new lives once I take you across the river to Jersey City."

After taking another sip of coffee, Ivan remarked, "I wonder what the odds are that we can pull this off?"

Even though Mike knew that Ivan and Shorty would never have an easy life, as long as men with badges were hunting them down, he did his best to sound as positive as possible when he looked directly at Ivan and said, "I told you a long time ago, there's no such thing as a perfect plan, just one that's better than the others. If you expect to survive life on the run you have to become Danny Gannon. The same goes for Shorty and his new identity as Gus O'Malley. As long as you boys continue to think like Ivan Larson and Francis Shorty Mc Ghee, you won't last thirty seconds in the real world without making someone suspicious. On the other hand, if you become Danny Gannon and Gus O'Malley you'll be able to buy every cop and MP you meet a cup of coffee or a drink and never come under suspicion."

After pausing to take a sip of coffee, Mike continued and said, "Long before you have to worry about that colored cop from the bank, you have to worry about everyone that you and Shorty ever had contact with who is willing to help the cops find you. Fortunately, we worked in a tight knit group, so there aren't that many people who know all that much about you boys. The bad news is, the cops will use every shred of information they get to their advantage. That's why you and Shorty need to get out of town as soon as possible, which is why I'm taking you boys to Jersey City to go through the induction process."

While Mike continued, he used his knife and fork to cut up and mix his dish full of eggs and Spam. "Fortunately, for you and Shorty, a crooked politician I did business with in the old days, who owes me more favors than you boys will ever know about, is a big shot on the draft board across the river. As far as this crooked politician is concerned, my two nephews moved back to live with my sister Clara and want to get into the Army. He took care of the rest no questions asked."

After pausing long enough to remove some hand written notes from his suit pants pocket, Mike spoke as he handed a piece of folded notebook paper to each of the boys. "I wrote everything down that you need to know about your new identity on this paper. Because you boys are cousins you need to memorize each others information. Once you commit this stuff to memory, I want you to burn the paper and flush the ashes down the toilet. This is serious shit so do what I tell you to do."

As Mike continued, he pointed to the sheet of paper that Ivan held in his hand as he continued. "You'll be using my sister Clara's place to hang your hat until its time to report. Remember this address, because this is your new home. All your mail needs to be sent to this address but only after you receive mail from me. I also want you to address your mail to me care of my sister's married name, which is Clara Connely Mac Carthy. As far as anyone is concerned, you and Shorty are her nephews which makes her your Aunt Clara."

After taking a sip from his coffee cup, Mike continued and said, "If and when the day ever comes that I can't drive to Jersey City, I'll send your mail to my sister's place and she'll forward it on to you. This will insure that you'll never be connected to this side of the river. As long as I think it's safe, I'll have my sister forward your mail to where ever I hang my hat. If for some reason I have to move around, I'll call my sister from a safe place and have her read your letters to me over the phone.

I'll also stop writing if I get wind that the cops are on to me. If that happens, you boys are on your own."

Once again Mike paused to take a sip from his coffee cup before he continued. "I know I don't have to tell you boys this but I'll say it anyway. It's the little things that can ruin a perfectly good plan." While the old man paused to pour a shot of whiskey into his coffee cup, he spoke as if everything was under control when he remarked, "I can't think of anything else to say so let's eat."

After reading Amos Washington's interrogation report, the Police Commissioner was even more convinced that the U.S. Army Provost Marshal's Task Force should be in charge of the manhunt for Ivan Larson and his associate. In addition to assigning Frank Angelone and Johnny Mc Donald to this task force, the Police Commissioner also agreed to assign Patrolman Parker to this unit to assist the investigators as required. The Commissioner approved this assignment because Patrolman Parker was the only police officer who could identify the gunman who murdered Tommy Mulray and Patrolman Murphy.

While Al Parker sat in a comfortable leather chair, he rubbed his sore arm while he waited to be called into the Police Commissioner's Office. Even though Al was determined to hunt down the gunman who killed Pat Murphy Jr., as well as his accomplice, the reality of the situation prevented him from doing so without help. This was the case because in 1943 the presence of a Negro police officer in a nationwide manhunt created certain complications that needed to be addressed. For starters, Al knew that he would never be permitted to enter an all white army base to interview or inspect white troops without an appropriate white escort.

The fact that our nation was involved in a world war further contributed to the complexities of this case, especially if the two fugitives had to be pursued overseas. Like it or not, in 1943, the land of the free and the home of the brave was a segregated nation, that would never allow a Negro policeman to operate in all parts of the country, in the same fashion as a white law enforcement officer. However, African Americans could fight and die on the same battlefield with white troops, providing that they immediately returned to their own area once the smoke cleared.

As soon as the door opened, Captain Pat Murphy Sr. stepped into the outer office and said, "You can come in now, Al."

Besides Captain Murphy and the Police Commissioner, Andy Dubrowsky, Lt. Colonel Fred Richmond and Major Beauregard were sitting in the PC's office. The moment Al entered the room, Captain Murphy spoke as he closed the door, "I have good news, Al. The Commissioner has approved my request to assign you to the Provost Marshal's Task Force to help hunt down Ivan Larson and his accomplice. You'll be working for Colonel Richmond and Major Beauregard for as long as it takes to get the job done or a decision is made to do otherwise."

After hearing what Captain Murphy had to say, Al responded in a respectful fashion and said, "Yes, Sir."

Lt. Colonel Fred Richmond was a true professional and proved it when he stood up and extended his hand as he welcomed Al into his unit. "Major Beauregard and Agent Dubrowsky told me you did an excellent job breaking Amos Washington. It's good to have you with us, Al."

As the two men shook hands, Al Parker once again spoke up and said, "Thank you, Sir."

After being welcomed into the unit by Major Beauregard and Andy Dubrosky, the Police Commissioner spoke as he walked around his desk and extended his hand to shake with Patrolman Parker. "Al, the entire department wishes you the best of luck in your new assignment."

Once again, Al said, "Thank you, Sir," as he shook hands with the PC.

Next in line was a sincere looking Captain Patrick Murphy Sr. As Pat Murphy Sr. shook Al's hand, he spoke in a very sincere tone of voice and said, "May God bless you on your journey to find these bastards." Then, after a brief pause, the veteran police captain added, "Promise me you'll be careful."

"I will, Captain," responded Al.

After telling Lt. Colonel Richmond that he would meet him back at the office, Jim Beauregard thanked the Police Commissioner and Captain Murphy before he extended his left hand toward the door while he looked at Al Parker and said, "After you, Al." While Colonel Richmond and Captain Murphy remained behind to continue meeting with the Commissioner, Al Parker, Jim Beauregard and Andy Dubrowsky left to get back to work.

With his wife crying her eyes out at the kitchen table Tommy Shea sipped his morning coffee before he read the headlines again out loud, "Bank Robber Kills War Hero Cop. Police Hunt Two Gunmen. City Offers Reward."

As Mr. Shea held the newspaper in his left hand, he looked across the kitchen table at his wife of three years and screamed, "For God sake woman stop your crying. It says right here in black and white that Terry Kelly was shot and killed during the robbery and a subject identified as Ivan Larson is wanted for killing Patrolman Patrick Murphy Jr., a highly decorated combat veteran of the fighting on Guadalcanal. A third subject who drove the getaway car and was armed with a Thompson Submachine Gun also managed to escape." After putting the paper down, Mr. Shea sneered and said, "Are you still gonna to tell me that your lousy no good son Francis wasn't involved?"

While her second husband poured a shot of Irish whiskey into his coffee cup, Mrs. Shea pleaded with him not to call the police. "Please Tommy, I'm begging you. Don't call the police. You have no proof that Francis was involved in this terrible crime," remarked the former Mrs. Mc Ghee as she held her Rosary beads in her folded hands.

As the dock worker from Queens slammed his fist on the table, his wife froze in fear rather than provoke him beyond his limits. Seeing him sneer the way he did as he said, "Quiet woman," was a clear indication that her second husband would resort to violence if she continued to defend her youngest son. Hearing the abusive alcoholic remark, "That bastard's no good," proved to be too much for the old Irish woman to take.

Even though she was defying her second husband and risking bodily harm, the former Mrs. Mc Ghee braced herself on the corner of the table as she stood up and screamed, "You'll not be calling my son a bastard. I was wed in a church and had all five of my children including Francis baptized by a priest." Before Mrs. Shea could say another word, her second husband flipped the kitchen table over and smacked her across the face so hard, he left a red welt several inches wide behind as evidence of his abuse. Tommy Shea then walked past his wife and used the phone to call the special number listed in the paper.

As the former Mrs. Mc Ghee held her face, she got up off the floor and went over to the sink. While Shorty's mother put some tap water on a dish towel and placed a cold compress on her badly bruised face, she regretted the day she married the merchant seaman turned dock worker. With five mouths to feed and her struggling to make ends meet, Mrs. Mc Ghee ignored the trouble signs and accepted his hand in marriage. No sooner did she take his name, did her new husband become an abusive drunk. One by one her children left until Francis was the only one living at home.

The day her son Francis tried to defend his mother with his fists, Tommy Shea beat the short stocky kid until he was a bloody mess and threw him into the street with a handful of his belongings. He then went on to destroy and discard every photograph and personal possession of the teenager known as Francis Shorty Mc Ghee, until the former Mrs. Mc Ghee had nothing except her memories to remember her son by. While Mrs. Shea listened to her worthless second husband turn her youngest son into the police, she prayed that the useless drunk would burn in hell for his sins.

Even though the media focused a great deal of attention on the war news, members of the press continued to file reports about the efforts that were being made to hunt down the bank robbers who were responsible for the death of Patrolman Murphy and the wounding of others. The fact that law enforcement officials made it known that these criminals were also wanted for violating other laws, including black market activities, helped to keep this case in the news.

As a result of the publicity that this case was receiving, leads were coming in from concerned citizens who said they could help. While police detectives and FBI agents fanned out to interview every tipster, other investigators manned the phones and spoke to a number of callers who claimed to have seen a Negro teenager traveling with white teenagers at different times in the last few months.

The police were especially grateful when one particular anonymous caller who turned out to be Shorty Mc Ghee's stepfather, wanted assurances that he would receive a reward if he fully identified one of the bank robbers. Although Thomas Shea had no real proof that his stepson was one of the bank robbers, he did know that Francis Mc Ghee was very close friends with Terry Kelly and a punk named Ivan. He also told the police that Francis or "Shorty" as he was called, was a no good trouble maker who assaulted him before he left home to live with his gangster friends. After receiving a verbal guarantee that he would be paid for his information, Mr. Shea gave the police his home address in Queens.

Shortly after receiving this call, Andy Dubrowsky and Johnny Mc Donald along with two detectives from the 108 Precinct executed a consent search of the home where Francis Shorty Mc Ghee was born and raised. An hour later a team of forensic specialists arrived to gather physical evidence that could be used to further identify the subject known as Francis Shorty Mc Ghee.

Unfortunately, the former Mrs. Mc Ghee was a cleaning lady by trade who did such a good job of cleaning her apartment that the police were unable to find fingerprints that belonged to her son. Worse yet was the fact that in a drunken rage, Tommy Shea ripped up and disposed of every photograph of his stepson when young Francis was thrown out of the house. While this search was being conducted, U.S. Customs Agent Joe Coppola, New York DA's Office Investigator Sal Jacobi, Army Investigator Lt. Don Lorenz and Lt. Jimmy Scott from Naval Intelligence continued to take turns watching John Miller's warehouse.

In order to follow up on the other information provided by Andy Gooding, Jim Beauregard and Frank Angelone met with officials at the Brooklyn Army Depot about the employee who was reportedly involved in the theft of cigarettes. Andy Dubrowsky and Kevin Kalb also met with Andy Gooding when their informant continued to try and call John Miller. During this same meeting Andy Gooding was also directed to arrange another delivery of black market gasoline from his contacts at the Staten Island Fuel Depot. This left Patrolman Al Parker to man the phones in the office.

Escaping from the police dragnet in New York City with the help of Mike Connely proved to be a "piece of cake" as the saying goes. Even with the reduction of traffic in the city due to gasoline rationing, Mike Connely waited for the right time to cross the river into New Jersey. Because he was a professional crook, the retired gangster knew that the cops were looking for two young punks, not an old man and his two nephews.

After telling the boys exactly how to behave, Mike Connely slowed down as he approached the police checkpoint. As soon as Mike brought the Buick Roadmaster to a stop, he rolled the driver's side window all the way down and sounded like a good citizen when he called out, "Good afternoon, officer."

When the state trooper leaned closer to the open window and asked, "Where you headed, Sir?" Mike spoke in a very friendly and respectful fashion as he answered the officer and said, "Bringing my nephews back home to my sister's house in Jersey. Our family's getting together before the boys report for training."

As soon as the state trooper looked at Ivan and said, "Army, Navy, Marines or Coast Guard," Ivan sounded like a real nice kid who was proud to serve his country when he responded in a very respectful tone of voice and said, "Army, Sir."

With no reason to be suspicious and a line of traffic beginning to form behind the shinny black Buick, the forty six year old state trooper nodded his head as if he approved then said, "Good luck, boys," as he stood up and waved Mike Connley through the roadblock.

After hearing Shorty remark, "I don't believe we made it," Ivan turned around in his seat and cracked a confident smile and said, "I told you Mike would get us through." While beaming with pride, old man Connely ignored his doctor's orders and fired up a brand new cigar as he drove Ivan and Shorty to his sister's house in Jersey City.

As soon as Mike finished changing lanes, the old man glanced back at Shorty and said, "You can rest easy, Mister O'Malley. The New York cops will never find you boys in Jersey." Between making it across the New York state line into New Jersey and hearing the old man call him by his new name, Shorty felt better about the chances of actually pulling off their escape plan.

CHAPTER 20

THE GOOD GUYS TEAM UP TO GO AFTER THE BAD GUYS

When a delivery truck arrived at John Miller's Manhattan warehouse at 1950 hours (7:50 PM), U.S. Customs Agent Joe Coppola turned to Investigator Sal Jacobi and said, "This has to be it, Sal." A moment later the driver of the delivery truck was observed knocking on the office door to the warehouse. When no one answered, the truck driver walked over to the large wooden garage door and knocked on that door as well.

While the driver stood in front of Miller's warehouse and used a box of matches to light a cigarette, Joe Coppola turned to Sal Jacobi and said, "Whether Miller shows up or not, we're not letting this guy get away."

After checking his watch Joe continued and said, "We have a decision to make, Sal. Either we wait for our relief to arrive to call this in, or one of us has to stay put, while one of us gets to a phone."

"We better not wait. I'll make the call." remarked Sal Jacobi as he opened the passenger side door to the unmarked car that was parked near the corner on the street that was due west of Miller's warehouse.

When Lt. Don Lorenz and Lt. Jimmy Scott arrived to relieve Joe Coppola and Sal Jacobi, they parked their Ford sedan behind Joe's Chevrolet. After exiting his vehicle, the U.S. Customs Agent met the two military officers on the sidewalk by the front of their car. "It looks like we're all working late tonight," said Joe who quickly added, "The delivery truck showed up a few minutes ago but Miller is no where in sight."

When Jimmy Scott asked if Sal went to call it in, Joe responded and said, "You just missed him. Unfortunately, the closest phone that's available this time of night is in the bar that's one block south of here."

While Don Lorenz looked at the delivery truck that was parked in front of Miller's warehouse, the Army Investigator remarked, "So far Andy Gooding's been right on the money."

"He sure has," responded Jimmy Scott who quickly added, "The question is, where's John Miller? You'd think he'd be here by now to take delivery of a truck load'a meat."

"We'll know a lot more about what's going on once we look inside that truck and we search Miller's warehouse," responded the U.S. Customs Agent who served in Army CID during World War I and had over twenty years of experience conducting criminal investigations.

When Don Lorenz passed around a roll of Lifesavers, Joe Coppola thanked the Army Investigator for the candy then said, "Why don't you guys sit on our friend while I pick up Sal."

"You're a good partner, Joe," remarked Jimmy Scott who continued as he returned the roll of candy to the Army Investigator. "If I went to call the office Don would make me walk back."

Ever since the Army football team played Navy there has always been a healthy competitive spirit between the two branches of the service. As a result, it wasn't uncommon for soldiers and sailors to tease each other as often as possible. The same type of rivalry existed between men who served in the Ground Forces and men who serves in aviation units.

In an effort to keep this competitive spirit alive, U.S. Army Investigator Lieutenant Don Lorenz opened the passenger door of their car, as he joked around with his partner from Naval Intelligence. "I know you Navy guys like to ride everywhere but God gave you those legs for a reason."

The fact that Al Parker knew Frank Angelone and Johnny Mc Donald, made it considerably more comfortable for him to sit around the conference room table and enjoy a cup of Army coffee with Major Beauregard and other members of the Army Task Force. So far, everyone seemed very friendly and welcomed Al into the unit.

Shortly after Jim Beauregard finished briefing Al about the need to motivate John Miller to cooperate and further identify Ivan Larson, Andy Dubrowsky and

Kevin Kalb returned to the office with the signed search warrant. After handing the warrant to Jim Beauregard, Andy poured himself and Kevin Kalb a cup of coffee while he filled everyone in. "Even though we still don't know where Miller hangs his hat at night and Andy Gooding was unable to get in touch with the crooked butcher to place another order, Judge Tyler signed a search warrant for Miller's warehouse and any vehicles that are suspected of transporting black market meat to the subject of this investigation."

As soon as Andy finished relaying the good news, Johnny Mc Donald remarked, "If we catch Miller in possession of one counterfeit meat stamp and a truck load of beef in violation of OPA regulations our crooked butcher and all of his pals will be in big trouble with the G."

After hearing what his partner had to say, Frank Angelone rubbed his hands together and said, "I can't wait to get my hands on this crooked butcher. I'll bet this prick has a thumb that weighs a pound."

While everyone in the conference room had a good laugh, Investigator Sal Jacobi called in from the field to bring everyone up to date on their surveillance of Miller's warehouse. After answering the office phone and listening to the investigator from the DA's Office file his report, Jim Beauregard said, "Good work, Sal. We're on our way with the search warrant. If the driver goes to leave the area, you know what to do."

As soon as the Major placed the phone back on the receiver, he looked around the table and said, "According to Sal, a delivery truck just arrived at Miller's warehouse. The driver tried banging on the door but so far no one answered."

After picking his pack of cigarettes off the table, the Major looked at Al Parker as he stood up and said, "Al, you can ride with me."

When Jim Beauregard and the others arrived at Miller's warehouse, Joe Coppola, Sal Jacobi, Lt. Lorenz and Lt. Scott had the truck driver up against the side of the building. "We moved in when we thought he was taking off, Major," remarked Joe Coppola.

As soon as the truck driver turned around and said, "You got no right to stop me. I'm lost that's all," Don Lorenz remarked, "Easy, pal," as he pushed Mr. Moore back up against the wall.

After handing the truck driver's wallet to Jim Beauregard, Joe Coppola turned the prisoner around and said, "Mr. Moore, this is Major James Beauregard from the U.S. Army Provost Marshal's Office. The other men working this case are with the New York City Police Department, the FBI, Naval Intelligence, U.S. Marshals, the DA's Office, the Post Office, the State Police and the OPA. I'm telling you this to let you know that you're in a great deal of trouble with the City of New York, the State of New York and the federal government."

As soon as the truck driver lowered his head and remarked, "I told you before. I got nothing to say," Andy Dubrowsky asked if they searched the truck yet.

"Not yet, Andy," responded Sal Jacobi.

While Joe Coppola continued, he pointed to the truck driver's wallet that Jim Beauregard held in his left hand. "We found Miller's phone number and the address of this warehouse in his wallet. There's also a name and phone number in his wallet from out west that the FBI and the OPA will be interested in checking out."

When a uniformed police sergeant and his driver arrived on scene, Jim asked Kevin Kalb to take charge of the prisoner. As soon as Jim walked over to the police car, he identified himself and explained that he and his men were executing a federal search warrant on a black market meat distribution operation.

After telling Eddie Evans from the Enforcement Division of the OPA to standby to drive the truck into the warehouse, Jim turned to Frank Angelone and said, "OK, Ange, get your tools and do the honors."

As soon as Frank removed a sledge hammer and a New York City Fire Department Ax from the trunk of his unmarked car, he asked Al Parker to hold onto the ax, while he put the sledge hammer to good use. A few seconds later the door that led to the warehouse office was wide open.

Once the members of the Provost Marshal's Office Task Force entered the warehouse, Johnny Mc Donald and Al Parker went to work searching the office, while Andy Dubrowsky and Frank Angelone led the rest of the search party deeper into the building. While the raiding party went about their duties, Jim Beauregard stood off to the side while Richy Olsen opened the large wooden garage door and motioned Eddie Evans to drive the delivery truck inside the warehouse.

When Richy Olsen opened the back door of the truck, Jim Beauregard and the other members of the Army Task Force, along with the two uniformed city cops, marveled at the sight of a delivery vehicle that was filled with sides of black market beef. As soon as Richy Olsen remarked, "I wonder how much meat is in this truck," Jim Beauregard responded and said, "More than any of us could eat in a week."

With meat rationing being what it was, Steve Klein couldn't resist and joked, "I don't know about you, Major, but I'd like to try."

"Me too," added Eddie Evans.

When Jim Beauregard heard Detective Angelone call out, "Hey, Major, we need you back here," the Atlanta cop turned Army Investigator could tell by Frank's tone of voice that something important was just discovered by the men conducting a thorough search of the warehouse. Immediately after Jim asked Steve Klein and Eddie Evans to inventory the contents of the delivery truck, Richy Olsen remarked, "I'll get my camera, Major." While Richy left the warehouse to get his camera equipment from the trunk of his car, Jim started walking toward the back of the warehouse.

As soon as Jim approached the men who were huddled around the open door to a room in the corner of the warehouse, Detective Angelone pointed inside and said, "If this is our crooked butcher we'll never squeeze him for information about Ivan Larson." While Jim stood in the open doorway to the meat locker, he pointed to the saw dust covered floor around the body and said, "Look at the drag marks in the sawdust. I'll bet whoever did this hit this guy on the back of the head out here in the warehouse, then dragged the body inside the meat locker to finish him off. After all, whoever shot this guy knew that no one would hear a small caliber handgun being fired inside such a well built meat locker."

While his colleagues agreed with his assessment of the crime scene, Jim knew the first order of business was to confirm the identity of the murder victim. Because it would take time to have one of his men pick up Andy Gooding and transport him into Manhattan, Jim turned to the only U.S. Customs Agent assigned to the Army Task Force, and said, "Do me a favor, Joe, and have Kevin bring that truck driver in here to see if he can identify the deceased? Also, ask the sergeant to notify the squad that we have a homicide on our hands and tell Richy we need him back here as soon as he's finished taking pictures of the truck."

As soon as Joe Coppola responded and said, "I'm on the way, Major," he headed toward the front of the warehouse, while Jim knelt in the open doorway and examined the body from a different perspective.

Jim Beauregard proved that he was also an experienced police detective who handled his fair share of homicides, when he looked at the victim's badly damaged skull and said, "I'll bet he was dead before he hit the floor. The bullet wasn't necessary but it was delivered anyway to make sure this guy never spoke again."

Immediately after Jimmy Scott nudged Don Lorenz on the side of his arm, the Naval Intelligence Officer pointed to the side of beef that was hanging inside the meat locker and said, "This guy had some operation."

As soon as Joe Coppola and Kevin Kalb delivered the truck driver to the open doorway of the meat locker, Agent Coppola pointed to the deceased and said, "We thought you might like to reconsider your position on cooperating, because this is now a homicide investigation, which is almost as serious as selling black market beef in time of war."

In order to motivate the truck driver to cooperate, Agent Coppola nudged the prisoner closer to the open doorway and said, "Why don't you take a closer look and tell us if you know who that is."

The second the truck driver looked at the dead body he changed his disposition and said, "That's John Miller."

When Andy Dubrowsky asked Mr. Moore if he was sure, the truck driver responded and said, "Yes, Sir, I'm sure."

As soon as the truck driver answered Andy's question, Jim Beauregard asked Mr. Moore about the last time he had contact with John Miller. While the forty five year old truck driver looked away from the body, he sounded as if he was telling the truth when he responded to the Major's question. "I was here two weeks ago with a truck load of beef but it wasn't enough to fill Miller's orders. When Miller said he needed another shipment, arrangements were made for me to make another run to New York. I was supposed to be here yesterday but I got a late start due to some bad weather out west."

After making eye contact with Kevin Kalb, Andy Dubrowsky cocked his head to the side to signal his fellow investigators to take their new informant out for some fresh air. While Kevin Kalb patted Mr. Moore on his back, the Deputy U.S. Marshal spoke in a friendly tone of voice when he said, "Why don't we step outside and get some fresh air."

Mr. Moore didn't need any coaxing to leave the crime scene and sounded relieved when he was offered the chance to be escorted out of the warehouse. "Thanks, I could use some air."

When Richy Olsen arrived with his Kodak camera in hand, everyone stepped aside as Jim pointed to the open door to the meat locker and said, "You know what to do, Richy. The body on the floor is John Miller."

"I guess we won't be interviewing this guy anytime soon," remarked the New York State Police Investigator as he began taking photographs of the crime scene.

"You're right about that," responded Jim before he turned to Frank Angelone, Joe Coppola and Sal Jacobi and said, "While you guys wait for the detectives from the local precinct, Andy and I are gonna see how the search of Miller's office is going."

As soon as Jim and Andy walked into the office, they could tell that the two city cops were conducting a thorough search when they saw the furnishings in the room, including a large wooden desk and a leather couch, were dragged away from the walls.

The moment Jim asked if they found anything interesting, Johnny looked up and said, "You're just in time, Jimmy. Al spotted a lose piece of molding when we pulled Miller's desk away from the wall."

While Jim Beauregard, Andy Dubrowsky and Johnny Mc Donald stood nearby, Al Parker was on one knee and used his bone handle pocket knife to pry the loose piece of molding away from the wall. As soon as Al removed the molding, he remarked, "Be careful, Johnny, this might be loaded," as he removed a black leather holster containing a German Luger Pistol from the secret compartment and passed it to Detective Mc Donald.

As soon as Johnny passed the holstered pistol to Jim Beauregard, Andy Dubrowsky remarked, "This case just got a lot more interesting."

While Jim unloaded the German Luger and placed it on the desk, Al Parker continued to remove items from the secret compartment. After passing a neatly folded Nazi flag to Johnny, Al removed a metal box containing photographs of John Miller with other men in German American Bund uniforms, as well as photos of Miller with another butcher at two different butcher shops. Al also found a list of former members of the German American Bund, a road map from out west that contained circled locations, a stack of German Marks, $2500 dollars in U.S. currency and Miller's Passport.

Once Al made sure that he removed everything from the secret compartment, he looked up and said, "That's it, Major," before he stood up and brushed the dust off his pants.

While Jim and Andy examined the items that Al removed from Miller's secret hiding place, Johnny Mc Donald remarked, "The rest of the office is clean as a whistle."

Under the circumstances, Jim was exceptionally grateful that the search of Miller's warehouse office produced some interesting results. He proved how grateful he was when he wasted no time in congratulating Al and Johnny. "If you and Johnny didn't pull this furniture away from the walls and if you didn't spot that lose board, we'd be leaving this place empty handed. In fact, you saved the day by finding this stuff."

After pausing to quickly light a cigarette, Jim continued while he slipped his Zippo lighter into his suit jacket pocket. "The reason you saved the day is because we found Miller's dead body on the floor of a meat locker on the other side of the warehouse. Whoever killed him struck him from behind and put a small caliber bullet in the side of his head."

While looking around the thoroughly searched office, Andy remarked, "I'll bet whoever killed Miller cleaned this office out as well."

"If that's true, we should consider ourselves lucky that whoever killed Miller didn't find everything," responded Jim as he examined the pile of evidence more closely. Even though Johnny agreed with Jim and Andy, he was more concerned about where to go from here. He proved that when he spoke up and said, "I hate to be the bearer of bad news, but now that Miller is dead we'll have to find his partner if we ever hope to get a list of their former customers."

"Maybe we'll find some more leads once we find out where Miller lived?" remarked Al.

"That's always a possibility," responded Jim Beauregard who went on to say.

"But in the meantime, we'll have to use these photographs, this list of names and this map to help us locate Miller's former business associate," responded Jim who continued as he examined Miller's Passport. "Who knows, maybe this passport will lead us in the right direction."

While Andy picked up the Nazi flag, he expressed another concern that he and his colleagues had to consider. "Even if we find Miller's former partner, he might not be willing to cooperate. After all, if he was a Bund member like Miller he might not be all that interested in helping the police, the FBI or the United States Army."

"We'll cross that bridge when we come to it," responded Jim, as he put his cigarette out in the ashtray on Miller's desk before he looked at Al Parker and said, "Do me a favor, Al, and get the rest of the men in here so they can see what you found. Also, tell Richy to bring plenty of film and flashbulbs for his camera. He's got a lotta pictures to take."

As soon as Al said, "You got it, Major," and he left the room, Jim looked at Johnny Mc Donald and said, "You better give Captain Murphy a call. He might want'a meet us to go over this evidence. As soon as you're finished, I call Colonel Richmond and give him the good news."

When Johnny Mc Donald picked up the telephone in Miller's office, Jim paused to light another Lucky Strike before he remarked, "This is one hell of a case."

As soon as Ivan Larson heard that John Miller was found murdered, he was convinced that Mike Connely killed the crooked meat supplier to keep him from talking to the police. Even though Miller could also implicate Mike Connely in black market operations, Ivan knew that Mike silenced the crooked butcher to protect him and for no other reason. Now that Miller was eliminated, Ivan could breath a sigh of relief and continue with his plan to join the Army with Shorty to evade arrest.

When Rudy Mueller read the morning newspaper he knew the police would be interested in speaking to him about his former partner. In fact, for all he knew, the police might consider him a suspect.

The fact that Mueller was also involved in a black market meat operation motivated him to remain unavailable to the police. Mueller also had good reason to be concerned, because the cattle rancher who supplied him with black market beef was related to the rancher who supplied Miller. In addition, Mueller had a legitimate reason to be concerned about the driver who was arrested at Miller's warehouse in possession of a truck load of black market beef.

Even though Mueller used his own drivers to transport black market beef from out west, he had to consider the possibility that the driver who was arrested at Miller's warehouse might know enough to bring both operations down. After discussing his concerns with his father-in-law, Mueller decided to travel out west to visit his supplier before the Wagner brothers picked up another shipment. Before doing so, Mueller sent his wife to live with her father, while he moved out of their apartment to make it harder for the police to find him.

While Jim Beauregard, Andy Dubrowsky and Joe Coppola met with Captain Pat Murphy Sr. and Lt. Colonel Richmond in the CID Office, the decision was made to have Andy handle the search for Miller's former partner. Joe Coppola was also asked to check Passport and U.S. Customs records to get as much background information as possible on John Johann Miller's travels from Germany to the U.S. Joe also said that he would check to see if any other Bund members on Miller's list had a passport and traveled internationally.

Pat Murphy Sr. proved to be a valuable asset to the CID Task Force, when he arranged for the two detectives who were assigned to handle the Miller homicide to assist Andy in this endeavor. Doing so enabled the limited number of men assigned to the Army Task force to focus on the search for Ivan Larson and Francis Shorty Mc Ghee.

Shortly after the article about John Miller's homicide was featured in the morning newspaper and on several radio shows, one of his neighbors responded to the request for assistance in locating Miller's place of residence. After calling the Army Task Force to report the address, Jim Beauregard, Andy Dubrowsky, Frank Angelone and the two detectives assigned to the Miller homicide conducted a thorough search of the victim's apartment.

With the exception of a cash box that contained $1200 dollars and a drawer full of matchbooks, train schedules, business cards, postcards and motel receipts from various locations out west, Miller's apartment was exceptionally clean. Once this evidence was listed in a report, a copy was forwarded to FBI and OPA offices out west so a collateral investigation could be initiated.

When Sister Danielle O'Rourke saw the front page of the Daily Mirror she held her rosary beads close to her chest and began to pray. As difficult as it was for her to listen to the radio reports about Ivan's involvement in the killing of Patrolman Murphy, Sister O'Rourke found it twice as hard to look at the police sketch of Ivan's face that was featured on the front page of the newspaper. After reading the front page news story, Sister O'Rourke hesitated before she picked up the phone and called the task force that was spearheading the search for Ivan Larson and his accomplice.

Thanks to Mike Connely and his contact across the river, Danny Gannon and Gus O'Malley received an expedited official notification to report to the draft board in Jersey City, New Jersey to go through the screening process for military service. In order to motivate his contact to help assist his nephews, Mike played the sympathy card with tremendous skill. While talking to the crooked politician that Mike compromised many years before, he described how Danny Gannon and Gus O'Malley had a personal motive for wanting to get into the fight, ever since their fathers were caught behind enemy lines in the Pacific and have not been heard from since December 7, 1941.

After receiving the expedited induction notices, Mike Connely drove Ivan and Shorty to the local draft board, so they could go through the screening process for national military service. The presence of a long line of eligible males waiting to enter the induction center, was enough to make Ivan and his sidekick swallow hard as Mike Connely parked his car across the street.

After hearing Shorty remark, "I'm glad you took us to Jersey, Mike. There's no way I would've been able to pull this off if I had to go through this ordeal on the New York side of the river."

While old man Connely cracked a smile, Ivan offered Shorty a cigarette and said, "This is it. Are you ready?"

As Ivan leaned over the front seat and offered his buddy a light, Shorty spotted a white haired patrolman on guard duty by the entrance to the induction center and said, "I feel a little naked going in without my Roscoe."

While reacting as if he was Shorty's straight man, Ivan looked at his partner in crime and remarked, "Don't worry, where we're going they give you all the guns and ammunition you can carry." Once again Mike Connely grinned after hearing Ivan's comeback.

After turning to make eye contact with Shorty, Mike faced Ivan and said, "Good luck, boys. I'll be out here waiting for you."

As soon as Ivan opened the front passenger door and said "Thanks Mike," Shorty started singing, "Off we go into the wild blue yonder," as he stepped out of the back of the car.

Once Ivan and Shorty walked across the street, they got in line behind an eighteen year old Polish American kid who lost his older brother during the Battle of Midway. As they milled around with the others, Ivan and Shorty exchanged small talk about the war and tried to act as gung ho as everyone else. When the Jersey City Police Department Patrolman twirled his baton as he walked by oblivious to their presence, Ivan turned to Shorty and whispered, "So far so good."

While Shorty was still a bit nervous, Ivan acted as if he was on his way to a new adventure. Fortunately for both young men, they were in very good physical condition and considered healthy enough to go on to the next battery of tests. When it came time to fill out the eight page questionnaire, Shorty was very careful to stick to the simple story that Ivan and Mike Connely helped him to remember.

Shorty Mc Ghee had a new lease on life by taking on the identity of an adopted Irish kid who was killed in a car accident, while traveling overseas with his adopted parents; a happily married couple that Mike Connely knew from his early days as a high rolling gangster. It also helped that the orphanage where the real Gus O'Malley was initially raised, was destroyed by fire and had the records lost before the war began. This made it possible for Shorty to fill in the blanks as best as possible with little or no concern that his answers could be questioned. The fact that the real Gus O'Malley was killed in an accident in a town in Europe, that was now under German occupation, also meant that the feds would never be able to challenge his story.

The scariest part of the entire process was when Ivan and Shorty were finger-printed and photographed. If there was ever a time when Shorty appreciated Ivan's attention to detail and insisting that they wear gloves and a mask before robbing the Lincoln Savings Bank this was it. With clean records and no fingerprints left behind at any crime scenes, both fugitives felt as if they were home free when the draft board official smiled and informed them that they were being classified as 1A.

The only unfortunate turn of events occurred when Ivan and Shorty received their intelligence test scores. To complicate matters, the two fugitives had to deal with the fact that the U.S. Army Air Forces had more men on its rolls than it actually needed. This meant, that even if they achieved higher scores, Ivan and Shorty would not have been selected to become aviators because the priority shifted in favor of filling vacancies in the Army Ground Forces.

After seeing another dejected face come his way, the classification clerk smiled in a friendly fashion and said, "I'm sorry it didn't work out for you, pal, but the Army needs foot soldiers not fliers."

As disappointed as he was, Ivan appreciated the kind words. While Ivan nodded his head and did his best to appear content with being selected to serve, as the clerk continued. "Even if you scored higher you'd still be going into the Ground Forces. Besides, you said you wanted to get into the fight. If you went to flight school you'd be stuck in the states for another year. Hell, with the way this war is going you might never see combat as a pilot."

While the classification clerk continued to process Ivan's induction papers, Ivan acted as polite as possible and asked, "Excuse me, Sir, but is there any chance that I can go though training with my cousin?" As the clerk stopped writing and looked up, Ivan was very respectful as he continued. "I hate to be a pest, Sir, but my cousin and I grew up together were hoping we could serve together."

The moment Ivan heard the clerk remark, "First of all, I ain't no Sir. I'm an enlisted man just like you're about to become but I do appreciate the fact that you're smart enough to show some respect for someone with stripes on their uniform." After pausing for a second to look around, the corporal faced Ivan and said, "Where's your cousin?"

While Ivan Larson aka Danny Gannon pointed to the other side of the room, he responded and said, "The last I saw him he was on the other side of this room. His name is Gus O'Malley."

As the classification specialist stood up, he put Danny Gannon's file under his arm and said, "Wait here and I'll see what I can do." before he walked to the other side of the room.

While Ivan waited in the crowded room, he did his best to act content with the way things worked out. When the classification clerk returned to his desk, he looked as if he was proud of himself for doing a fellow G.I. a favor. As the corporal stood behind his cluttered desk, he leaned forward and said, "I spoke to your cousin's classification clerk. We're sending you to the same reception center. From there it's anyone's guess where you might end up. If you get real lucky they might keep you together. It's the best I could do."

Even a hard case like Ivan Larson could not stop from smiling at the sound of such good news. As Ivan said, "Thanks," the classification clerk sat down and made a final notation on the file before he stamped it approved and said, "Welcome to the United States Army. Good luck." After smiling wide and feeling relieved that he had made it through the induction process, Ivan walked over to find Shorty.

While Ivan waited patiently in the hallway, Shorty finished up with his classification clerk and left the interview room with the weight of the world off his shoulders. As Ivan approached his partner in crime, he quickly glanced around to see if anyone was close enough to hear what he had to say before he remarked, "Did we get lucky or what?" Shorty couldn't believe it. If it wasn't for Ivan they would be heading to different reception centers.

As Shorty stepped closer to Ivan, he tried to contain himself as he whispered, "They were just about to send my ass to a different reception center when your classification clerk showed up and had a private talk with my guy. The next thing I know I'm going to the same reception center as you. What the hell did you do, pay the guy off?"

After cracking a smile, Ivan teased his partner in crime and remarked, "I can have it changed if you like?"

Shorty was so impressed by what Ivan managed to do he ignored the ribbing and said, "I don't know how you did it but you kept us together."

As happy as he was that things worked out the way they did, Ivan knew that they were taking it one step at a time from now on. In an effort to prepare Shorty for the day when the U.S. Army would piss on their parade, Ivan remarked, "I don't know how long our lucks gonna hold out so enjoy it while it lasts."

After Ivan ushered Shorty over to the wall to let a pair of doctors pass by, an Army staff sergeant walked over and said, "If you men are finished you can leave."

As soon as Ivan responded and said, "Yes, Sir," the Staff Sergeant stopped, turned around and remarked, "First off, I'm a Sergeant not a Sir, but you boys will be learning all about that once you get to basic training. Second, don't forget to report to the reception center on time or we'll come looking for you!"

While both fugitives responded appropriately and said, "Yes, Sergeant," Ivan grabbed Shorty by the arm and ushered his buddy out of the induction center.

The moment Ivan and Shorty stepped outside, they were surprised to be met by the smiling face of the Jersey City Police Patrolman who was standing guard by the entrance to the building. As soon as the old Irish cop said, "Well, boys, how did it go?" Shorty was at a loss for words, while Ivan acted like a true patriot when he responded in a very enthusiastic tone of voice. "They took us, Officer. We're in the Army now."

After seeing the patrolman smile as if he was truly proud of them, Shorty Mc Ghee found the courage to force a smile. Shorty was twice as surprised when the uniformed patrolman patted Ivan on the back and said, "Good luck, boys," when the two fugitives walked by the old beat cop.

After being accepted for military service, the two fugitives were anxious to report for duty. The faster they got trained and shipped overseas the faster they would feel safe, even if it meant they had to fight a war in order to make their way to freedom. Unfortunately, instead of being ordered to immediately report for duty, the Army was giving all new recruits a brief furlough before they had to report for processing at a reception center.

While every other newly inducted soldier was grateful for the furlough, Ivan and Shorty were pissed off to no end that they were not immediately transported to a training base. As the two fugitives walked to Mike Connely's car, Shorty became unglued and remarked, "Do you believe this shit? They tell us how hard up the Army is for replacements at the front and they're not even in a hurry to train us and send us overseas."

Ivan couldn't believe it either. As they crossed the street with a group of new recruits, Ivan turned to Shorty and said, "Welcome to the United States Army, Pal."

Since Shorty did not share Ivan's dream of becoming a pilot, he had no problem with the Army's decision to fill the ranks of the infantry and armored units with as many able body men as possible. Still, Shorty was curious to find out exactly how disappointed Ivan was that he would not be getting his wings. As the two fugitives walked to Mike Connely's car down the crowded street, Shorty tried to sound as sympathetic as possible when he said, "Are you sore about not being selected to serve in the Air Corps?"

Seeing Ivan shrug his shoulders meant that he wasn't terribly broken up about the recent turn of events, especially when he remarked, "It would've been nice, but the corporal who kept us together told me the war might be over before I finished all the training required to serve in the Army Air Forces."

After hearing Shorty remark, "All that matters is that we get overseas as soon as possible," Ivan proved that he agreed when he offered Shorty a cigarette and said, "That's the plan."

CHAPTER 21

FOLLOWING LEADS

After taking the call from Sister Danielle O'Rourke, Jim Beauregard grabbed his hat and left his corner office in search of a partner to take along on what might prove to be the second most important lead of the day. As the Major put on his fedora and pulled the brim down, he looked around the squad room and saw that everyone including Detective Angelone was busy handling calls.

As a career law enforcement officer, Jim Beauregard knew that it was proper protocol to team up with a member of the New York City Police Department, when it came time to follow up on a lead that could further identify the fugitive who was wanted for killing Patrolman Pat Murphy Jr. Rather than break with tradition and because no one else from the city police was available, the Major turned to Al Parker as he hung up the phone on his desk and said, "Hey, Al, feel like taking a ride?"

As surprised as he was to be asked to partner up with the Major, Al stood up and said, "Yes Sir," as he grabbed his suit jacket from the back of his chair.

Even though he was a beat cop and not a detective or a federal agent, Patrolman Parker's exploits as a veteran street cop, who was a war hero to boot, were well known by the members of the Provost Marshal's Office Task Force. His first contribution to the fugitive manhunt investigation actually occurred during the bank robbery, when Al got a good look at the face of one of the robbers before he was shot. Al made his second contribution to this case when he arrested Amos Washington. Al also played a significant role in getting Amos to cooperate. His contribution to this case continued when Al assisted an FBI artist sketch create an accurate likeness of Ivan Larson. In addition, Al Parker was credited with finding valuable evidence during the search of John Miller's warehouse.

Even though Al only briefly saw Ivan Larson's face, he was 110% confident that the sketch that was created with his input was an accurate rendering of the killer of Pat Murphy Jr. Al proved to be right on the money, when the same artist sat down with Andy Gooding and produced an almost identical sketch of the same subject. When Andy Gooding, Curly Gooding and Amos Washington were shown the two composite sketches, everyone agreed that the drawing that was made with the help of Patrolman Parker was the most accurate rendering of Ivan Larson.

While Jim Beauregard held the office door open for Al, the Major filled him in on the reason for their trip into the field as he said, "A Catholic nun just called and said she raised Ivan Larson at St. Mary's Orphanage."

As Al stepped into the hallway, he spoke in a confident tone of voice and said, "I know St. Mary's, Major. I brought a few runway kids back there over the years."

Even though Jim Beauregard knew how to get to midtown Manhattan, the Major proved that he was happy to have a local cop along when he remarked, "I'm glad one of us knows where we're going."

Despite his long standing career as a police officer, Jim Beauregard was not used to working with a Negro cop. Even though the City of Atlanta employed a number of Negro police officers, Jim had very little to do with these officers, unless there was a serious crime committed in the Negro section of town that required the attention of a white detective. The simple truth was that Jim Beauregard was like other white folks who secretly struggled with the issue of segregation and racism but figured that he was powerless to change the way things were.

Once America went to war in December of 1941, Jim believed that the conditions were right for the issue of race relations in America to change for the better. Jim felt this way because during the early years of his childhood, he learned a great deal about the contribution that was made throughout history by American Negro soldiers. Jim received this education by listening to the colored men who worked on his grandfather's farm. Much to Jim's surprise these men were war heroes, or the sons of soldiers who served the United States in uniform. After hearing about the exploits of Negro combat veterans, young James Beauregard wondered why these men were not permitted to come and go as they pleased, even though they were technically free.

Jim learned even more about the contribution of colored soldiers, when he became friends with a one legged Negro man who lost his leg in combat during the Spanish American War. When he wasn't in school, Jim often rode on the wagon to and from the fields with the Negro known as Mister Smith. During their time together, Jim listened intensely about how several of Mister Smith's relatives served during the Civil War and how his father was a Buffalo Soldier with the 9th Cavalry.

Like most white kids his age, Jim had no idea that so many brave colored men had sacrificed so much for the United States of America. It was twice as puzzling for Jim to understand why such brave men were treated so poorly, after they served so honorably. Even though Jim was grateful that he was made privy to such seemingly classified information, it troubled him to no end that the contribution made by American Negro soldiers did not receive the public recognition that it deserved. Worse yet, even when the accomplishments of certain Negro military units were publicized, their heroic exploits were never enough to change the way colored folks were treated.

From the moment they met, Mister Smith had a captive audience and began introducing young Jim to other Negro field hands who had relatives who served the flag or were veterans themselves. Naturally, when Jim mentioned his new found knowledge at the dinner table, his grandfather was surprised to hear him speak so eloquently about the contributions made by Negro soldiers. Instead of leaving well enough alone, Jim put his grandfather on the spot when in his innocence he asked why colored folks were still treated differently if they did so many brave things in battle. Seeing her husband at a loss for words, brought Jim's grandmother to say that such matters should not be discussed at the dinner table.

While Jim continued to eat his supper, he made eye contact with his grandfather. From that point on, it was a case of you know that I know, that you know that I know what's going on. On that day, Jim Beauregard took a giant step toward manhood. Unfortunately, the very next day Mister Smith and the other Negro workers bowed their heads in a respectful fashion and kept going without speaking a word to their young white friend. It was blatantly obvious that they were afraid to speak to young Jim and he knew why.

As soon as Jim Beauregard returned his attention to the mission at hand and he offered Al Parker a cigarette, Al held up his left hand as he removed a cigar from his shirt pocket and remarked, "No thanks, Major, I've been a cigar smoker ever since I became a cop."

After lighting his cigarette, Jim Beauregard exhaled and said, "I just want you to know that Colonel Richmond and I appreciate everything you're doing to help with this investigation."

Even though Al Parker did not need a pat on the back to be motivated work on this case, he appreciated the Major's kind words. While Al said, "Thanks Major," he removed a box of wooden matches from his suit jacket pocket in preparation of lighting his cigar.

After lowering the passenger side window all the way, Al used two matches to light a cigar. While Al puffed on a fresh White Owl, he sat back and wondered who would speak next. Al's question was answered when the CID car stopped at a traffic light and the Major seemed lost in thought as he stared at the road ahead. When the light changed and the sound of a honking truck horn failed to motivate the Major to snap out of his trance, Al leaned to the left and said, "The light's green, Sir."

After recovering quickly, Major Beauregard engaged the clutch and quickly worked his way through the gears as he made up for lost time. Rather than let the opportunity to say something go by the wayside, Al spoke up and said, "Excuse me for asking, Major, but is something bothering you, Sir?

So many things were troubling Jim Beauregard he didn't know where to begin. Even though he did not know Patrolman Parker for very long, Jim felt very comfortable being in Al's presence. In a way, Jim felt the way he did when he was a young boy sitting on a farm wagon, while Mister Smith talked about feats of bravery in far off lands. While Jim remembered the smiling face of the first and only colored friend he ever had, he felt as if a switch was flipped in his heart that made him feel good about trying to cultivate a personal relationship with another brave Negro.

As soon as Jim Beauregard pulled the CID car over to the curb in front of the orphanage, he turned sideways and looked directly at Al Parker as he spoke in a very down to earth tone of voice. "I didn't join the Army to be a cop. I wanted to fight like my two sons are doing but the Army had other plans for me because of my police background. I figured once I got in I'd be able to transfer out of the MPs but all I did was end up being made even more of an Army cop when they transferred me to the Provost Marshal's Office. When I pushed the issue again with Colonel Richmond, I was told that my request for transfer would be reconsidered by headquarters after this case was solved, or we could prove that the subjects of our investigation were confirmed to be dead or captured by the enemy."

After seeing that he had Al Parker's undivided attention, the Major continued and said, "I'm sorry about Patrolman Murphy. I also feel bad for his family and for you, Al. I also know what you did during that bank robbery. We all do. You're a very brave man and it's an honor to serve with you, so please don't take this the wrong way when I tell you that I would rather be leading men in battle, than being the lead investigator on this case, even though this manhunt is the most important manhunt that the U.S. Army is currently working on."

The moment that Al Parker started to respond Jim Beauregard held up his right hand and cut him off as he said, "Excuse me, Al, but let me get the rest of this off my chest before we go any further."

While Al gently puffed on his cigar, he could tell by the expression on the Major's face and the tone of his voice that he was being very sincere. After picking up where he left off, the Major continued and said. "Even though I wish I was serving in a different capacity, I have every intention of working this case to the best of my ability. I feel this way because I've been a cop long enough to know that cop killers need to be captured or killed if they resist being taken into custody. I also know that it's not gonna be easy for us to work this manhunt, especially if we have to travel together. I say this because you know as well as I do what it's like out there, so let's not fool ourselves into thinking that if we have to take this show on the road, that it will be easy because we can't do this without you." After pausing long enough to take one last drag on his cigarette, the Major continued while he crushed the remains of his Lucky Strike out in the car's ashtray. "I also miss my wife and I'm worried about my two sons so I hope you understand if I get a little grouchy at times."

With the exception of the Murphy clan and a few cops like Frank Angelone and Johnny Mc Donald, Al Parker had never had such a down to earth conversation with a white man, especially a gentleman from the south. While it's true that Al usually got along well with most white folks, he also knew his place and only crossed the line when invited to do so. The fact that Al was a decorated police officer and World War I Army veteran gave him a special standing of sorts among a number of Caucasian officers. Unfortunately, once out in the civilian world, Al Parker was just another colored man who had to tow the line and never forget his place. After a lifetime of living under these bizarre and unfair social rules of engagement, Al Parker was torn between having hope that things would change for the better in his lifetime and having no hope that race relations would improve as a result of World War II.

Al Parker also had a lot to say but chose to keep his response brief. While speaking in the same tone of voice that he used when he had heart to heart talks with Pat Murphy Jr., Al felt very comfortable about responding to the Major's remarks. "I don't know what to say, Major. Part of me is glad to be alive and the other part of me would like to trade places with my young friend. Regardless, I'm grateful for the chance to help find the men who robbed that bank and killed Patrick."

While pausing long enough to tap the ash from his cigar in the car's ashtray, Al picked up where he left off and said, "I know it won't be easy, but we do have something in common besides the fact that we're both cops."

The second the Major said, "What's that, Al?" Al smiled then said, "I also have two sons in the service. My oldest son is training to become a fighter pilot and my youngest is a military policeman assigned to the 761st Tank Battalion. I worry about them all the time."

After hearing what Al had to say, Jim nodded his head in agreement before he opened the driver's side door and said, "Come on, Al, we've got a witness to interview and two fugitives to catch."

CHAPTER 22

SISTER DANIELLE O'ROURKE

Sister Danielle O'Rourke was visibly upset when she entered the main office in the orphanage and the Mother Superior introduced her to Major James Beauregard and Patrolman Al Parker. As she stood facing the Army investigator and the city policeman, Sister O'Rourke felt even more despondent because she knew that a million novenas would never undue the trouble that Ivan was in.

Once the introductions were made, the Mother Superior instructed Sister O'Rourke to have a seat and tell the two investigators from the Army Task Force everything she could about Ivan Larson. While Major Beauregard sat silently next to Al Parker, he could not help but notice how dreary the orphanage was. It was also quite evident that while Sister O'Rourke appeared to be a very kind and attractive young woman, the older Mother Superior was stern faced and strictly business.

The moment Major Beauregard finished filling the sisters in on the background of the case, the Mother Superior wasted no time in saying, "I always knew that boy was no good." After hearing the Mother Superior's last comment, Al Parker and Jim Beauregard were convinced that the nun in charge of St. Mary's Orphanage actually enjoyed the fact that Ivan Larson was wanted for murder, bank robbery and black-market operations.

After seeing the expression on Sister O'Rourke's face, Al could see that the younger nun was dying a slow and painful death when she heard the Mother Superior make such a harsh statement about Ivan Larson. Even though Larson was a murderer and a thief, he had a past that included a very troubled childhood. Just being an orphan was enough to start someone off on the wrong foot. Seeing her reaction brought Al Parker to politely interrupt the Mother Superior and say, "Excuse me, Mother Superior, but I'd like to ask Sister O'Rourke a question."

As much as the Mother Superior did not like being interrupted, she sat silently while Al turned to his right and said, "Excuse me, Sister, but I couldn't help but notice the look on your face when the Mother Superior expressed her feelings about Ivan Larson."

Sister O'Rourke knew that she did not have a very good poker face. With nothing to hide except her affections for Ivan, Sister O'Rourke faced Patrolman Parker while she spoke with an Irish brogue that was laced with a bit of sarcasm and said, "Far be it from me to contradict the opinions of the Mother Superior."

Sisters from a religious order were a lot like policemen. Patrolmen did not make a habit out of challenging the opinions of their superior officers, any more than sisters in the Catholic Church contradicted the feelings of a Mother Superior. Still, this was a very serious matter and no investigator worth his salt could let a question like this go unanswered.

After seeing Sister O'Rourke's reluctance to say more, Major Beauregard spoke up and said, "What Patrolman Parker is trying to say, Sister, is that you might be able to help us catch Ivan before he hurts someone else, if you tell us everything that you know about him."

While picking up where he left off Al added, "We know how you must feel, Sister, but like Major Beauregard said, Ivan is wanted for killing two men including a policeman, as well as other serious crimes. His involvement in black-market activities alone in time of war are serious enough for us to find him."

While looking at her stern faced Mother Superior, Sister O'Rourke cleared her throat and spoke up, "May God forgive me for what I am about to say."

Hearing her subordinate's invocation brought the crusty old Mother Superior to stand behind her desk and speak in a stern voice. "I suggest you chose your words, Sister."

After years of faithful service, Sister O'Rourke was tired of living in such bondage. Her vocation to God was marred by the presence of viscous women who cloaked themselves in black and took their frustrations out on the innocent children who were placed in their care and custody.

As she vaulted out of her uncomfortable straight back chair, Sister O'Rourke faced the Mother Superior with clenched fists, as she leaned on her oversized wooden desk and began her remarks with a salvo of well spoken words. "How dare you say Ivan was no good. Who beat the spirit out of that boy as well as the other children! Go ahead, Mother Superior tell these policemen who whipped Ivan until you became physically unable to continue. Why don't you tell these policemen that no matter how hard you beat that boy he never cried. May Almighty God have mercy on your soul for what you and the other nuns have done to the children in this orphanage!"

After calming down Sister O'Rourke turned to a shocked Major Beauregard and an equally surprised Patrolman Parker and said, "Major Beauregard, Patrolman Parker, I'm ashamed of myself for not speaking up sooner. The boys in this orphanage have been terribly mistreated in the past and are still being mistreated as we speak. Although I make no excuses for his despicable behavior, I am not surprised that Ivan turned to violence." Then, without so much as pausing to catch her breath, Sister O'Rourke continued as she looked at Major Beauregard and Patrolman Parker. "I would appreciate it if you gentlemen would give me a few minutes to pack my things before you take me to your office, so I can tell you everything you need to know about Ivan that may help you find him."

As both men stood up, the Mother Superior slowly sat in her chair and remained silent. Just as Sister O'Rourke went to leave, she paused long enough to face the Mother Superior to inform her that she would be asking Father Cavanagh for another assignment.

Once Mike Connely made sure the boys were safely in his sister's house, he promised to return after he took care of some business back in New York. Even though Mike told Ivan and Shorty not to get too cocky and walk around Jersey City, the boys eagerly volunteered to go to the store for Clara Connely Mac Carthy when the chain smoking old Irish widow ran out of smokes. Since the old lady wasn't much of a cook, Ivan also thought it might be a good idea if they grabbed something to eat at a local diner.

After spotting two Jersey City policemen walking a beat across the street, Ivan reached out and gently patted his partner on the back as he spoke in a low but firm tone of voice and said, "Easy does it. Those are Jersey City cops not New York bulls."

"I don't care. A cop is a cop," remarked Shorty.

Even though Ivan wasn't surprised at his friend's behavior, he was getting tired of always having to reassure Shorty that everything was going to be OK. After hearing Shorty remark, "The cops have radios you know. Hell, even the Jersey papers have an article about us," Ivan responded and said, "I thought you got over being a nervous wreck?"

Despite his command performance at the induction center, Shorty was still very concerned about running into a cop who would see through their cover story. Even though he was a little more confident than he was before, Shorty knew that he had good reasons to be worried. Shorty also knew that he had a much better chance of escaping if he stayed close to Ivan. He felt this way because Ivan had a gift of gab and a pair of balls to match. While Shorty considered his own inadequacies, he lowered his head deep into his shoulders as he apologized for being such a burden. "I'm sorry for being a pain in the ass. You'd better off without me."

Even though Shorty could be a royal pain in the ass at times, Ivan knew that his partner in crime made it possible for him to escape being captured during the bank robbery in Brooklyn. Despite the fact that Ivan knew that he could make it on his own, he preferred to execute his escape plan in the company of the last surviving member of his gang. Ivan also knew that if they separated, Shorty could help the police identify him if he was ever picked up. As a result, it made sense for Ivan to stay as close to Shorty as possible. Besides, Ivan didn't have the heart to kill his partner in crime. Even though Shorty had moments when he wasn't as confident about their escape plan, he was just as loyal to Ivan as Amos Washington and Terry Kelly.

In an effort to bolster Shorty's confidence Ivan patted his buddy on the back again and said, "Don't be so hard on yourself. If it wasn't for you I'd either be in jail or in my grave by now."

While Shorty buttoned his sports jacket, he showed Ivan that he appreciated his kind words by smiling then saying, "Thanks."

After looking around to make sure that no one was paying any attention to their conversation, Ivan continued as he faced his friend and said, "Mike's right. There ain't a cop in New York who's gonna find us in Jersey. Besides, we're not fugitives. We're two new recruits on our way to a reception center to be processed into the Army. Once that happens we're on our way to basic training."

Ivan's pep talk seemed to have a positive impact on his partner's moral when Shorty removed a pack of smokes from his jacket pocket as he remarked, "I guess you're right."

While Shorty used his Zippo to light an unfiltered cigarette, Ivan pointed to the nearby diner and asked his buddy if he was still hungry. After exhaling a lung full of tobacco smoke, Francis Shorty Mc Ghee aka Gus O'Malley nodded his head and said, "Of course I'm hungry. Mike's sister is a nice old lady but she can't cook for shit."

As Ivan led the way into the diner, he cracked a smile then remarked, "I agree but don't tell that to Mike."

By the time they finished their lunch, Ivan and Shorty read every newspaper article on the police manhunt to locate the fugitives who held up the Lincoln Savings Bank in Brooklyn and killed Patrolman Patrick Murphy Jr. The story they read in the newspaper also made Ivan and his gang of teenage criminals sound like traitors for participating in black market activities that resulted in the death of Tommy Mulray. Although it took some doing, Ivan managed to calm Shorty down when he pointed to the front page article about the hunt for New York City's most famous fugitives and remarked, "This story will be old news in a matter of days."

Shorty ignored everything that Ivan said, the moment he spotted a Jersey City Patrolman enter the diner and have a friendly exchange with a cab driver who handed the uniformed cop a folded copy of the local newspaper. While Ivan looked out the window then back at Shorty and said, "If you don't relax you're gonna make that cop curious why you're so nervous."

To reinforce his point, Ivan pointed to the composite sketch of the subject known as Ivan Larson, that was featured on the front page of the local newspaper and said, "Take a look, Mister O'Malley. Do you know anyone who looks like this anymore?" Shorty had to admit that a haircut and a clean shave was enough to change the way that Ivan looked. Shorty also knew that they managed to get through the induction process and get past a local uniformed cop, so whatever they were doing to blend in must be working.

Even though the newspapers reported that Patrolman Al Parker got a good look at the robber who killed Patrolman Murphy, Ivan was confident that outside of running into this Negro cop, he could pass muster as Danny Gannon. The moment of truth came, when the patrolman took a seat at the counter and he began to read the newspaper, while a waitress delivered a hot cup of coffee to the local beat cop. Fortunately, all those years of hanging out in movie theaters made Ivan a consummate actor. While Ivan looked across the table at Shorty, he continued to speak just above a whisper as he said, "Watch this."

With the look of complete shock on his face, Shorty leaned across the table and whispered, "What are you gonna do?"

Even though Ivan wanted to give Shorty a ration of shit for being so petrified, he held his tongue as he spoke just above a whisper and said, "Would it make you feel any better if I walked right up to that cop and asked for directions to the nearest police station?"

Ivan knew that he had Shorty's undivided attention, when he saw his cohort's eyes bulge out of his head as Shorty responded in an equally low tone of voice. "Are you crazy?"

As Ivan stood and said, "Pay attention, 'cause I'm only gonna do this once," Shorty sat back in complete shock as if a floor show was about to begin.

Without making himself look obvious, Ivan stood by the table and patted his pockets as if he was looking for something. While playing his part to the hilt, Ivan turned to Shorty and said, "I'll be right back, Gus, I gotta get some matches."

As soon as Ivan made his way to the front of the diner, he glanced back and saw that Shorty was paying very close attention to everything he did, when Ivan leaned over the counter and politely asked the waitress for a book of matches. Shorty could not believe his eyes as he watched Ivan Larson, a fugitive from justice, stand one stool away from an officer of the law and act as calm as a cucumber.

Immediately after he took a sip of hot coffee, the Jersey City Patrolman looked to his right and made eye contact with the clean cut looking young man who was standing less than two feet away. The moment their eyes met, Ivan smiled politely and said, "Hello, Officer." After receiving the right kind of nod from the Jersey City cop, Ivan knew he was home free.

Regardless of the jurisdiction that they represented, police officers were the same all over. It was well known that most cops made it a habit never to smile at strangers. If anything, cops were famous for giving a civilian who addressed them in a respectful fashion, a quick nod of the head that was supposed to take the place of a verbal acknowledgment.

The moment Ivan thanked the waitress for the book of matches, the waitress smiled and said, "You're welcome, soldier." As Ivan used the fresh book of matches to light a cigarette, his brain raced for clues to figure out how the waitress knew that he was in the Army, even though he was not wearing a uniform. Then it hit him. He and Shorty were carrying their induction papers with them as proof of their new identity. As Ivan exhaled, he remembered that he put his induction papers on the table in the booth when the waitress served their pancakes and coffee.

In his most convincing tone of voice Ivan responded by saying, "No more diner food for us, Ma-am. In another week and my buddy and I will be eating Army chow." Even Shorty couldn't believe it when the stone faced cop relaxed the expression on his face and swiveled around on the stool to face Ivan as he said, "We're all proud of you, son. Give 'em hell."

As cocky as he was, even Ivan became weak in the knees when he faced the veteran patrolman longer than he originally expected. While Ivan did his best to appear as appreciative as possible, he nodded in a respectful fashion and said, "Thank you, officer," before he turned and started to walk to the back of the diner where Shorty was seated. All the way back to his table, Ivan had very mixed emotions about what just transpired. In a strange sort of way what started out to be a test of sorts turned out to be a very unusual experience.

As soon as Ivan sat down across from Shorty, he looked as if he had seen a ghost. There was no other way to put it. Having people be so nice to him for doing something as simple as joining the Army was a new experience for Ivan Larson. This also wasn't the first time since the robbery, that Ivan wished that he wasn't wanted by the police.

While Shorty chain smoked another cigarette, he looked across the table and said, "Don't ever do that again." Meanwhile, at the other end of the diner, the patrolman finished his coffee and slapped a dime on the counter as he stood up. As the cop turned to leave, he tossed the two fugitives a casual salute, before he left the diner to go back out on patrol. Seeing Ivan smile and return the salute encouraged a stunned Francis Shorty Mc Ghee to watch this unusual event unfold in complete amazement.

While the two fugitives sat in a booth by the bay window, they watched the patrolman walk across the street. "Somebody pinch me. I think I'm dreaming," remarked Shorty as Ivan picked up the check and led the way to the front of the diner. After paying the check and handing their waitress a nice tip, Ivan and Shorty behaved like polite soldiers as they said goodbye and left the diner.

While her two customers headed down the street, the waitress turned to the short order cook who was taking a break and said, "Such nice boys. I hope they survive this horrible war."

After Mike's sister Clara went to sleep, Ivan and Shorty stayed up for most of the night smoking cigarettes and listening to the radio. By 3 AM the two fugitives were fast asleep in strange beds as they spent another night on the lam. Unlike his sidekick, Ivan was wide awake at 7 AM and ready to start the new day. When Ivan saw that Shorty was still out like a light, he tried to be as quiet as possible as left the room on the second floor and headed for the bathroom to hit the head and wash up.

Even though the accommodations left a lot to be desired, Ivan was grateful that he was still a free man. After using the old lady's bathroom to wash up and change, Ivan admired himself in the cracked mirror. Being clean shaven with shorter hair made him look and feel like a new man. His new look also gave him the confidence that he needed to appear in public with little or no fear that anyone would identify him as the bank robbing cop killer from Brooklyn.

After interviewing Sister O'Rourke, Major Beauregard and Al Parker were able to put together an accurate profile of Ivan Larson. Their evaluation was aided by the information that was obtained when the Major and Al Parker conducted another interview of Amos Washington and Andy Gooding. Based on the second debriefing of Amos Washington, as well as the recovery of the revolver that he used to shoot Patrolman Parker, Detectives Angelone and Mc Donald were able to close the open case on the armed robbery of Mr. Sweeney's Liquor Store.

Once Major Beauregard finished talking privately to Colonel Richmond, he took a sip of coffee from his favorite mug before he began the early morning briefing. As Jim looked at the faces of the investigators under his command, he knew he had everyone's undivided attention when he spoke up and said, "I thought I'd begin this briefing by letting you know that Captain Murphy and Eddie Evans are going through Andy Gooding's records, to see if they can come up with additional leads that can help us further identify Ivan Larson and anyone else that he's associated with. In addition, our resident FBI Agent will be spearheading the search for John Johann Miller's former business partner, another German American Bund member identified as Rudolf Mueller. Thanks to our distinguished representative from U.S. Customs we know a little bit more about these guys." After pausing to take another sip from his coffee mug, Jim added, "The FBI and the OPA are also looking into the evidence that we found in Miller's warehouse and in his apartment. Unfortunately, it could take time to check out all of the information that we sent out west."

Jim continued the briefing while he put his mug down on the corner of an empty desk in the squad room. "Another matter of importance involves the search for the two fugitives." After quickly lighting a cigarette, Jim went on to say, "Due to the fact that Mrs. Shea is a cleaning lady by profession, the team that searched her home in Queens was unable to find any fingerprints of her son."

When New York District Attorney's Office Investigator Sal Jacobi spoke up from the back of the squad room and said, "I wish Mrs. Shea would come over to my place and help out. My wife can't clean a house for shit," the room exploded in laughter. Even Jim Beauregard grinned from ear to ear, as the seasoned investigator tossed him a sloppy salute and called out, "Sorry, Major, I couldn't resist."

As Major Beauregard put up his right hand to signal the roomful of lawmen to calm down, the veteran Atlanta Police Captain turned U.S. Army Investigator continued with his briefing. "You also know that thanks to Mr. Shea's temper we also don't have any photos of Francis Mc Ghee aka Shorty."

After pausing briefly to take another drag on his cigarette, the Major continued and said, "Yesterday, Al Parker and I interviewed Sister Danielle O'Rourke at St. Mary's orphanage. The Sister was kind enough to come back here and spend some time filling us in about Ivan Larson. Needless to say we learned a lot." Rather than give this part of the briefing himself, Major Beauregard caught Al Parker by complete surprise when he turned to him and said "Al, would you fill everyone in on what we learned from Sister O'Rourke."

Despite his status as an experienced street cop, Al Parker felt like a school boy who was not all that comfortable about being called on to speak in front of the class, even though he knew the answer to the question. After taking a sip of coffee that he wished was laced with a shot of Irish whiskey, Al stood up and tried his best to conceal the fact that he was a bit uneasy about addressing a roomful of fellow officers, especially white cops.

As nervous as he was, Al realized that he had waited his entire life for a moment like this. Because of the significance of this moment, Al knew that he had no choice but to suck it up and give a good account of himself or risk looking like a fool. After looking to the front of the room and acknowledging Colonel Richmond, Al turned to Major Beauregard, nodded his head and said, "Thank you, Major," before he turned and made his impromptu presentation to the other members of the task force.

As Al spoke he remembered to sound confident and professional. "According to Sister O'Rourke, Ivan Larson was an orphan child of a Times Square prostitute. All we know about his father is that he was a sailor. In fact, two of the most important things we learned about Ivan Larson is that he hates sailors and he once told the sister that he'd like to become a pilot like Charles Lindbergh. This was confirmed by our interviews with Amos Washington."

After clearing his throat, Al continued. "We also know that Larson was repeatedly beaten in the orphanage by several of the older nuns and that Sister O'Rourke was the closest thing to a decent mother that he ever had. According to the good Sister, Ivan Larson liked to fight, which she believes was a disposition that was brought about by the mistreatment that he received at such a young age. Sister O'Rourke also admitted helping Larson steal money from the orphanage when he ran away at age 15. She thought it was the least she could do considering how the boy was mistreated."

So far Al could see that he made a good impression when he noticed some of the investigators in the room nodding their heads while others took copious notes. While speaking in a matter of fact tone of voice, Al added, "Sister O'Rourke has agreed to help us find Larson before he hurts anyone else. Right now we have her looking at photographs of recently inducted U.S. Army personnel."

When Al finished his remarks he felt a lot better about standing in front of a room to speak. As Al turned to the front of the room, the Major said, "Thanks, Al," before he continued his end of the briefing. "As Johnny Mc Donald likes to say, the good news is we have no choice but to proceed under the assumption that Ivan Larson and Shorty Mc Ghee have been inducted into the United States Army. The bad news is there are over 200 training camps and forts throughout the United States where Ivan Larson and Shorty Mc Ghee could be hiding. The Army Air Forces alone has 17 training bases spread out all over the United States. Our fugitives could also end up attending one of the contract training schools that are run by civilian flight instructors."

After pausing to tap the ash from his cigarette into a nearby ashtray, the Major added, "There's also no guarantee that Ivan Larson and Shorty Mc Ghee were accepted into the Army Air Corps."

"Is that good news or bad news, Major," asked Frank Angelone.

After holding up his right hand to signal that he had something to say, Colonel Richmond stepped forward and addressed the group by saying, "The Army needs riflemen now not pilots. Even if Larson and Mc Ghee scored high enough to get selected by the Army Air Forces, they would more likely be assigned to serve in the Army Ground Forces. If that's the case we could have a much harder time finding them."

""Either way we have our work cut out for us,"remarked Johnny Mc Donald.

"That's correct," responded Colonel Richmond as he sat back down on the corner of a nearby empty desk and continued puffing on his pipe.

While Jim Beauregard stepped back in front of the squad room he continued the briefing by saying. "In addition to the reception centers that process thousands of men a day into the Army, every base we need to inspect holds an average of 30,000 to 75,000 men. If we concentrate on Army Air Forces training bases we might never find them if they ended up in a Ground Forces unit.

After quickly stamping his cigarette butt out in an ashtray, Jim Beauregard continued and said, "In fact, knowing the Army the way I do, our two fugitives could training to become infantrymen, paratroopers, artillerymen, tank drivers, medics, engineers, cooks and as crazy as it sounds MPs. If they managed to get inducted by now, they're in basic training, which narrows down the number of bases that we need to inspect. If we don't find Larson and Mc Ghee by the time they complete basic training, it will be a lot harder to find them unless we develop some worthwhile leads. This means that for the next fifteen weeks or so we'll focus our attention on reception centers, as well as on the camps and forts where newly inducted soldiers receive basic training."

Jim had one last thing to say before he dismissed the men. "A schedule will be posted assigning one member of this task force to answer the phones, respond to emergencies and handle other duties as required on a daily basis. If you have the duty and you can't be in the office for any reason, you need to let me or Colonel Richmond know so we can get a replacement to cover your absence. Also be advised that new field assignments will be posted within the hour." Then, after pausing for a split second, Jim did his best to sound like a coach giving his team a pep talk when he said, "Gentlemen, let's get these sons a bitches before they kill someone else."

CHAPTER 23

A WELL DESERVED THREE DAY PASS

In addition to being a family man, Lt. Colonel Fred Richmond knew from his long career in the FBI that men needed a break after working weeks straight with little or no time off. Immediately after he finished work on Friday night, Jim Beauregard made his way to Pennsylvania Station to catch a late night train home to Atlanta.

During the train ride home, Jim ended up sitting in the dining car next to two Army officers from an armored unit who were expressing their opinions about colored troops. After hearing an Army Captain with a southern accent remark, "I'm telling you those niggers don't belong in a tank battalion any more than they belong flying fighter planes," Jim felt bad for the old Negro porter who walked by just as this racist remark was made.

With little or no concern for being overheard, the shorter of the two Army officers made the situation worse when he spoke up and said, "If our CO caught you making a pass at his daughter, you'd be on your way to the 761st where you'd be knee deep in fried chicken and colored boys for the duration."

While both men laughed and acted more like fraternity brothers than Army Officers, Jim Beauregard put his newspaper down as he leaned across the isle and said, "Excuse me, gentlemen, but did I hear you mention the 761st Tank Battalion?"

The moment the two captains realized that their remarks were overheard by the Major sitting at the next table, they responded in unison by saying, "Yes, Sir."

"I see," said Major Beauregard, who paused briefly before he said, "It's just that I have a friend of mine who has a son in that unit."

When the taller of the two Captains assumed that the Major was referring to a white officer who had the misfortune of being assigned to a colored tank unit, he remarked, "I feel sorry for your friend's son, Major. No white officer should have to spend the war baby sitting a bunch of cotton picking loafers."

As Jim Beauregard stood up he removed a money clip from his pant's pocket and left a handsome tip on the table, before he turned to the two loud mouthed armored unit officers and said, "Actually, my friend's son is an enlisted man not an officer."

While the two Captains appeared to be somewhat dumbfounded, the shorter of the two Captains remarked, "Are you sure you're talking about the 761st Tank Battalion, Sir? That's a colored outfit."

Once again Major Beauregard sounded like he knew what he was talking about when he said, "The same 761st that was stationed at Camp Clayborne in Louisiana before it was transferred to Camp Hood, Texas."

"But I don't understand, Sir. The only white men in that unit are officers," responded the taller of the two confused captains."

Seeing his cue, Major Beauregard leaned over and addressed the two Army officers in a low but stern tone of voice, while the same Negro porter cleaned off a nearby table. "I suggest you gentlemen choose your words more carefully when you speak in a raised tone of voice in public. Those colored soldiers that you have such disdain for are biting at the bit to get into combat so they can prove themselves. The two of you should be so lucky to serve with such brave men." Then, as Jim stood up straight, he nodded once then remarked, "As you were."

While being assigned to the Provost Marshal's Office in New York City, Jim Beauregard understood the meaning of the expression that absence makes the heart grow fonder. As far as Jim was concerned, his wife Bea never looked more beautiful as he admired her from across the dance floor. While Jim appreciated the fact that his father-in-law organized a welcome home party on his behalf on such short notice, he would have preferred to have spent the night alone with his wife.

After picking up two glasses of champagne from the bartender in his father-in-law's mansion, Jim made his way through the roomful of family members and friends. As soon as Jim reached his wife's side, he presented Bea with her drink as he undressed her with his eyes. Even a dignified Southern Bell like Beatrice Beauregard was frustrated by the fact that ever since her husband got off the train, their time together was monopolized by everyone from her father to half the Atlanta police force.

Fortunately, dinner and dessert went by quickly and by 9 PM Jim and his wife Bea were making mad passionate love to each other in their bedroom. While the couple remained locked in a warm embrace, Bea still couldn't believe how lucky she was to have her husband home on leave.

Even though her husband made mad passionate love to her as if he was a man half his age, Bea knew that Jim had a lot on his mind from the moment she met him at the train station. The fact that Jim always shared his work with his wife, made Beatrice Beauregard worry less because it helped to visualize what Jim was doing, as opposed to having her mind wander. Bea also knew that Jim was deeply troubled that his request for a combat command was rejected. Even though Bea wanted Jim to accept the Governor's appointment to head the highway patrol, she knew that she had no right to complain because her husband was just as safe by being an investigator for the Army as he was being a police chief in Georgia.

When Bea considered the horrible wounds that soldiers were sustaining in combat overseas, she also knew that she had no right to complain when she learned that her husband was grazed by a bullet across his scalp line during a shootout in Brooklyn. As the wife of a career law enforcement officer, Beatrice Beauregard was used to the risks of her husband's profession. The fact that Jim had plenty of close calls as an Atlanta cop, also conditioned Bea to accept the risks that were inherent with her husband being a policeman in the Army. Besides, whenever Bea began to worry, she reminded herself to be grateful that her husband would likely be stationed stateside for the duration of the war.

Even though Bea felt the way she did, she tried not to act overly happy that husband's latest request for a combat command was denied. Still, like most good wives, Beatrice Beauregard knew when her husband wasn't sharing all of his feelings with her. Since Bea knew Jim was holding back, she decided it was time for her to do a little probing to see if she could get her husband to open up.

While Bea caressed her husband's chest and told him how handsome he looked in his uniform, she was just about to ask him how things were going at the office when Jim looked directly into her eyes and said, "I love you, Bea. I mean I really love you." As Bea melted into Jim's arms, she decided not to risk spoiling the moment by asking him a laundry list of questions. Instead, Bea decided to let Jim work certain issues out in his own mind before he discussed these matters with her.

When morning came Jim seemed more relaxed as he walked up behind his wife and kissed her gently on the side of the neck before he said, "Good morning, Bea." As soon as Bea turned around, she kissed her husband passionately on the lips and told him how grateful she was that he was granted leave when so many other wives weren't as lucky.

The moment the couple pulled apart and Jim said "Why don't we forget breakfast and go upstairs," Bea smiled coyly before she responded and said, "Why, Major, if you would've said that before I started cooking, I would have allowed you to sweep me off my feet but since this food is almost ready I suggest we eat first."

While Jim sat at the head of the kitchen table opposite his wife, he poured himself a cup of freshly brewed coffee and said, "I can't tell you how tired I am of eating out all the time. I shouldn't complain because the food is usually pretty good. It's just that I miss your cooking."

As Bea delivered a mountain of food to the table with the skill of a professional short order cook, she responded and said, "You just sit tight, because I made you your favorite breakfast. Fortunately, we can still get fresh pork and chickens, as well as eggs, milk and all the fruit and vegetables that we need from your grandfather's farm. One of the best decisions we ever made was to keep that place and let your cousin Jack run it after he retired from the sheriff's office."

Beatrice Beauregard was like other wives in 1943 who cooked, cleaned, kept house and raised children. Even though Bea was employed by her father's private business that had a war department contract, the fact that she made her own hours made it possible for her to enjoy the best of both worlds for a woman of that era.

While Jim filled his plate with food, Bea poured herself a cup of coffee and said, "I can't tell you how many times I read your letters over and over again. You're a wonderful writer, Jim. When I read your letters I can actually imagine traveling with with you in New York City. I really hope you take the time to write a book about the cases you've been working on. People have no idea how important the Provost Marshal's Office is to the war effort."

As Jim devoured his wife's cooking like a man who spent a month at sea in a life raft, Bea decided that it was time to probe a little deeper. The moment his wife asked how his latest case was going, Jim took a quick sip of coffee before he looked across the table and said, "Working in New York City has been an eye opening experience. Between what I've seen as a cop in Georgia and what I've seen in New York, I'm ashamed of myself for not doing more to make things right."

After pausing long enough to take another sip of coffee, Jim continued and said, "I gotta tell ya, Bea. I don't like the way colored folks are treated in this country. It's a disgrace and something has to be done about."

Like most people who lived in the south in the 1940s, Beatrice Beauregard accepted the way things were as far as race relations were concerned, even if there were certain aspects of this issue that she personally found distasteful. As the wife of an Atlanta Police Captain and the daughter of a wealthy politician, Bea also had a responsibility to be as politically correct as the times demanded. Clearly, this was viewed as a necessary course of action to take to insure her family's status in the community.

When Bea reminded her husband that he was a good man who always treated Negroes with kindness, Jim went on for five straight minutes about how hypocritical it was that the United States was fighting a racist regime like the fascist Nazis, as well as the fanatical Japanese militarists, with a segregated army.

As Jim paused long enough to light a cigarette, he finished his remarks by saying, "I mean it Bea. It doesn't make any sense that colored soldiers have been fighting and dying for our country since the War of Independence and they're still not truly free men. I know I told you this when we first met but I feel twice as strongly about this now because the people in this country have had over twenty years since the last war to fix things and they haven't done so. Heck, I'm working with a Negro cop who saved the lives of two white cops and got wounded trying to save a third and he still can't go to most of the places that I can."

While Bea refilled her husband's cup with more coffee and a splash of milk she remarked, "And here I was thinking that you were upset about not getting a transfer to a combat unit."

"That's another story, Bea," said Jim as he sat across the table from his wife and tapped the ash from his cigarette into a nearby ashtray.

Even though Beatrice Beauregard was a strong woman, she barely held it together whenever she read or heard about the war because it reminded her of the perils that their two sons were facing. To have her husband enlist at his age and volunteer to serve in a front line unit would be more than she could handle. Since she knew Jim was a persistent individual, she sat up straight and said, "Don't tell me you intend to make another request for a combat assignment?"

As Jim answered his wife, he tried to sugar coat his response as much as possible when he said, "With the way this case is going I doubt if the Army will ever honor my request for reassignment."

The moment Beatrice remarked, "You didn't answer my question," Jim knew that he had to come clean and tell her the truth.

After taking sip of coffee, Jim looked across the table at his wife and said, "You know I can't lie to you, Bea. The answer is yes. As soon as this case is over, I intend to request another transfer to a front line combat unit unless victory has been achieved."

Without saying a word, Bea stood up and took her coffee cup over to the sink. Jim had been married long enough to know that his wife of many years was upset with him. As Jim stood up and walked over to the sink, he did his best to plead his case, while he stood facing his wife's back and said, "Look Bea, I know how hard this must be for you. I also know that you weren't happy when I decided not to take that job with the highway patrol so I could accept a commission in the Army, but this was something I felt I had to do."

After hearing his wife say, "Let's not relive the past. What's done is done," Jim debated whether or not he should push his luck and continue to defend his decision to join the Army or move on to another topic.

As Jim walked over to the open window that faced the back yard of their home, he spoke in a somber tone of voice and said, "Bea, I can't handle the fact that our sons are in harms way and I'm not there to protect them. I'm their father. It's ingrained in me that my job is to keep them from getting hurt and this is the first time in my life when I can't do a damn thing to keep them safe." Then, after a quick pause, Jim added, "And it must be just as bad if not worse for you because you're the mother of our two sons. Heck, when I was working all those crazy hours, you were the one who raised those boys and made it possible for them to become fine young men."

While Bea turned to face her husband, Jim continued as her eyes filled with tears. "I also admit that even if I didn't have two sons who were old enough to fight, I'd still want'a serve. I say that because the people we're fighting in this war are hell bent on dominating the world and it's gonna take all hands to stop them. That means that retreads like me are gonna have to pitch in and help out. I know it stinks but that's the way it is."

As Jim turned around and faced his wife, he continued and said, "I'm no hero, Bea. I'm just a guy who wants to do everything I can to help end this war as fast as possible."

While Bea embraced her husband she rested her head against his chest, as she responded to his remarks in a soft tone of voice. "I know it's not right to be selfish, not with all the crazy things that are going on in this world. I also know how you feel about being a soldier. You've been at it a long time and you believe that you can save lives if you're in the thick of it. All I hope and pray is that our sons are lucky enough to serve under an officer like you. If that happens they'll come home safe and sound."

After hearing his wife's kind words all Jim could say was, "Thanks, Bea."

Even though Bea wanted things to be different, she knew that an untold number of lives were being negatively affected by the double menace that threatened the free world on a daily basis. The thought of being enslaved by the Nazi's or the Japanese was enough to make Beatrice Beauregard prepared to use the family shotgun if need be to defend Atlanta from attack.

As Bea regained her composure, she felt an intense surge of passion fill her body from head to toe. Rather than waste the most precious gift of all, Bea gently grabbed her husband by the hand and said, "Follow me, Major and that's an order."

As his wife led the way upstairs to their bedroom, all Jim could say was, "You're in charge, Bea."

CHAPTER 24

THE FUGITIVE SOLDIERS

T he contingent of military police who were assigned to screen the new recruits were genuinely overwhelmed by the sheer volume of men who arrived for processing. Even the additional presence of several police detectives and FBI Agents, was not enough to produce the hoped for results when it came to locating two fugitives among the massive number of newly inducted recruits.

Fortunately for their sake, Ivan Larson and Francis Shorty Mc Ghee managed to stay together and get assigned to the group that was heading to Camp Wheeler near Macon, Georgia on the evening train. By being extremely polite and playing the, "I'm with my cousin card," Ivan and Shorty were able to stick together, especially when they acted as if they were happy about serving in the infantry so they could get into combat as soon as possible.

While the two fugitives waited to board a southbound train to Georgia, Ivan turned to Shorty and whispered, "So far so good," as a pair of military policemen strolled by. As usual, Shorty was unable to enjoy the fact that they were finally about to escape the intensive efforts by the New York City Police, the FBI and the U.S. Army to locate them.

Shorty proved that he was considerably more rattled about living life on the run than Ivan, when he faced his buddy and said, "You're right. So far so good but what about tomorrow and the next day?"

When Ivan remarked, "Just try taking it one day at a time," their train pulled into the station.

As soon as the train came to a stop, Shorty did his best to live for the moment when he turned to Ivan and said, "This is it. We're on our way."

After getting settled in their seats, Ivan turned to his buddy and asked if he felt better. "I don't know why you put up with me," responded Shorty.

While the train load of new recruits got settled in their seats, Ivan cracked a smile then said, "I guess it's because you're the only friend I have left."

While meeting with Lt. Colonel Richmond in his office, Captain Patrick Murphy Sr. and Andy Dubrowsky brought the Provost Marshal for New York up to date on the investigation into the evidence that was found in Miller's warehouse and apartment. Andy Dubrowsky began the briefing by saying, "I just got back from Germantown, PA with one of the detectives assigned to the Miller homicide. Thanks to the passport that Al found in Miller's warehouse and the work that Joe Coppola did, we confirmed that John Johann Miller and Rudolf Mueller used the same address in Germantown on their passports. When we checked that address, we found ourselves standing in front of a butcher shop that matched one of the photos that were recovered from Miller's warehouse. After we did some further checking, we confirmed that Miller and Mueller were partners and owned this business before they moved to New York City and opened the M&M Butcher Shop on the west side."

As a high ranking FBI supervisor on military leave, Fred Richmond was just as familiar with the German American Bund as Andy Dubrowsky. When the Colonel asked if the Bureau had any information about the involvement of Miller and Mueller in the Bund, Andy replied, "Luckily for us, one of the names on the list that was found in Miller's warehouse was an informant who worked for Dan Phillips. From what I heard, this guy did an outstanding job infiltrating the Bund and helping our agents round up enemy aliens after the attack on Pearl Harbor. Dan thinks he still might be serving in the Merchant Marine. If that's the case, he could be anywhere in the world. Either way, we'll find him."

Fred Richmond proved that he knew exactly who Andy was referring too when he spoke up and said, "Dan's informant also did some excellent intelligence work for us in Germany before the war. If anyone can help us find Mueller he can."

After removing the cigar from the corner of his mouth Andy added, "Agents out west are still looking into the laundry list of leads that we found in Miller's warehouse and in his apartment. That includes the locations that were circled on Miller's road map. Unfortunately, like Jim said, it's gonna take some time to check all this out."

When Fred Richmond asked if they were canvassing the area in midtown where the M&M Butcher Shop was located, Captain Murphy spoke up and said, "The area on the west side where the M&M Butcher Shop was located is filled with bars, restaurants and small hotels. There's also several hack outfits that aren't all that far away from the address where the M&M Butcher Shop was located. After considering our options, Andy and I agreed that we should hold off on flashing badges and asking questions in that neighborhood until we know more about Miller and Mueller."

As soon as Fred Richmond agreed, he added, "No sense in tipping our hand, especially if this is an area where Ivan Larson conducted his black market activities.

While the Colonel packed his pipe with a fresh bowl of tobacco, he asked if they had any leads that could be pursued locally. After hearing the question, Captain Murphy wasted no time in responding. "Outside of helping the FBI make cases against Andy Gooding's contacts at the Staten Island Fuel Depot and the Brooklyn Army Depot, we've been unable to use the information in Andy Gooding's records to develop any meaningful leads that can help us further identify Ivan Larson or any of his associates. The only shred of a lead that we've been able to pursue, is to look for the black 1937 Suburban with the dented left rear fender that Ivan Larson used to pick up black market merchandise from Andy Gooding."

"You never know. We could get lucky. It's happened before," remarked Fred Richmond.

Pat Murphy Sr. finished his remarks about the 1937 Suburban by saying, "Even though I know it's a long shot, I've got every beat cop and uniformed sergeant in the department looking for this vehicle but so far it hasn't been found. I even have our men calling in the license plates and locations where they find Suburbans of a different color that don't have a damaged fender. I figured it wouldn't hurt to do so, just in case the registered owner had his vehicle painted and patched up since it was used by Larson to deliver black market merchandise." Then, after pausing, the Captain added, "Unless something changes, all of our chips are riding on the evidence that was found in Miller's warehouse and in his apartment."

Fred Richmond knew that not all leads were like brightly painted signs that led investigators directly to the evidence that was needed to make a case. While doing his best to sound encouraging, Lt. Colonel Richmond looked directly at Captain Murphy and said, "Have faith, Pat, you never know what might come up while we keep digging."

Even though he was frustrated by the lack of progress that was being made to find the two fugitives, Captain Murphy agreed with Fred Richmond. "You're right, Fred. I'll keep my fingers crossed for both of us."

As soon as Fred Richmond stood up behind his desk, he picked up his mug and invited Pat Murphy Sr. and Andy Dubrowsky to join him in the conference room for a cup of coffee. While Captain Murphy and the veteran FBI Agent followed Colonel Richmond down the hallway, Andy Dubrowsky noticed that every desk in office was empty, now that every man assigned to the task force except the duty agent was in the field.

After hearing Andy Dubrowsky remark, "I think we need more men, Colonel," Fred Richmond stopped by the entrance to the conference room and faced the veteran FBI Agent and the city police captain and said, "Sorry, Andy, but unless we uncover the lead of the century, we're it. Despite the importance of this case, no additional personnel will be assigned to this task force on a full time basis. That means we have to take whatever help we can get when we operate in the field as an unexpected bonus."

Now that Ivan Larson was on the run and John Miller was dead, Murray Silverman lost his contact for black market gasoline, cigarettes and high quality beef. Fortunately, he still had a large supply of cigarettes that he intended to hang on to, unless he needed to give a carton to a court clerk, a court officer or a judge when he needed a favor.

Rather than do without or with less, Murray decided to do a little trading on his own and swap premium brand cigarettes for a few gallons of gasoline that one of the court officers in Manhattan was able to periodically obtain. Unfortunately, the amount of gasoline that Murray was able to get his hands on, was barely enough to keep his late model 1941 Oldsmobile sedan on the road.

Murray's secretary and girlfriend Silvia Krause also had no choice but to limit the amount of driving that she did as well. Doing so created the perfect excuse for Murray to drive his secretary to and from work everyday. When Murray's wife went away to care for her sick father for six weeks, Silvia was able to spend day and night with the man that she had been having an affair since she was hired to work in his law firm.

As soon as FBI Supervisor Dan Phillips heard that the New York CID Task Force needed help in locating Rudolf Mueller and other former German American

Bund members, he immediately began trying to locate Willie Gunderson. In all his years in the Bureau, Dan Phillips considered Willie Gunderson to be one of his absolute best informants. The reason for this was because Willie volunteered to help the FBI because he hated Nazis. In addition to being an American patriot, Willie was well motivated to assist the FBI because he was raised by a grandmother who was Jewish.

From the first day they met, Dan Phillips and Willie hit it off and became a team. Initially, Willie infiltrated the Friends of New Germany, the organization that predated the German American Bund. When the Bund was formed in 1936, Willie was considered a well respected supporter of National Socialism by his fellow Bund members.

The fact that Willie was a merchant seamen enabled him to participate in a variety of Bund activities in between shipping out on different cargo vessels. During Hitler's rise to power, Willie also intentionally accepted assignments on merchant vessels that were bound for German ports. Doing so served two purposes. In addition to serving as the eyes and ears of the FBI, Willie was able to entertain his fellow Bund members with stories about the "wonderful" things that were happening back home in the Fatherland.

With no immediate family members to contact, Dan began to track Willie down by finding out which ship he was serving on. After making several phone calls, Dan Phillips learned that his 60 year old former informant was assigned to a Liberty Ship that was delivering supplies to Allied controlled ports in North Africa and Southern Italy. The next report that Dan received stated that Willie's Liberty Ship was attacked by German aircraft and sustained battle damage. A week later Dan was notified that Willie Gunderson was wounded in the air attack on his ship.

When Dan Phillips learned that Willie Gunderson was wounded while supporting the Italian Campaign, he asked his contacts at the CID Task Force to locate his old informant. After making numerous inquiries, Lt. Scott determined that Willie Gunderson was a patient in the British Army Hospital in Bari, Italy and was scheduled to be transported back to the United States on a hospital ship.

Rather than wait for Willie to return to the states, a request was made to have a U.S. Army CID Agent serving in the Italian Campaign interview Willie to determine if he was willing to help the FBI locate Rudolf Mueller and his associates. Unfortunately, when U.S. Army CID Agents arrived at the British Army Hospital in Bari, they were unable to locate Willie Gunderson.

As soon as Andy Dubrowsky was notified that Willie Gunderson was not in his hospital bed, he contacted Dan Phillips to give him the bad news. "I'm sorry, Dan, but your informant is no where to be found."

"How can that be?" remarked Dan who quickly added, "Not only is Willie 60 years old but he's was wounded when his Liberty Ship was attacked by the Luftwaffe."

Once again Andy shared everything that he knew with the FBI Supervisor from the Newark, New Jersey Field Office. "All I know, Dan, is that a British Army doctor in Bari told CID that Chief Gunderson was still recovering from multiple shrapnel wounds and is no condition to be limping around Italy in a hospital robe and slippers."

After lighting a cigarette, Dan remembered something that might help and said, "I don't know if this helps, Andy, but Willie became friends with an Italian merchant seamen who was seriously injured when cargo was being unloaded from his freighter. According to Willie, he gave his buddy the money to open a restaurant in the port city of Taranto after his arm was crushed in a deck accident. Based on what he told me, his buddy not only paid him back but gave him a piece of the action. Unfortunately, Willie's plans to retire in Italy were delayed because of the war."

Andy Dubrowsky knew exactly what needed to be done and said, "I'll ask Fred Richmond to send a message to CID Headquarters requesting that British Army MPs look for Willie. After all, how hard could it be to find a 60 year old American merchant seamen with a bad leg, who left a British Army hospital wearing a bathrobe and slippers and is hanging out in a restaurant in Taranto, Italy like the Humphrey Bogart character in Casablanca."

After liberating some clothes from the hospital laundry, Willie Gunderson limped his way through Bari with the aid of a cane, until he was able to hitch a ride south to Taranto on a British Army truck. Once he arrived in the port city of Taranto, Willie found the building that he was looking for. Willie was familiar with this location because The Marina Ristorante was owned by his good friend, Amato Maduch Della Vecchia, a retired Italian merchant seamen he met during his first port call in the boot of Italy. That was over ten years ago.

The day that crated cargo shifted on deck and crushed his left shoulder and arm, the 48 year old Italian merchant seaman known as Maduch was forced to stop going to sea. When his friend lost his livelihood, Willie offered to give his buddy the money to open a bar restaurant in an ideal location in Taranto. Being a proud man, Maduch refused the generous offer. When Willie insisted, Maduch agreed on the condition that Willie share in the profits, even after he was paid back for his initial investment. Rather than argue with his friend, Willie accepted the terms and looked forward to every trip that he made to Southern Italy.

Thanks to his American friend, Maduch and his family were able to start a business and prosper when all seemed lost. Even when Italy joined the war against the Allies, the Della Vecchia family was able to survive by fishing and growing their own food on the small farm that they owned on the outskirts of town. Owning a bar restaurant in a port city also helped to keep the family from falling on hard times. Once the British 8th Army landed in Taranto, Brindisi and Bari, the Della Vecchia family was able to breath a sigh of relief now that the worst of the war was behind them.

After spending time in a British Army Hospital, Willie needed a drink, some decent food and an old friend to talk to about their combined sea going adventures. The second Willie limped into the place called, The Marina Ristorante, his old friend could not believe his eyes. As soon as Maduch made his way across the dining room section of the restaurant, the two men embraced each others like long lost brothers.

While Maduch helped his injured friend into the kitchen, the British military personnel and merchant seamen who were customers in The Marina Ristorante couldn't help but notice the touching reunion between the two older men. Even though Willie wore an assortment of British military clothing, no action was taken to report his presence because he appeared to be in pretty bad shape and looked like he needed a drink more than a trip to the stockade.

Lt. Colonel Richmond couldn't have been more proud of the men under his command when they volunteered to work over the Thanksgiving and Christmas Holidays to continue searching for the two fugitives. While Lt. Scott from The Office of Naval Intelligence was assigned to supervise the screening of troops who were being transported overseas, Major Beauregard directed the contingent assigned to search Army camps that were located outside of New York. After attending a morning briefing, several teams of task force personnel left for Pennsylvania Station and various Ports of Embarkation to continue to search for Ivan Larson and Francis Shorty Mc Ghee.

Willie was in a lot worse shape after he made the trip from Bari to Taranto on a badly wounded leg. After moving Willie to the family farm on the outskirts of town, Maduch arrived to tell his friend that the British Military Police were looking for him.

"What do they want with me? I don't work for them," remarked Willie who continued and said, "Don't they have anything better to do than look for a 60 year old man, who left his hospital bed to visit an old friend and get some decent food?"

While Maduch sat next to Willie's bed, he seemed a bit excited when he spoke in a mixture of broken English and Italian, while using his hands to emphasize what he had to say. "Two times this week the British Polizia Militare come into the ristorante to look for the 60 year old primo ufficiale di copereta, how do you say the Americano Merchant Marina Capo, como si dice, Chief'a Mate by the name of Willie Gunderson. When they ask these questions I tell them, if you see this old man you take him with you. Then I give them a glass of wine and they leave."

Even though Willie was still in bad shape, he was in a much better place mentally now that he was being cared for by the Della Vecchia family. Of all the places Willie visited in his travels, Italy was his absolute favorite. Because his plans to retire in Italy were derailed due to the war, Willie didn't have to think twice when Maduch asked his old friend to remain in Taranto rather than ship out again and risk getting killed.

For someone who never had a family, Willie was deeply touched when Maduch reassured him that by the time he recovered, the British military police would be busy looking for another patient who left their hospital in Bari without permission. Once that happened, they could run the restaurant together and have a good life.

Before Maduch left to return to Taranto he removed two brown glass bottles from his pocket and said, "I give'a customer from the English Navy free food and free wine if he brings me farmaco, how you say, medicine. You take and sleep. I com'a back two days."

In January of 1944 the United States Army established the Criminal Investigative Division known as CID. By reactivating the unit that was last utilized during World War 1, the Army established a command under the Provost Marshal General's Office that was solely dedicated to conducting criminal investigations. Due to his background and his current assignment, Major James Beauregard, as well Lt. Colonel Fred Richmond and a few other investigators from the Provost Marshal's Office received new credentials that identified them as U.S. Army CID Agents.

After several months of not turning up any significant leads, the men in the CID Task Force were beginning to feel the strain of their unusual assignment. Even with all that they knew about Ivan Larson and Francis Shorty Mc Ghee, the men assigned to the New York CID Task Force were no closer to apprehending the two fugitives than they were when they first began their investigation.

Throughout their time in basic training, the soldier known as Danny Gannon found life in the Army to be relatively easy, while the G.I. known as Gus O'Malley was having a rough time adjusting to the daily routine. Getting up at 5:55 AM and being given twenty five minutes to hit the head, wash, get dressed and make his bed before he had to march to the mess hall, was no way to start the day as far as Francis Shorty Mc Ghee was concerned. Even when they were just about to complete their training, Ivan was a fully indoctrinated soldier, while Shorty was still a civilian at heart.

After giving up on his dream of becoming a hot shot Army aviator, Ivan accepted the fact that he was destined to become a rifle toting infantryman. As soon as he accepted this change in his destiny, Ivan envisioned himself as being a real Sergeant York type; an infantryman who was able to fight well with others, or by himself when the situation called for him to act aggressively on his own. Even though Shorty had more experience using a Tommy Gun than anyone else in their training class, Gus O'Malley hated everything about the Army, except the fact that Camp Wheeler was a little closer to Mexico than New York.

Because his partner in crime was having a difficult time adjusting to Army life, Ivan had his hands full trying to keep Shorty from going over the hill. As grateful as he was that he and Ivan managed to get stationed together, Shorty was determined to get out of the infantry at all costs. While Ivan liked Army life and was looking forward to being stationed in a front line fighting unit, Shorty would love nothing more than to hear that the war was over. If they were stateside when that happened, they would make a bee line for Mexico. Even the idea of making their way to Ireland, sounded like a much better alternative than serving another day as a ground pounding infantryman in the U.S. Army.

With a weekend pass in hand, Ivan was about to leave the base for a night on the town when an excited Shorty Mc Ghee ran into the barracks with a flier in hand. When Shorty arrived by Ivan's bunk, he was soaked with sweat and wearing a pair of filthy herringbone fatigues after another day of company punishment for screwing up. So far, nothing except chow time seemed to motive Shorty to get excited over anything that the Army had to offer.

While the dapper looking Danny Gannon pushed his tie up to form a perfect knot, he glanced over to his sweaty sand covered friend and said, "Don't tell me. You won an honorable discharge in a crap game."

While Shorty ignored Ivan's joke, he smiled wide as he held out the flier and said, "Check this out, pal."

After closing his locker, Ivan turned to Shorty and relieved him of the paper flier that he held in his hand. The flier was a recruiting poster that offered anyone interested in becoming a glider pilot a chance to earn Army aviator wings, even if they had no prior flight training. The more Ivan read the more he became excited. Based on the information in this flier, Ivan finally had a way to realize his childhood dream and become an Army combat pilot. As far as Ivan was concerned, he was ready to sign on the dotted line, even if it meant that he had fly a plane that had no engine and wasn't armed in order to earn his wings.

While Shorty used his Zippo lighter to light a cigarette, Ivan sat on the corner of his bunk and continued reading the glider pilot recruiting poster. The moment Shorty saw that Ivan was finished reading the flier, he spoke up and said, "You owe me, pal."

After ignoring Shorty's comment, Ivan looked up and said, "Where'd you get this?"

As Shorty looked around to make sure that they were still alone, he spoke in a confident tone of voice while he stood between his cot and Ivan's bunk and said, "The company clerk gave it to me. He's another Yankee like us who knows that we tried to get into the Army Air Forces but ended up in the infantry. He also knows how much I hate this place. He said the job is ours if we want it."

While Ivan quickly read the contents of the flier over again, he shook his head and remarked, "They must really be hurting for glider pilots for the Army to lower the standards like this. Hell, according to this if you can walk and chew gum at the same time you can get into the glider program."

After taking a drag on his cigarette, Shorty exhaled and said, "Well, what do you say?"

Without hesitation Ivan said, "I'll do anything to get a shot at becoming a pilot, even if I have to fly a plane with no engine in order to do so."

As Shorty extinguished his cigarette in a red fire brigade bucket that was filled with sand, he looked at Ivan and said, "Good, 'cause the fix is in. We'll be outta this dump before you know it."

Because he was anxious to hear more, Ivan stood up and faced his friend as he said, "How long before we get our wings?"

When Shorty responded, he sounded like an authority on the subject. "Because we didn't enter the Army with a pilot's license we have to complete ground school and flight training in a single engine puddle jumper. If we survive flight school, we get sent to Basic Glider School and Advanced Glider Training. There's a few other schools that last four to six weeks that we have to attend as well. Best yet, we get to do this as staff sergeants before we become Flight Officers. Some guys who complete this training are even getting commissioned as Lieutenants."

After hearing what Shorty had to say, Ivan sounded a bit disappointed when he remarked, "But that means we won't get overseas for several months depending on how spaced out all this training is."

"If you want'a fly this is your ticket outta the infantry," remarked Shorty who quickly added, "The choice is yours."

As happy as Ivan was about the prospects of finally getting his wings, he couldn't help but wonder why Shorty was so enthusiastic about becoming a glider pilot. Even though Ivan knew that Shorty hated Camp Wheeler and was having a bad run of luck pissing off their red neck sergeant, he never figured that he would be in such a hurry to get airborne.

After standing up, Ivan looked around to make sure they were still alone before he faced his buddy and said, "I know you're a mechanical genius and one hell of a shot with a Tommy Gun but do you really want'a learn how to fly and become a glider pilot? Without hesitating Shorty remarked, "I gave up on the idea of going to Mexico because I know you like this man's army too much to go with me. Besides, I figured as long as our luck is holding out I might as well tag along."

While Ivan appreciated Shorty's sense of loyalty, he was still wondering why his partner in crime was so anxious to learn how to fly. As Ivan patted Shorty on the side of his left arm and said, "Thanks," he paused for a second before he asked his buddy if he was ready to go through flight training.

Under the circumstances, Shorty knew that he had some explaining to do. Once again Shorty sounded unusually confident when he responded and said, "I can't explain it but this feels like the right move for us to make. Besides, you were right. Pilots get respect. This buck private shit is for the birds. If I have to stay in this man's Army to keep you company, I'm not gonna do it in the damn infantry."

Just to be sure that Shorty was totally on board with this decision, Ivan asked, "Even if you have to fly a glider to do so?"

After nodding his head, Shorty responded in an enthusiastic tone and said, "I don't care what we fly as long as we get the hell outta this red neck shit hole."

After being well cared for on the Della Vecchia farm, Willie decided to travel into Taranto with Maduch to bring a barrel of homemade wine to the restaurant. Unfortunately, Willie's visit was short lived when a pair of British Army MPs entered The Marina Ristorante and found him sitting at the bar talking to Maduch after he opened for business.

When the MP Sergeant asked if he was an American, Willie decided it would be in poor taste to respond in German so he remarked, "100% red blooded."

"Can I see some identification, Sir," asked the British MP.

Willie Gunderson had been going to sea long enough to know that anything could happen at anytime. As a result, he made it a habit to always carry his papers, wallet, his favorite pipe, a pouch of tobacco, a Zippo cigarette lighter and a pocket knife. In addition, he wore a small leather pouch around his neck that contained fifty dollars in U.S. Currency and a gold coin that could be used to buy provisions, a few drinks or a place to sleep if he ended up on dry land longer than expected. When the war began Willie also made it a habit to wear his U.S. Maritime Service metal identity tag around his neck at all times.

As soon as Willie produced his identity tag and he asked the MP why he was looking for him, the British Sergeant checked his "dog tag" and remarked, "All I know, Sir, is that an American FBI man by the name of Daniel Phillips asked us to find you and take good care of you because he needs your assistance back in the states. In fact, your Agent Phillips has been driving our embassy chaps in Washington crazy with a flurry of requests that we tear this town apart if necessary to locate you."

Once Willie heard that Dan needed his help, he told Maduch that he would be back as soon as he finishing helping his friend from the FBI. While the two men hugged each other and said goodbye, the British MP Sergeant sounded very polite when he remarked, "We better go, Sir. Whatever it is, it must be important."

After being examined by a Royal Navy Doctor in Taranto, Willie Gunderson was issued medication and a Chief Petty Officer's uniform before he was transported to the U.S. Army 15th Air Force Headquarters in Foggia, Italy. As soon as Willie arrived, a U.S. Army CID Agent asked Willie a series of questions that were forwarded to CID in Italy from Dan Phillips and Andy Dubrowsky. When Willie confirmed that he could help the FBI locate Rudolf Mueller and his other associates, the CID Agent handed him a set of priority transportation orders for Mitchell Field in New York. After being issued a travel bag with toiletries and some extra clothing, Willie was escorted to the C47 that would take him on the first leg of his journey home.

The day Willie arrived at Mitchell Field, he wasn't surprised to find FBI Agent Dan Phillips and another agent waiting for him on the tarmac. As soon as the two men greeted each other, Dan remarked, "I'm sorry for dragging you halfway around the world but we need your help, Willie." After introducing Willie to Andy Dubrowsky, Dan picked up Willie's travel bag and said, "Let's grab something to eat while we fill you in."

As soon as Dan Phillips finished telling Willie why they needed to find Rudolf Mueller, the 60 year old merchant seaman responded and said, "When I first met Miller and Mueller they were talking about selling their butcher shop in Germantown, PA to open a butcher shop either in New York or New Jersey. At the time, Mueller was dating the daughter of another Bund member by the name of Gunther Kessler. I was actually surprised to see them together because Mueller is a lot older than Kessler's daughter."

While Willie continued, he pointed to one of the photographs of Mueller, Miler, Gretchen Kessler and Gunther Kessler that Andy Dubrowsky brought to the meeting. "Kessler's daughter changed her name from Gretchen to Greta when Hitler declared war on our Allies in Europe. You also need to know that when Gunther Kessler wants to Americanize his name he calls himself Gary. Kessler is a baker by profession and had a bakery in Bayonne. After his wife died, his daughter stayed on to handle the customers and help her father with his bookkeeping."

After taking a quick sip of beer Willie continued and said, "The last time I had anything to do with Bund members was right after Pearl Harbor when you asked me to make the rounds to see if any of these characters were up to no good. That's when I found out that Mueller was engaged to Kessler's daughter and was looking for a location in New York to open a butcher shop with his pal Johann Miller. After that I shipped out again and made runs to England and Russia until I was torpedoed off the coast of North Carolina. That put me on the beach for a month until I was able to go back to sea. From there I ended up in Malta, North Africa and Italy where I got torpedoed again, bombed and strafed."

When Andy showed Willie another black and white photograph he identified every person without hesitation. While Willie pointed to four former Bund members, he continued to fill Dan and Andy in. "If you're looking for Mueller you'll increase your chances of finding him, if you find his father-in-law, the Wagner brothers and Max Hoffman. Even if all you do is find his father-in law, once you find Kessler's daughter you'll find Mueller."

As soon as Dan asked Willie what the Wagner brothers and Hoffman did for a living, Willie responded and said, "When I knew 'em they were truck drivers. The Wagner brothers were long haul drivers, while Max Hoffman drove a beer truck around Jersey. The last time I saw Bruno and Henry Wagner they were looking to move to Secaucus or Hoboken. Hoffman also moved and was living with his sick mother in Union City. Mueller and his future young wife also got a place of their own, not far from where Hoffman's mother lived."

Dan didn't have to ask but he did anyway, "Do you think you could help us find these guys?"

Once again Willie responded without hesitation. "I'm all yours, Dan. My days in the Merchant Marine are over. As soon as I can, I plan on returning to Italy to live out the rest of my years in peace. In the meantime, I'll do whatever I can to help you and Mister Hoover."

As Dan stood up, he picked up the check and remarked, "Thanks Willie. At the very least, the FBI owes you a trip back to Italy. Who knows, when this war's over maybe I'll come and visit you."

Traveling with a Negro partner in 1944 was also no easy task for a white officer assigned to the Army's Criminal Investigation Division. With restaurants, hotels and military bases segregated, Major Beauregard and Patrolman Parker could not eat at the same lunch counter, share the same motel room, drink from the same water fountain, visit the same bathroom or stay in the same rail road sleeper car while traveling on official business. Still, both men understood the rules and never complained. It was almost as if Al knew what he had to do to make this partnership work as much as Jim Beauregard did.

Although their mission was a noble cause, trying to find Ivan Larson and Francis Shorty Mc Ghee among millions of soldiers, was proving to be a mission that had little hope of coming to a successful conclusion. The fact that on one day alone over 14,000 new recruits arrived at a reception center to get processed into the U.S. Army, was a prefect example of why this manhunt was the equivalent of looking for two small needles in a huge haystack.[7]

Conducting this investigation in 1944 also proved to be an ordeal, especially when you consider the logistics involved of traveling by train, plane and car to inspect massive numbers of troops at various training camps and forts throughout the United States. Despite the odds of success, the investigators assigned to this case did what cops do best, regardless of the title they carried or the agency they worked for.

In 1943 and 1944 the U.S. Army Air Forces was doing everything possible to train thousands of men to fly an aircraft without an engine into battle. When not enough volunteers signed up to fly gliders, the Army lowered the standards and opened the doors to enlisted men and commissioned officers who previously did not qualify. According to the new rules, glider pilot candidates did not have to have a valid or recently expired civilian pilot's license and were not required to pass the same screening process as power pilots or other aviators. In general, Class B students, as they were called, were all eager to fly, even if their options were limited to flying a less flashy glider.

Even though the requirements for glider pilots were lowered, every candidate had to successfully complete a course in basic flight instruction in a small single engine aircraft before he could continue in his glider pilot training. In other words, just because it was easier to get into the glider program, did not mean that it was easy to successfully complete the required training and get assigned to a Troop Carrier Squadron. In other words, U.S. Army flight school and glider training was just as demanding to complete as it was before, even if the requirements to get accepted into the program were loosened up a bit.

While pilots who flew the fighter aircraft and bombers were often considered the cream of the crop, the job of flying a C47 transport plane or a glider was often considered a much less flashy assignment. Despite this image issue, the simple truth was that flying a fabric covered glider that had to be towed into combat behind a transport plane was no easy task. In addition to delivering badly needed supplies and equipment to forward areas, glider pilots who flew the American made GC-4A Waco Glider were also responsible to transport up to thirteen fully equipped troops into combat.

Despite their importance, glider pilots who did not posses a commission in the Army received the rank of Flight Officer once they completed their training. This meant that while some glider pilots eventually received commissions, most of the 6000 men who served as glider pilots did so as Flight Officers. To accommodate this new rank, the Army designed an insignia that became known as the Blue Pickle.[8] This new insignia was a blue enamel bar that was similar in design to the insignia worn by a Warrant Officer.

In addition, all fully trained glider pilots were issued a slightly modified pair of silver colored pilot's wings that displayed a large initial G in the center of the insignia. These new wings were designed to distinguish a glider pilot from a "regular" pilot. When asked by other servicemen what the letter G stood for, most glider pilots learned to respond, "The G stands for guts."[9]

Lieutenant Billy Davis was a veteran C47 pilot who saw combat in North Africa and Sicily before rotating stateside to help train glider pilots. Of all the men in the current training class, it was only natural that Billy Davis would become friends with Danny Gannon and Gus O'Malley. This happened because Billy was from New York City and his two new army buddies were from Jersey City, New Jersey.

While serving in North Africa, Billy Davis dropped American paratroopers from the 509th Parachute Infantry Battalion over Youks les Bains Air Field. The mission was a success and the paratroopers were able to seize a vital transportation link from the enemy. Just prior to the Invasion of Sicily, Billy Davis was promoted to 1st Lieutenant and was given command of his own plane and crew. As he would soon find out, the Invasion of Sicily proved to be a baptism of fire for the newly promoted pilot in command.

As a pilot with the 51st Troop Carrier Wing, Billy Davis towed an American GC-4A Waco glider flown by a British pilot and a volunteer American co pilot by the name of Mike Kirby during Operation Ladbroke as the Invasion of Sicily was called. Unlike other tow plane pilots who released their gliders off shore, Billy Davis flew his C47 through a sky full of enemy anti aircraft fire and searchlight beams until it was safe to signal the British Glider Regiment Pilot in command of the GC4A to cut loose and make his decent. Once the glider they were assigned to tow was safely delivered to Sicily, Billy Davis and his crew returned to base.

As far as Billy Davis was concerned, it was almost as exciting to have the chance to see different parts of the United States as it was to be stationed overseas. After all, to most New Yorkers the Jersey Shore was considered the deep south. In fact, until the war began, most Americans rarely if ever traveled away from home. Once a civilian joined the armed forces, it was anyone's guess where they would train and serve. While some military bases were in dismal locations, most installations were located near or fairly close to populated areas and offered troops a town or even a major city to travel to when they were on leave.

After a rocky and slow start, the glider program was in full swing by 1943. As 1944 rolled around, the Army Air Forces had an impressive number of glider pilots and ground crew personnel trained and ready to serve. The mistakes of the past were now part of the training doctrine that was used to teach glider pilots how to successfully compete their missions under adverse conditions. Likewise, the accomplishments of the past became the beacon that guided glider pilots to safely reach their intended destinations.

The fact that a glider was not equipped with an engine, meant that a glider could only remain airborne for a relatively brief period of time. Flying a combat glider mission became even more dangerous when you came under fire, when you flew a night mission, when your tow rope snapped before you reached a suitable landing area and when you had to land on terrain that was flooded, filled with obstacles, filled with mines or with enemy troops.

One of the first things that Major Mike Kirby did when he took command of advanced glider training at South Plains Army Air Field, was arrange a transfer for Lt. Billy Davis so he could help him train glider pilots. Major Kirby did so for two reasons. First, Billy Davis was a decorated C47 pilot who knew what it was like to deliver a GC4A Waco glider to its intended destination under combat conditions. The Major also wanted to repay his favorite tow plane pilot for keeping his Waco glider out of the sea and for delivering him and their British allies to a landing zone that enabled them to complete their mission.

The day Billy Davis received his travel orders to return to the states for a TDY to South Plains Army Air Field near Lubbock, Texas everyone in his squadron was anxious to hear how he pulled this assignment off. While smiling wide, the young lieutenant from Brooklyn surprised his power pilot buddies when he remarked, "I was nice to a glider pilot once and kept his feet dry." Then, as Billy cracked a devilish grin, he continued and said, "You see, the poor bastard can't swim."

While Ivan Larson lived for the day when he would fly his first combat mission, Shorty Mc Ghee joined the glider program to stay with his partner in crime and get as far away from the infantry as possible. Shorty was also motivated to join the glider program because the food and accommodations were said to be better in the Army Air Forces. In addition, the Army Air Forces also offered more opportunities for advancement.

Even though Shorty was generally more mechanically inclined than Ivan, it was due to Ivan's tutoring that Shorty was able to successfully complete motorized flight school in a single engine aircraft. Ivan accomplished this by taking the time to explain how each part of a single engine aircraft made it possible for a pilot and his plane to defy gravity. Once Ivan appealed to the side of Shorty's brain that liked to tinker with mechanical objects, his partner in crime was able to become one with his aircraft and complete basic flight school. Even when Shorty had to shut the engine off in his aircraft, he was able to successfully perform the required number of dead stick landings.

Thanks again to Ivan's tutoring, Shorty was also able to complete Basic Glider School. One reason for this was because landing a glider was similar to safely landing a lightweight motorized aircraft once the engine was shut off. In other words, if you could complete basic motorized flight training, you should also be able to complete basic glider training.

Unfortunately, Shorty's problems started after he graduated motorized flight school and basic glider training and he arrived at Advanced Glider School in Lubbock, Texas. As soon as the glider landing scenarios became more complicated, Gus O'Malley was singled out as a potential candidate to be dropped from the program. With the pressure on to produce capable glider pilots, the instructors were ordered to fail anyone who couldn't cut the mustard. As far as the U.S. Army was concerned, there was no shortage of volunteers who wanted to be a combat aviator, even if it meant they had to fly a glider in order to earn their wings. The U.S. Army Air Forces also had a large number of pilots who were normally assigned to fly single engine and multi-engine aircraft, who could be pressed into service to fly gliders in combat.

Since the U.S. Army Air Forces invested a great deal of time and money in everyone who went through flight training, they gave everyone who entered advanced glider training a certain amount of time to learn how to fly a GC4A Waco glider under more demanding conditions. While the instructors did everything humanly possible to get their glider pilot trainees to complete the required training, anyone who failed to cut the mustard was reassigned to other duties.

The deciding vote to fail a student at the Advanced Glider School at South Plains Army Air Field was in the hands of one man. Major Kirby was a combat tested glider pilot who was assigned to command the advanced glider training at South Plains Army Air Field in early 1944. Mike Kirby took this mission seriously because he knew from experience that glider pilots were part aviator and part commando.

With most of the instructors ready to drop Gus O'Malley from the program, the Major stepped in to evaluate the one glider pilot trainee in the current class who seemed destined to fail. In order to perform a fair and impartial evaluation, Major Kirby decided to fly the next training mission to personally observe Gus O'Malley in action.

While Major Kirby stood in front of the class, the flight line was busy with activity as thirty CG- 4A Waco gliders and an equal number of C47 transport planes were made ready to fly another practice mission. With his voice raised an octave, Major Kirby addressed thirty glider pilot trainees as he stood in front of his jeep. "The practice mission today will involve half the men in this class. The purpose of this exercise will be to simulate a combat glider resupply mission in a landing zone behind enemy lines. In order to make this exercise as fair as possible, we'll fly the same practice mission bright and early on Monday morning, with the pilots of Chalks 1 through 15 switching places with the pilots who fly Chalks 16 to 30. Once you complete these training flights, the remaining thirty pilots in your class will get a chance to do the same."

After pausing briefly when a fuel truck drove by and left the flight line, the Major continued and said, "Remember, gentlemen, if this was a real combat mission the troops on the ground would be in desperate need of the ammunition, fuel, rations and medical supplies that you will be delivering into the designated landing zone. I also want you to remember that if flying a glider in combat was easy, every pilot in the Army would be a glider pilot." Immediately after hearing some of the men laugh at his last remark, Major Kirby added, "The assembly area is on the Northeast corner of the LZ. You all know what to expect, so let's look sharp out there." After pausing long enough to check his watch, the Major looked at the thirty glider pilot candidates and said, "Pilots, man your planes."

As the group of prospective glider pilots began to disperse, Lt. John Jay Keating offered Ivan Larson a stick of gum and said, "Today's your lucky day, Danny. We've got the lead ship for round one, which means we fly the tail end Charlie position on Monday morning."

While Ivan walked with his flight instructor to the glider known as Chalk 1, he remarked, "Chalk 1 it is," as he strained his head to see what position Shorty drew.

As far as Ivan was concerned, the scene looked a lot like a Friday night dance, as the instructors approached their students and began walking to their gliders in pairs. The last thing Ivan wanted to see was Major Kirby sitting in the passenger seat of his jeep as he called out, "O'Malley, you're with me in Chalk 30." Of all the flight instructors, Major Kirby was the strictest, even if he had a reputation for being very fair. Still, more glider pilot trainees washed out because of Major Kirby than any other instructor.

While Ivan walked to the far end of the flight line, the entire contingent of glider pilot trainees and their instructors watched as the Major's driver raced down the taxiway in the opposite direction with a sad faced Gus O'Malley sitting behind the man known as Killer Kirby.

After seeing the expression of concern on Danny Gannon's face, Lt. Keating remarked, "Don't worry about Gus, the Major is strict but fair."

While the fugitive who adopted the identity of Danny Gannon conducted a thorough pre-flight check of his glider, he did his best to sound like a team player when he agreed with Lt. Keating. "You're right, Lieutenant. Major Kirby is strict, but fair."

After completing his pre-flight check, Ivan entered Chalk 1 and inspected the ballast that was lashed down in the cargo compartment behind the cockpit. This was done to make sure that the simulated load of cargo was properly secured to the plywood floor. After all, the last thing a glider pilot wanted to have happen, was to make a perfect landing and get killed because the cargo that he was carrying broke lose and smashed into the cockpit when his glider came to a sudden stop.

After securing the door and checking the emergency exits, Ivan buckled himself into the pilot's seat before he checked the rudder pedals and controls. Once the ground crewman attached the tow line and Ivan was satisfied that the fitting was securely fastened, he released the parking brake and looked to the left and right to make sure that the ailerons were in the neutral position. After making sure that he completed the Army Air Forces Form No. 1G and 1AG Ivan was ready to get airborne.

In addition to the fact that he personally liked Danny Gannon, Lt. John Jay Keating was an experienced flight instructor who knew when he was assigned to train someone who was a natural born flier. Because this was the case, Lt. Keating did not want Danny Gannon's performance to be negatively affected because he was worried about his cousin.

With little time to spare before takeoff, Lt. Keating turned to his left and said, "I hate to preach, Danny, but I want you to put everything out of your mind and make believe that this is the real Mc Coy. Remember, you're the lead ship in a serial of thirty gliders that have to deliver supplies that are badly needed by U.S. Army troops who are holding a critical position behind enemy lines. As you'll see once we reach the LZ, there will be no room for error on this mission, especially for the gliders that make up the last half of this serial. If you and the other pilots in this class think this is a difficult training mission, wait until you have to fly training missions with fifty or a hundred gliders during the day and at night. As a result, I suggest you remain focused because nothing else matters right now."

Even though Ivan knew his instructor was referring to his concern for his cousin Gus O'Malley, this was the time to be selfish and concentrate on flying the best mission possible. In order to let Lt. Keating know that he appreciated the good advice, Ivan did his best to sound as convincing as possible when he said, "I understand."

Once U.S. combat glider operations began to evolve, more and more gliders had telephone lines installed to facilitate communications between the tow plane pilot and the glider crew. After picking up the intercom phone, Ivan grinned when he heard Lt. Billy Davis remark, "Hey, Danny, I forgot how to start this thing? Any suggestions?"

As soon as Ivan Larson aka Danny Gannon turned to his right and repeated what Lt. Davis just said, Lt. Keating shook his head and smiled over the antics of Billy Davis. While Lt. Keating made a notation on his clip board, he spoke up and said, "Answer that nut so we can get this show on the road."

Even though they only recently met, Billy Davis was quickly becoming Ivan's closest army buddy next to Shorty Mc Ghee. Ivan Larson aka Danny Gannon proved that he also had a good sense of humor when he spoke into the intercom phone and said, "You're asking me? I'm flying a plane with no engine."

Immediately after Billy Davis was heard laughing, the C47 pilot flying the lead ship in the formation called out, "Clear!" just before the line went dead and the number one engine on his tow plane came to life. By the time the second engine on Billy's C47 turned over, other C47s on the flight line began to rumble to life and prepared to take off.

During this training mission, the C47 at the end of the formation was being flown by Lieutenant Lenny Tucker and his co pilot Lt. Carl Guliver. Lt. Tucker was a native of Richmond, Virginia who was raised in a very strict home where he grew up calling his father by his official title rather than refer to him as father, dad or pop. The fact that his family heritage included a number of decorated Confederate Army officers and a father who served in World War I, helped cement the Tucker family's standing in local politics for some time to come.

As far as his father was concerned, the chance to serve in World War II enabled his only son to prove his worth as a man and establish a solid reputation, that would translate to votes for any member of the Tucker family who ran of office. Judge Tucker also saw the build up to support the war effort, as a tremendous economic boom for the southern states, which included Virginia.

With his entire future already mapped out by his overbearing father, Lenny Tucker cut classes at the University of Virginia on December 7, 1941 to enlist in the United States Army. Like other men from his generation, Lenny Tucker had high hopes of serving as a fighter pilot or bomber pilot. Unfortunately, the Army had other plans for the newly commissioned Second Lieutenant Leonard Tucker and sent him to learn how to fly a twin engine C47 transport plane. Lt. Tucker felt even more depressed when his father became furious and called the Yankee Army every name in the book, for denying his son the right to fly a more glamorous fighter plane or a front page stealing four engine bomber like the B17.

While feeling completely disgraced and worthless, it took some doing for Lt. Tucker to try and convince his father that he would do his best to seek glory and distinguish himself, while flying a lumbering transport plane in combat. Hearing his disappointed father remark, "But it doesn't even have guns, son," was enough to make the young man who could never seem to make his father happy consider committing suicide. Instead, Lt. Tucker braced himself for a long winded dissertation about how he should conduct his affairs and do everything possible to make sure that he got into the thick of it as soon as possible. Then, in a completely selfish moment, his overbearing father reminded him that this was an election year and that it would help his success at the poles if he had a war hero for a son.

Since Lenny Tucker was perpetually in a bad mood, he had no close friends in the U.S. Army. The young man who was called "Grumpy and The Judge's Son" behind his back also had no use for Billy Davis. This feud existed because Lt. Davis was the most popular pilot in his squadron and a Yankee to boot. The fact that Billy Davis was also very friendly with enlisted men and glider pilots, also infuriated the stuck up pilot from Virginia who believed that commissioned officers were a higher class of people.

While Lt. Tucker's thoughts drifted away from his duties, Lt. Carl Guliver nudged him on the right arm to remind him that it was time to go. As soon as the engine run up and take off check list was completed, Lt. Tucker and his crew were ready to get airborne. After applying just enough power to inch his C47 forward, Lt. Tucker felt the distinctive tug on the tow rope that signaled that he was beginning to pull Chalk 30 behind his aircraft.

While Lenny Tucker applied enough power to move his C47 into position behind Chalk 29, he did his best to act like a regular guy when he spoke up and said, "Just think, Carl, in a few weeks we'll be leaving this God forsaken outpost and be on our way to England."

Carl Guliver was just as happy to be getting shipped to the ETO, even if it meant that he had to fly combat missions with a stuffed shirt who had the personality of a first class redneck prick. Because he knew how much Lt. Tucker disliked Lt. Davis, a man he preferred to fly with, Lt. Guliver couldn't resist and acted as if he and Lenny Tucker were asshole buddies when he said, "I know you have a lot on your mind with us going overseas to England and all, but I thought you should know that we're towing the absolute worst glider pilot in the class on today's mission."

The moment Lt. Tucker heard what his co pilot had to say, he fell for Carl Guliver's antics hook, line and sinker and remarked, "That's all we need. If this sad sack breaks the tow line Major Kirby better not blame us."

The only satisfaction that Carl Guliver had since he was assigned to fly with Lt. Tucker, was that he knew which buttons to push to provoke his pompous pilot in command and frustrate him to no end. While doing his best to act like a genuinely concerned friend, Lt. Guliver put on a straight face and said, "Rumor has it most of the instructors in this class want'a clip this guy's glider pilot wings. I also heard that the reason this guy hasn't been grounded is because Billy Davis asked the Major to give his buddy another chance."

The mere mention of Lt. Davis was enough to boil Lt. Tucker's blood. Carl knew that he did an excellent job of provoking Lt. Tucker when the exasperated aircraft commander limited his response to saying, "Unbelievable."

In order to add more wood to the fire, Carl continued and said, "Based on what I heard, Billy Davis became friends with this guy because they grew up across the river from each other back east in New York and New Jersey." Then, after pausing long enough to slip a stick of spearmint chewing gun into his mouth, Lt. Guliver added, "I also heard that if this guy screws up today even Billy Davis won't be able to save his buddy from being reassigned."

After hearing what Carl had to say, Lt. Tucker kept his right hand on the throttles as he remarked, "Major Kirby has taken more pilots out of the sky than the damn enemy. Whoever this want'a be glider jockey is, he better fly a perfect mission or he'll be packing a rifle in the infantry."

After doing an excellent job of provoking his aircraft commander, Lt. Carl Guliver stretched his neck a bit as he looked down the flight line and said, "It looks like Lieutenant Davis is getting ready to go."

While Lt. Tucker waited for his turn to take off, he thought about the flight across the Atlantic that he and his crew would make in order to get to England. Even though Allied troops were fighting in a number of locations around the world, all anyone seemed to talk about was the impending invasion of mainland Europe. Despite the fact that the details of the invasion were top secret, it was common knowledge that the Allies were preparing to mount a cross channel invasion of mainland Europe. This meant that once Lt. Lenny Tucker and his crew left Lubbock, Texas they would be on their way to war.

As the Waco glider identified as Chalk 1 lumbered down the runway behind its tow plane, Ivan forgot about the fact that he was a fugitive and became one with his aircraft. While his tow plane continued down the runway, Ivan rotated his glider into the air when the indicated airspeed reached 75 Miles Per Hour. Once the C47 being flown by Lt. Billy Davis reached 120 MPH, the twin engine tow plane also went airborne and towed Chalk 1 to an altitude of 1500 feet. At that altitude, the tow plane and glider combination leveled off and proceeded to the designated landing zone.

As soon as the C47 in front of him began to pull the glider known as Chalk 29 into the air, Lt. Tucker became very businesslike as he applied power and motivated the twin engine work horse of the Army Air Forces to pull Chalk 30 down the runway. With the other tow planes and glider combinations already airborne, Lt. Tucker tried to ignore the fact that he was flying the tail end Charlie position, with the worst glider pilot in the class attached to his plane by a 350 foot nylon rope.

The moment the rope went slack, Lenny Tucker knew that Chalk 30 was airborne and flying about twenty feet behind and above his plane. When the time was right, Lt. Tucker rotated his C47 into the air and climbed to the prescribed altitude with Chalk 30 in tow. After leveling off and adjusting the trim on his aircraft, Lenny Tucker waited for Carl Guliver to finish with his radio work before he remarked, "I can tell this guy can't fly for shit by the way we're dragging him through the damn sky."

Carl Guliver felt very proud of himself for provoking his prima donna for an aircraft commander. Just as he expected, Lt. Tucker continued to express his frustrations and remarked in a sarcastic tone, "Who is this guy anyway?"

As Lt. Guliver continued to play Lt. Tucker like a fiddle, he responded and said, "I don't know his name, but if you really want'a piss him off all you have to do is call him Shorty Number 3. He got that nickname when Billy Davis started calling the three shortest pilots in this class Shorty Number 1, Shorty Number 2 and Shorty Number 3. I also heard this guy hates being called Skinny, a nickname he got because he's so scared of flunking out and being grounded he stopped eating. You'll also be happy to hear that as close as Major Kirby is to Billy Davis, I heard the Major actually told Lieutenant Davis to tone it down as far as his joking around is concerned. According to Billy's co pilot, this unofficial counseling session took place when Lieutenant Davis started giving nicknames to other pilots in the class, including a few that weren't all that flattering."

While Lt. Lenny Tucker flew his aircraft with perfection, he looked to his right and remarked, "You'll have to point this character out to me so I can wish him well when Killer Kirby sends him packing without his glider pilot wings."

"I'll be happy to do so," said Lt. Guliver as he offered Lt. Tucker a piece of gum and quickly added, "Providing of course that this guy doesn't kill himself and Major Kirby when he tries to land in an LZ that's jam packed with twenty nine other gliders."

Once the C47 flying the lead position reached the release point, Lt. Davis instructed his crew chief to signal Chalk 1 with the green light. The moment Ivan spotted the green flashing beacon, he pulled down on the tow line release mechanism that cut the nylon rope and allowed him to make his decent into the LZ.

Deep down inside Ivan was screaming at the top of his lungs. Once Ivan completed Advanced Glider Training and he attended ground combat and tactical training courses that were specifically geared for glider pilots, he would be fully certified to fly combat missions in a glider. In the meantime, he had a training mission to fly.

Flying an aircraft that was not equipped with an engine made glider pilots know what it was like to be an angel, even though in Ivan's case he was an angel with a dirty face. With nowhere else to go but down, it took a tremendous amount of skill to keep the right amount of air flowing over the wings, as a glider pilot steered his glider toward a suitable landing area. The goal was to descend quickly but safely and land in an open space without killing yourself or any of your passengers. Naturally, this maneuver was even more dangerous when it was performed in actual combat.

While Ivan made his approach over the field, he executed a textbook S turn to bleed off air speed, before he leveled off at just the right time to enable him to land at the farthest end of the LZ. Doing so made it possible for the other twenty-nine pilots to have an ample amount of room to land in a confined area.

While the Waco glider identified as Chalk 1 slid to a stop, the sound of dirt, rocks and scrub brush scrapping along the undercarriage was music to Ivan's ears. Then, in a hearty hi ho silver, Ivan's glider came to a complete stop at the far end of the Landing Zone.

After congratulating his student for a job well done, Lt. Keating quickly unbuckled his seat belt and said, "Come on, let's bail out before we get nailed in the ass." By the time Ivan and his flight instructor exited their aircraft, Chalk 2 was already sliding to a stop, while Chalk 3 was making its descent and Chalk 4 was being released over the field. One after another, the entire flight of CG-4As came in for a landing and began to fill up the available open ground in the confines of the designated landing zone.

As soon as the other pilots began to reach the assembly area, Ivan and his flight instructor watched as the C47 known as Old Virginia towed Chalk 30 to the release point. While Ivan used his Ronson lighter to light his instructor's cigarette then his own, Lt. Keating looked up and said, "Here comes Gus."

Immediately after Ivan looked up into the sky and said, "Come on, Gus, you can do it," he turned to his flight instructor and said, "Gus is worried the CO's gonna ground him."

When Lt. Keating asked, "Is that why Gus stopped eating?" Ivan remarked, "He actually stopped eating before we got here. I'm surprised Gus hasn't passed out since all he's been living on is coffee and cigarettes."

After taking a drag on his cigarette, Lieutenant Keating spoke in a matter of fact tone of voice and said, "Tell me, Danny. Do you think your cousin can cut it as a glider pilot?"

As difficult as it was for him to do, Ivan had to admit that Shorty was having his fair share of difficulties operating a glider under stressful conditions. While trying his best not to sound like he was sandbagging his cousin behind his back, Ivan defended Shorty as best as he could when he said. "Getting through flight school and basic glider training was a piece of cake for Gus compared to this school. He's just worried about injuring or killing other glider pilots or troops on the ground, if he screws up when he lands in an LZ that's filled with other gliders."

Lt. Keating agreed with Ivan's assessment and added, "Unfortunately, glider pilots can't count on the luxury of landing in an empty cow pasture or on a long runway, especially in combat."

As hard core as it sounded, the U.S. Army was not interested in the reasons why people failed to successfully complete a required training program. All the Army wanted to know was that you were able to meet their standards and safely operate a glider under combat conditions. Anyone who passed the prescribed training received their wings. If you failed, the Army assigned you to other duties. After all, the Army had a war to win and no time to coddle those who failed the required training.

Nice guy or not, Lt. Keating was responsible to train glider pilots to serve in Troop Carrier Command combat operations. Teaching men to make difficult decisions was just as important, as teaching them the technical aspects of how to fly a glider during the day and at night under demanding conditions. As a result, Lt. Keating was not about to let a perfect opportunity to make an important point go by the way side.

After changing his tone and sounding more like a typical flight instructor, Lt. Keating pulled no punches when he addressed Danny Gannon and said, "You know the drill, Danny. Suppose this was a real combat mission and suppose we were short on pilots and Gus had to fly a mission by himself? I also ask you to consider how well Gus would perform, if this mission involved hundreds of gliders instead of thirty? Worse yet, suppose this was a night mission? Would you sit in the back of a glider with confidence, while Gus handled the controls with no one up front who was qualified to help him out?"

As much as Ivan hated to admit it, the Lieutenant was right. After shaking his head from left to right Ivan responded in a solemn tone of voice. "No, I couldn't do that. But I would let Gus fly as my co pilot. There's also a chance that Gus will do a lot better once he gets more flight time. After all, even if he remains the worst pilot in this class, every class has someone who graduates dead last."

While Ivan was doing his best to defend his friend, Shorty had his hands full as he gripped the controls with sweaty palms and scanned the crowed landing zone for a place to land Chalk 30. Having Major Kirby sitting silently in the co pilot's seat proved to be almost as nerve racking, as trying to find a place to land in landing zone that was already filled with twenty nine other gliders.

As Shorty did his best to pay attention to the mission at hand, the last thing he needed to hear was Major Kirby speak up and say, "Make believe I'm not here, O'Malley and I promise I won't take the controls unless you try and kill me." After hearing the Major's comment, Shorty was torn between wanting to quit on the spot and show Killer Kirby that he could pull this off.

So far, Shorty survived the take off and the flight to the LZ without screwing up. All he had to do to get Killer Kirby off his back was land Chalk 30 in one piece. While Shorty took a quick look down at the crowded LZ, he felt as if the deck was stacked against him. As far as Shorty was concerned, even an experienced glider pilot like the Major would have a tough time landing a glider in a designated location that was already occupied by twenty nine other GC4As.

Even though Shorty was not completely comfortable landing a GC-4A Waco glider in a crowded landing zone, he had no choice but to pass Advanced Glider Training if he hoped to stay close to his "cousin" Danny Gannon. On an exceptionally bad day, Shorty regretted not staying in the infantry. Had Shorty stayed in the infantry, he would either be dead, wounded, captured or fighting on some God forsaken battlefield that was far away from the clutches of the New York City Police, the FBI, the military police, Army CID and Killer Kirby.

With over the bulk of the instructors ready to clip his glider wings, Shorty knew that he was already teetering on the brink of being dropped from the program. This meant that Shorty had a lot riding on the performance that he put on for Major Kirby.

Every pilot who went through glider training became familiar with the term "the point of no return." This term applied to the moment when you cut lose from your tow plane, so you could glide an aircraft that had no engine to the ground for the purposes of making a safe landing. Knowing what was about to happen was enough to churn Shorty's stomach, especially since he hadn't eaten anything close to a decent meal since he began flight training, especially advanced glider training.

As soon as Shorty saw the flashing green light, he reached up and pulled down on the release mechanism that cut the tow rope that connected Chalk 30 to his tow plane. Despite the gung ho attitude that Shorty had when he signed up for glider training, he quickly learned to dislike the odds of surviving a combat glider mission. Shorty was twice as concerned about flying a long mission over water and three times as worried about flying a night mission.

As far as Gus O'Malley was concerned, there were simply too many ways for a glider pilot to get himself and others killed for this duty to be sought after by anyone of sound mind. At least when you were flying a small single engine aircraft, you were never expected to land in an open field that was filled with other aircraft. Only if your engine failed would you have to act like a glider pilot and try to make a dead stick emergency landing.

The moment Major Kirby broke his rule of silence and said, "Remember, O'Malley, the ground is coming up fast," Shorty resisted the urge to panic when he observed a crowd of glider pilot trainees and instructors watching his every move from the collection point on the northeast side of the LZ. When the Major observed Gus O'Malley looking at the crowd below, he barked, "Forget about them and fly the damn mission!"

The moment Major Kirby observed Gus O'Malley misjudge the approach into the LZ and he called out, "I got it," the Major backed off when Shorty responded in an unusually confident tone of voice and said, "Please, Sir, let me do it."

The second the Major let go of the controls, Shorty did his best to salvage an otherwise bad situation as he made his decent. While doing a good job of avoiding Chalk 29 and 27, Shorty aimed for the only patch of open space that was left in the LZ. Unfortunately, it was a tight fit and Shorty flared his glider a tad too soon. Doing so caused Chalk 30 to bounce off the top of Chalk 26 and go airborne again.

When Ivan saw what was happening, he cringed and said, "Oh no," just as several pilots began wagering on the outcome. As soon as Chalk 30 slammed down on the ground, the glider nosed over, crashed upside down and landed on top of the tail section of Chalk 24. After running to the crash site, Ivan and Lt. Keating pulled Shorty from the damaged glider, while other instructors and members of the training class rescued Major Kirby from the wreckage.

Even though Shorty would suffer from a number of aches and pains after surviving such a hard landing, Major Kirby sustained the most serious injury when he lost his footing and badly sprained his right ankle while he was being pulled from the damaged glider. The fact that Major Kirby originally sprained the same ankle while serving in the Sicily Campaign made a bad situation worse. In addition to his hurt pride, Gus O'Malley walked away from the crash with a sore back and neck.

After leaning on Lt. Keating for support, Major Kirby sized up the damage to Chalk 30 and the two other GC-4A's that Gus O'Malley crashed into while executing his version of a glider landing. As the crowd of pilots and instructors remained quiet, Major Kirby removed the cigar from the corner of his mouth as he turned to Gus O'Malley and asked if he was all right.

Even though Shorty would hurt a lot more in 24 hours, he stood tall and told the Major that he was OK. While Major Kirby continued looking at the pilot he knew as Gus O'Malley, he spoke in a raised tone of voice when he said, "Don't bullshit me, O'Malley. I asked how you feel and I expect the truth."

Without sugar coating his response, Shorty rubbed his neck as he responded to the Major's question and said, "I'm a little sore, Sir, but I'll be OK." Then, after pausing for a split second, Shorty added, "I'm sorry about your ankle, Sir."

As far as Shorty and his fellow classmates were concerned, the medical jeep could not have arrived at a better time. While Corporal "Doc" Mel Keller and Lt. Keating helped Major Kirby over to the nearby jeep, Ivan offered his friend a stick of gum and said, "The good news is, you didn't kill Major Kirby. The bad news is, you're still alive."

Once the Major was helped into the front passenger seat of the jeep, he called out, "O'Malley, front and center!" All eyes were on Gus, as he slipped the piece of gum into his pocket, while he walked over to the jeep to face his Commanding Officer.

As Doc Keller sat in the driver's seat of the jeep, Shorty stood by the passenger side and said, "O'Malley reporting, Sir."

While doing his best to ignore the pounding pain of his badly sprained ankle, Major Kirby removed the cigar from the corner of his mouth and said, "I know you can fly O'Malley or you wouldn't be here. The question is, can you be counted on to fly a glider into a landing zone that is jammed packed with other gliders. I also feel obligated to tell you, that if you think my presence in the cockpit makes you uncomfortable, just wait until you fly your first combat mission during the day or at night while you're being shot at."

After pausing to reposition his leg, the Major continued and said, "Let me give it to you straight, O'Malley. I'm still not sure if you can cut it in the glider program but I'm willing to give you one more chance to prove me wrong. Instead of flying the lead ship on the practice mission that's scheduled for Monday morning, you'll fly the tail end Charlie position again with Lt. Keating. That will give you the weekend to recuperate and think about what you need to do to remain in the glider program."

After pausing for a split second to remove a piece of tobacco from the tip of his tongue, Major Kirby looked at the badly rattled glider pilot trainee and said, "You look like shit, O'Malley. I want you to get yourself checked out by the Flight Surgeon and that's an order. I also heard you're not eating. To rectify this situation and put an end to you being called Skinny I expect to see you in the chow hall with a full tray of food, comprende?"

While the fugitive masquerading as Gus O'Malley stood frozen at attention, he could feel his heart pounding through his perspiration soaked uniform as he responded and said, "Yes, Sir."

As soon as Shorty presented the Major with a snappy salute, Major Kirby returned the salute while Doc Keller started the engine and said, "Excuse me, Sir, but we need to take care of your ankle."

The moment the Major said, "OK, Doc," Doc Keller put the jeep in gear and drove away. Within a matter of seconds, Gus O'Malley was surrounded by his fellow class mates who anxiously wanted to know what Killer Kirby had to say.

Even Ivan chimed in and said, "Come on, Gus. Tell us what the Major said. Are you in or out?"

Even though Shorty was calmer now than he was before, he was still a little shook up from the experience of crash landing a glider in such a violent fashion. As Shorty pulled a pack of cigarettes from his flight suit pocket, he looked at his class mates and said, "Yea, I'm still in but if I don't shape up I'll be shipping out. You boys can also stop calling me Skinny 'cause the Major just ordered me to fill my mess tray with a full load of food and start eating again." While the entire class of glider pilots began clapping, whistling and cheering, a good number of their stoic looking instructors stood off to the side and seemed troubled by the news.

Once the FBI confirmed that Gunther Kessler closed his business in Bayonne, the decision was made to start looking for Kessler in other cities. In an effort to locate Mueller and his associates, the FBI also checked Department of Motor Vehicle records in New Jersey. Unfortunately, New Jersey DMV records did not produce the desired results when FBI Agents determined that Mueller and other subjects of their investigation recently moved.

CHAPTER 25

THE RAILROAD STATION

As soon as the U.S. Army truck drove up to the railroad station, the military policeman sitting in the back with the German Prisoners of War jumped out before the GMC deuce and a half came to a complete stop. After shouldering his 12 gauge Winchester pump shotgun, the tallest MP in this detail stepped aside as he ordered the POWs to exit the U.S. Army vehicle. "OK, boys, Mach schnell. It's chow time."

When Al Parker spotted the German Prisoners of War line up next to the truck, he couldn't believe his eyes. Not since Al served in World War I had he seen a German soldier up close. In fact, just seeing these German POWs being transported under guard in a town down south made Al feel as if victory was on the horizon.

As Al turned to Major Beauregard, he snickered then remarked in a loud tone of voice, "They don't look like the master race to me."

While two military policemen escorted the German prisoners toward the railroad station, Jim Beauregard agreed with Al and said, "They sure don't."

With the exception of the Mexican guerrillas that Jim ran into during the Punitive Expedition in 1916, this was the first time that he had the chance to see an enemy soldier up close. Even though they were wearing baggy American fatigues with a large P painted in white on their backs, the Major tried to imagine these men in their flashy German uniforms adorned with all sorts of decorations. With many of them having blonde hair and blue eyes, the POWs fit the profile of a typical Nazi storm trooper.

What impressed Jim Beauregard the most was when he received a pair of casual salutes from the two MPs who were guarding the column, followed quickly by eight very smart salutes from the entire contingent of German POWs. Once Major Beauregard returned the military courtesy, Al remarked in a sarcastic tone, "I'll say one thing for these SOB's. They know how to salute."

As the column walked toward the train station, Jim caught the eye of an enemy officer and nodded his head. Even though no words were spoken, a great deal was said. Rather than let an opportunity like this pass by, the Major called out, "Excuse me, Sergeant." After halting the formation, the MP Sergeant walked over to Major Beauregard and Al Parker, while the other MP stood with his shotgun in hand in front of the column of German Prisoners of War.

After snapping to attention and offering a much smarter salute, the MP Sergeant said, "Yes, Sir, how can I help the Major?"

As Major Beauregard presented his CID credentials he said, "I'm curious, Sergeant. What are you doing with these prisoners in town?"

After glancing over to the column of prisoners, then looking back at Major Beauregard, the MP Sergeant responded in a matter of fact tone of voice and said, "This is where we feed German POWs, Sir. We have a contract with the restaurant in the train station to provide lunch for prisoners who work under guard on local farms."

After nodding his head, the Major asked the MP which branch of the service the Germans were from?"

Without hesitating, the Sergeant said, "All eight are U Boat men, Sir."

With his curiosity satisfied, the Major remarked in a friendly tone, "Thank you, Sergeant. Carry on."

Once again, the Sergeant saluted the Major then pivoted around like he was taught and returned to the column. As the MP Sergeant waved his hand and called out, "OK, Harry, move 'em out," the other MP motioned the POWs to proceed into the railroad station.

While the German POWs were being escorted into the railroad station, a bus pulled up to the curb where Al Parker and Major Beauregard were waiting for their ride. As soon as the twelve Negro soldiers spotted Major Beauregard, they started saluting in a chain reaction as they walked off the bus and followed the enemy prisoners into the train station. This time Al's remark was more tongue in cheek when he snickered and said, "At this rate you're gonna wear out that arm before this day is over."

After returning the last salute, Jim Beauregard turned to Al as the Negro soldiers filed by and remarked, "Remind me to wear civilian clothes the next time we go into the field."

Rather than take a taxi to their destination, Major Beauregard phoned ahead and arranged for the local CID Agent to pick them up, as soon as his meeting with the local police chief was concluded. While the Major checked his watch and remarked, "I wonder what's holding up our ride," a commotion was brewing inside the train station that spilled out into the street.

By the time the Major used his Zippo to light the end of a Lucky Strike cigarette, the entire contingent of Negro soldiers that just arrived by bus, were being pushed out of the terminal by a railroad policeman and a civilian who was wearing a white apron.

After almost being knocked off balance by the retreating group of Negro G.I.s, Major Beauregard called out, "What seems to be the problem here, officer?"

The moment the Negro staff Sergeant spotted Major Beauregard, he immediately turned to his men and called out, "Attention shun!"

Once again Major Beauregard was being shown a military courtesy that went along with his position as a commissioned officer in the United States Army. While the twelve Negro soldiers and their sergeant came to attention and waited to see what the white major would do about their predicament, the railroad cop pushed his way through the crowd to present himself to the one person who was in a position to offer some badly needed assistance.

"Am I glad to see you, Major," said the white patrolman as he walked up to Major Beauregard with the railroad station restaurant owner in tow. After repeating himself again and asking the railroad cop what the problem was, the uniformed railroad police officer began to respond when the man wearing the white apron interrupted the officer and said, "It's these colored boys, Major. They know they can't eat inside but they came over to the counter anyway."

After hearing Mr. Johnson's response, Major Beauregard turned to the Negro staff sergeant and said, "What's your side of the story, Sergeant?"

Al Parker couldn't have been more proud of another Negro when Staff Sergeant Theodore Jefferson III identified himself and responded to the Major's question. "Sir," all we wanted was to get something to eat before we got on our train. The only reason we went up to the counter was because it was empty, Sir. We weren't trying to cause trouble, Sir. Once we paid for our food, we intended to eat in the alley behind the station while we waited for our train."

After nodding his head Major Beauregard said, "I see."

A split second later, one of the Negro privates called out from the back of the formation and said, "Hey, Sarge, tell the Major about them Kraut prisoners."

After hearing one of the Negro G.I.s use the slang word that was synonymous for the word German, Major Beauregard turned to the Staff Sergeant Jefferson and said, "What about the German POWs, Sergeant?"

Almost as if he was too embarrassed to speak, Sergeant Jefferson lowered his head for a second before he looked up and said, "As soon as we entered the station, Sir, we spotted some German POWs and two of our MPs sitting at tables near the counter. When we saw the waitress taking their order, we figured it wouldn't be a problem if we ordered some food at the empty counter. After all, Sir, we're American soldiers. Unfortunately, we figured wrong. They'll serve the enemy, but they won't serve us, Major."

While Major Beauregard ignored the remarks that were being muttered in the ranks by some of the more disgruntled colored soldiers, the Negro sergeant turned to his men and called out, "Quiet in the ranks. Show this officer respect or I'll have your stripes!" Immediately, the dozen Negro troops snapped to attention again. After appreciating the display of proper protocol, especially under such demanding circumstances, Jim Beauregard remembered the comments that he made to his wife Bea about the racial problems that faced our nation.

While speaking in a very official tone of voice, Major Beauregard spoke directly to Mr. Johnson and said, "If the enemy can eat in your restaurant why can't uniformed soldiers of the United States Army order food at your counter, especially if the counter is empty?"

Under the circumstances, the restaurant owner could not believe that a U.S. Army Major with a southern accent was questioning the way that things operated down south. Without hesitating, the railroad station restaurant owner who was classified as 4-F or unfit to serve in the armed forces, responded in a matter of fact tone of voice and said, "You know the way it is, Major. The law says I don't have to feed colored folks at the white counter. If they want'a buy food from my restaurant, they have to go 'round back and I got a sign posted right out front that says so."

Even though Major Beauregard was very familiar with the regulations involving segregation in the south, this was the first time in his life that he was personally involved in an obvious act of discrimination involving uniformed Negro troops. Southerner or not, Jim Beauregard found it hard to believe that such discrimination was still taking place in the United States.

Just like Jim told his wife, he believed that it was twice as hypocritical for the world's greatest democracy to enforce its own segregation laws with a vengeance, while trying to rid the world of the Axis nations that were determined to enslave the planet through a racist and hateful agenda. The fact that enemy prisoners of war could be treated with such respect and courtesy and our own troops were refused a meal and a cup of coffee at the same counter was simply unforgivable. Even though the law permitted segregation, Jim Beauregard saw this act of discrimination as the straw that broke the camel's back as far as he was concerned.

While Jim pondered what to do, he remembered the time his grandfather retaliated against Mr. Smith and the other Negro military veterans who worked his land because they had the audacity to educate his grandson about the heroism displayed by Negro soldiers in combat. Back then Jim was powerless to affect change but today was different. Even though Jim had no authority to eliminate racism, segregation and discrimination from American society, he did have the ability to speak up for the Negro soldiers who wanted to purchase food in a restaurant that had no problem feeding enemy prisoners of war.

While Major Beauregard put his arm around Mr. Johnson, he gently ushered the railroad station restaurant owner away from the others for a private chat. Al Parker was especially sorry that he wasn't close enough to hear what was being said, when he saw the Major and the restaurant owner going back and forth in what appeared to be a spirited discussion.

After the Major looked around to make sure that no one could hear him, he leaned closer to Mr. Johnson and said, "You listen to me and do exactly what I say or I'll have some friends of mine in the War Department lose your contract to feed German POWs and it won't be found until long after this war is over."

After hearing the restaurant owner remark, "You can't threaten me, Major. The law's on my side," Jim squeezed the little man's shoulder while he said, "You listen to you little prick. I guarantee that the U.S. Army will inspect your kitchen and will find a dozen reasons why you should lose your contract. If you want'a put me to the test be my guest. If you want this matter to come to a peaceful resolution for all parties involved you're gonna serve me, while the Negro Sergeant stands nearby and accepts the food for his men. This way, all you're doing is handing me food and I'm paying you. Is that clear?"

Even though the white restaurant owner agreed to the Major's terms, he wanted to know why an Army officer with a southern accent was so interested in helping a group of colored soldiers. After making the mistake of asking the Major to explain his actions, Jim Beauregard leaned closer to the little man and sneered as he remarked in a disgusted tone of voice and said, "Get outta here before I forget that I'm an officer and a gentleman."

As the pissed off restaurant owner walked back into the train station, Major Beauregard returned to the group of Negro troops and said, "Mister Johnson has agreed to a compromise and allow me to act an intermediary and pass your food to you at the counter. As a smile crossed the faces of every man present, including Al Parker, the Major turned to the Negro Staff Sergeant and said, "Sergeant Jefferson, bring me your order as soon as you have it ready. I'll be inside having a cup of coffee, while I keep an eye on Mr. Johnson." The Major then turned to the stunned railroad policeman and said, "Officer, I would appreciate it if you would escort Sergeant Jefferson inside the station so he can bring me his order. These men need to be fed before their train leaves the station."

Even though the railroad cop wasn't quite sure if he should be helping an Army Major circumvent the law, he nodded his head in agreement and said, "OK, Major."

The Major then turned to Al Parker and said, "Do me a favor, Al and keep and eye out for that CID Agent. I'll be back in a few minutes."

As Al nodded his head and said, "Sure thing, Major," Jim Beauregard headed into the train station.

Once he arrived at the counter, Major Beauregard ordered a cup of coffee for himself and a cup for the railroad police detective who came over to find out what the commotion was all about. Less than a minute later, the Negro Army Sergeant entered the train station with a railroad police escort and handed the Major a lunch order and a ten dollar bill.

As the Major read the order to Mr. Johnson's waitress, he appreciated the fact that the Negro troops limited their request to 12 bottles of soda pop and 12 sandwiches. While a curious crowd of onlookers began to notice something strange happening at the food counter, Major Beauregard sipped coffee with a railroad police detective, while the Negro Sergeant stood nearby with the uniformed railroad cop. As soon as the order was ready, a box containing the requested items was delivered to the Negro Sergeant by Major Beauregard, just as the German Prisoners of War finished their meal and were escorted back to the Army truck by the two military policemen.

While the Negro Staff Sergeant and the Major watched the German POWs march by, they knew the enemy soldiers observed the entire event, including how a white officer came to the rescue and made sure the colored American troops were fed from the white counter, even if they had to stand off to the side to pick up their food. This spectacle proved to the Germans that even though

America wasn't perfect, it was a nation that would never surrender to the ways of the Nazis.

When the Negro Sergeant spotted the ten dollar bill inside the box, Major Beauregard remarked, "Lunch is on me, Sergeant." Since this was a moment worth remembering, Sergeant Jefferson couldn't resist and politely asked the Major what his name was. After the Major identified himself, Sergeant Jefferson placed the box of food down on the counter and saluted the officer from Army CID. As soon as the Major returned the salute, Sergeant Jefferson picked up the box of food under the watchful eyes of a very pissed off Mr. Johnson. After thanking the Major again, Staff Sergeant Jefferson was escorted out of the station by the uniformed railroad cop.

By this time a small crowd had noticed what the white Major did. While some folks were shocked, others smiled in approval, as Major Beauregard left the station and found all twelve Negro soldiers lined up and saluting him as he walked by. After returning the salute and seeing the Army sedan pull up to the curb, Major Beauregard nodded his head and said, "Carry on, men," as he joined Al Parker and CID Agent Alan Ellis by the Army sedan.

After Agent Ellis introduced himself and apologized to the Major for being late, Al and Major Beauregard watched the contingent of Negro soldiers walk into a nearby alley to enjoy their food.

As soon as Al remarked, "You did the best you could for those boys, Sir. If it wasn't for you this situation might'a got out'a control," Jim Beauregard opened the door to the Army sedan and remarked, "Thanks, Al, but my best wasn't good enough."

While FBI Agents out west continued to visit diners, motels and tourist courts to determine if anyone remembered John Miller, Rudy Mueller or any their associates, another team of agents used a small aircraft to fly over the locations that were circled on the map that was found in Miller's warehouse. Back in New Jersey, another team of FBI Agents along with Willie Gunderson checked every bakery from Perth Amboy to Ft. Lee. Willie also worked with an FBI artist to prepare composite sketches of Mueller and his associates. These sketches were used to augment the photographs that were recovered from Miller's warehouse.

CHAPTER 26

CHALK 14

As a kid growing up in Queens, New York, Francis Shorty Mc Ghee was a loner who was a favorite target of the bullies in his neighborhood. In fact, his strong faith was shredded when no amount of prayers made young Francis any taller or braver when he had to deal with his childhood enemies. As a result, all Francis Mc Ghee ever thought about was being able to get back at the people who picked on him about his size. Even his drunken stepfather found him easy prey, when the mood struck the abusive Irishman to take his miserable life out on his youngest stepson.

Things seemed to change for Francis Shorty Mc Ghee the day he met Terry Kelly. Terry was the first big kid who was kind to him. For that reason, Shorty looked up to Terry as a surrogate older brother. In fact, it was Terry who encouraged Shorty to develop his skills as a mechanic and made it possible for Francis to work in the garage that Mike Connely owned that was used to process stolen luxury cars for resale.

When the invitation was made to join their gang, Shorty agreed and never looked back. Then came the day when Shorty felt like a giant among men, when he effectively used a Thompson Submachine Gun to fend off a small army of police officers while Ivan killed a cop, wounded at least one other and robbed a bank in Brooklyn of thousands of dollars. While joining the Army wasn't Shorty's idea, he had to admit that if doing so kept him from being arrested, he was better off in an Army uniform than in standard prison garb.

Once Shorty had the opportunity to fly a small single engine aircraft and a glider, he preferred to fly a plane that was designed to remain airborne on its own power and land on a paved runway or in an open field. Even the idea of coming under fire in a small power plane, didn't bother Shorty as much as the thought of being shot at in a glider. Shorty felt this way because a pilot flying a plane with an engine could try and evade enemy fire, while a glider offered little or no protection from enemy ground fire.

While Francis Shorty Mc Ghee aka Gus O'Malley struggled to get through Advanced Glider Training, he proved that he was a very talented mechanic when he began spending his off duty hours helping Sergeant Lawrence Peavy repair and maintain everything from vehicles to Waco gliders. Major Kirby first became aware of Gus O'Mally's talents as a mechanic, when he was told by Billy Davis that it was his buddy Gus who repaired the Major's personal car. Even a hard ass like Killer Kirby had to admit, that anyone who could make his old jalopy roadworthy again might prove to be useful to the Army glider program. The Major was twice as impressed when he was told that Gus O'Malley insisted that Sergeant Peavy should be given the full credit for repairing the Commanding Officer's personal vehicle.

As dependent as Shorty was on Ivan Larson, the fugitive who went by the name of Gus O'Malley felt that the time had come for him to do something that would make up for his obvious lack of glider flying abilities. Shorty realized what he needed to do, when Sergeant Peavy told him about a devastating crash that took place the week before he arrived at Advanced Glider Training. This particular accident involved a Waco glider known as Chalk 14 that broke its tow line and crashed in a remote location.

According to Sergeant Peavy, the trip to the crash site included driving off road in very demanding terrain in an area east of the base near the small town of Dickens, Texas. Once they finally arrived at the crash site, it took time to extract and stabilize the two casualties. After spending the night at the crash site, the decision was made to transport the injured aviators to a nearby secondary road, so a pair of single engine Cessna L4s could be brought in at first light to take the injured airmen to the hospital.

While Sergeant Peavy continued to describe the difficulties of conducting a recovery effort at the crash site, Shorty began to visualize how they could recover the wrecked glider if they worked as a team. After describing his plan to the one man in the Army Air Forces who was just as much of a loner as he was, the most talented grease monkey at South Plains Army Air Field remarked, "That might work, Gus."

Knowing that the Army failed to recover the now famous Chalk 14 gave Shorty the incentive to succeed. After conferring with Sergeant Peavy, the two left the base well before first light in a pair of U.S. Army 4x4 vehicles that were equipped with trailers filled with spools of wire and rope, assorted pieces of lumber, boxes of nails, pulleys, an assortment of tools, lanterns, sandwiches, three thermoses full of hot coffee, four 5 gallon Jerry cans full of extra fuel, two 5 gallon Jerry cans of drinking water, six cotton canvass tent quarters, army blankets, a medical kit and two M1 Carbines for use against aggressive wildlife.

When O'Malley and Peavy failed to return by sunset, Major Kirby notified the duty officer to call him at his residence as soon as they returned. The duty officer was also instructed to launch an air search if O'Malley and Peavy failed to return by 0500 hrs on Sunday morning.

Private Lester Dumont was the first to spot Gus O'Malley and Sergeant Peavy returning to base at 2215 hours, while towing the remains of a wrecked glider behind a Dodge power wagon and a 1942 Willys Jeep. As soon as Private Dumont picked up the phone in the guard shack and called Major Kirby's residence, the 19 year old soldier said, "Sir, O'Malley and Peavy just returned." After a brief pause, the excited enlisted man continued speaking in a high pitched tone of voice. "It's no wonder they're getting back so late, Sir. They're towing a wrecked glider back to base at a snails pace. That's right, Sir, yes, Sir."

Shorty after the man on guard duty hung up the phone, a number of glider pilot trainees and instructors not on leave began to assemble by the administration building to see what all the commotion was about. By the time Shorty stopped the Dodge Power Wagon, a small group of Army personnel began to examine the salvaged remains of a badly damaged Waco glider that were secured to the truck and its trailer with bailing wire and rope.

As Shorty turned sideways and slid his exhausted and bruised body out of the cab of the Dodge truck, he ignored the laughter when one joker called out, "Hey, Gus, you're not supposed to practice without permission." While Shorty ignored the snide remark, he rubbed his sore back as he walked over to the slow moving jeep that was just entering the base.

The moment Private Peavy drove through the front gate, another glider pilot trainee examined the badly damaged fuselage more closely and called out, "Hey, fellers, these parts are from Chalk 14." Suddenly, the crowd went dead silent when everyone realized, that Gus O'Malley and Lawrence Peavy managed to accomplish an incredibly difficult recovery operation without help.

With his chest inflated with pride, Gus O'Malley limped over to the entrance of South Plains Army Air Field to join Sergeant Peavy as the senior enlisted man brought his Jeep to a stop. A moment later the crowd of onlookers came to attention when a military policeman driving a staff car delivered Major Kirby to a parking space in front of the administration building.

While Gus O'Malley and Sergeant Peavy stood in between the two vehicles, Major Kirby exited the Ford sedan with great care and used the aid of crutches to walk over to the remains of Chalk 14. After turning first to Sergeant Peavy then to Gus O'Malley, the senior instructor barked, "Explain yourself, Mister."

With all the confidence in the world, the fugitive masquerading as Gus O'Malley replied, "Sergeant Peavy and I recovered Chalk 14, Sir. We also repositioned the glider that landed on the outskirts of Lubbock so it won't interfere with local traffic."

As Captain Walter Beaver started to grin, the Major proved that he was in no mood for bullshit when he leaned closer to Gus O'Malley and said, "What I want to know O'Malley is who gave you permission to risk such an operation when you knew the United States Army was still evaluating the feasibility of recovering Chalk 14?"

This time Shorty answered the question with more of an explanation. "No one gave us permission, Sir. We did this on our own, but not until Sergeant Peavy and I studied the situation very carefully."

Even Major Kirby had to admit that he was impressed. After seeing the Major relax his stance, Shorty added, "I assure you, Sir, that at no time did I endanger myself or Sergeant Peavy when we recovered the badly damaged glider."

Even though he was wearing a fatigue cap, Shorty was unable to hide the fact that he had a blood stained bandage wrapped around his head. Major Kirby proved that he was a stickler for details when he pointed to the blood soaked bandage and said, "No one was in danger uh? What happened to your head?"

Under the circumstances the fugitive masquerading as Gus O'Malley knew he had no choice but to respond. As Shorty lifted his cap, he did his best to sound as truthful as possible when he responded. "It was an accident, Sir. A pulley collapsed when Sergeant Peavy and I were removing one of the damaged wings from Chalk 14. After Sergeant Peavy patched me up, we reinforced the pulley system that we rigged at the crash site and were able to remove the other parts of Chalk 14 without incident."

After Major Kirby examined the remains of the heavily damaged glider, he turned his attentions back to Gus O'Malley and his equally quiet assistant. While speaking in a much nicer tone of voice Major Kirby said, "I expect a full report on this after chow in the morning, O'Malley."

While Shorty enjoyed one of the proudest moments of his life, he stood at attention and saluted Major Kirby as he responded and said, "Yes, Sir."

Much to everyone's amazement, after Major Kirby returned the snappy salute, he leaned closer to Shorty and remarked, "Not bad for a guy who almost got me killed."

While Shorty remained at attention, he looked at his superior officer and said. "Thank you, Sir."

After turning his attention to the senior enlisted mechanic Major Kirby remarked, "Congratulations, Sergeant Peavy. I'll see that you'll get bumped up in rank for this."

Immediately after the otherwise timid Sergeant Peavy thanked his Commanding Officer, the Major spoke as he limped back to his staff car, "Captain, make sure these men are well fed and have Doc Keller take care of that cut on O'Malley's head before he hits the sack. I also want Chalk 14 moved into a hangar for a detailed inspection at 0800."

As Major Kirby eased himself into the back seat of the staff car and signaled the MP to drive him back to his quarters, Captain Beaver acknowledged the order with a crisp, "Yes, Sir."

The moment the Major left the area, the crowd of glider pilots, mechanics and instructors converged on Gus and Sergeant Peavy with a deluge of questions and congratulations. While Captain Beaver patted Shorty on the back, the Executive Officer said, "Come on, Gus. You and Peavy must be starving. I'll have the cook open up the mess hall for you. Then, we'll get your head looked at."

As Gus O'Malley and Sergeant Peavy devoured a large pot of reheated beef stew, a half a loaf of bread and a pot of hot coffee, all Shorty could think about was what Ivan would say when he returned from his weekend pass. By recovering Chalk 14 Gus O'Malley managed to dramatically improve his standing in the eyes of every pilot and instructor at the Advanced Glider School, including Major Kirby. As far as Shorty was concerned, if Ivan could gain a reputation as an outstanding glider pilot, then he could develop his own reputation in the glider program, one that was befitting his mechanical capabilities.

CHAPTER 27

PISSING UP A ROPE

With military policemen standing guard by the exit and several others milling around outside, Major Beauregard and Al Parker followed the Provost Marshal into the first barracks to be inspected on a sunny day in the spring of 1944. The moment they entered the building a drill sergeant turned to his platoon of Army Air Forces enlisted men and gave the command, "Attention!"

After stepping up to the front of the formation, the Provost Marshall stood at parade rest as he addressed the curious faces of the men they were about to inspect. "Gentlemen, my name is Major Fleming. I'm the Provost Marshal on this post. I know you have a lot to do today so I'll keep this brief. Army CID along with the New York City Police Department and the FBI are looking for two fugitives who enlisted in the United States Army to avoid capture. With me today is Major Beauregard from Army CID and Patrolman Parker from the New York City Police Department. You will stand at attention and answer any questions you are asked. Wanted posters of the two fugitives will be passed around. If any of you have seen either of these men we expect you to speak up."

As the Provost Marshal went to turn the inspection over to Major Beauregard, he turned back to face the formation of soldiers and said, "In case you're wondering, these men are wanted for several serious crimes including killing a police officer and wounding others during a bank robbery. The subject identified as Ivan Larson is also wanted for killing an accomplice during the hijacking of a truck load of tires."

As soon as the Provost Marshal turned to Major Beauregard, he nodded his head and said, "Major," before he stepped aside and turned the floor over to Major Beauregard and Patrolman Parker.

With an entire base to inspect Major Beauregard wasted no time in addressing the troops. "Patrolman Parker is an eyewitness who can identify one of the killers. You will remain at attention while Patrolman Parker gets a closer look at you."

Just like he did during numerous other inspections, Al walked up and down the two rows of men stopping on a few occasions to take a closer look at the soldiers who had the same basic build as Ivan Larson and matched the description of Francis Shorty Mc Ghee. After completing his inspection, Al walked up to the front of the room and shook his head from left to right.

Without saying anything to Al Parker, Major Beauregard stepped forward and addressed the group of young G.I.s again. "If at any time you become suspicious of anyone you meet or observe who meets the description of the two fugitives you are under standing orders to report your suspicions to the military police or CID. Thank you."

As Major Beauregard and Al Parker walked out of the barracks, the Provost Marshal turned to the drill instructor and said, "They're all yours, Sergeant."

While Major Beauregard, Al Parker and the Provost Marshal followed their military police escort into the next barracks to repeat the process again, Major Beauregard turned to Al Parker and Major Fleming and said, "Trying to find two fugitives in this man's Army is like pissing up a rope."

After inspecting troops in ten different barracks buildings, Major Beauregard and Al Parker were given a small room to use as an office before they left the post. While Al sat in front of the only desk in the room, the Major sat behind the large wooden desk that offered a window view of the base.

As soon as the Major removed a pack of cigarettes from his pant's pocket, he sounded tired and frustrated when he remarked, "It's days like today that make me wonder if we'll ever be able to find Larson and Mc Ghee."

"I know what you mean," responded Al, who quickly added, "But I don't know what else we can do, Sir. After all, we're looking for two wanted men in an awfully large Army."

After lighting a cigarette, Jim stood up and looked out the window while he continued lamenting about the case at hand. "I lost count of the number of Army camps and forts that we inspected since January. After all this work we still don't have one decent lead to follow. I hate to say it, Al, but Larson and Mc Ghee could be anywhere by now. They could even be dead."

Al Parker was just as tired and frustrated by the lack of success that they were experiencing after months of hard work. If there was one aspect of this investigation that improved Al's morale, it was knowing that he wasn't alone in his pursuit of the two fugitives. In addition to what Jim Beauregard and Lt. Colonel Richmond were doing, teams of investigators from various agencies were were still committed to this manhunt. Even Captain Pat Murphy Sr. was working overtime to assist the members of the CID Task Force when they operated in New York City, as well as when they pursued leads in other parts of the country.

After using a wooden match to light his cigar stub, Al removed the two wanted posters from his suit jacket pocket and remarked, "Maybe we ought'a do something about these wanted posters. After all, Army life can change the way a man looks."

Outside the base was bristling with activity. While men were training for war, Jim Beauregard was assigned to perform the duties of a police detective for the U.S. Army. As Jim continued to gaze out the window, something told him that Al Parker just said something profound, even if he wasn't quite sure what it was. After turning to face his partner, Jim spoke in an apologetic tone when he said, "I'm sorry, Al. What did you say?"

With his cigar sending a stream of smoke billowing up to the ceiling, Al repeated his remarks about the dated wanted posters that they were still using. When Al finished repeating what he just said, he added, "I also doubt Ivan Larson is telling his Army buddies that he's an orphan from Manhattan. We also have to assume that Shorty Mc Ghee adopted a new identity as well."

As soon as Jim forgot about the fact that the war was passing him by and he started thinking like an experienced police detective, he was able to focus on the case at hand. Al was right. They had to consider the fact that the wanted posters were no longer an accurate description of the two fugitives. Jim also agreed that they needed to figure out how Ivan Larson and Shorty Mc Ghee were blending in with their fellow soldiers, especially since CID described the two fugitives as an orphan and a loner who was no longer in contact with his family.

As soon as the Major sat back down, he gave Al his full attention when he responded and said, "You're right, Al. While Army life can't make a man taller or shorter, a clean shave, a haircut and the loss of a few pounds could easily make it possible for Ivan Larson and Shorty Mc Ghee to avoid coming under suspicion. We also have no idea what bullshit story they concocted to make themselves sound like red blooded Americans. Worst yet, we have no idea if anyone has helped them or is still helping them to maintain a new identity. The question is what do we do about it?"

While Jim stamped his cigarette out in a nearby ashtray, he looked at Al and said, "I'm not saying this to get rid of you, Al, but do you still think you can identify Ivan Larson after all these months, especially if he looks like a clean cut G.I.?"

Al Parker had been waiting for someone to ask him this question for some time. "If I ever get within a hundred feet of that son of a bitch he's gonna shit in his pants and make a run for it," responded Al.

While Al continued he leaned closer to the desk and tapped the ash from his cigar into the ashtray. "I don't care how much hair Ivan Larson cuts off his head, how close his shave is, or how much weight he loses or gains. I'll never forget what that killer looks like." The second that Al saw Jim Beauregard nod his head in agreement, he knew his position as the principle witness in this investigation was still rock solid.

As soon as Jim stood up and said, "What'a you say we pick up some chow in town and eat in the car down by beach before we head over to our next stop? I'm buying," Al knew that the Major was doing his best to deal with the fact that it was socially unacceptable for them to sit together in a restaurant.

Even though Al didn't like the way things were, he knew that Jim Beauregard was making a concerted effort to avoid having to deal with uncomfortable and embarrassing situations that he had no control over. Since their options were limited, Al did his best to make light of the situation by saying, "You know, Major, I get twice as hungry when it's your turn to buy."

While Al stood up and removed his suit jacket from the back of the chair, Jim walked around the desk and said, "Don't worry, Al. We'll get 'em. It's just a question of time."

As serious as this case was, Al proved that he still had a sense of humor when he responded and said, "I know we will, Major, but in the meantime we gotta eat."

By civilian standards the private meeting that Gus O'Malley was having with Major Kirby was considered a "father and son" chat. After telling Gus to take a seat, Major Kirby got right to the point. "I asked to see you, Mister O'Malley, because the time has come to discuss your future in the Army Air Forces. Before we go any further, I want you to know that I asked the other instructors to provide me with a written assessment of your glider flying abilities. Based on this assessment, the time has come for you to consider your options."

As soon as Major Kirby removed a cigar from a nearby ashtray, he committed himself for the record and said, "I said you could have one more chance to prove to me and the other instructors that you should continue to be allowed to complete advanced glider training. Before you fly the Monday morning mission, I feel obligated to let you know that even if you manage to impress the heck out of me with your performance, the training will get progressively more demanding in the coming weeks. I also want you to know, that if you feel uncomfortable flying a glider under more demanding conditions and you still want a fly, you can request to serve as a Liaison Pilot and fly a single engine L4 or L5 aircraft. The fact that you didn't do well in Advanced Glider School won't be held against you."

While the Major paused long enough to light his cigar, Shorty knew that he had no interest in flying a single engine aircraft when doing so would separate him from Ivan. As Shorty did his best to sound sincere, he responded to the Major's offer and said, "I'm sorry I didn't work out for you, Sir. I know how bad the Army needs glider pilots." Shorty then poured on the charm and added, "With your permission, Sir, I'd really like to stay in a glider unit even if I have to clean latrines in order to do so."

Hearing Gus O'Malley express such esprit de corps for the glider program made it even easier for Major Kirby to continue. After taking two quick puffs on his cigar, Major Kirby sounded like a reasonable man when he said, "I'm glad you feel that way, because I'd like to make you an offer that I think you'll be interested in. Because you made it this far and you proved that you possess impressive mechanical skills, I've decided to recommend that you be trained to serve as an Assistant Glider Engineering Officer with the rank of Warrant Officer. If you agree to do so, I'll enthusiastically endorse your request to transfer to duties that you are better suited to perform."

When the Major continued and said, "If you accept this new assignment, I also promise to do everything I can to get you assigned to the same Troop Carrier Group as your cousin," Shorty knew that he was being offered a deal that was too good to pass up. Shorty also knew that recovering Chalk 14 was paying huge dividends for him in a moment of need.

The U.S. Army Air Forces glider program was also receiving a great deal of notoriety, especially when he was told at breakfast that the command staff at South Plains Army Air Field wanted to exploit the fact that glider personnel salvaged a heavily damaged GC-4A Waco Glider that was paid for by hard working patriotic American citizens. Based on what Gus heard so far, the local newspaper and radio station was biting at the bit to cover the story of how personnel under the command of Major Mike Kirby recovered a badly damaged glider that would be rebuilt into a flyable aircraft. There was also every reason to believe that this would become a story that would receive nation wide publicity.

Major Kirby seemed to be in an exceptionally good mood when he continued and said, "I'm sure you'll be happy to know that the local newspaper and radio station are going crazy over the story about how you and Sergeant Peavy salvaged Chalk 14 and our efforts here at South Plains Army Air Field to keep as many gliders in the air by cannibalizing the wrecks. Rather than wait for Chalk 14 to be restored to flying condition, the decision was made to exploit the public relations value of this story for all it's worth. This means that members of the press will be given access to Chalk 14 while it's being repaired, as well as when this badly damaged GC4A is restored to flyable condition. In addition to reporters from The Stars and Stripes and Yank Magazine, a number of civilian reporters and radio commentators will be interviewing you, me and Sergeant Peavy while Chalk 14 is being repaired. Photographers will also be on hand to take pictures as well."

Even though the entire base was well aware that the Army made the story available to the wire services, Shorty never expected to become a celebrity over the recovery of a badly damaged glider. While sounding more like a proud father than a strict disciplinarian, Major Kirby added, "Even though I had to make a call about your capabilities as a glider pilot, I have to admit that you're a natural born Glider Engineering Officer. I also hope you enjoy the publicity because in a few days you and Sergeant Peavy will be famous."

After hearing what the Major had to say, Shorty knew exactly why Killer Kirby was being so nice to the only pilot in the class who would not be completing Advanced Glider School. By this time in their conversation it had also become painfully clear to Shorty, that his efforts to show everyone that he could do the impossible had backfired beyond his wildest imagination.

While Shorty began to feel trapped, he became very concerned about the consequences of being photographed for articles that would be published in U.S. Army and civilian newspapers. Shorty also felt his stomach tighten when he considered how Ivan would react, when he told his partner in crime that he was going to be featured in a nationwide publicity campaign for his involvement in the recovery of Chalk 14.

After pausing long enough to place his cigar in an ashtray, Major Kirby continued and said, "The good news is that I changed my opinion of you and that other mechanical genius of a loner who pulled Chalk 14 out of that God forsaken terrain in the ass end of no where. I also know that you've been helping Sergeant Peavy fix and maintain everything from vehicles to gliders and even a few L4s and L5s on your own time and that you're the one, not Sergeant Peavy, who got my old Ford running again." Then, after breaking off a piece of chocolate from a half eaten Hershey Bar, the Major added, "The bottom line, Gus, is that you redeemed yourself by showing me where your true talents lie."

As bizarre as it sounded, Major Kirby was now calling the worst glider pilot in the current class by his first name. The fugitive who adopted the identity of Gus O'Malley was twice as surprised when Major Kirby asked him how he felt, after Doc Keller used over a dozen stitches to sew his scalp together.

While Shorty relaxed for the first time since he was in the presence of his commanding officer, he responded and said, "I'll be as good as new, Sir, once the stitches come out. Doc Keller said I made it easy for him to patch me up because I've been shaving my head ever since I was a kid." Even though Shorty started shaving his head to change the way he looked to avoid capture, this bullshit story sounded like it was the truth and that's all that mattered.

After having this rather friendly exchange with Major Kirby, Shorty did his best to sound like a team player when he said, "With your permission, Sir, I'd like to take you up on your offer to serve as an Assistant Glider Engineering Officer. I promise I won't let you down, Sir"

Besides the fact that he admired loyalty in a man, nothing pleased a superior officer more than when a subordinate took his advice and went along with the program. With plenty of administrative matters to address, Major Kirby stood up with the aid of his cane and extended his right hand in a friendly fashion as he remarked, "Good luck, O'Malley. I'll let you and Sergeant Peavy know when we can expect the reporters and the photographers from Stars and Stripes to arrive. As far as your current status is concerned, you won't be required to fly any training missions due to the fact that you're still recovering from a head injury. In fact, effective immediately you can continue to work with Sergeant Peavy until you're ready to leave for training at Shepard Field."

After shaking hands with his commanding officer and saying, "Yes, Sir, Thank you, Sir," Shorty remained standing while he saluted Major Kirby. As soon as the Major returned the salute, Shorty pivoted smartly and walked out of his CO's office with some troubling news to share with Ivan.

FBI Agents out west received their first break when they located a waitress in a diner who remembered serving John Miller on several occasions in 1943. The reason it took so long to find this waitress, was because she just returned to work after spending time with a daughter who's husband was killed while serving in Burma.

After canvassing motels in the vicinity of the diner where Miller was identified as a customer, an FBI Agent and Eddie Evans located a motel clerk who remembered meeting Miller. A check of the register books confirmed that a John Miller from New York City was a guest in The Roadway Motel the month after meat rationing was imposed in the U.S.

As a result of the cooperation of Mr. Moore, the FBI also confirmed that Charlie Dobbs was the rancher who supplied black market beef to John Miller. Unfortunately, Mr. Moore had no knowledge of Charlie Dobbs being involved with anyone identified as Rudy Mueller. After the death of John Miller, Charlie Dobbs notified Mr. Moore that he would no longer need his services because he was selling his ranch.

The day before he was scheduled to leave for Glider Engineering School, Gus O'Malley was told to make himself available to be photographed in front of Chalk 14. While everyone else in the bar was congratulating Gus O'Malley, the fugitive hiding out in the Army under the name of Danny Gannon was privately fuming over the attention that Shorty brought on himself by salvaging Chalk 14.

After several hours of drinking copious amounts of alcohol, most of the glider pilot trainees who were attending advanced glider training in Lubbock, Texas were either drunk or paired up with the local bar girls. Once Ivan saw that everyone was either three sheets to the wind or preoccupied, he decided to make his move.

After asking his buddy Gus to step outside, Ivan walked into the alley behind their favorite hangout and looked around to make sure they were alone. Once Ivan was sure the coast was clear, he grabbed Shorty by the front of his uniform shirt and said, "Well, Joe hero, how does it feel to be responsible for fucking up a perfectly good escape plan?"

Although Shorty wasn't blind stinking drunk, he was feeling no pain after consuming his fare share of alcohol. Even though Shorty was capable of defending himself, he decided not to resist being manhandled because he knew Ivan had a legitimate reason to be upset. Drunk or not, Shorty was smart enough to know that having his picture published in The Stars and Stripes Newspaper, Yank Magazine, as well as in numerous civilian newspapers, could seriously jeopardize their escape plan.

The fact that millions of G.I.s, including CID Agents and military policemen, read military and civilian newspapers and magazines was reason enough for Ivan to be concerned about Shorty being photographed by the press. All it would take is one Army flatfoot or one suspicious soldier to make the connection between Gus O'Malley and Francis Shorty Mc Ghee and Ivan and his partner in crime would be back on the run or in custody.

Ivan and Shorty also had good reason to be concerned because Amos Washington knew that Ivan wanted to be an Army pilot. Amos also knew that Shorty agreed to follow Ivan in their escape plan that involved joining the U.S. Army. If Amos remembered these plans and if he provided this information to the authorities, the military and civilian police would be crazy not to concentrate their search for Ivan Larson and Francis Shorty Mc Ghee in the U.S. Army Air Forces.

While Ivan tried to keep his voice down, he finished berating his friend by saying, "Having a picture of a member of the Army Air Forces who's assigned to glider training by the name of Gus O'Malley featured in The Stars and Stripes, Yank Magazine and various civilian newspapers is like sending an engraved invitation to the New York City Police, the FBI and the Army cops to come and arrest us."

The moment that Shorty lost his patience and said "You act as if I did this on purpose," Ivan tossed his friend to the ground in disgust, before he kicked a pile of empty wooden crates that were stacked up against the wall behind the bar.

As Shorty looked up from the ground, the liquor in him clouded his mind enough to make him forget the need to be discrete. The second Shorty remarked, "Fuck you, Ivan." a pissed off Ivan Larson lunged at his partner in crime with a vengeance. While the two fugitives traded punches, they kicked up a small cloud of dust as they rolled around on the ground. Although a couple of Shorty's punches hit the mark, Ivan ended up standing over his friend with badly bruised knuckles and a split lip. Shorty wasn't so lucky.

After remarking, "Go to hell," Shorty rolled on his side and moaned, as he gently felt his swollen right eye and a bloody but not broken nose.

As Ivan collapsed on the ground next to his friend and remarked, "Don't ever call me that again," Shorty put his handkerchief to work to stop the bleeding and said, "Don't worry, I won't."

While Ivan sat on the ground next to his friend, he wasn't sure if he heard right when Shorty mumbled, "Maybe I should change the deal I made with Killer Kirby." After checking his front teeth to see if they were loose, Ivan spoke up and said, "What's that's suppose to mean?"

While Shorty paused long enough to adjust his position on the ground, he continued speaking as he half faced Ivan. "That so called stunt I pulled recovering Chalk 14 is the main reason why I'm still in the glider program. In fact, the only reason I'm going to Shepard Field to train to become an Assistant Glider Engineering Officer, is because I turned down an offer to become a Liaison Pilot and fly a single engine hedge hopping observation aircraft. If I took that route we'd be split up for sure. Instead, I played ball with Major Kirby and he promised to do everything possible to get me assigned to the same Troop Carrier Group as you."

While Shorty explained every detail of his conversation with Killer Kirby, Ivan felt like shit for reacting so harshly to the news that the Army was launching a nationwide publicity campaign to promote the recovery and restoration of Chalk 14. In a gesture of friendship, Ivan removed a cigarette from the crushed pack in his shirt pocket and slipped it in between his lips before he offered one to Shorty.

After waving his right hand to refuse the cigarette, Shorty gently dabbed his bloody nose with his handkerchief before he looked at Ivan and said, "What could I say to the old man. I'm sorry, Sir, I can't be photographed because I'm wanted by the police." As soon as Ivan put the flame from his Ronson lighter to the tip of his Camel cigarette, he filled his lungs with tobacco smoke and exhaled, while Shorty continued and said, "To tell you the truth I'm glad things worked out the way they did, because I'd rather fix those canvass coffins than fly 'em. Gliders give me the fucking creeps."

Seeing Ivan grin encouraged Shorty to continue. Before he spoke he dabbed his nose with his hanky again. "You're the one who always wanted to be a pilot, not me. Hell, I'm surprised I like flying a plane with an engine as much as I do. The only reason I made it through flight school was because you helped me to understand how planes with engines are able to defy gravity. Once I understood the mechanics, I was a lot more comfortable in the air. Unfortunately, I don't feel the same way about gliders."

As Shorty took the burning cigarette from Ivan's hand and took a drag, he exhaled and said, "I tried. I really did. You gotta give me credit for that. It's just that I don't like the idea of trying to figure out how I'm gonna land one of those death traps in a landing zone that's jammed packed with other crash landed gliders, especially while the enemy is trying to kill me."

After hearing Ivan remark, "I know what you mean," Shorty felt reassured that things were back to normal between them.

As disturbing as it was that he and Shorty would have to split up for a relatively short period of time, Ivan knew that Major Kirby was a man of his word. If Killer Kirby said that he would do his best to get Shorty assigned to the same Troop Carrier Group as his cousin, Ivan believed that the Major would keep his word. Ivan was also impressed by the way Shorty was taking the news. Quite frankly, Ivan was surprised that Shorty was as calm as he was and wasn't talking about going AWOL. Who knows, thought Ivan, maybe Shorty also found a home in the Army and was growing up.

To prove the fight was over and they were still friends, Ivan reached out and grabbed Shorty by the arm as he said, "Come on, let me help you up."

Resisting at first Shorty pulled back and said, "What about the photo for the newspapers?"

After saying, "We'll work it out," Ivan lifted his friend up and added, "Come on, let's get off the ground and get cleaned up before the local cops or the MPs show up." While Shorty stood facing Ivan he had a brainstorm. It would hurt but it would be worth it. The moment Shorty pointed to his undamaged left eye and said, "Hit me," Ivan thought his buddy was punch drunk.

While Ivan dusted off his suntans (tan colored summer uniform) and remarked, "Are you outta your mind," Shorty stood his ground and waited for his partner in crime to comply with his request.

As sore as he was, Shorty stood up as straight as possible and said, "The Army wants to photograph me with Major Kirby and Sergeant Peavy in front of Chalk 14, right?" Without waiting for Ivan to respond, Shorty answered his own question. "It's simple. If you do a number on me there ain't a newspaper in the country that would use my picture and even if they did no one will be able to recognize me."

Ivan had to admit that Shorty made perfect sense. As Ivan sized up the damage he did so far, he squinted his right eye as he tried to figure out how he could do this without causing any permanent damage to his willing accomplice. In order to make sure that Shorty really wanted to be hit again, Ivan asked, "Are you sure you want me to do this?"

To prove his determination, Shorty extended his chin toward Ivan as he leaned forward and pointed to his face and said, "Try not to miss."

Without warning, Ivan hauled off and punched his partner in crime in the left eye and knocked him almost unconscious. As Ivan bent over and helped Shorty up, he sounded sincerely concerned when he made sure his friend was all right.

After being knocked on his ass twice in the same day, the tough Irish kid from Queens held onto Ivan with both hands, as he walked with spaghetti legs toward the rear entrance of the bar and asked, "How do I look?"

While Ivan sized up the damage, he looked at Shorty and said, "You look like you got knocked on your ass twice in the same day."

Even though it hurt like hell, Shorty forced a grin as he looked up at Ivan with a squinted left eye that would be swollen completely shut in under an hour and said, "I need a drink."

After getting one look at Gus O'Malley's face, Major Kirby refused to include his photograph in any newspaper article that was intended to promote a positive image of the Army Air Forces glider program. Major Kirby had good reason to feel this way because Gus O'Malley looked like he was in Chalk 14 when it crashed in a remote location of the Texas Panhandle.

Although Major Kirby was officially perturbed that two of his men got into a street brawl, he knew his boys were a rough bunch who didn't react kindly to other servicemen who refused to believe that glider pilot's were real Army aviators. With Gus O'Malley off the hook, a smiling Major Kirby was photographed with Sergeant Peavy in front of the famous glider that was being restored.

After leaving South Plains Army Air Field on their flight cross country, Lt. Guliver decided to pass the time by provoking Lt. Tucker, with more tales about the ever popular Lt. Billy Davis. While Lt. Guliver sat in the co pilot's seat, he explained how Major Kirby was influenced by Billy Davis to allow his Army buddy from back east to transfer to glider engineering duties.

When Lt. Guliver continued, he did his best to make it sound as if he was sharing top secret scuttlebutt when he said, "Best yet, according to Lt. Keating, Billy Davis got his buddy promoted to Warrant Officer."

Nothing bothered Lenny Tucker more than to hear a man get a break, when he should have endured the disgrace of being officially considered a failure. After saying, "What's this world coming to," Lt. Tucker sounded even more disgusted, while he continued to handle the controls and said, "I can't believe Major Kirby has turned soft on us." A frustrated Lt. Tucker then added, "While I fully acknowledge that Lt. Davis is a brave man, I can't understand why he would go to bat for such a Sad Sack."

Although he was not surprised to hear Lt. Tucker make such harsh remarks, Carl Guliver could not believe that he was serving with such a screwed up human being. In a last ditch effort to explain the realities of life to his stuck up senior pilot, Lt. Guliver explained that the service was no different than civilian life when it came to giving people nicknames. While some nicknames were derogatory in nature, others were a compliment or meant to label someone for a particular trait, a capability or a certain physical feature.

Lt. Guliver also mentioned that Billy Davis respected the pilot that he dubbed Shorty Number 3 because he was a tough son of a gun who refused to give up. Billy was even more impressed with his buddy from back east, when he found out that he stopped eating in order to get through flight school and glider training. That's the reason why in this guy's case being called Skinny was considered a compliment."

As Lt. Guliver continued, he added, "I know how you feel about Billy Davis and I agree that he jokes around more than anyone else in the Army Air Corps, but in this case he did the right thing when he tipped off Major Kirby that his buddy was living on a steady diet of coffee and cigarettes because he was afraid of being grounded."

"I'm still not impressed, Carl," responded Lt. Tucker who quickly added, "I like a good joke just as much as anyone else. Unfortunately, for someone who has flown combat missions, you would think Billy Davis would spend less time giving people nicknames and joking around and more time helping to train Army aviators to go to war."

While trying his best to behave like a true blue friend who had more scuttlebutt to pass along, Carl Guliver remarked, "I know what you mean. Billy Davis doesn't know when to quit with the jokes. In fact, after this aspiring glider pilot recovered Chalk 14 with Sergeant Peavy, I heard Billy Davis tell his co pilot that they should start calling his buddy Stitches, because he had to be patched up after he cut his head open while pulling that wrecked glider out of the ass end of Texas."

After all that Carl Guliver had to say, Lt. Tucker sounded as snobby as ever when he remarked, "I'm sorry, Carl, but that guy has more nicknames than anyone else in this man's Army. The good news as far as I'm concerned, is that whether this Sad Sack is called Shorty Number 3, Skinny or Stitches he won't be flying anymore."

Rather than try to make Lt. Tucker understand that is was possible for a man who failed in one pursuit to excel in another, Lt. Guliver decided to change the subject and offer his aircraft commander a sandwich and a cup of coffee. As Lt. Guliver retrieved their lunch, Lt. Tucker transformed himself into a first class gentleman from the south when he asked Carl to take the controls while he took a break.

While Lt. Tucker thanked his co pilot for making sure that their crew had plenty of food, hot coffee and soda pop to make the long journey from Texas to the east coast, Carl Guliver gave up on the idea that Lenny Tucker would ever change for the better. Even though Lt. Tucker was an outstanding C47 pilot, the man known as Grumpy and The Judge's Son had some serious personal problems that motivated him to have complete contempt for anyone who did not measure up to his expectations.

CHAPTER 28

COLLATERAL DAMAGE

While Major James Beauregard and his team of investigators from various agencies scoured numerous Army bases, a number of incidents took place when soldiers thought they identified one of fugitives wanted by CID. In one instance, a fight broke out when the son of a New York City Police Lieutenant tackled a 19 year old recruit at Ft. Dix, who in his opinion looked like Francis Shorty Mc Ghee. By the time the MPs responded, the fight turned into a brawl between two training companies. Once this incident was under control, the "suspect" was identified as a soldier who was completing his first year in Seminary School, when the two fugitives were robbing the Lincoln Savings Bank.

In another incident, a Negro soldier was badly beaten by five white soldiers when their plans to go on leave were delayed, because a colored cop by the name of Al Parker inspected their barracks. After visiting the Negro Private in the base hospital, Al Parker was driven back to the Provost Marshal's Office by an Army MP.

As soon as the MP Sergeant transported Al back to the Provost Marshal's Office, Al decided to smoke a cigar while he waited outside for Major Beauregard. While Al paced back and forth and puffed on his cigar, all he could think about was how he would have handled this incident, if he apprehended any of these punks back in New York City. Unfortunately, instead of being on his home turf, Al was inspecting a U.S. Army base in the deep south in 1944, a place where race relations would not improve for several decades to come.

When the Major emerged from the building, Jim wasted no time in asking Al how Private Carlton was holding up? As angry and upset as he was, Al tried not to take his frustrations out on Jim Beauregard.

After pausing long enough to gain control of his emotions, Al looked at the Major and said, "He won't be eating solid food for some time to come, thanks to those bastards."

Even though Jim knew that such things happened, it still boggled his mind that five white soldiers could justify beating a Negro soldier, because a Negro cop

266

who was searching their barracks for two dangerous fugitives delayed their plans to go on leave. After pausing to light a cigarette, Jim spoke in a friendly tone of voice as he started to walk away. "Come on, Al, it's late. Tomorrow's another day."

Instead of putting the matter to rest, Al stood still while the Major began walking to the room where they were spending the night. The moment Jim stopped and turned to see what was holding up his partner, Al spoke in an equally friendly tone of voice and said, "Working this case is a lot harder than I thought it would be."

As soon as Jim walked back over to where Al was standing, he nodded his head ever so slightly before he agreed. "It certainly hasn't been easy."

Between the normal difficulties of trying to find two fugitives in an army that contained millions of men, the fact that this investigation had to be conducted in a segregated society made a bad situation worse. When Jim continued he looked directly at Al and said, "Don't think for one minute that I don't see the look on your face every time we see a sign that says whites only. I'd like to say that I know what it must be like for you to deal with the way things are but I can't. All we can do is hope that this war will change things for the better. In the meantime, the only thing that we can do is our job. It won't be easy, but we either continue as best as possible, or we pack up and go back home empty handed." Then, after pausing for a split second, Jim added, "I also know that Pat Murphy Jr. was a very lucky man to have you as his friend. The same goes for Captain Murphy and every man assigned to the CID Task Force, including me."

As Al Parker stepped closer to Jim, he could see the reflection of the moonlight in the metal insignia on the Major's neatly pressed Army uniform when he said, "Some days I'm filled with hope that things will change for the better once we win this war. Those are the good days. Unfortunately, I also have plenty of bad days, when I have absolutely no faith that things will change for the better once the shooting stops and people go back to living their lives." After pausing to massage his tired face, Al remarked, "You're right. We either go on, or we go home empty handed. I say we go on."

Ever since he started working with Al Parker, Jim was never the same again. In a way, neither was Al Parker. The simple truth was, that Jim Beauregard and Al Parker carried a burden that was made even more cumbersome to bear because they were unable to effect social change.

While Jim field stripped his cigarette, he looked at his partner and said, "Come on, Al. I have a bottle of scotch in our room. I'll buy you a drink."

As both men walked back to the converted storage room on base where the Major and Al were spending the night, Al Parker thought to himself that there was hope for mankind yet, as long as men like Jim Beauregard, Frank Angelone, Johnny Mc Donald, Andy Dubrowsky, Fred Richmond, Sal Jacobi, Steve Klein, Joe Coppola, Jack Donovan, Don Lorenz, Jimmy Scott, Kevin Kalb, Richy Olsen, Eddie Evans and the members of the Murphy family were around.

CHAPTER 29

THE TWO FUGITIVES CONTINUE
TO TRAIN FOR WAR

S ince it was often said that people with opposite personalities were attracted to each other, it was obvious why an outgoing guy like Danny Gannon would be as close as he was to a guy like Gus O'Malley. As far as their new identities were concerned, Ivan let their fellow soldiers know that Shorty's mother and Ivan's mother were sisters and that they were both raised by their Uncle Mike after their mothers died.

Their cover story also garnered a great deal of sympathy, when they let it be known that their fathers served together as merchant seamen, before they went to work on construction contracts in the Pacific and haven't been heard from since the war began. The fact that they let it be known that their "fathers" ended up in Japanese held territory, made everyone who heard their fabricated sob story view Danny Gannon and Gus O'Malley as patriotic young men who had a personal reason to kick some Axis ass. Even something as simple as receiving mail from their Uncle Mike's home in Jersey City, New Jersey, was enough to prevent any of their fellow soldiers from suspecting that Danny Gannon and Gus O'Malley were the famous fugitives who were being hunted by Army CID, the FBI and the New York City Police.

In addition to representing themselves to be cousins, Danny Gannon and Gus O'Malley acted as if they were as close as brothers. This behavior fit their personalities because Danny Gannon acted like a typical older brother, while Gus O'Malley behaved more like a younger brother.

The only problem the two fugitives had was with Shorty's height. Even though Ivan and Shorty were able to successfully avoid detection by adopting new identities, they were no taller or shorter than they were when they were inducted into the U.S. Army. Despite this fact, the two fugitives managed to make it all the way to the Advanced Glider School before anyone called Gus O'Malley "Shorty."

Fortunately, the fugitive who adopted the identify of Gus O'Malley was the taller of the three pilots who Lt. Davis jokingly referred to as Shorty Number 1, Shorty Number 2 and Shorty Number 3.

To counter this potential problem Ivan decided that he had to start using another nickname to refer to his partner in crime. Calling his buddy Skinny, instead of Shorty seemed like a good fit, especially when Ivan let it be known that his cousin Gus stopped eating because he was afraid of failing flight school. The fact that Shorty lost even more weight and became considerably more physically fit, made it easy for Ivan to give his buddy a new nickname as a way to get Billy Davis to stop calling Gus O'Malley "Shorty Number 3." Fortunately, when Gus O'Malley began training as an Assistant Glider Engineering Officer, he left all of his nicknames behind at South Plains Army Air Field.

As soon as Billy Davis returned from a weeks leave, he wasted no time in looking up his buddy Danny Gannon. Billy Davis was like everyone else who served in the Army, who looked forward to meeting other soldiers who were born and raised in the same part of the country. Even if someone came from a city or a small town that was a hundred miles away, he was still considered from back home. In fact, being from Brooklyn and meeting two guys from Jersey City, New Jersey was the equivalent of running into your next door neighbor.

The United States Army was a mirror image of the nation, a melting pot of people from every nook and cranny of the country. While many of the men were from small towns others were from big cities. Even the level of education between men in the same unit varied from one extreme to another. The different branches of the Armed Forces were also filled with married men and single men, including those who had different levels of experience with women. The bulk of the different branches of the service were also made up of citizen soldiers, sailors, airmen and marines who had no intention of remaining in the military once the war was over. These men served because their lives depended on their survival in battle and because it was expected of them.[10]

Because all of the other instructors in Texas were from down south or out west, Billy Davis took an immediate interest in two particular glider pilots who were the only members of the class from his neck of the woods. With Gus O'Malley in Glider Engineering School, Billy Davis had all the more reason to look up Danny Gannon.

After leaving his quarters at South Plains Army Air Field, Billy Davis walked over the Day Room to locate his buddy Danny G. from Jersey City. Now that Danny was half way through Advanced Glider School, Billy was anxious to fill his buddy in on what happened behind the scenes after Gus and Sergeant Peavy recovered Chalk 14.

Even though there was a rivalry between glider pilots and tow plane pilots, there were also plenty of instances when one group had a reason to admire the other. This was especially the case when C47 crews performed incredible feats of heroism in order to deliver their assigned glider to the proper release point. In fact, Lt. Billy Davis was a perfect example of a tow plane pilot who earned the respect of others because of his exploits in combat.

After reviewing his notes, Ivan looked up just in time to see his favorite C47 pilot enter the Day Room. As the most popular C47 pilot on base, Billy Davis was a celebrity of sorts who loved to joke around with the men that he would one day tow into combat behind his troop carrier aircraft.

While Billy made his way over to where Danny Gannon was sitting, he had a few friendly exchanges with some of the glider pilots who acted like hecklers in a night club as he walked by. One particular glider pilot from South Carolina was louder than the rest when he called out, "Hey, Flatbush, what are you doing back in Texas with all of us Johnny Rebs?"

Without stopping Billy responded as he walked by. "As a native New Yorker I've been sent to Lubbock, Texas to make sure that you gentlemen from the south are enjoying your stay in the Yankee Army. I've also been instructed to inform you that if you have any complaints you can tell your problems to Jesus 'cause the Chaplain went ashore."

While some of the pilots attending the Advanced Glider School who came from southern states began laughing, others continued making jokes as Billy Davis cracked a smile and crashed down in a comfortable chair next to the pilot he called Danny G. As the banter between pilots from southern states and pilots from states that sided with the Union died down, Billy Davis leaned over and shook hands with the man he knew as Danny Gannon as he said, "How's it going, Danny G.?"

Ever since they became friends, Ivan called Billy Davis by his first name when ever they were alone. Otherwise, he was known as Lieutenant.

"I'm OK, Billy," said Ivan.

"You're doing better than that, pal," responded Billy Davis. "The way I hear it, you're rated as the number three pilot in your class. That's not bad considering this school is a lot harder that the basic course."

As hard as it was for Ivan to believe, the orphan from St. Mary's found his niche in life, even if he did so while being a fugitive from justice with a manufactured past that was as fake as a counterfeit ten dollar bill. Even though Ivan liked to hear people say nice things about his flying abilities, he really wanted to talk to Billy about what happened between Major Kirby and Shorty.

After seeing the expression on his friend's face, Billy Davis remarked, "Let me guess. You miss Shorty Number 3 or are you still calling him Skinny?"

Just hearing the nickname Shorty was enough to make Ivan's hair stand up on the back of his neck as he remarked. "Come on, Billy, you know how much Gus hates to be called names. You should'a heard him when me and the other guys started calling him Skinny when he stopped eating."

Once again Billy Davis lived up to his reputation as a young man who liked to joke around when he said, "You think Skinny is bad. I came real close to calling Gus "Stitches" after he cut his head open while recovering Chalk 14."

"Thank God you never spread that one around. That's all Gus needed was another nickname," responded the fugitive masquerading as Danny Gannon.

While Billy Davis made a pushing motion with his hands to signal Danny to calm down, the veteran C47 pilot sounded like a true blue Army buddy when he said, "Relax, Danny, Gus can't hear me."

While thinking fast, Ivan decided to make a joke out of the situation by saying, "I know, but I'm just as bad about this name calling business as everyone else. After all, I've been teasing Gus ever since we were kids. I'm not even gonna tell you what every kid in the neighborhood called him when he started shaving his head with our Uncle Mike's razor." Then, as Ivan Larson cracked a devilish grin, he leaned closer to Billy while he continued and said, "I wonder who told Major Kirby and

Lt. Keating that Gus stopped eating because he was petrified about flunking out of advanced glider training?"

"You know I did that for his own good," responded Billy who quickly added, "In fact, I think we should continue to call Gus "Skinny," although "Stitches" isn't a bad nickname for a guy who had to have his head sewed up after recovering the famous Chalk 14. Either way, both of those nicknames sound a lot nicer than Shorty Number 3."

After shaking his head from left to right, Ivan remarked, "You're intolerable." When Billy continued he became a tad more serious. "Now that we joked around let me fill you in on what happened behind the scenes between Major Kirby and our buddy Gus."

While Ivan Larson aka Danny Gannon gave his favorite C47 pilot his undivided attention, Billy looked directly at his buddy and said, "Gus did himself a big favor when started helping Sergeant Peavy keep everything from the Major's old Ford to all kinds of vehicles and gliders operational. Pulling Chalk 14 outta the boondocks of Texas was the cherry on the top of the cake, that saved his ass when it looked like he wasn't going to make it through advanced glider training. Between what I told Major Kirby about Gus's mechanical abilities and what the Major saw for himself when Gus and Sergeant Peavy recovered Chalk 14, our buddy was destined for a transfer to Glider Engineering School that included a promotion to Warrant Officer."

After listening to Billy Davis fill him in, Ivan remarked, "You did that boy a favor. Gus would've had a heart attack if he was here when we had to fly our first training mission at night."

After cracking a devilish grin, Lt. Billy Davis remarked, "That was Major Kirby's concern as well."

Under the circumstances Ivan played along and said, "Gus tried...you have to give him credit for that."

As soon as Billy Davis remarked, "I agree," he continued briefing the glider pilot known as Danny Gannon. "The second I heard that Gus was having problems landing in a crowded LZ I started letting the Major know that Gus was spending all of his free time helping Sergeant Peavy. Gus scored his first points with Killer Kirby when he insisted that Sergeant Peavy take the credit for making CO's old Ford roadworthy again. When the Major thanked him, Peavy gave Gus up and said that it was Gus who performed the impossible and fixed his car. It also helped that Major Kirby got a huge pat on the back from the brass after the story got published about how Chalk 14 was salvaged and would be made flyable again."

After pausing for a split second Billy Davis sounded like a man who was speaking between the lines when he continued and said, "Who knows, maybe you, me and Gus will luck out and get stationed with Killer Kirby once we get shipped overseas."

Even though Billy Davis seemed to know more than he was saying, Ivan didn't pry. Instead, Ivan sat quietly in his chair, while Billy smiled then said, "Have faith my friend, have faith."

After making some small talk about how much they missed the east coast, Ivan became somewhat serious and spoke in a very polite fashion when he said, "I hate to ask, Billy, but now that I'm getting close to graduating, I was hoping you would tell me what it's like to fly a combat mission." While Billy Davis sat back in his chair, Ivan explained his reason for asking such a personal question. "I'm not trying to pry but I'd like to know how bad it can get so I can prepare myself for combat."

Ivan Larson aka Danny Gannon was like every other military pilot who was training to fly in harms way. He wanted to know what it was like to fly in combat, while being shot at by enemy troops who were determined to prevent you from successfully completing your mission. While Billy considered Danny's request, he packed his pipe with a fresh bowl of tobacco.

Billy decided to talk about things that he rarely if ever spoke about, because he knew Danny Gannon was eager to learn. Billy also knew that he might be able to help Danny to survive, if he provided him with some insight into flying combat missions in a glider. After looking around the room, Billy faced his Army buddy as he leaned forward and said, "You want'a know what it was like? OK, Danny, I'll tell you."

While Ivan used his Ronson to light a cigarette, he gave Billy Davis his undivided attention when the veteran C47 pilot began to speak. "Always remember that anything can happen at any time. This includes always being prepared to fly the mission that you end up with and not the mission that they tell you about in a briefing session. You also need to expect to see some horrific things take place in combat. When I say horrific, I mean the stuff that nightmares are made of. This includes everything from seeing planes on fire and shot out of the sky, to seeing men falling through the sky when their parachutes don't open. You also need to remember your training. Whatever you do don't panic and don't cut any corners. If you get scared take a deep breath and keep going. In other words, never give up."

Ivan was never more serious in his life. His only regret was that he was a man on the run. He liked the Army and the Army seemed to like him. As Billy Davis finished his remarks, he looked directly at the fugitive masquerading as Danny Gannon and said, "Danny, you're a natural born glider pilot. Once we get you some twin engine time you'll also be an outstanding C47 pilot. If I were you I'd consider staying in the Army after this war is over because you have the makings of a good leader."

After pausing to light his pipe, Billy Davis continued and said, "Also, don't believe this bullshit that we're fighting now so our kids won't have to go to war in the future. Our Uncle Sam said the same thing to soldiers like my father who served in World War I and they'll be telling soldiers the same line of bullshit in every war that we fight when this one is over. The simple truth is, there's never been peace on earth for anything even remotely close to a long period of time, so be prepared to fight this war and the next one 'cause the U.S. Army will need good pilots just as much in the future as it does now."

While Billy Davis puffed on his pipe, Ivan considered what his friend had to say. Even though there were times when Ivan thought about making a career in the Army, he knew the odds of doing so were slim to none, especially as long as the authorities were aggressively looking for him and Shorty.

As Ivan tried not to dwell on negative thoughts, Billy Davis sat back in his chair and said, "You know something, Danny. Gus kind'a grows on you. You two remind me of how me and my brothers are with each other."

While Ivan tapped the ash from his cigarette in a nearby ashtray, he nodded his head in agreement and said, "I miss him too."

With his pipe billowing a stream of fragrant smelling smoke, Billy Davis put his pouch of pipe tobacco away then stood up and said, "Come on, I'm thirsty. How 'bout a Coke? I'm buying."

Once Ivan grabbed his notebook and stood up, he followed Billy Davis through the crowded Day Room. Just as they expected, on the way to grab a Coke, a group of glider pilots joked that the two Yankees were going steady. "Don't mind them," remarked Billy Davis who quickly called out, "Remember what happened in 1865. I'd hate to have to pull rank on you southern boys."

Thanks to Willie Gunderson a team of FBI Agents were able to locate Max Hoffman as he left his mother's house in Union City, New Jersey. After keeping tabs on Hoffman for several days, Willie and the two agents he was assigned to work with spotted the Wagner brothers meeting Hoffman outside a bar in Hoboken, New Jersey. Unfortunately, it was proving harder to locate Rudy Mueller who moved from his last known address in Union City.

After inspecting another dozen Army camps and forts, the entire multi-agency CID Task Force returned to the office to take a break and exchange information. While Major Beauregard stood in front of the squad room he finished his opening statement by saying, "Al Parker suggested that we come up with a new set of wanted posters. I agree with his suggestion. Unfortunately, we have no idea how much Ivan Larson and Shorty Mc Ghee have changed after being in the Army for several months."

While the Major continued speaking, he walked over to the other side of the room and stood by a large window. "An FBI artist will be spending some time with Al to come up with some new sketches of our two fugitives. Even though this won't be easy, we have to try and come up with some new wanted posters that reflect how Larson and Mc Ghee look after getting a haircut, a clean shave and a daily regiment of physical training. Any questions?"

The second Frank Angelone raised his hand Jim Beauregard acknowledged the police detective. "Ange."

While the veteran detective removed a stick of gum from his shirt pocket he spoke up and said. "I don't mean to put the cart before the horse, Major, but what happens if we develop a lead that needs to be followed up overseas. Will we be allowed to take this show on the road, in order to conduct our investigation?" It was an excellent question, one that everyone in the room, especially Al Parker wanted answered.

After turning to face Lt. Colonel Richmond, Jim Beauregard asked the commanding officer of the New York CID Office if he would respond to this particular question?" As the distinguished looking Lt. Colonel Richmond removed the pipe from the corner of his mouth, he took a few steps closer to where Jim was standing and said, "According to the War Department, Major

Beauregard and a contingent of Army CID Agents and MPs will pursue all leads on foreign soil, especially if a lead involves traveling anywhere near the fighting. Once the prisoners are transported back to the United States, the New York City Police Department, the FBI and federal marshals will assume responsibility for Larson and Mc Ghee."

As soon as Major Beauregard made eye contact with Al Parker, he could see that he was extremely disappointed by the news that only CID Agents and military policemen were authorized to continue this manhunt overseas.

The moment Colonel Richmond started to leave the squad room, that was also known as the bull pen, he turned to his second in command and said, "Carry on, Jim."

After nodding his head, Jim Beauregard said, "Yes, Sir," before he faced the other members of the CID Task Force and remarked, "OK, men, let's get back to work."

Jim Beauregard didn't have to be a mind reader to know how Al Parker felt about being denied the opportunity to pursue Larson and Mc Ghee to the ends of the earth. The Major could see by the way Al rammed a freshly lit cigar in the corner of his mouth that he was pissed. Without waiting to hear Al voice his complaint, Jim walked over to where the veteran New York City cop was seated and said, "I'm sorry, Al."

Al Parker knew better than to speak his mind when he was beside himself and frustrated by circumstances that were beyond his control. Instead, Al stood up and brushed by the Major, while the other members of the task force went back to work. Halfway to the door, Al turned around to address Jim Beauregard. After removing the smoldering cigar from his clenched teeth, Al looked directly at the Major and said, "I'm gonna hunt Larson and Mc Ghee down if I have to enlist in the damn Army to do so."

After saying his peace, Al turned and started to walk out without waiting for a response from the CID Agent in charge of the fugitive investigation. Rather than let Al leave in such an obvious bad mood, Jim went after the man that he had become friends with and gently grabbed him by the arm as he walked through the door and into the hallway.

After closing the door so they could speak in private, Jim Beauregard sounded very sincere when he said, "I know how you feel, Al, but the U.S. Army can't let a New York City cop look for two fugitives in any location where the enemy is shooting at American soldiers."

With all the confidence that he could muster, Al Parker leaned closer to Jim Beauregard and responded in a very determined tone of voice when he said, "We'll see about that."

CHAPTER 30

WARRANT OFFICER GUS O'MALLEY MAKES A NEW ARMY BUDDY

As far as Gus O'Malley was concerned, Glider Engineering School was turning out to be a piece of cake compared to flight school and training to become a glider pilot. While everyone else in their class was enjoying some time off, Shorty spent the evening installing a Griswold protection device over the front of a new glider with Lt. Steve Perkins.

While Lt. Perkins wiped his hands on a shop towel, he walked over to his new found friend and said, "The CO's gonna be very happy with us when he sees we finished putting this bird together on our own time."

After putting his foot up on the front bumper of their jeep, Shorty faced his friend and proudly remarked, "The last CO I had rode my ass like you wouldn't believe. That guy scared the crap out of me so much I stopped eating. Meanwhile, the CO of this school loves me. That's the Army for you."

As much as Shorty missed Ivan, he felt pretty good about being on his own. Hitting it off with Lt. Steve Perkins helped a lot. With the way things were going at Glider Engineering School, Shorty Mc Ghee was feeling a lot less like a fugitive and more like a soldier.

In many ways, Shorty Mc Ghee was a lot like Ivan Larson. While Ivan grew up in an abusive orphanage, where his only nurturing came from one Catholic Nun, Francis Shorty Mc Ghee had a loving mother who ended up marrying an abusive alcoholic who drove him out of the house at a young age. Even though he was a wanted criminal, Shorty had enough of a conscience to feel bad about the torment that he put his mother through, especially when she learned that he was involved in a bank robbery that cost the life of a New York City policeman who happened to be Irish.

In order to forget the past and focus on the future, Shorty tried to stay as busy as possible. Today was no different. When Lt. Perkins suggested they call it a night,

Shorty field stripped his cigarette and tossed the remains in a nearby bucket that was filled with sand while he remarked, "Sounds good to me."

After getting behind the wheel of their jeep and starting the ignition, Shorty drove back to their barracks while Lt. Perkins spoke at a slightly raised tone of voice so his buddy could hear him as he shifted gears. "I heard we're going overseas as soon as we graduate."

"That suits me fine," responded Shorty as he remembered to watch the speed limit, while he drove through Camp Shepard on the way back to their barracks.

While Lt. Perkins carried on a one way conversation about the war, Shorty's thoughts drifted to the last time that he saw his mother. As Shorty down shifted and prepared to negotiate a right turn, he started to get a bit choked up when he thought how proud his mother would be, if she could see him now that he was making up for his sins by serving as a soldier in time of war.

The moment Lt. Perkins realized that his buddy Gus seemed to be in another world, he turned to his left and said, "Are you all right, Gus?"

As soon as Shorty snapped out of his trance and said, "I'm OK," he pulled over to the curb and stopped the jeep in front of their barracks.

Immediately after Shorty shut the engine off, Steve looked at his buddy and said, "You didn't hear a word I said, did you?"

After shaking his head from left to right, Shorty put on a friendly face and remarked, "I'm sorry, Steve, I was just thinking about an Irish girl I used to know."

The day Willie sat in an FBI car and he identified Gunther Kessler as he left his combination grocery store and bakery in Newark, Eddie Evans learned that Charlie Dobbs had a cousin who was a cattle rancher in the neighboring state. As soon as Eddie heard about the rancher identified as Paul Moran, the retired police detective who was now serving with the OPA recommended that businesses in the vicinity of this ranch should be canvassed.

Within thirty six hours of expanding their search, Eddie Evans and an FBI Agent interviewed a motel owner out west who remembered renting rooms to John Miller and Rudy Mueller. While checking registration records, Eddie Evans and his FBI Agent for a partner found an entry that confirmed that a John Miller from New York City and a Rudy Muller from Union City, New Jersey stayed at

The Fairway Motel two months after meat rationing was imposed. This particular motel was located over fifty miles away from the Dobbs ranch in a neighboring state. The next day, Eddie Evans and his partner located a waitress in the State Line Diner who remembered serving Miller, Mueller and the Wagner brothers on several occasions. The same waitress also recalled that Miller and Mueller had breakfast with a local rancher by the name of Paul Moran.

After canvassing other motels and tourist courts, Eddie and his partner from the FBI also determined that Mueller and the Wagner brothers were also registered guests at The Happy Trails Motel in July of 1943. Rudy Mueller also stayed in The Happy Trails Motel shortly after Miller was found murdered in his warehouse. On two other occasions in 1943 and on three occasions in 1944, including as recent as three weeks ago, the Wagner brothers also stayed in this motel.

On June 5, 1944, the FBI secured the cooperation of a warehouse manager in Newark, who had a contract with the government that supported the war effort. Due to its location, this warehouse provided the FBI with an excellent view of Kessler's grocery store and bakery.

After pulling the FBI car inside by the loading dock, Willie was taken upstairs to the third floor to keep an eye on Kessler and his daughter, while also watching out for Mueller. While Willie Gundrerson sat by the window and smoked his pipe, he spotted Rudy Mueller entering Kessler's store at 0900 hours. Thirty minutes later Mueller left the store and entered the warehouse next door. After calling the local field office, two additional FBI Agents were dispatched to help monitor Rudy Mueller's activities.

CHAPTER 31

D DAY AND MORE MEN GO OFF TO WAR

O n the morning of June 6, 1944, Beatrice Beauregard called her husband the moment she heard the news that a massive Allied invasion force landed in Normandy, France. "I just heard," remarked Jim as he rubbed his tired face and leaned on his desk while his wife said, "I keep thinking about Michael. God, I hope he's all right."

Even though Jim was just as concerned, he tried his best to reassure Bea that their youngest son was alive and well. "I have a good feeling, Bea. I can't explain it but I know Michael is OK."

As strong as she was, Beatrice Beauregard was no different than other mothers who had sons serving in the armed forces during World War II. Her baptism of fire came when their oldest son Peter was slightly wounded when his PT Boat was shot out from under him in the Solomon Islands. Even a strikingly beautiful woman like Beatrice Beauregard seemed to age a few years, when she received the telegram from the War Department that notified her and her husband that their oldest son was wounded in action. After being notified that Peter was recovering from his wounds, the Beauregards learned to take life one day at a time, especially when their oldest son informed his parents that he was returning to his PT Boat Squadron. While Jim understood why his oldest son was returning to his unit, his wife had a difficult time coping with the fact that Peter was not taking advantage of the leave that was given to all men who lost a ship in combat.

When their youngest son enlisted the day after he graduated from high school, Beatrice Beauregard went to her room and cried uncontrollably for herself and for all the other mothers who had sons who went off to war. As a Private assigned to the 327th Glider Infantry Regiment of the 101st Airborne Division, Michael Beauregard landed on Utah Beach while armed with a variety of weapons and a chest full of courage. Even though Michael trained to fly into combat in gliders, his unit went ashore in landing craft due to a shortage of suitable aircraft. Regardless, on June 6, 1944 Private Michael Beauregard became a combat veteran.

While his mother sat in the kitchen back home and talked to his father on the phone, Michael Beauregard was digging in near the beach, while he and his fellow glider infantry troops waited for the rest of their unit to come ashore. After promising to call his wife as soon as he heard something, Jim hung up the phone and buried his face in hands while he prayed for his youngest son and the other brave men who were fighting in Normandy.

When Colonel Richmond appeared at the door of his office with a concerned look on his face, Jim looked up just as his superior officer said, "Are you all right, Jim?"

Since Jim had been told that he did not have to stand when his CO entered a room, he remained seated when he shared his concerns with Colonel Richmond. "That was my wife on the phone. She heard about the landings in Normandy. She's worried about our son, Michael and to tell you the truth, Sir, so am I."

As concerned as he was about his own sons, Jim knew that Colonel Richmond had a son-in-law, as well as another young man who was engaged to his second oldest daughter who were scheduled to participate in the invasion of France whenever it occurred. Seeing the old war horse appear as calm as he was, made Jim feel as if he was overreacting until the Colonel smiled a bit then said, "My wife just called me too. We're worried as well, but there's nothing we can do except pray and hope that all of our loved ones and friends survive this ordeal."

As Colonel Richmond walked over to Jim's desk and picked up the phone, he looked at his second in command and said, "Your son's in the 101 right?"

"Yes, Sir," 3rd Battalion 327th Glider Infantry Regiment," responded Jim.

After the Colonel asked the operator to connect him to a telephone number at the Pentagon, he held his hand over the receiver and remarked, "Let me see if I can find out if there's any news about our boys."

While Jim used his Zippo to light a cigarette, Colonel Richmond transformed himself from a fellow law enforcement officer and a father figure to a professional Army officer as he spoke into the phone and said, "This is Colonel Richmond from CID New York, let me speak to Colonel Danvers."

Without haste the female Army telephone operator said, "Yes, Sir," and put his call though.

While waiting to be connected, Colonel Richmond turned to Jim and said, "Danvers is a retread like me. If anyone can find out what's going on over there it's him." The moment Colonel Danvers answered the phone in his office, Jim sat at the edge of his chair while Colonel Richmond inquired about the landings in France.

The first casualty of the D Day Invasion of Normandy, France among family members of the men who served in the New York CID Task Force was the oldest son of Sal Jacobi. After leaving medical school to enlist, Sal's oldest son lost his left leg from the knee down while treating wounded soldiers on Omaha Beach. Lt. Colonel Richmond's family also received a telegram informing them that his son in law was wounded while fighting as a first lieutenant in the 82nd Airborne Division. The young man who was engaged to one of Colonel Richmond's twin daughters survived the invasion while serving with the 1st Infantry Division.

The day Steve Klein's only son landed on Utah Beach while serving with the 4th Infantry Division, the U.S. Coast Guard LCI (Landing Craft Infantry) ship that his nephew was serving on was sunk by German gunners off the coast of Normandy. Joe Coppola also had one son serving in Normandy, France as a military policeman and another son being trained for war. Jack Donovan's oldest son was also fighting in France with the Second Armored Division.

After being wounded on his 14th bombing mission over Germany, Andy Dubrowsky's nephew, Thomas Dubrowsky, returned to his flying duties once he recovered from his shrapnel wounds. Andy's nephew would be shot down on his 19th mission over Germany and would spend the rest of the war in a German POW Camp.

Elsewhere in the war, Johnny Mc Donald's oldest son Matthew was a U.S. Marine who survived the fighting on Tarawa, but sustained a minor wound during the invasion of Saipan. Johnny Mc Donald's youngest son Erin was a Gunner's Mate (GM) serving on a U.S. Navy destroyer escort in the Southwest Pacific Area.

While Keven Kalb's oldest son was a U.S. Marine assigned to the 1st Tank Battalion, his youngest son was on his way to fight in the Battle of Guam as a soldier with the 77th Infantry Division. Richy Olsen's oldest son was serving with the 4th Marines and saw combat on the Kwajalein Atoll in early 1944. On July 24, 1944, Richy's son would land on Tinian Island and would be evacuated from combat when he was wounded in his left hand.

Because Frank Angelone's oldest son Nick had a year of college and spoke fluent Italian, he was recruited into the Office of Strategic Services (OSS) and served in Italy. Frank's youngest son Anthony also spoke fluent Italian and served with the 10th Military Police Battalion in the Italian Campaign.

While Eddie Evans had two sons serving on the New York City Police

Department, his youngest son and his 18 year old grandson served in U.S. Army combat units. In mid June of 1944, Eddie's youngest son was leading soldiers from the 6th U.S. Army Infantry Division against Japanese positions in the Battle of Lone Tree Hill in Dutch New Guinea. Eddie's 18 year old grandson would arrive in the ETO in time to serve in General Patton's 3rd Army during the Allied Invasion of Germany in March of 1945.

While Jim Beauregard's oldest son Peter continued to serve in the Pacific, his youngest son Michael survived the fighting in France and was back in England by July of 1944.

After graduating second in his class behind Lt. Perkins, Warrant Officer Gus O'Malley became a newly minted Assistant Glider Engineering Officer. As a graduation gift, the fugitive known as Gus O'Malley and Lt. Perkins received official notification that were assigned to serve in the 440th Troop Carrier Group under the command of the recently promoted Lt. Colonel Mike Kirby. Until they left for the ETO, Warrant Officer Gus O'Malley and Lt. Steve Perkins were asked to accept a temporary detail with the training cadre at Shepard Field. This assignment kept them busy and enabled the rest of the men who would serve in their engineering section to be properly trained before they left for Europe.

Once his orders to ship out to the ETO finally arrived, Shorty was a happy camper now that he had official confirmation that he was being sent overseas to serve with Danny Gannon and Steve Perkins. The only question that Shorty was unable to get answered, was whether he would be making the trip to the European Theater of Operation on the same troop transport as Ivan, or if he and Steve Perkins would be traveling overseas on a different vessel.

The night before he left Shepard Field, Shorty decided to accept an invitation to have a few drinks with the other men in his engineering section to celebrate receiving their orders to join the war in Europe. This was also the first time that Shorty was in a large social gathering without Ivan being present. Between graduating second in his class and the notoriety that he received as the man who recovered Chalk 14, Shorty was a celebrity of sorts among his fellow glider engineering personnel. In fact, these two achievements made it possible for the fugitive who was now known as Gus O'Malley to feel comfortable among his peers.

After several hours of drinking and carousing at a local bar, Shorty ended up a bit inebriated and feeling no pain. When Lt. Perkins nudged him on the shoulder and said, "Come on, Gus, it's time to go," Shorty made one of the worst mistakes in his life when he brushed his buddy aside and mumbled, "You go, Ivan," before he quickly recovered and acted as if he had a bad case of indigestion before he added "hoe is staying put."

Even though Shorty managed to catch himself and think quickly by turning the name Ivan into Ivanhoe, Steve Perkins wasn't sure what his buddy said and remarked, "What did you say Gus?

"I said you go. Ivanhoe is staying put," responded Shorty, who continued to act more intoxicated that he was. As Shorty continued he completed his comments by saying, "When I was a kid I wanted to be a knight in shinning armor like Ivanhoe. You should'a seen me, Steve. I had a wooden sword and used my bicycle as my horse. I was the best knight in shinning armor in New Jersey."

As Lt. Perkins smiled wide and disregarded the antics of his drunken classmate, he grabbed Shorty by the arm and said, "Let's go knight in shining armor. We gotta get back to camp."

Both Andy Dubrowsky and Dan Phillips believed that far too much was at stake to approach Rudy Mueller and ask him to cooperate, now that there was good reason to believe that Mueller and his associates were involved in a black market meat operation. Their position was based on the information that was gathered to date by FBI Agents and OPA officials out west, as well as by the observations that were being made by the agents who were working this case in New Jersey.

Even though it wasn't a crime to travel, none of the locations out west that were visited by John Miller, Rudolf Mueller and the Wagner brothers were famous vacation destinations. The FBI also determined that the Wagner brothers had good jobs as truck drivers on the east coast, that kept them busy enough without having to travel all the way out west to haul cargo. In contrast, Mueller didn't seem to have a legitimate source of income, even though he was observed on several occasions making what appeared to be sales calls to a number of local bars, restaurants and butcher shops in different cities in New Jersey.

FBI Agents also followed Max Hoffman when he left Mueller's warehouse in a truck, including at night, and made deliveries to many of the same businesses that Mueller visited on previous occasions. After making these observations, FBI Agents in New Jersey were convinced that the subjects of their investigation were involved in a black market meat supplying operation.

Now that it seemed that the FBI and the OPA would be able to make a case against Rudy Mueller and his associates, the decision was made to increase the coverage that was given to the subjects of this investigation. While the FBI Field Office in Newark, New Jersey directed the main focus of the surveillance operation on Mueller and his warehouse, agents also kept tabs on the Gunther Kessler, the Wagner brothers and Max Hoffman.

After completing tactical training at Laurenburg Maxton Army Air Base in North Carolina, Flight Officer Danny Gannon received his orders to report to the European Theater of Operation. After a well deserved forty eight hour pass, Ivan Larson aka Danny Gannon and a group of his fellow glider pilots were transported by train to Camp Kilmer in New Jersey.

When Beatrice Beauregard called and told her husband that their son Peter decided to use his survivors leave and come home for a visit, Lt. Colonel Richmond handed Jim a three day pass and had Lt. Lorenz take his second in command to Pennsylvania Station. Even though his visit was short, Jim was able to bond with his naval officer son and spend some time relaxing with his wife and family.

Between having Peter back home and knowing that Michael was back in England after fighting in France, the Beauregard family had a great deal to be thankful for. After a wonderful visit, Jim walked through the railroad station with his wife and his oldest son as the conductor notified the passengers bound for New York City to board the northbound train.

As Jim turned to Peter, he tried not to think that this might be the last time they saw each other. Jim knew from his discussions with his oldest son, that once his survivors leave was over, Peter was being promoted and reassigned to serve on a destroyer. Knowing that his oldest son was returning to a combat command was enough to make this a difficult moment for a parent to experience. Jim also believed that Fred Richmond was right when he said, "Sometimes all you can do is pray."

The Navy Cross and the Purple Heart ribbons that were appropriately displayed on his oldest son's uniform were a clear indication that Lt. Peter Clayton Beauregard was a fighting man in the truest sense of the word. Even though this was the case, Jim and his wife Bea were typical parents who would always remember the days when their two sons were infants and little boys. Having these memories made it considerably more difficult to see a child that you raised from birth to manhood go off to war.

As soon as Jim shook his son's hand, he pulled Peter close to him and patted him on the back while he said, "Don't ever forget how proud I am of you, son." Even though many fathers in 1944 were not known for openly displaying affection for their children, James Beauregard was a man ahead of his time.

As soon as father and son pulled apart, Jim looked at his oldest son and said, "Promise me you'll be careful."

"I promise, Dad," responded Peter who quickly added, "And don't worry about Michael. He's a tough kid. He'll be OK."

While Beatrice wiped the tears from her eyes with an embroidered cotton handkerchief, Jim did his best to appear in control of his emotions as he nodded his head in agreement and limited his response to a simple, "I know."

To prove to his father that he was just as concerned about his safety, Peter ran his right index finger across the same section of his own scalp line where a bullet grazed his father's forehead and said, "You be careful too, Pop. You've seen more action stateside than some of the guys who are stationed overseas."

"I see your mother gave me up," remarked Jim, as he tried to make light of the fact that he sustained a minor gunshot wound while performing his duties as an Army Investigator.

"Don't let it happen again, Dad," remarked Peter.

When Jim responded he said the only thing that made sense under the circumstances. "How 'bout I say that I'll do my best to be just as careful as you and your brother."

As a combat veteran of the Pacific War, Peter Beauregard knew exactly what his father meant. No matter how hard a serviceman tried to avoid being killed or wounded, bad things happened to good people every day. To let his father know that he got the message, Peter limited his response to a simple, "OK, Dad."

The moment the conductor walked by and said, "All aboard, Sir," Jim turned to his wife and gently grabbed her right hand as he said, "I have to go, Bea."

While acting as if she was a loved starved teenager, Beatrice Beauregard draped her arms around her husband's neck and told him how much she loved him before she kissed him passionately on the lips. As the train began to slowly pull out of the station, Bea stepped back and said, "You better go."

After saying, "I love you, Bea," Jim grabbed his bag from his son and jumped on the slow moving train. While holding on to the railing in between the cars, Jim sounded more like a father when he looked back and called out, "Take care of your mother and don't forget to write."

During World War II, the United States went from being an isolationist nation to the Arsenal of Democracy and a full fledged partner in the war against fascism in the span of a few short years. Once the Japanese attacked Pearl Harbor on December 7, 1941, and war was declared against the Axis forces, the U.S. expanded its military might to meet the demands of fighting a two front war.

In order to facilitate the transportation of troops and equipment overseas, the United States developed a network of Ports of Embarkation or POE. Servicemen from all over the United States were funneled to an embarkation base, where they would remain for a short period of time before being transported to a nearby port where a merchant vessel would take them overseas.

Camp Kilmer was an embarkation base located near Brunswick, New Jersey. This camp was ideally suited to serve as an embarkation facility, because it was a relatively short distance by train and ferry from Camp Kilmer to various piers on the New York and New Jersey side of the harbor. With the camp shut off from the outside world, the troops who were destined to travel overseas were under strict orders not to leave the base. Although the majority complied with the strict security procedures, some men slipped past the military police for a last night out on the town before they shipped out.

While Ivan Larson kept an eye on the two MPs, two of his fellow glider pilots debated whether they should slip though the hole in the fence and to enjoy the local nightlife before they left for the ETO. As soon as Flight Officer Mike Butler turned to Ivan Larson aka Danny Gannon and asked if he was going along, Ivan responded and said, "I think I'll stay behind and hit the sack early tonight. Besides, I don't think anything's changed since I left this part of the country and joined the Army."

Under the circumstances Ivan had no intention of tempting fate by traveling into any city in New Jersey or New York. Besides, after months of training, Ivan was looking forward to getting into combat as soon as possible. Ivan was also hoping to meet up with Shorty and pick up where they left off. If they were lucky they would survive the war and live happily ever after in Europe.

The only rumor that disturbed Ivan was that the war in Europe would be over by Christmas. The moment Ivan heard this rumor he feared being stationed in the U.S., while the War Department prepared to invade Japan. As a result, no one was more relieved than Flight Officer Danny Gannon when he received orders to ship out to the ETO. As far as Ivan was concerned, the U.S. Army wasn't sending every available glider pilot to Europe just to bring them home for the holidays. While Ivan watched Flight Officer Butler and Flight Officer Romero successfully crawl through the hole in the fence, he knew he made the right decision to remain behind. He felt this way because in the morning he would be on his way to Europe. Even though Ivan knew that he could still be pursued overseas, once his troop transport left the dock he would be on his way to completing an important part of his escape plan.

After wondering where Shorty was, Ivan thought about all that had transpired since he became a wanted man. Ever since Ivan heard that Shorty would be going to Glider Engineering School, he became concerned about his buddy being on his own. While Ivan had his fictional life memorized, he was always concerned that Shorty could be broken in a matter of minutes if the military or civilian police ever questioned him about his past.

Ivan and Shorty also knew that Army CID was looking for an orphan and a teenager who left home after having a falling out with his stepfather and never returned. Once again, Mike Connely was right. It was the little things that got you arrested. Making up a believable past and being able to remember your cover story was critical for a fugitive. It was also just as important to blend in and appear to be as law abiding and patriotic as everyone else. Thanks to Mike Connely, the two fugitives looked like typical red blooded Americans whenever they received a succession of letters, food parcels, newspapers and junk mail from home during mail call.

While acting as if Shorty was his cousin, Ivan made people ignore them as suspects when the word spread that CID was looking for an orphan and a runaway. The fact that Danny Gannon and his cousin Gus O'Malley spent the bulk of their life growing up in New Jersey, further protected them from being identified as the two fugitives who were from New York City. Again, as Mad Mike Connely said, it was the little details that kept you from coming under suspicion.

While Ivan stamped his last cigarette out for the night, he wondered if Shorty would be boarding a troop transport to the ETO any time soon. Even when Ivan heard that a glider engineering unit was scheduled to travel to the ETO in the next few days, Ivan was unable to locate Shorty among the thousands of troops who passed through Camp Kilmer on any given day. It was also possible that Shorty was sent to a different embarkation base. This meant that unless Shorty made a grand entrance by the time his train left the station, Ivan would be going to Europe without his partner in crime.

CHAPTER 32

TURNING UP THE HEAT

While a heavy rain fell on New York City, Al Parker finished reading the most recent letter from his oldest son for a third time. As a U.S. Army fighter pilot, Lt. Jack Parker was based in Italy while flying combat missions in a P51 Mustang.

While beaming with pride, Al Parker could hardly contain himself, as he looked across the conference room table at Detective Angelone and remarked, "Hey, Ange, good news from Italy. My son Jack just shot down his second German plane."

As the sarcastically irreverent Frank Angelone closed the case file that he was reading, he looked across the conference room table at Al and said, "That's great, Al, but do me a favor and tell flying Jack Parker to watch what he's shooting at over there 'cause I still got family on the other side. That includes my two sons who got sent to Italy 'cause they speak the lingo."

After cracking a smile, Al responded and said, "Sure thing, Ange," as he placed the letter back into the envelope before he put the letter in his suit jacket pocket.

When a soaking wet Johnny Mc Donald walked into the conference room carrying a large wooden crate that was filled with food from his parent's bar, Frank Angelone remarked, "Look, Al, a wet Leprechaun."

As soon as Johnny Mc Donald put the box on the table, he hung up his rain soaked hat and trench coat and said, "It would be the luck of the Irish that it was my turn to pick up our supper during a thunderstorm."

The moment he heard his partner complain about the weather, Frank Angelone stood up behind the conference room table and motioned Johnny to move faster as he said, "Chop chop, stop complaining and deliver the goods, will ya? Me and Al are starv'in."

While Johnny removed their supper from the wooden crate, Al Parker finished setting the table while he remarked, "You know, Johnny, your Mom makes the best bar food in New York City."

After thanking Al for complimenting his mother's cooking, the happy go lucky Irish American police detective continued and said, "When my mother heard we were working late again, she made us an extra pot of boiled potatoes with sliced hard boiled eggs and onions to go with a big batch of grilled Spam sandwiches on homemade bread."

When Frank Angelone remarked, "What, no dessert?" Johnny produced a metal tin that was filled with a batch of his mother's signature oatmeal cookies with raisins and said, "Are you happy now?"

As soon as Frank spotted the pile of homemade cookies, he rubbed his hands together and acted like a kid in a candy store when he remarked, "Look, Al, the famous Mrs. Mc Donald's homemade oatmeal cookies with raisins."

While Al admired their dessert, he smiled then said, "I can't wait to have one of those babies with a hot cup of coffee"

After seeing how Frank and Al reacted to the sight of their desert, Johnny acted like the only adult in the room when he moved the tin of cookies away from his two colleagues and said, "No dessert for you two until after we eat."

While Johnny Mc Donald and Al Parker finished setting the table, Frank Angelone became serious as he picked up the pot of coffee and filled three mugs. "The Major's been looking at the new wanted posters for over an hour. Maybe we should let him know the food's here."

Al Parker agreed and sounded genuinely concerned. "I'd hate to see him go without supper when we have a full night of work ahead of us."

As soon Johnny spoke up and said, "You boys sit tight. I'll get him." he headed for the door to the conference to let Jim know that he was back with their supper.

While Johnny could be heard telling Jim Beauregard that it was chow time, Frank Angelone placed a mug of coffee where his partner was sitting, before passing one to Al. "Here you go, Al. Be careful, it's hot."

Anywhere else in the world an African American would never be served by a white man. As outspoken as he was, Frank Angelone never forgot his roots and knew how hard it was for him and his relatives to make it in a city that was controlled by the Irish. Even though Johnny MC Donald was like a brother to him, Frank had a long standing general distrust of the Irish that went back to his childhood. He felt this way because the Irish could be clannish bastards who took care of their own and went out of their way to screw the dagos. In fact, as crazy as this would sound to some people in 1944, there were times when Frank believed that he had more in common with Al Parker than he did with most Irishmen. Naturally, this didn't apply to people like Johnny Mc Donald and his family or members of the Murphy clan.

As a full blooded Italian American, Detective Frank Angelone grew up believing that the Irish had a short memory and forgot what it was like to be the low man on the totem pole. Once the Irish came to power, through their methodical takeover of the police and fire departments, they ruled as if they were preordained to be in charge of the city's public safety services. If you were Irish you were protected and taken care of. If you were white but not Irish you had to settle for the leftovers and be grateful for everything you got. It was also no day at the beach to be Jewish. If you were colored, you were really screwed. Even when Fiorello LaGuardia became Mayor and politics in New York City began to change for the better, the Italians and other ethnic groups would never control the police department or the fire department the way the Irish did.

As soon as Al thanked Frank for the coffee, Johnny returned and said, "He's on the way."

While the three city cops who were assigned to the Army CID Task Force began passing food around the table, Al Parker placed a sandwich in his dish before he looked out the window at the falling rain and said, "I wonder where our two fugitives are right now?" A second later the pouring rain was accompanied by flashes of bright white lightening and a barrage of thunder over the city.

After taking another look at the latest artist conceptions of what Ivan Larson and Shorty Mc Ghee might look like, Jim Beauregard figured that they had nothing to lose and everything to gain by publishing these sketches in various publications, including in The Stars and Stripes Newspaper and Yank Magazine. Jim felt this way because the alternative was to take no action at all and allow potential witnesses to forget about this investigation.

By continuing to publish information about this investigation, Jim and his men were hoping to keep this case alive and increase the chances that someone in the U.S. Army would become suspicious of the two fugitives. Under the circumstances, anything was better than continuing to print outdated wanted posters of two men who no doubt looked different since they became soldiers. After collecting the four best composite sketches off his desk, Jim Beauregard left his office and walked down the hall to the conference room.

As soon as the Major entered the conference room, Johnny Mc Donald called out, "You're working too hard, Jimmy. Have a seat and join us. The food is still warm."

After admiring the array of food that was laid out on the conference room table, Jim seemed anxious to eat as he sat at the head of the table and said, "Well, Johnny, I can see your mother's been working overtime in the kitchen again."

While Johnny Mc Donald remarked, "Supper tonight is simple fare but we've got plenty to go around," he and Al Parker passed pots and plates of food to the Major, while Frank filled Jim's mug to the brim with some freshly brewed coffee.

As soon as Jim thanked his men for the food and the hot coffee, he continued as he handed Frank Angelone the folder that contained the new wanted posters. "Nice work, on the new sketches, Al."

Immediately after Al thanked the Major, Detective Angelone admired the art work and remarked, "Gee, Al, I didn't know you could draw," before he passed the sketches to Johnny Mc Donald.

While Al Parker cracked a smile, Johnny Mc Donald examined the new composite drawings before he passed the folder containing the sketches back to Jim Beauregard as he added his own two cents to the conversation. "These new sketches are a definite improvement over the drawings that we've been working with. At the very least these new wanted posters should help motivate soldiers to keep talking about this case." "I agree," said Frank Angelone who quickly added, "Anything we can do to keep this case alive has to produce results at some point."

After taking a bite of his grilled Spam sandwich on homemade bread, Jim Beauregard sipped some coffee before he looked at the others and said, "According to our contact at the War Department, the new composite sketches will start getting published with an updated article about this case in Army publications in two to three weeks. It will also take about the same amount of time to distribute the new wanted posters to every military police unit in the states. Naturally, it will take longer to get these new sketches to units overseas, especially to units in forward areas. The good news is that local newspapers around the country will start receiving copies of the new wanted posters along with an updated article about this case in less than a week."

Al Parker knew that a lot could happen in the span of a few weeks, especially during a world war. After seeing a concerned look on Al's face, Jim said, "I know how you feel, Al. Unfortunately, whenever Colonel Richmond and I mention the importance of this case to our superiors and we ask for more assistance we get reminded that there's a war on."

While Al Parker looked directly at Jim Beauregard he responded and said, "There's no doubt in my mind, Major, that everyone involved in this case wants to see Larson and Mc Ghee taken into custody as much as I do. I was just thinking that we might be able to come up with other ways to move this case along, beyond circulating the new composite sketches of Larson and Mc Ghee. I guess what I'm trying to say, is that we need to make the search for the two fugitives more than just a newspaper story or a set of wanted posters."

While the Major scooped up another fork full of food, he looked over at Al and said, "What do you have in mind, Al?"

Al Parker was further encouraged to speak his mind when Johnny Mc Donald said, "Go ahead, Al," and the colorful Frank Angelone remarked, "Yea, Al, spit it out." After being encouraged to continue, Al responded and said, "I know this may sound like a crazy idea, Major, but maybe we should consider broadcasting information about this case on a radio program as a way to get the word out and keep G.I.s interested in this manhunt."

After months of pursuing the two fugitives to no avail, Jim Beauregard was open to any suggestions that made sense. "That's an excellent idea, Al," remarked Jim Beauregard who quickly added, "I mean it. That's a good one."

As soon as Al said, "Thanks, Major," Jim considered what Al just said as he thought of another way to keep this case in the news and make life miserable for Ivan Larson and Francis Shorty Mc Ghee.

While Jim looked around the table, he shared what he had in mind with the others. "Soldiers also watch newsreels when they go to the movies. If we can get some civilian and Army camera crews to give us a hand, we can produce some film footage that will make it look like every CID Agent, MP, Shore Patrolman, G Man and cop in the country is looking for Ivan Larson and Francis Shorty Mc Ghee."

After hearing what Al and the Major had to say, Detective Angelone remarked, "Since we're tossing ideas around, why don't we ask the War Department to authorize a 30 day furlough for any military personnel who provide information that leads to the arrest of the two fugitives. After all, unless things have changed since I was in the Army, most soldiers would give up their own mother to have 30 days away from their Uncle Sam."

Jim proved that he liked what he was hearing when he agreed with Frank's suggestion and said, "We could have the most popular Armed Forces Radio Program of the entire war, if we offered a reward of a 30 day furlough to any military personnel who provide information that leads to the arrest of the two fugitives."

"That's it then," remarked, Johnny Mc Donald, who quickly added, "It's time to go on the air, so we can let Larson and Mc Ghee know that we're doing everything possible to hunt them down."

Frank Angelone was the next man at the table to speak up and said, "Just imagine the pressure that Larson and Mc Ghee will be under, when the soldiers they serve with start listening to radio broadcasts about this case and they watch newsreel footage that shows the effort that's being made to locate the two most famous fugitives of this war."

Once again Al spoke up and reminded everyone that they could have their radio programs recorded right here in New York City, then shipped overseas in time to coincide with the publication of a series of articles in The Stars and Stripes Newspaper and Yank Magazine.

After hearing what Al had to say, Jim finished sprinkling salt on his plate of food before he looked at the others and said, "I also think it's time to expand our screening operation in the POE. Instead of just using military police, shore patrolman and the few of us who are available to screen troops leaving for overseas, I think it's time that we put our witnesses back to work. In addition to using our witnesses to screen troops before they board ships in the port, we'll also use our limited number of witnesses to help us inspect troops as they enter and leave embarkation camps."

Before Jim continued he took a sip from his coffee mug. "When we used our witnesses during the early stages of this investigation, we had them looking at photographs of newly inducted G.I.s from New York City and screening troops at a few reception centers but we never publicized the fact that we did so. Maybe that was a mistake."

After picking up where the Major left off, Johnny Mc Donald was quick to comment. "No matter how much Larson and Mc Ghee may have changed since they became soldiers, they might decide to go AWOL rather than risk coming face to face with the witnesses who can identify them."

As soon as Al asked, "When do we start?" Jim responded without hesitation. "Whether he likes it or not Andy Gooding will be picked up tomorrow morning at 0600 by Lt. Lorenz and Richy Olsen to begin screening troops who are heading overseas from the New York POE. I'll also ask Keven Kalb and Steve Klein to pick up Tommy Shea bright and early and get that useless SOB out to the port for screening duty. If Mr. Shea complains one bit we'll lock him up in the city jail for being drunk and disorderly until he agrees to cooperate."

When Al Parker asked about using Amos Washington, the Major responded, "Don't worry, Al, he'll be out there. I just have to ask Captain Murphy if he can assign two patrolman to escort Amos Washington from the city jail to the port on a daily basis for as long as we use witnesses to screen departing troops."

After pausing for a split second to take another sip from his coffee mug, Jim continued addressing the others and said, "As soon as we finish eating, I'll start making calls."

When Frank Angelone asked about using Curly Gooding to screen departing troops, the Major responded and said, "That kid's been through enough, Ange, but we'll include him in some newsreel footage just to let Ivan Larson think that we're using every available witness to hunt him down."

The Major then turned to Al Parker and said, "How 'bout giving the good Sister a call in the morning and see if she can help out. If she's free take my car and pick her up. Once you explain what we're trying to do, you and I can run Sister O'Rourke over to the port to start screening troops as they board ships."

As usual, Al was quick to respond. "You got it, Major," Jim then turned to Frank Angelone and said, "Ange, I need you to call our contact at the Office of War Information. We need him to come into the office as soon as possible to help us get the word out about our intensified effort to hunt down Larson and Mc Ghee."

"My pleasure, Major," said Frank."

As Jim looked around the table he continued. "I'll talk to Colonel Richmond in the morning about requesting approval from the War Department to authorize a 30 day furlough as a reward in this case. We also need to meet with the Commanding Officer of the MP detachment in the port to let him know what we're up to."

After pausing to light a cigarette, Jim continued and said, "I'll also talk to Captain Murphy about using his contacts to get us some newspaper coverage and newsreel footage of the intensified effort by the CID Task Force to apprehend Ivan Larson and Francis Shorty Mc Ghee. In addition to the help that we get from the civilian press, I'll ask the Colonel to get us an Army camera crew that can take film footage of our people canvassing embarkation bases like Camp Kilmer and Camp Shanks."

As the Major continued, he turned to Al Parker and said, "Al, you, me and Andy Dubrowsky are about to become the stars of the CID Radio Show. In order to do this right, I need you to use the case file, as well as your notes, to draft a number of detailed outlines that can be used as the basis for a series of radio show interviews. We'll kick things off by describing what happened the night Ivan Larson killed Tommy Mulray and Tony G. After that we'll cover the raid on Gooding's garage and highlights of the various field trips that we took to locate the two fugitives. We need these radio broadcasts to be just as interesting as an episode of Dick Tracy and Terry and The Pirates."

While Al acknowledged his instructions, Jim took a drag on his cigarette before he continued addressing the only cop who could identify Ivan Larson. "I hate to ask you to do this, Al, but if we're gonna use a radio program to let troops know how dangerous Larson and Mc Ghee are, it would help a great deal if we dedicated an entire episode on the bank robbery in Brooklyn. In order for this broadcast to be effective we need G.I.s all over the world to have their ears glued to their radios, when they listen to you describe everything that happened during that robbery. That includes how Ivan Larson shot and killed Patrolman Patrick Murphy Jr., a police officer who was a highly decorated U.S. Army Sergeant who was medically discharged after being wounded on Guadalcanal. We also need troops to hear how ruthless Francis Shorty Mc Ghee was, when he blazed away at a small army of policemen with a Thompson Submachine Gun."

Once again Al proved that he was a team player when he spoke up and said, "Don't worry, Major. I'll do whatever is necessary to catch these bastards. All I hope is that Ivan Larson and his submachine gun toting sidekick are listening when I end my interview by telling them that we're coming to get 'em."

After thanking Al for agreeing to relive what happened during the robbery on a radio show, Jim continued and said, "In the next episode we'll feature the story about how you and Captain Murphy arrested Amos Washington. We'll end that episode with a description of the interrogation of Amos Washington and our efforts to screen troops departing for overseas. If he's up to it, I'd like Captain Murphy to participate in these broadcasts. Last but not least, I also plan on asking Sister O'Rourke to let us interview her on our radio show."

After hearing what Jim had to say, Al Parker remarked, "I'll bet a months pay that it will piss Ivan Larson off to no end to hear Sister O'Rourke describe how she gave him up for his own good."

As soon as Johnny Mc Donald and Frank Angelone agreed, Jim concluded his remarks as he looked around the table. "In order to make this a real radio program, I'll ask Colonel Richmond to get us a well known celebrity to handle the actual interviews. After all, we're cops not radio personalities."

As promising as all this sounded, cops like Al Parker, Frank Angelone and Johnny Mc Donald were still pissed off at the Army, for excluding "civilian" law enforcement officers from pursuing the two fugitives overseas. They felt this way because men like Frank Angelone, Johnny Mc Donald and Al Parker were veteran street cops who worked every case and every call they handled from beginning to end until they completed their assigned task. If this meant they had to work without sleep or on a day off, they did so and never complained, especially when the fruits of their labor resulted in the arrest of a dangerous criminal.

The same was true for Special Agent Andy Dubrowsky and every other member of the CID Task Force who was considered a "civilian" law enforcement officer. Being told by the U.S. Army that police officers and federal agents would not be allowed to pursue the two fugitives on foreign soil, made absolutely no sense to a group of hard charging civilian law enforcement officers who routinely went in harms way for a living.

While being as brutally honest as he was respectful, Detective Angelone spoke up and said, "Nothing personal, Major, but none of us so called civilian cops are happy about being excluded from this case, especially if we develop leads that indicate that Larson and Mc Ghee are overseas. In fact, we all believe the War Department's position on this issue stinks in plain English."

As a U.S. Army officer who also happened to be a cop from Georgia, Jim didn't like the War Department's official position on this issue either. Since Jim knew that the non military law enforcement officers who were assigned to the CID Task Force were not happy with the Army's official position on this matter, he decided to come up with a few ways to address this issue with the War Department.

Jim knew that he had everyone's undivided attention when he looked around the table and explained what he had in mind. "I have two ways that I intend to address this issue. First, I plan to file a written request through the chain of command that explains the need to have additional sworn civilian personnel who are familiar with this case available to assist CID Agents and military police, if and when it becomes necessary to conduct this investigations overseas."

After pausing long enough to take one last drag on his cigarette, the Major looked at all three New York City cops as he continued. "If necessary, I also intend to justify my request by reminding our Uncle Sam, that the War Department allows civilian war correspondents to serve with U.S. military personnel in combat units, so why not authorize federal agents and city police officers to travel overseas, including in and around forward areas, to locate and arrest two dangerous fugitives?"

The first to comment was Johnny Mc Donald. "Excellent idea, Jimmy."

Frank Angelone was next to comment and said, "If civilian war correspondents can travel with our troops, I see no reason why a few cops and G Men can't go overseas to help capture two fugitives who are hiding out in the Army?"

Al Parker also agreed, then quickly added, "Besides, no one knows this case better than we do."

After stamping his cigarette butt out in a nearby ashtray, the Major continued and said, "Before we raise this issue with the Army again we have to develop a lead that's worth pursuing overseas. In order to do so, we have to exhaust every option available to us, while we make the lives of our two fugitives as miserable as possible. Larson and Mc Ghee need to be constantly worried that they'll either be spotted by a witness, or a fellow soldier will get suspicious enough to turn them in to CID or the MPs."

As soon as Frank Angelone opened four bottles of Rheingold beer and passed them around the table, Johnny Mc Donald raised his bottle of beer in the air and proposed a toast. While Jim Beauregard, Frank Angelone and Al Parker raised their beer bottles, Johnny Mc Donald remarked, "Ivan Larson and Francis Shorty Mc Ghee here we come."

After taking a sip of beer, Jim removed a small notebook from his shirt pocket and spoke as he passed the book to Frank Angelone. "This notebook contains the names of every Army camp and fort that we inspected, as well as every ship that had its passengers screened before it was allowed to leave a POE. In addition, this book also contains notes about the effort that's being made by a small army of FBI Agents and OPA officials, including Andy Dubrowsky and Eddie Evans, to locate Rudy Mueller."

As soon as Frank finished examining the pocket size black notebook, he handed the book to Johnny Mc Donald and said, "It's hard to believe that after all this hard work we still haven't found these guys."

"You're right, Ange," responded Jim who quickly added, "A lotta water has gone under the bridge since this case began and it's not over yet. Even so, I still believe the day's gonna come when we're gonna get our hands on Larson and Mc Ghee."

As Johnny Mc Donald leaned across the table and handed the notebook to Al Parker, the only cop who knew what Ivan Larson looked like spoke up and said, "I have my bad days, but overall I still have a good feeling about this case."

Even though Al Parker was just as frustrated by the lack of success as everyone else, he knew that they had to keep plugging away if they wanted to make any headway in this case. While doing his best to sound as positive as possible, Al handed the notebook back to Jim Beauregard as he remarked, "Who knows, maybe we'll get lucky tonight."

"Let's hope so, Al," responded Jim Beauregard before he checked his watch as he stood up then said, "As soon as I make a few calls, we'll head out to Mitchell Field to screen the air crews who'll be departing for the ETO in the next few days."

Between the physical evidence that was gathered to date and the observations that were made in the field, the FBI and the OPA believed that at some point Mueller and his associates would need to acquire another shipment of black market beef from out west. Once that happened, the FBI and OPA would be in a position to catch Mueller and his associates red handed.

Up until now Willie Gunderson served a valuable purpose by helping the FBI to identify and locate Mueller and his associates. After discussing their options, Dan Phillips and Andy Dubrowsky agreed that the time was right for Willie to run into some of his old friends. Just as Dan expected, Willie agreed to serve in an undercover capacity and suggested that the FBI make it possible for him to have a "chance" encounter with the Wagner brothers.

In order to build a believable cover story, the decision was made for Willie to be moved into a furnished room near Hoboken. Arrangements were also made for Willie to be offered a civilian job in the Port of Embarkation.

CHAPTER 33

IVAN LARSON-SHORTY MC GHEE AND THE QUEEN MARY

After spending a week at Camp Kilmer in New Jersey, Ivan Larson was ready to ship out to the European Theater of Operation. With breakfast out of the way, the glider pilots who were destined to serve in the ETO assembled under the watchful eyes of a contingent of military policemen. The moment it became time to move out, Ivan and his fellow glider pilots were turned over to the transportation officers for the train ride to Jersey City, New Jersey. Once they arrived in Jersey City, Ivan and his fellow glider pilots were scheduled to travel by ferry to the actual port where they were slated to board a ship for their trip to the ETO.

After a tense moment that involved passing by a formation of MPs, Ivan boarded the train with a mixture of trepidation and adrenaline rushing through his veins as he took his seat. Ivan received a second jolt to his system when he heard that there was a change in plans and that he and his fellow glider pilots were being taken to a pier in Manhattan, instead of to a pier on the New Jersey side of the harbor. If one thing gave Ivan the confidence to carry on, it was the fact that between his uniform, the helmet that he wore and the equipment that he carried, he should be able to blend in with the thousands of other men who were traveling to New York City to board a troop transport for Europe.

Once the train lurched forward, Ivan felt a strange feeling consume him from head to toe. It was finally happening. After months of serving in the U.S. Army under an assumed name, Ivan Larson aka Danny Gannon was making his way to the ship that would take him to Europe. While Ivan carried on a conversation with another glider pilot, he thought to himself, so far so good.

After loading their gear on the British troop transport, the American soldiers who were destined to cross the Atlantic on a pathetically slow ship got the break of a lifetime. Although most of the passengers were still topside when it happened, those who were below decks were ordered to abandon ship in an orderly fashion when an electrical fire broke out in the vessel's radio room. When a second electrical fire broke out in the adjoining cabin, a New York City Fire Department boat responded to provide assistance in case the fire spread any further.

As disappointed as the crew was to see their vessel damaged in this fashion, the American troops were glad to hear the order to grab their gear and assemble on the pier for further instructions. Within a matter of minutes the pier was filled with American soldiers, who were glad to get off a ship that was famous for serving mutton and oatmeal with raisins for breakfast, lunch and dinner. Once the decision was made to have the troops destined for the ETO board another ship, a U.S. Navy Convoy Control Officer ordered the contingent of U.S. Army Air Forces personnel to move out.

While Ivan marched away from the damaged British ship, he did his best to conceal the fact that he was pissed beyond belief, that he would have to go through another checkpoint in order to board another troop transport. Ivan was also worried about Shorty, especially since his partner in crime was the nervous type and would not fair well, if he was questioned by the authorities when he was so close to making his way to Europe.

As the contingent of U.S. Army Troop Carrier personnel made their way to another pier, men began placing bets among each other about the size and nationality of the next ship that they would be ordered to board. After being told to quiet down, the men returned to being good soldiers and followed the U.S. Navy Convoy Control Officer in an orderly fashion to another section of the port.

After walking some distance, Ivan and his fellow glider pilots were elated to see the Queen Mary getting ready to set sail. Painted for war, the most famous ocean liner in the world was capable of making 19 knots and reaching Europe in six days. Even though her decks were jam packed with other soldiers, the massive ship known as The Queen seemed big enough to handle a few more. This was one time when no one had any complaints. Whether by accident or design, every soldier learned to accept any positive turn of events with a smile whenever good things came their way.

While Ivan waited his turn to board the Queen Mary, he looked up at the excited faces of other American soldiers who packed the railing to greet the new-comers. Between the patriotic music that was being played over a loudspeaker and the presence of Red Cross ladies handing out treats, the process of going to war seemed to be a rather festive occasion.

As Ivan inched forward in line, he hoped that someone would remember that his unit was already screened before he was forced to go through another checkpoint. The closer he got to the gangway, the more Ivan began to wonder how far he would get if he broke from the ranks and tried to make a run for it. Even though he was armed with a pistol and a carbine, Ivan knew that he would have little or no chance of making his way back to Mike Connely's hideout, if he got into a shootout with the military and civilian cops who were stationed on every pier in this section of Manhattan.

While Ivan was grateful that there wasn't a Negro cop in sight, he felt his stomach tighten in knots when he spotted a Military Police Jeep carrying Andy Gooding and two cops in plainclothes heading his way. As Ivan turned his head ever so slightly to the left, he continued conversing with a fellow glider pilot, while he listened for the sound of a Jeep coming to a screeching halt and Andy Gooding screaming, "That's him!" When the Jeep continued on its way to an another pier, Ivan was relieved that Andy Gooding never spotted him in the column of soldiers who were on their way to board the Queen Mary.

While Ivan prepared himself to act as unconcerned as everyone else, his stomach tightened again when he spotted civilian cameramen setting up their equipment. Even if Ivan was lucky enough to get past the scrutiny of another checkpoint, he also had to worry about being photographed for newspapers and newsreel footage that would be shown in movie theaters all over the USA, as well as to troops overseas. Ivan felt another lightening bolt of fear grip his spine, when he spotted Amos Washington standing by the gangway while being guarded by a pair of uniformed city policemen.

Ivan's situation was made worse when a tough looking cop in plainclothes pointed to a short stocky glider pilot who was immediately pulled out of line by an Army MP. After comparing the soldiers face to a series of wanted posters, an MP Lieutenant checked the soldier's dog tags, while the cop in plainclothes examined the young glider pilot's identification card. The final level of scrutiny took place, when the cop in plainclothes asked the two patrolman to bring their prisoner over, to take a look of the pilot who matched the description of Francis Shorty Mc Ghee.

Ivan knew that the man they pulled outta line was a glider pilot by the name of Thomas Reed, a young man from Kansas who was Shorty's height but a good ten pounds heavier. Seeing a somber looking and handcuffed Amos Washington limp over to where Flight Officer Reed was being held for questioning, was a disturbing sight for Ivan to witness. If anyone ever wanted to serve his country in time of war it was Amos Washington. Just seeing the way that Amos was being manhandled was enough to boil Ivan's blood.

The final level of embarrassment that Amos was subjected to, took place when the cop in plainclothes pointed to F.O. Reed and said, "Is this him?"

Without saying a word Amos responded by shaking his head from left to right. As soon as Flight Officer Reed was allowed to board the ship, the U.S. Navy Convoy Control Officer waded through the crowd and informed the detail of military and civilian police that this group was already screened and were cleared to travel overseas.

While the U.S. Navy Convoy Control Officer showed his clipboard to the MP Lieutenant, he finished his remarks by saying, "The Royal Navy troop transport that this group was cleared to board had to be evacuated when a fire broke out in the radio room. When that happened I was told to bring 'em here."

While Ivan stood ten rows away from coming under the scrutiny of Amos Washington and a much more thorough group of law enforcement officers, he felt the weight of the world lift from his shoulders, when the MP Lieutenant in charge of the detail instructed his men to return to the command post for reassignment. As the two uniformed cops placed Amos Washington in the back of a Jeep, Ivan desperately wanted to take a quick look at the only Negro friend he ever had before he was taken away. The moment the pair of Jeeps filled with military and civilian cops and their prisoner left check point, Ivan decided not to tempt fate and turned away just as the Jeep carrying Amos Washington drove by his place in line. What the most wanted man in the U.S. Army didn't know at the time, was that his trusted Negro friend was sure he just spotted his buddy Ivan standing in line waiting to board the Queen Mary. Even though this soldier looked a bit different, something told Amos that Ivan Larson was on his way to war. As the Jeep drove away from the screening area, Amos kept the sighting to himself and thought, "Ba ba bye I I Ivan. Ga ga good la luck."

After turning to the glider pilot standing to his left, Ivan remarked, "I hate to say it but it looks like the U.S. Navy got all the smart officers."

While the glider pilot standing next to Ivan cracked a smile, the U.S. Navy Convoy Control Officer sounded especially polite when he addressed the British Royal Navy Boarding Officer. "Sorry about the delay, Lieutenant. They're all yours."

After saluting his American ally, the British Navy Lieutenant began to walk down the line of American troops as he called out and said, "OK, lads. As you Yanks like to say...the show is over. Let's move smartly up the gangway. We wouldn't want to be late for the war."

After straining his eyes against the morning sun, Ivan lowered his head as he walked at a snails pace behind a long line of men in uniform who were on their way to war. Suddenly he felt alone and very vulnerable. As hard as it was for Ivan to admit, he missed his partner in crime. Even though Shorty could be a royal pain in the ass, Ivan would rather endure this ordeal with his buddy by his side than do so alone.

As soon as Ivan wondered when he would see Shorty again, he was nudged forward by the man behind him when a Royal Navy sailor remarked, "Come on Yank, you're holding up the line."

With his M1 Carbine slung over his right shoulder and his duffel bag over his left, Flight Officer Danny Gannon took another quick look at the rather impressive looking ship before he stepped onto the gangway. When a traffic jam up ahead caused the boarding process to stop, another British sailor held up his left hand and called out, "Hold it up, lads."

As soon as the British sailor motioned the Americans on the gangway to board the ship, Ivan looked up and thought he saw a familiar face. After being ordered to move up with the others, Ivan was almost all the way up the gangway when the line of men in front of him came to a stop. While taking advantage of the delay, Ivan looked up to see if his suspicions were correct. The second Ivan spotted Shorty waving like a crazy man and calling down to him, he cracked a smile and gave his buddy the thumbs up signal as he completed the boarding process and entered the ship.

By the time Ivan found Shorty, the tug boats were moving into position to ease the Queen Mary away from the dock. After yelling, "Gus!," at the top of his lungs, Ivan pushed his way through the crowd until he stood facing his partner in crime.

While Ivan enthusiastically gripped Shorty by his shoulders, he smiled wide and said, "It's good to see you, Pal. I looked all over Camp Kilmer for you."

After hearing Ivan mention Camp Kilmer, Shorty remarked, "That's because at the last minute my unit was taken to Camp Shanks."

As soon as Ivan remarked, "I was worried I'd have to win this war without you," Shorty responded, "I don't think so, fly boy." A split second later the two fugitives hugged each other like brothers. After all they had been through, they were finally reunited and on their way to Europe.

By now the tug boats were in position to guide The Queen Mary out of her berthing area and into the channel. Due to the number of troops who were anxious to get one last look at New York City, the crowd that formed along the railing was several rows deep. Rather than ask Shorty how he managed to get past the cops who were screening the departing troops, Ivan motioned his buddy to follow him so they could speak in private.

Even though the Queen Mary was packed with well over 10,000 troops plus a full crew, Ivan and Shorty managed to find some privacy below decks. After looking to make sure they were alone, Ivan leaned closer to Shorty and spoke just above a whisper as he said, "When you boarded this ship did you see an older guy dressed like a garage mechanic standing by the gangway with the military and civilian cops?"

"Yea, I saw him," said Shorty, who quickly added, "He was checking everyone out who boarded this ship in front of my engineering unit, before he went with the MPs and two dicks to take a smoke break over by the Red Cross ladies. Why... who's he?" As soon as Ivan explained who Andy Gooding is, a shocked Shorty Mc Ghee reacted by saying, "Thank God I never met that guy."

After pausing to let a British sailor walk by, Ivan continued as he leaned closer to his buddy and said, "Trust me when I tell you, I died a thousand deaths when that prick drove by me in an MP Jeep. Fortunately, I spotted him coming my way in time to turn my head to the left, while I was talking to one of the other pilots. It also probably helped that I'm wearing a helmet and was standing in a long column of troops who look alike." Once again Ivan paused as he casually looked around before he continued and said, "I guess it was meant to be for us to make our way to Europe together."

Even though Andy Gooding was obviously helping to locate Ivan Larson among the troops who are heading overseas, the military and civilian cops who were manning the gangway check point were just as interested in apprehending Francis Shorty Mc Ghee. Since Ivan was well aware that this was the case, he was surprised that Shorty seemed to be in such good spirits.

The moment Ivan asked his partner in crime how he managed to get by the reception committee, Shorty presented a devilish grin then said, "When I heard the Chaplain's Assistant was in the hospital with a bad appendix, I offered to help the Padre carry his gear to our troop transport. I figured it wouldn't hurt to be by his side when I boarded the ship to England. I felt even better about being with our Chaplain when we began boarding the Queen Mary and a group of MPs and civilian cops started checking dog tags and IDs.

After pausing to catch his breath, an excited Shorty Mc Ghee continued and said, "When two cops and an Army MP pulled three of our tech sergeants outta line to check them out, our Chaplain turned to me and said he couldn't believe that the MPs in the port didn't know that the men in our unit were already cleared by the military police in our own command. Needless to say, this was news to me. As soon as I said, "I didn't know that, Padre," our Chaplain went to rescue the three enlisted men who were being given the third degree."

As soon as Shorty looked around to make sure that they were still alone, he continued and said. "While two detectives were grilling the shit out of all three tech sergeants who look a lot more like you than me, our Chaplain told them that the military police already checked out every man in our unit before we got to Camp Shanks. In fact, according to the Chaplain, the MPs started checking every man in our unit when we were at Shepard Field. After hearing what the Chaplain had to say, the cops assigned to screen troops boarding the Queen Mary took a break until the unit behind us reached the gangway. Like I said before, even your buddy Mr. Gooding went with 'em. Once the line of G.I.s in front of me boarded the ship I was up the gangway and home free."

After pausing briefly to look around to make sure they were still alone, Shorty continued and said, "As soon as the next unit arrived on the pier to board the Queen, the MPs and the two cops along with your pal Andy Gooding returned to the gangway and continued screening troops destined for the ETO. The only time I got concerned was when I saw the two uniformed cops and an MP who were escorting Amos get off the transport that was tied up to the pier across the way. They must'a had Amos checking troops who boarded that ship before I boarded the Queen Mary."

When Shorty asked Ivan if he thought Amos would have identified them if he had the chance to do so, Ivan didn't need to think twice about his response. "I don't think he would've."

"Are you sure about that?" said Shorty.

Without hesitating Ivan responded in a tone of voice that was laced with complete confidence. "Remember, Amos was one who came up with the idea that we join the Army to get away from the cops. It was also his idea that we join the Air Corps."

Once again Ivan paused to let a pair of British sailors walk by before he continued. "Even if the cops tricked him into telling them about our unusual escape plan, I believe Amos would'a been happy to see us wearing these uniforms and on our way to Europe. Besides, Amos didn't look all that happy being forced to screen troops who were on their way to war."

Ivan proved that he was finally starting to relax after his close call when he leaned closer to Shorty and said, "You know, I'd almost like to send the cops who are chasing us all over hell and creation a letter, so I can tell 'em that an Army Chaplain and a Navy Convoy Control Officer helped the two of us to escape overseas. I'm also sure our Uncle Sam would like to know that two of their cracker jack witnesses just missed getting a good look at us before we boarded a troop transport to the ETO."

While Shorty pointed his right index finger at Ivan and said, "Don't kid around like that," he spoke just above a whisper as he continued filling his buddy in. "I got something else that you need to hear so listen up. Our Chaplain is a huge fan of detective novels and loves to hang out with the MPs, which is how he found out that the military police checked out every man in our engineering unit and notified CID that the two fugitives they're looking for were not members of our command."

After pausing to let another Royal Navy sailor walk by, Shorty seemed even more excited when he continued and said, "According to our Chaplain, the MPs started checking the mail that every member of our glider engineering unit received, starting when we went through training at Shepard Field. They did this because the taller of the two fugitives is an orphan who has no family and the shorter fugitive is a runaway who has no family to correspond with. This means that our Uncle Mike has been keeping us from being suspected by sending us mail from "home" on a regular basis."

Ivan had to admit that in addition to being impressed by Shorty's improved level of confidence, it sounded like the military and civilian cops had no idea where they were stationed or if they were still alive. Clearly, this was good news and made Ivan look forward to a relaxing cruise to England on the former luxury liner, now that he knew that the authorities were no closer to catching him and Shorty than they were back in 1943. As a relieved Ivan Larson patted his buddy on the side of his left arm, he cracked a smile then said, "Come on, Mister O'Malley, let's get one last look at New York while we can."

While Al Parker drove Sister O'Rourke along the Hudson River to the CID Office at 90 Church Street, he spoke as he pointed to the large ship that was leaving the harbor. "Take a look at that, Sister. That's the Queen Mary making another run to Europe." As Sister O'Rourke looked to her right, she admired the luxury liner turned troop transport and remarked, "Look at all of those men going off to war."

After admiring the Queen Mary make its way through the harbor, Sister O'Rourke turned to her left and said, "Tell me, Officer Parker, what are the chances that Ivan went to war on such a magnificent ship?"

While Al continued to drive the unmarked Army sedan toward Church Street, he did his best to provide a detailed response to the Sister's question. "If Ivan Larson is on the Queen Mary, Sister, it means the military and civilian police officers and federal agents who are assigned to screen troops before they boarded that vessel failed to spot him. The same goes for Francis Shorty Mc Ghee."

As soon as Al Parker changed lanes to go around a slower moving delivery truck, he continued and said, "Until we develop a lead that indicates that Ivan Larson and Francis Shorty Mc Ghee made their way overseas, we have to do everything possible to stop them from getting on a troop transport. In order to do so, we need to use every available witness who can identify the two fugitives to help us screen troops before they leave the country."

When Sister O'Rourke asked, "Would I be intruding if I asked how many other witnesses are available to help you and the other policemen look for Ivan and his accomplice?"

After changing lanes again, Al Parker continued filling Sister O'Rourke in on the complexities of the case at hand. "Including you and me, Sister, we have a handful of witnesses who can identify Ivan Larson. One of witnesses who had dealings with Larson is a disabled Army veteran but because of his war wounds, the Major decided to limit how we use him. We also have one witnesses who can only identify Francis Shorty Mc Ghee."

After pausing briefly, Al finished answering the Sister's question. "Two of our witnesses started screening troops heading for Europe early this morning. A third witness was transported from the city jail to the port at 0800. With you helping us out, we'll have every available witness except the one who's a disabled Army veteran screening departing troops before noon today."

As soon as Sister O'Rourke remarked, "It sounds like a great deal of effort is going into the process of locating Ivan and his companion," Al said, "You're right about that, Sister."

After pausing long enough to change lanes, Al continued briefing Sister O'Rourke about the complexities of working this case. "Unfortunately, the biggest problem we have is that there are a limited number of us assigned to the CID Task Force to follow leads and inspect numerous Army camps and forts. Even with all the help that we receive from MPs, civilian policemen and federal agents in other states, we still don't have enough people to inspect every Army camp or screen ever ship and plane that's heading overseas. In fact, it's a full time job for us just to try and cover the Port of Embarkation in New York." As Al finished his remarks, he glanced to his right and said, "The simple truth is, that once Ivan Larson and Shorty Mc Ghee managed to get into the Army, they became two needles in the a huge haystack."

After listening to Patrolman Parker, the Sister spoke up and said, "So what you are saying, Officer Parker, is that Ivan and his accomplice could very well be passengers on the Queen Mary or might already be in combat overseas."

"That's correct, Sister," responded Al, who added, "It's possible that Larson and Mc Ghee managed to get by our search teams and made their way overseas. They could also be stationed in the states, in a hospital, in a prisoner of war camp, or killed in action. They could even be AWOL and we wouldn't know it, because we don't know the phony names they're using. Regardless, we intend to keep looking for 'em."

While Sister O'Rourke took another look at the Queen Mary, Al remained silent as he drove the government sedan to the CID Office. Although it was impossible to make out any faces, it was easy to see that the converted luxury liner's deck was awash in a sea of American soldiers who were dressed for war.

As the Queen Mary slowly cruised by Ft. Hamilton and the tip of Staten Island, Ivan Larson leaned on the railing along the stern of the vessel and thought about the night he gunned down Tommy Mulray. So much had transpired since that night, that Ivan no longer felt like the person he once was. Even though the police considered him a two bit gangster turned cop killer, Ivan had a much different opinion of himself by the summer of 1944.

As the giant troop transport continued on its journey, Ivan regretted not sneaking back into the city to see Mike Connely before he shipped out. In addition to making it possible for him and Shorty to escape to New Jersey and get through the induction process, Mike Connely also sent them enough mail and food parcels "from home" to prevent Ivan and Shorty from coming under suspicion.

Since hindsight was 20/20, all Ivan could think about was how he would give anything to have the slate wiped clean of everything that he ever did wrong in his life. While Ivan took one last look at the Ft. Hamilton section of Brooklyn, he told himself over and over again that killing Tommy Mulray was something that had to be done. When his thoughts drifted back to the day when he and his gang held up the Lincoln Savings Bank, Ivan remembered how surprised he was when that off duty cop gunned down his best friend. Looking back, Ivan knew that he shot that cop because he killed Terry Kelly and because Patrolman Pat Murphy Jr. was blocking his escape from the bank.

The moment that Shorty heard Ivan mutter, "It was him or me," he knew his friend was taking another frightening stroll down memory lane. After making sure that none of the other servicemen on deck were paying attention to their private conversation, Shorty nudged Ivan with his elbow and brought him back to reality. Seeing Ivan grin and remark, "Thanks, Gus," meant that his cohort was back to reality. Just to make sure Shorty asked, "Are you all right?" As soon as Ivan nodded his head, he spoke in a low tone of voice that was partially muffled by a light breeze that blew across the fan tail. "So far so good."

As the tug boats peeled away from their escort duties, the converted luxury liner made her way past the security of New York Harbor and ventured out into the open ocean. With tears in his eyes, Shorty Mc Ghee leaned on the railing and whispered, "Goodbye, Mom."

While Ivan patted Shorty on the back, he did his best to comfort his buddy by saying, "I'll bet she's real proud of you for doing the right thing and joining the Army." "I hope so," remarked Shorty, as he took one last look at the place that he called home. Once again Ivan acted like a true friend, as he patted Shorty on the back again as he said, "I know so."

Unlike his partner in crime, Ivan was unable to shed any tears after leaving New York City behind. The main reason for this was because Ivan was elated about being a free man. So far their plan was working, even if it took a lot longer for them to leave the United States because they volunteered for the glider program instead of remaining in the infantry. Even Shorty had to admit that it was worth the wait.

As Shorty looked out to sea, he sounded very sure of himself when he remarked, "I'm glad we did this. I mean stick it out."

"Me too," remarked Ivan."

As the two fugitives took one last look at the fading coastline of New York, they wondered if they would survive the war and live happily ever after in Europe once victory was achieved. Like most G.I.s, Ivan believed that it would be the other guy who would get killed or seriously wounded. Shorty on the other hand was convinced that his days were numbered. His Irish Catholic upbringing also ingrained in him a tremendous sense of guilt, one that made it difficult for Shorty to believe that he was truly forgiven for his mortal sins.

Now that the ship was underway, it was time to receive their berthing assignments. As the Queen Mary picked up speed, its massive number of passengers began moving below decks to learn the routine of the ship. With an average of four to six men to a cabin, the accommodations that were designed for 2000 guests made for some very close living conditions.

The Wagner brothers couldn't believe their eyes when they spotted their old friend Willie Gunderson standing at the bar while he leaned on a cane. When the bartender let Willie know that some friends of his wanted to buy him a drink, Willie put on an Academy Award performance as soon as he made eye contact with Bruno and Henry Wagner.

While acting as if he was sincerely happy to see his old friends, Willie limped over and greeted both men with a big smile and a hearty handshake. The moment Willie made contact with the Wagner brothers, one of the FBI Agents who was covering Willie casually left the bar to call Dan Phillips.

While using the expense money that was provided by the FBI, Willie invited the Wagner brothers to join him for late night supper. When Bruno Wagner asked Willie what brought him to Hoboken, the 60 year old FBI informant explained that he recently rented a furnished room nearby because he was scheduled to start working in the Port of Embarkation. Even though this was pure bullshit, the Wagner brothers accepted what Willie said on face value. The Wagner brothers were also very interested in Willie's sea going exploits.

When Willie asked about the old gang, he acted genuinely surprised when he was told that Johann Miller was murdered back in 1943. After asking about everyone else, the Wagner brothers told Willie that Gunther Kessler opened a small grocery store and bakery in Newark, that Rudy Mueller was in the process of opening another butcher shop and Max Hoffman was still driving a delivery truck. When Bruno stood up and said that he was going to call Rudy to give him the news about Willie's return, Willie continued talking to Henry Wagner about his travels to far off lands.

As soon as Bruno returned, he was all smiles when he sat down and said that Rudy Mueller was happy to hear that the oldest member of their group survived the war and was back home. When Bruno extended an invitation for him to join the old gang at Kessler's home for Sunday dinner, Willie felt as everything was going according to plan.

After telling Willie that they would pick him up at 2PM, they had one more drink before they called it a night. Rather than have Willie make his way home on his own, Bruno Wagner offered to give the old man a ride. Little did the Wagner brothers know, that during the entire evening they were under surveillance by the FBI.

CHAPTER 34

THE TRIP TO THE ETO

W hen heavy seas sent food trays flying, most of the troops on board the Queen Mary took refuge in their bunks or spent time filling buckets and toilets with vomit. While Shorty Mc Ghee was sick as a dog, Ivan Larson had an excellent pair of sea legs for an American soldier who was forced to remain below decks during a storm at sea. Due to the rough sea conditions, Ivan had no choice but to sit tight and wait for smoother weather, while his seasick sidekick died a thousand deaths.

Just when things seemed to be going exceptionally well, Glider Engineering Officer Lt. Steve Perkins made his way over to Shorty Mc Ghee's bunk to check on his sick friend. By now Ivan was fully aware who Lt. Perkins was after Shorty introduced him to the only other friend that he had in the Army. As Ivan looked up, the young Lieutenant appeared genuinely concerned when he asked how Gus was doing.

After standing up to face the Glider Engineering Officer, Ivan tossed the copy of Yank Magazine on his bunk as he answered Steve Perkins in a friendly tone of voice and said, "He's been sick as a dog since last night, Lieutenant, but he'll live."

As soon as Steve Perkins leaned over to get a closer look at his seasick buddy, he looked up and said, "Is he dead or just asleep?"

Ivan proved that he was a good actor when he grinned and said, "Don't worry, Gus has nine lives."

Ever since they became friends Steve Perkins knew that Danny Gannon and Gus O'Malley grew up together. As a result of his friendship with Gus, Lt. Perkins also knew a great deal about his hot shot glider pilot cousin from Jersey City. After making some small talk, Lt. Perkins said, "I guess you'll be flying 'em while Gus and I fix 'em."

Ivan knew exactly what the young officer was referring too. As glider engineering officers, Steve Perkins and Gus O'Malley were responsible for supervising the ground support personnel who assembled gliders, maintained gliders and prepared gliders for combat missions. Glider Engineering Officers and maintenance crews were also responsible to repair gliders that were damaged.

While Ivan sat back down on his cot and picked up his copy of Yank Magazine, Steve Perkins looked at the man he knew as Gus O'Malley and remarked, "Seeing Gus like this reminds me of the night we celebrated graduating from Glider Engineering School. Gus was so drunk he called me Ivanhoe and started talking about knights in shinning armor."

Immediately after hearing the Lieutenant's remark, Ivan, acted as if he wasn't paying attention as he looked up and said, "Did you say something, Lieutenant?"

As Steve Perkins reminisced about the day Gus called him Ivanhoe and explained that he wanted to be a knight in shining armor when he was a kid, Ivan Larson did his best to conceal his concern for Shorty's slip of the tongue. Being the quick witted gangster that he was, made it easy for Ivan to think of something appropriate to say. "At least he didn't call you Lady Marion." While Steve Perkins smiled, Ivan continued and said, "I can't tell you the number of times that me and Gus had sword fights with homemade wooden swords, while we rode around the neighborhood on our bikes as if we were knights jousting on horseback."

In order to change the subject Ivan thought fast and said, "Between you and me I think Gus is a lot more homesick then he lets on. In fact, I'll bet a month's pay he's been thinking a lot about the days when we grew up in Jersey City."

While Steve Perkins nodded his head ever so slightly up and down and he appeared to be very receptive of everything that Ivan Larson had to say, the fugitive from justice masquerading as Danny Gannon continued and said, "It's not easy for Gus to talk about it but our Uncle Mike is pretty sick. He did a hell of a job of raising us after our moms died." Then, after pausing for a split second, Ivan continued in a more somber tone and said, "I don't know how much Gus told you, but we didn't see our fathers much when we were growing up because they were in the merchant marine. Just before the Japs attacked they got jobs building bases in the Pacific. We haven't heard from them since the Japs went on the warpath."

After hearing Lt. Perkins comment that he knew about their family situation and that he would pray for their fathers safe return, Ivan did his best to appear grateful. As Lt. Perkins looked down at that young man he knew as Gus O'Malley, he asked Danny Gannon to let Gus know that he stopped by to see how he was doing. After telling Lieutenant Perkins that he would relay the message, Ivan did his best to conceal his reaction to Shorty's slip of the tongue.

As soon as Lt. Perkins left the cabin, Ivan started to figure out the best way to eliminate the young glider engineering officer. The more Ivan thought about Shorty's screw up the more upset he got. It was moments like this that convinced Ivan that Shorty Mc Ghee would be the death of him yet.

A blinding rain storm was a welcomed relief for the passengers and crew of the Queen Mary because the heavy rain dampened the size of the waves and had a calming affect on the open ocean. Unfortunately, the smell of overflowing toilets, vomit and mutton permeating through the ship, was enough to make most of the Americans on board the Queen Mary look forward to serving in combat. The moment that Shorty woke up he found Ivan Larson pacing back and forth in the gangway outside their cabin. Between the never ending cloud of swirling cigarette smoke, the stench of body sweat and the overpowering odor of vomit, the berthing area below decks on the Queen Mary was the equivalent of hell on earth. With his stomach still growling after a rough night, Shorty braced himself as he stood up to make sure the ship was no longer swaying in a stormy sea.

As soon as Shorty stepped out of his cabin, he was totally unprepared to face a furious friend. If looks could kill Shorty's lifeless body would have dropped to the floor. The second they made eye contact, Shorty knew that he was in trouble, even if he had no idea why. After stepping aside to let another G.I. pass by, Ivan was tempted to strangle Shorty for his apparent slip of the tongue. Worse yet, Ivan had to wonder how many other times Shorty slipped and used their real names. Even using a variation of the name Ivan had the potential of ruining their escape plan.

After glancing around quickly to see if any of the other soldiers were paying attention to him and his fellow fugitive, a pissed off Ivan faced Shorty and spoke just above a whisper when he said, "You're gonna be the death of me yet."

Since Shorty had no idea why Ivan was angry with him he became defensive and said, "What's your problem?"

Again, Ivan looked around before he leaned closer to Shorty and said, "Guess who I had a long talk with while you were asleep?"

While Shorty had a completely dumbfounded look on his face, he shrugged his shoulders and said, "Who?"

"Lt. Perkins," responded Ivan as he placed his hands on his hips and stepped aside as a British sailor walked by.

After hearing Shorty remark, "So," as if he was still confused why Ivan was so pissed off, Ivan leaned forward and poked his right index finger in Shorty's chest as he said, "So, your friend told me about the day you got shit faced and called him Ivan-hoe."

The moment Shorty heard what Ivan had to say, he lowered his head and didn't look back up for a good two seconds before he responded just above a whisper and said, "At least give me credit for sobering up fast enough to catch my mistake when I called him Ivan and I quickly added "hoe" to the end of it. You gotta admit, it's a lot better than if I didn't catch myself and I called him Ivan."

As Shorty swallowed hard, Ivan knew by the size of the lump in his throat that his buddy was guilty as charged. After not knowing what else to say, Shorty lowered his head again as Ivan said, "After listening to your friend tell me about your childhood infatuation with Ivanhoe and the Knights of the Round Table, I told him a cock and bull story about how we used to ride around Jersey City on our bikes while fighting with wooden swords." I also told your friend that you're homesick and worried about our Uncle Mike 'cause he's real sick. Even though he knows about our fictitious past, I laid it on thick about our mothers dying and our fathers being Missing in Action ever since the war began."

Shorty proved that he appreciated everything that Mike Connely did to help them make their escape and not come under suspicion when he looked at Ivan and said, "I have to admit..the bullshit story Mike made up for us is a real tear jerker, especially the part about our fathers not being heard from ever since the Japs started this war."

"I agree," said Ivan who continued and said, "But that doesn't change the fact that you made a mistake that could put the cops hot on our trail and may end up doing so if your buddy ever puts two and two together." After Ivan looked around to make sure that it was safe for him to speak his mind, he leaned closer to Shorty and whispered, "Your friend's going over the side tonight and you're helping me do it or you're going with him."

Despite their friendship and all that they had been through together Ivan Larson walked away from Francis Shorty Mc Ghee in complete disgust. While Ivan stepped through the water tight door to gain entrance to the next compartment, he felt like a fugitive again instead of a U.S. Army Flight Officer who was anxious to get to Europe so he could start flying combat missions.

Just as they had been in the past, Gunther Kesseler and his daughter were gracious hosts and welcomed Willie into their home. While the men started drinking ice cold beer, Greta began making supper in the kitchen. After settling down in the living room, Gunther raised his glass of beer and proposed a toast, "To Willie, welcome home."

In the conversation that followed, Gunther told Willie how Rudy called him as soon as he heard that he was back from the war. When Gunther asked Willie how he was feeling, Willie responded and said, "I can't complain after what happened to some of the men that I served with."

The fact that Rudy Mueller was running late made Willie even more anxious to meet the obvious leader of the group. Once Rudy Mueller arrived carrying a large box containing their supper, Willie knew why Mueller was late. As soon as he greeted Willie, Rudy opened the box and displayed a dozen freshly cut thick steaks and said, "Tonight we celebrate the return of an old friend in style."

Under the circumstances, Willie acted as natural as anyone else who knew that seeing such a pile of premium grade meat was a sight to behold, now that beef was heavily rationed and not available in this quantity to civilians. "Oh my, that's a beautiful sight," was all that Willie could think to say.

While his friends had a laugh at his expense, Kessler carried the steaks into the kitchen while Rudy became serious and asked Willie how he was feeling. After Willie repeated most of what he said to the Wagner brothers, he added a few remarks that were highly critical of FDR and Congress for how they failed to provide the same benefits to merchant seamen as they did for the men who served in the armed forces. Willie also joined Mueller and the others in a spirited conversation about politics, one that centered on how America's real enemies were the Russians, not the Germans.

When Mueller asked Willie why he chose to find a place to live near Hoboken, the old man who was working for the FBI said, "Now that I'm retired from the Merchant Marine, one of my old skippers got me a job as a civilian employee with the Quartermaster Corps in the Port of Embarkation. I figured I'd take it until the war was over, then move to Florida so I could live near the beach."

As soon as dinner was served, Willie devoured his perfectly cooked steak and side dishes like a man who had been eating more than his fare share of hospital food. Willie knew he was in business when Rudy suggested that he think about working for him on a part time basis. According to Rudy, doing so would allow Willie to make more money than he would make working full time in a civilian government job.

While doing his best to seem interested and grateful, Willie asked Rudy what he had in mind. "A sales job with a salary and commissions," responded Mueller who quickly added, "If you're interested I'll move you to Newark so you can be close to my new butcher shop. In fact, you're just in time because I expect to be doing a lotta business in the next few weeks. In the meantime, I'll put you on the payroll and introduce you to our customers. You can even use my car to make your sales calls."

After pausing to sip some beer, Mueller sounded as confident as ever when he continued and said, "Who knows, Willie, you might want to stay on and work with me and the boys once this war is over, especially now that we have the contacts that we do in the meat business."

After being cooped up for almost two days and nights, the soldiers traveling to the ETO were allowed to go up on deck in groups. Although smoking on deck was not permitted, everyone appreciated the opportunity to get a breath of fresh air, after spending days and nights in the stench of vomit, flooded gangways and backed up toilets.

While Ivan Larson smoked a cigarette below decks, he waited patiently for Shorty to return from his trip around the ship to locate Lt. Perkins. The fact that Lieutenant Perkins seemed to be oblivious to the efforts that were being made by military and civilian law enforcement authorities to locate Ivan Larson and Francis Shorty Mc Ghee was no longer important. As distasteful as the decision was, Shorty reluctantly agreed that they could not risk having Lt. Perkins become suspicious and notify the military police. Even though killing a man at sea was not necessarily a difficult thing to do, the two fugitives knew that executing such a crime would not be easy on a ship that contained thousands of troops plus a large crew.

After spotting Shorty making his way through a crowded gangway, Ivan put his cigarette out in a nearby sand filled metal bucket and began to walk toward his friend. As Ivan stepped through an open water tight door, he met Shorty by the entrance to the mess hall. While Shorty looked around to make sure that they were alone, he spoke in a low tone of voice and said, "I found him. He's getting something to eat. I told him I was gonna get some air and would meet him on deck by the lifeboat station where we hang out in between storms at sea."

Finding privacy on the Queen Mary was virtually impossible given the fact that over six times the normal number of passengers were onboard. While Ivan and Shorty stood next to the steel bulkhead, they spoke just above a whisper to avoid being overheard by the steady stream of soldiers and sailors who were constantly walking by in both directions. Even though Shorty reluctantly agreed to go along with Ivan's plan, he proved that he was concerned about how they were going to throw Steve Perkins overboard on such a crowded ship when he said, "Do you have any idea how we're gonna do this?"

Without hesitating Ivan remarked, "Without getting caught."

With less than a few hours left to go before they arrived in England, Lt. Steve Perkins was just as anxious as everyone else to support the war effort. After eating a bowl of British oatmeal and prunes that was washed down with a strong cup of British tea, Lt. Perkins made his way topside to meet with his friend Gus.

As Shorty leaned on the guard rail, he seemed lost in thought as the Queen Mary cut through the Atlantic Ocean like a knife though butter. After being sick for most of the trip, Shorty was just starting to feel better when his classmate from Glider Engineering School stood next to him and said, "Feeling better?"

Shorty was too numb to be startled as he glanced to his right and calmly remarked, "I feel like ten pounds of shit in a five pound bag."

Seeing Steve Perkins smile wide was a clear indication that he wasn't the least bit suspicious about Gus O'Malley or Danny Gannon. Still, Ivan was right. Even though Lt. Perkins was a nice guy, he could easily put two and two together at a later date.

After snapping out of his trance, Shorty looked out to sea and remarked, "I can't wait to get on dry land. This ocean voyage crap is for sailors not soldiers."

"You and me both, brother," said Lt. Perkins, who paused for a split second before he added, "Hey, Gus, where's that glider pilot buddy of yours? Don't tell me he caught what you had?"

As soon as Shorty turned to face Steve Perkins, he did his best to sound as down to earth as possible. "You mean Danny? He's all right. He's down below. He said he'd rather lose ten pounds then eat another bowl of oatmeal or smell the stench of lamb being cooked by the Limey cooks on this tub."

Seeing Steve smile again was another good sign, especially now that Ivan and Shorty were concerned that they might have made Lt. Perkins a little suspicious, when they asked him to join them up on deck, after the Brits ordered everyone to remain below.

Hearing Steve Perkins remark, "I guess a lotta guys got a little claustrophobic last night," was Shorty's cue to explain the reasons why he and Ivan tried to get Lt. Perkins to join them on deck when the conditions got rough again.

"Claustrophobic nothing, did you smell the stench down there last night? I don't know what was worse the BO, the smell of vomit, or the backed up toilets in our section." Then, in a more sarcastic tone, Shorty added, "I don't know about you, Steve, but me and Danny needed some air. In fact, I don't know how you stayed in your bunk last night."

Why some people got along and others didn't was one of the great mysteries of life. Despite their obvious differences, Steve Perkins was a lot like Gus O'Malley and was a young man who desperately wanted to be accepted as one of the guys. Even though the teenagers that Lt. Perkins wanted to hang out with were light weights compared to the thugs that Shorty ran around with, the fact that Steve Perkins and Francis Shorty Mc Ghee were loners made them gravitate to each other when they first met. Steve Perkins and Gus O'Malley were also drawn to each other because they both had a passion to fix things.

In order to shed his reputation as a bookworm, Steve Perkins began tinkering with anything mechanical until he eventually became a first class grease monkey. When it came time to report to the local draft board, the fact that Steve Perkins was enrolled in college and had experience as a mechanic motivated the Army to offer him a commission as a Second Lieutenant. Even though he lacked an interest in flying, Steve was eager to serve as an aviation engineering officer. As the glider program expanded, Steve Perkins was sent to Glider Engineering School where he ended up meeting Gus O'Malley.

Even though Shorty only slipped once, Steve Perkins never forgot the night that his friend Gus O'Malley got drunk and called him Ivan-hoe. Lt. Perkins also remembered the chat that he had with Danny Gannon. Since this was the first time they had to talk in private since Shorty recovered from seasickness, Steve Perkins wanted to let his friend Gus know that he was there for him if he needed someone to talk to.

As Lt. Perkins leaned on the railing next to his buddy, he spoke in a serious tone of voice when he said, "Danny told me about your Uncle Mike getting sick. We also talked about you fathers being Missing in Action. I'm sorry, Gus." While Shorty continued to look out to sea, he thanked his friend for his concern.

As soon as Steve Perkins removed a pack of chewing gum from his pant's pocket, he offered a piece to Gus while he tried to cheer his friend up. "At least you and Danny had each other when you were growing up. I grew up alone and didn't have any friends until I started fixing cars for the bullies in town." The moment an upbeat Steve Perkins patted his buddy Gus O'Malley on the back and said, "I sure could'a used a friend like Ivanhoe when I was a kid," Shorty realized that his partner in crime was right. This guy had to go.

Unfortunately, Ivan and Shorty agreed that it was virtually impossible and not worth the risk, to kill Steve Perkins and throw his body over the side on such an overcrowded ship. Instead, the two fugitives decided to wait until they reached dry land to deal with Steve Perkins.

On August 27, 1944, the recently promoted Sergeant Calvin "Cal" Parker left Camp Shanks in Rockland County, New York and proceeded with his unit by train to the POE in Manhattan to board a troop transport to the ETO. Between the smell of salt water and the overbearing mixture of diesel fumes and strange foods being prepared by Royal Navy cooks, the air along the waterfront was far from inviting for the American soldiers who were on their way to Europe.

While Al Parker had his silver patrolman's shield pinned to the lapel of his sports jacket, Jim Beauregard showed his Army CID badge and identification card to the pair of U.S. Navy Shore Patrolmen who were posted by the gangway of the Royal Navy troop transport. Once the Shore Patrolman knew who they were, Jim Beauregard and Al Parker were permitted to remain on the pier, while a long line of Negro G.I.s were slowly boarding the British troop transport in perfect order.

The last person that Cal expected to see while he waited his turn to board the H.M.S. Esperance Bay was his father and a his white partner. The moment Al spotted his son and called out, "Hey, Cal," a young Negro private who was good friends with Cal Parker said, "Who's that, Sarge?"

While smiling wide, a surprised Calvin Parker responded and said, "That's my father and his partner."

As soon as Cal smiled and waved to his father, Private Thomas Davies made a face as he adjusted the position of the M1 Carbine on his shoulder and said, "His partner? Your old man is a New York City cop and he's got a white Army Major for a partner?"

"Crazy isn't it," said Cal as he reached the gangway, just as a U.S. Navy Shore Patrolman stepped aside and motioned him to pass so he could meet more privately with his father without holding up the flow of traffic.

As Al Parker did his best not to get emotional, he enthusiastically shook his son's hand while he gripped his left arm and said, "It's good to see you, son." Then, as Al held his son by the shoulders and admired him in his uniform, he smiled proudly and remarked, "Look at you. I wish you mother was here to see how sharp you look in your uniform. She sends her love you know. So does everyone else in the family."

Ever since Cal was a little boy he knew his father was full of surprises. It all started one Christmas when a red bicycle mysteriously appeared under the tree despite the presence of a blizzard in New York City. Since Al was the type of father who loved to tease his sons, he told them when they were very young that every police station had a telephone that went direct to the North Pole. The purpose of this special telephone was to enable policemen to tell Santa Claus who the good boys were and who the bad boys were.

As soon as Cal and his older brother heard this story, they hounded their father on the days leading up to Christmas, to make sure that he called Santa Claus to let Chris Kringle know that the Parker boys deserved to receive every toy that they requested in their letter to the North Pole. Naturally, Al would intentionally drive his sons crazy by telling them that he forgot to call Santa to let him know that his sons were good boys.

Year after year Al would wait until Christmas Eve to finally let his sons know that he called Santa to let him know that they were good kids. On Christmas morning all was forgiven when the Parker boys found every toy they wanted resting under the tree. After realizing that their prayers to heaven and their letters to the North Pole were answered, the Parker boys were convinced at a very young age that their father was personal friends with God and Santa Claus. The Parker boys also believed that their father was the bravest man they ever knew. Besides being a decorated war hero, who saved a white Army officer in the trenches of France, their father was also a decorated policeman who put his life on the line on many occasions.

Unlike other Negroes who were less fortunate, the Parker boys had a good life and knew that not all white folks were racists. Even though segregation was incredibly painful to endure, Cal and his brother were raised to think positive. The Parker boys grew up believing in the old adage that you had to start somewhere. If the Murphy family could be their friends, then other white folks could be their friends as well.

As a result of growing up in a home that was blessed with the security of a civil service job and the extra income of their father's side business, Cal and his older brother learned to appreciate the value of hard work. They also grew up in home that fostered a strong faith and a love of family. To insure their future, the Parker boys were given the best education possible. As a result, Cal and his brother Jack lived well and were a happy lot.

Once America was attacked, Jack Parker did not hesitate to leave college and enlist. As soon as Cal graduated from high school, he signed up and fought hard to get assigned as a military policeman. Cal wanted to be an Army MP to kill two birds with one stone and serve his country, while building his resume so he could follow in his father's footsteps and join the New York City Police Department as soon as the war was over.

When the 761st Tank Battalion was ordered to the ETO, Sergeant Calvin Parker and the other military policemen who were responsible to protect this armored unit were assigned to travel with their tank crews on the same ship. Just like their father and other relatives in their family, the Parker boys enlisted in the Army to fight, not to be a stewards or laborers.

As soon as Cal heard his father say, "There's someone I want you to meet," his son snapped to attention when the man he knew to be his father's partner stepped over to where they were standing. "Son, this is Major James Beauregard, my commanding officer at the CID Task Force," remarked Al, as a long line of troops continued to board the British ship that was tied up to the pier behind them.

After returning the salute, Jim Beauregard smiled as he extended his hand and said, "It's nice to meet you, Cal. Your father told me a great deal about you and your brother." Then, as Jim pointed to the buck sergeant stripes that were neatly sewn on Cal's uniform, he added, "Congratulations on the promotion to sergeant."

While speaking in a respectful tone of voice, Cal Parker thanked the Major before he turned to his proud father and handed him a letter that he recently received from his brother as he remarked, "Peter told me to send this to you after I read it. I don't want to spoil the surprise, Dad, but he shot down another German plane. Two more and he's an ace."

As Al slipped the letter in his jacket pocket, he found it hard to speak because he knew their time was short. Fortunately, Cal broke the silence when he asked his father how he found out what ship his unit would be taking to ETO. After pointing at Jim Beauregard, Al said, "The Major pulled a few strings and found out your date of embarkation and the name of the troop transport you'd be leaving on. Don't tell Army CID but your mother bribed the Major with a batch of her apple corn muffins if he got me down here to see you off before you shipped out."

Just like other Negro men who served during the war, Cal Parker knew from experience that the problem of racism in the United States, especially in the south, was not improving, even though the nation was at war. In fact, there were times when it was hard to be enthusiastic about the future, when you had every reason to believe that even if you survived the war, you would return to a country that still treated you like a second class citizen. Even though this was the case, Negro troops like Calvin Parker had no intention of shirking their responsibilities.

Regardless of the current status of race relations in the United States, Sergeant Calvin Parker knew enough about Major James Beauregard to like and respect him as much as he liked and respected the white commanding officer of the 761st. After thanking Major Beauregard for making it possible for him to see his father before he shipped out, Cal asked about his mother and spoke briefly about how his unit was eager to get into the fight against the Germans.

Like other good fathers, Al Parker felt obligated as a parent to give his son a few pearls of wisdom before he went off to war. While speaking in a serious tone of voice, Al looked directly into his youngest son's eyes and said, "Remember, Cal, getting shot at and doing the shooting is serious business. Pray hard and fight hard....whatever you do always give a good account of yourself. Never drink from your canteen or eat before your men have been taken care of and always lead from the front. Always be respectful of rank, even when you're right and the Officer you're dealing with is dead wrong. Write as often as you can and don't let what you see change you too much."

When Jim Beauregard noticed that the last of the troops were about to board the ship, the Major interrupted Al and said, "Excuse me, Al, but it's almost time to go. I'll be over there waiting for you." Since time was short, Jim Beauregard smiled as he extended his hand and said, "Good luck, Cal."

After thanking the Major again, Cal Parker saluted his father's commanding officer before Jim Beauregard walked over to visit with a Negro Lieutenant from the 761st, who was standing by the gangway while the last of the men in his unit boarded the ship.

While father and son stood facing each other, Al spoke first and said, "I'm not letting you go without giving you a hug from your mother." As Al embraced his youngest son, Cal knew that the bear like hug that he was receiving was also a display of affection from his dad.

As thousands of soldiers looked down from the decks of two nearby ships, Al Parker patted his youngest son on the back and said, "I love you, son." Hearing his youngest son say, "I love you too, Dad," was enough to strike a cord deep inside Al Parker's body, mind, heart and soul.

As Al stepped back a trickle of tears rolled down his cheek, as he nodded once and remarked in a soft tone of voice, "You better go. The Royal Navy's waiting."

Even though his father was not in the service and he did not warrant a salute, Cal Parker stood at attention and saluted his father as the British sailor stood ready to cast off the bow line. After receiving a more casual salute from his father, Sergeant Calvin Parker turned and walked up the gangway without looking back.

After watching a pair of tug boats maneuver the H.M.S. Esperance Bay away from the pier, Al Parker and Jim Beauregard returned to their duties. Despite the odds of success, teams of military and civilian law enforcement officers continued screening the massive number of troops who departed a Port of Embarkation for an overseas assignment. Only time would tell if their efforts would result in the capture of Ivan Larson and Francis Shorty Mc Ghee.

After being notified that his next shipment would be delayed for a few weeks, Rudy Mueller used the time to get Willie acquainted with their customers. Doing so gave enabled Willie to spend a great deal of time with Mueller under the watchful eyes of the FBI and OPA.

Shortly after Ivan and his fellow glider pilots arrived in England all available Flight Officers were notified that they would be participating in Operation Market Garden. While Shorty and Lt. Perkins were preparing to leave for detached service with the 26th Mobile Repair and Reclamation Squadron, the unit that was responsible for assembling gliders for the invasion of Holland, Ivan Larson aka Danny Gannon was temporarily assigned to fly a combat mission for the 439th Troop Carrier Group.

After getting dressed for war, Ivan headed over to the chow hall for something to eat. While Ivan walked through the tent city, he felt a sense of pride that he never felt before. Instead of watching a flying picture in a movie theater, Ivan Larson would have a front row seat to some real life action, now that he was scheduled to fly his first combat mission as an Army aviator.

When Ivan reached the entrance to the mess hall he paused for a minute to look up into the morning sky to check the weather. As long as the weather remained clear, his trip to Holland should prove to be a relatively pleasant ride. After entering the mess hall Ivan picked up a metal tray and got on line to get something to eat. While the Private on KP duty filled his tray with food, Ivan was busy thinking about what it was going to be like once he landed behind enemy lines. After accepting a cup of black coffee, Ivan turned toward the crowded tables in search of his partner in crime.

After listening to the first CID radio broadcast about the Army's intensified efforts to hunt them down, the last thing that Ivan and Shorty wanted was for them to be assigned to different units, even if these assignments were only temporary. There was also the issue of Ivan going off to war that complicated the situation and made it impossible for the two fugitives to escape together, if the need arose to do so while they were on detached service.

As soon as Ivan located Shorty, he found him sitting with Lt. Perkins because they were scheduled to leave for the 26th Mobile Repair and Reclamation Squadron at Cookham Common immediately after breakfast. In order to insure that they would have a private moment together, Ivan asked his buddy Gus if he could do him a favor and mail a letter for him before he left for the 439th.

After finishing his breakfast, Shorty stood up and turned to Steve Perkins and said, "I'll meet up with you as soon as I grab that letter from Danny."

As Steve Perkins stood up, he smiled and extended his hand across the table and wished Danny good luck. Even though the Glider Engineering Officer gave no indication that he suspected Danny Gannon or Gus O'Malley of being anything other than patriotic Americans, Ivan still considered Lt. Perkins to be capable of figuring out who they really were under the right circumstances.

After saying goodbye to Steve Perkins and promising to bring him and Gus some German souvenirs, Ivan left the mess hall with Shorty to have a private moment before they parted company. Once they got outside and made sure they were alone, Ivan spoke in a low tone of voice and said, "That guy sticks to us like glue. I thought we'd never get rid of him."

Rather than talk about Steve Perkins, Shorty decided to put their limited time together to better use by wishing Ivan good luck. After he shook hands with his partner in crime, Shorty continued and said, "We should be back together again under Killer Kirby's command before you know it. In fact, I just heard that we'll be returned to our regular assignments as soon as this operation is over."

As soon as Ivan removed a letter from his field jacket pocket, he presented it to Shorty and said, "I know you don't want'a have this conversation but I'm gonna say it anyway. I don't want you to mail this unless I don't come back. I'd also appreciate it if you ended this letter for me by telling Mike as much as you can. If anything happens to me I also want you to use my half of our money to take good care of yourself and your mother. I also want you to know that I had my G.I. insurance changed so my cousin Gus O'Malley is the beneficiary."

Saying goodbye to Ivan was proving to be a lot harder for Shorty to deal with after hearing what his partner in crime had to say. After swallowing hard, Shorty did his best to change the subject, while he slipped Ivan's letter into his field jacket pocket before he continued and said, "To tell you the truth I'm more worried about Mike than I am about you. We haven't heard from him since we left the states."

Since they didn't receive any mail during the last mail call, Ivan had no choice but to agree with Shorty and said. "Yea, I know."

After realizing that this was a bad time to make Ivan worry about Mike Connely, Shorty tried to lift his buddies spirits by saying, "You know how the mail is. I'll bet you a candy bar that we have a stack of mail waiting for us by the time we both get back."

"You're probably right," remarked Ivan before he checked his watch and said,

"I better grab my gear. It's time for me to go."

While the two fugitives faced each other, they tried not to think about the fact that Ivan could get killed, wounded, captured or listed as Missing in Action while participating in the up coming combat glider mission. Shorty's attempt to appear upbeat failed miserably when he displayed a concerned look on his face. Even Ivan found it difficult to say goodbye to the only real friend that he had in this world, next to Mad Mike Connely. While Ivan shook hands with Shorty, he did his best to sound confident when he said, "Relax will ya. I'll be back."

On September 17, 1944 fifty gliders of the 439th Troop Carrier Group departed England at 0930 hours carrying carry 216 troops, eight 57 mm anti tank guns, nine jeeps and two trailers full of ammunition. All over England on 24 different Air Fields 1545 Allied troop carrier planes, 451 tow planes and 451 gliders lifted off carrying men and equipment under a protective shield of 1130 American and British fighter planes and headed northeast over London for occupied Holland.[11]

Although others would follow in the days to come, this was the first wave of the Allied airborne armada that would participate in Invasion of Holland. While flying one of the gliders from the 439th TCG, Flight Officer Danny Gannon was responsible for the lives of thirteen members of the 82nd Airborne Division. Even though everyone else on board was experiencing a case of pregame jitters, Ivan displayed the disposition of an experienced combat veteran, while he flew his glider toward the assigned objective. As far as Ivan was concerned, after committing cold blooded murder, robbing a bank and being a fugitive he had little or no fear about flying a Waco glider to LZ N behind enemy lines in Holland.

Although it took some time, Ivan finally calmed down after being cheated out of his chance to get into combat. This occurred when the tow line that connected Ivan's Waco glider to his tow plane snapped during the flight to Holland. As soon as this happened, Ivan had no choice but to ditch his GC-4A in the sea. The fact that everyone onboard survived the ditching was credited to Ivan's capabilities as a pilot. Once Ivan and his passengers were rescued by the British Air Sea Rescue Service, they made the trip back to England by boat, while an armada of Allied aircraft flew overhead.

Even though Ivan never made it to LZ (N) November, he felt like a half assessed combat veteran after surviving a water landing with a full compliment of troops on board. With no missions of any importance to fly, except a few medical evacuation flights to the static front line, Ivan had time to think about eliminating Steve Perkins. While England was too civilized of a place to cut a man's throat or execute him mob style using a .45 caliber pistol, Ivan was convinced that it would be a lot easier to kill a man and get away with it now that they were stationed in France.

As soon as Ivan got cleaned up after participating in another ground combat training session, Shorty handed his buddy a stack of mail from "home" in front of a roomful of other glider pilots. "You owe me one candy bar," remarked Shorty before he added, "And I expect to be paid in full before close of business today."

When Ivan accepted the pile of letters and a package from their Uncle Mike, he grinned then said, "Don't worry, cousin, you'll get your candy bar as soon as I see how the family is doing back home."

The second Ivan opened the package, he played his part as a patriotic American from a good family to the hilt when he passed the box of homemade cookies around and said, "Help yourself, boys, homemade cookies from our Uncle Mike and Aunt Clara."

Even though Mike Connely had Mrs. Mc Namara bake the cookies for him, no one was the wiser when Ivan passed the box around the room. As far as their fellow Troop Carrier personnel were concerned, Danny Gannon and his cousin Gus O'Malley could always be counted on to share their goodies from home with their Army buddies. As crazy as it might sound, performing a simple act of kindness, like sharing a batch of cookies from home, helped to prevent anyone from becoming suspicious of the two fugitives.

Later that night Ivan Larson wrote a letter to Mike telling him that he survived the Holland mission and was back in France with Shorty. Even though he was risking a great deal by doing so, Ivan included a photograph of him standing next to the CG4A Waco Glider that he flew during Operation Market Garden. Ivan figured that the old Marine would get a kick out of seeing the name Mad Mike written on the side of his "nephews" glider in large white letters. Ivan also included a note from Shorty as well in the envelop.

CHAPTER 35

DEAR JOHN TO THE RESCUE

O ne of the most demoralizing things that could happen to a soldier was to receive a Dear John letter. Although some couples found comfort in the old adage, "absence makes the heart grow fonder," others found the long separations unbearable. While some servicemen handled news of a breakup better than others, no one liked to hear that their girlfriend left them for someone else. Servicemen in a combat zone had an even greater burden to bear because they had to continue fighting whether they were in a good mood or not.

The day Lt. Steve Perkins learned that his fiance left him for a naval officer he became thoroughly despondent. No matter what Shorty Mc Ghee aka Gus O'Malley said to raise his friend's spirits, Steve Perkins rocked back and forth while he sat on the edge of his bunk and repeated, "That fucking bitch," over and over again.

Immediately after Ivan entered the Lieutenant's tent, he was surprised to see the otherwise mild tempered Steve Perkins pounding his right fist into his right leg while he cursed the day his former girlfriend was born. As soon as Shorty explained the situation to Ivan, the fugitive masquerading as Warrant Officer Gus O'Malley continued to console his devastated friend. In contrast, Ivan Larson saw the receipt of a Dear John Letter as an opportunity to eliminate Lt. Perkins without raising suspicion.

While Flight Officer Danny Gannon did his best to sound like a true blue Army buddy, he leaned over and patted the distraught Glider Engineering Officer on the back as he said, "Come on, Steve. Rip that letter up and come out and tie one on with me and Gus."

After hearing what his favorite glider pilot had to say, Steve Perkins stood by the edge of his bunk and ripped the letter up. While Steve stuffed the pieces into the stove, he sounded like a changed man when he said, "Let's go! The drinks are on me!"

As soon as Lt. Perkins stormed out of his tent, Ivan picked up the most recent issue of The Stars and Stripes Newspaper that had another feature article about the cop killing bank robbing fugitives who were being pursued by military and civilian law enforcement authorities and asked, "Did he see this?"

While Shorty shrugged his shoulders and said. "If he did he didn't say anything about it to me."

The more he thought about it, the more Ivan was convinced, that the receipt of a Dear John letter provided the perfect opportunity to eliminate the one person he feared would eventually figure out who they really were. With no time to waste, Ivan shut the flu on the stove to put out the fire before he knelt down in front of the Lieutenant's foot locker and said, "You better go and keep him company."

While speaking in a nervous tone of voice Shorty asked, "Why? What are you gonna do?"

As soon as Ivan opened the Lieutenant's foot locker, he removed the engineering officer's .45 caliber pistol before he looked up at Shorty and said, "Saving your ass and mine." After slipping the pistol under his jacket and into his waistband, Ivan shut the foot locker, stood up and said, "Are you still here?"

When the body of Lt. Steve Perkins was found in a wooded area on the outskirts of Orleans, France the military police immediately identified the cause of death as suicide. The fact that the deceased was found with his pistol clenched in his right hand and a single bullet hole in the side of his head that contained powder burns, was ample evidence to prove that the intoxicated young officer took his own life.

The MPs were further convinced that Lt. Perkins committed suicide, when they found a ripped up Dear John letter from home, that was partially burned in the stove in the officer's tent. The case file was officially closed after the military police interviewed a French prostitute, who confirmed that she was unable to raise the Lieutenant's spirits because he was very distraught after losing his fiance to an American naval officer.

As a formality, Assistant Glider Engineering Officer Gus O'Malley was also interviewed, since everyone on base knew that he was the deceased Lieutenant's best friend in the ETO. Under normal circumstances the MPs would get suspicious whenever they interviewed such a nervous witness. Fortunately for Shorty McGhee, the military police found it understandable that Warrant Officer Gus O'Malley was deeply distraught by the unexpected loss of such a close friend.

The fact that Shorty had a shaved head, a mustache and was in excellent shape, changed his appearance enough to make it very hard for anyone who didn't know the real Francis Mc Ghee to suspect that he was one of the two most wanted fugitives in the U.S. Army during World War II. This was confirmed when the Military Police stationed at the 440th Troop Carrier Group failed to make the connection and suspect that Gus O'Malley was really a fugitive from justice. Even when Flight Officer Danny Gannon was interviewed in the field next to the body of Lt. Perkins, none of the MPs suspected any wrongdoing or that they were talking to a wanted man.

By the time Shorty Mc Ghee left the Provost's Marshal's office he felt considerably more sure of himself. The fact that the military police told Shorty that they planned to notify Army CID in Paris that Lt. Steve Perkins died from a self inflicted gunshot wound, further convinced him that he and Ivan managed to commit the perfect crime.

As Shorty made his way to the mess hall, Ivan Larson had to walk at a brisk pace in order to catch up to his partner in crime. When Ivan asked how things went with the MPs, Shorty acted as if being interviewed by the military cops was no big deal, as an unusually cocky Gus O'Malley shrugged his shoulders and said, "Piece a cake."

If this experience did anything it filled Shorty with an overdose of confidence. While walking taller than ever, Shorty was no longer gripped by the fear that possessed him ever since he had his fingerprints and photographs taken at the induction center in New Jersey. Ivan was even more surprised when Shorty stopped short then turned and said, "I should'a been interviewed by the MPs a long time ago. I feel fucking great. The bastards still don't know what we really look like. All they have are those stupid police sketches from New York hanging on the wall in their office. I'm telling you, we're home free."

Of all people, Ivan could not believe the transformation. As impressed as he was that his little buddy had finally grown a pair of balls, Ivan was still concerned that Shorty could blow it if the right pressure was applied. Rather than leave anything to chance, Ivan grabbed Shorty as he started to walk into the mess hall and whispered, "I'm glad you're back to normal, but remember, your best friend in the Army next to me just blew his brains out, so try not to act so happy in public for a while, OK."

As Shorty entered the mess tent, he nodded his head once then said, "No sweat," as he changed his disposition and did his best to look like he was in mourning.

Now that Willie was able to infiltrate Mueller's organization, FBI Agents and OPA officials based in New Jersey had a reliable informant who knew every aspect of Mueller's black market operation. This included having face to face meetings with every local businessman who placed orders for black market beef from Mueller.

Prior to Willie being involved, all the FBI and OPA managed to document was suspicious activity and circumstantial evidence. Once Mueller took Willie to meet his customers, the feds had exactly what they needed to make a case against both ends of this illegal meat supplying operation.

Having Willie involved also enabled FBI Agents and OPA officials out west to know when they could expect the Wagner brothers to arrive to pick up their next shipment. Since people tended to be creatures of habit, the agents out west made arrangements to observe the Wagner brothers when and if they checked into The Happy Trails Motel or stopped to eat at the State Line Diner.

All that was needed to bring this case to a successful conclusion, was to have the FBI and OPA catch Mueller and his associates in possession of a truck load of illegal possessed beef. Once that happened, a series of raids would be executed and a major black market operation would be shut down. In the process, Rudolf Mueller would face a series of federal charges that should motivate him to cooperate with members of the U.S. Army CID Task Force.

After receiving the signal from Willie, teams of FBI Agents and OPA officials had plenty of time to get ready to follow the Wagner brothers. Willie also managed to let Dan Phillips know the size of the shipment that the Wagner brothers were scheduled to pickup, as well as when they were expected to return to Newark.

CHAPTER 36

GOOD THINGS COME TO THOSE WHO WAIT

After several months of searching Army camps and screening soldiers who were in the process of being transported overseas, the men assigned to the New York CID Task Force needed a break. The same was true for the witnesses who were helping to screen departing troops. Once again the problem was manpower. Despite the importance of the fugitive investigation, there never seemed to be enough sworn personnel available to conduct searches and screen the massive number of troops who were stationed in the states or heading overseas. This effort was further stymied by the fact, that there was a limited number of witnesses available who knew Ivan Larson and Shorty Mc Ghee before they became soldiers.

To top all this off, there were occasional leads that needed to be pursued that involved sightings of the two fugitives. When these leads involved interviewing witnesses in the states, Jim Beauregard had to travel to different parts of country to conduct an investigation with an FBI Agent or a CID Agent who was stationed in the immediate area. In those instances when the lead involved a witness who was stationed overseas, CID Agents and MPs based in foreign countries were tasked with the responsibility to conduct the follow-up investigation. On two other occasions Scotland Yard Inspectors were called in to interview British troops who thought they spotted one of the famous American fugitives in a pub in England. In both instances, the results of the follow-up investigations proved negative.

In the months that passed since Jim Beauregard and his men recovered evidence from John Miller's warehouse and apartment, Andy Dubrowsly and other FBI Agents, along with members of the OPAs Enforcement Division, pursued every lead possible while conducting a thorough investigation. Good news came in October of 1944, when Andy Dubrowsky called Jim Beauregard to give him an update about the federal case that was being made against Rudolf Mueller and his associates. While everyone else was sent home after a long day of searching embarkation camps and screening troops in the POE, Jim Beauregard, Al Parker, Johnny Mc Donald and Frank Angelone remained behind to hear what Andy had to say.

As soon as Andy arrived in the office, he found Jim Beauregard and the others drinking coffee laced with Irish Whiskey while they sat at various desks in the squad room. When Frank Angelone asked if Andy liked his coffee with our without a splash of Irish Whiskey, the veteran FBI Agent responded and said, "It's been a long day, Ange. Coffee with a shot sounds good."

Once Andy finished hanging up his hat and trench coat, he sat at his desk and took a quick sip of spiked coffee then remarked, "That hit the spot." Andy then removed a cigar from his suit jacket pocket and began briefing his colleagues. "I just finished meeting with my boss and Dan Phillips from our field office over in Newark. Even though it took a lot longer than any of us expected to wrap this case up, I think you're gonna like the results."

After taking another sip from his coffee mug Andy looked at his fellow task force members and said, "As Jim knows from my periodic briefing sessions, early on we made a decision not to waste our time interviewing any of the former members of the German American Bund who were on the list that Al found in Miller's warehouse. We made that decision for two reasons. First, we couldn't risk having one of these characters contact Mueller to tip him off that we were interested in him. Second and more important, one of the names on that list was a man who infiltrated the German American Bund and gathered valuable intelligence information for the Bureau before the war. Unfortunately, we had to find this guy before we could locate Mueller, his wife, his father-in-law and three of his closest friends who were also on Miller's list."

As a result of the briefings that he received, Jim knew that Andy and the other agents who were pursuing Rudy Mueller experienced a number of setbacks that kept them from making progress until recently. After lighting a cigarette Jim looked at Andy and said, "One thing is certain, Andy. Nothing about this case has been easy."

"You're right about that," remarked Andy Dubrowsky, who paused to take another quick sip from his coffee mug before he continued. "The informant I'm talking about is an old sea salt who's been in the Merchant Marine since he was a kid. When Dan Phillips heard his old informant was wounded while serving in the Italian Campaign, he asked Jimmy Scott to help find the old man. It took some doing but Jimmy located Willie in a British Army Hospital in Bari, Italy."

After hearing what Andy just said, an excited Frank Angelone remarked, "Hey, that's where my family's from."

"That's good to know, Ange," responded Jim Beauregard who quickly added, "When we send this guy back to Italy we'll have you take him."

Because Frank knew that Jim was kidding around he limited his response to saying, "My bags are always packed, Major."

As soon as Andy finished lighting his cigar, he continued briefing his colleagues.

"According to what Jimmy Scott was able to find out, Willie was wounded in the leg when his Liberty Ship was attacked by the Luftwaffe. When CID Agents based in Naples went to the hospital in Bari to see if Willie could help us, he was no where to be found. Turns out, the old man liberated some clothes from the hospital laundry and hitched a ride to the port city of Taranto so he could visit a retired Italian merchant seamen he became pals with back in the early '30s. British Army MPs eventually found Dan's old informant in the restaurant that he helped his Italian buddy to buy when a serious injury forced him to stop going to sea."

After quickly tapping the ash from his cigar in the ashtray on his desk, Andy went on to say, "Once we had Willie flown back to the states, he filled in a few blanks and told us a few things that we didn't know. In addition, he agreed to help us locate Rudy Mueller and the other people on Miller's list who he was closest too. The first major break we got was when Willie helped us find Mueller's father-in-law, a former Bund member by the name of Gunther Kessler. One of the reasons it made sense to find Kessler, was because his daughter is married to Mueller. When we checked the location in Bayonne where Willie said Kessler owned a bakery and he wasn't there, we decided to check every bakery from Perth Amboy to Ft. Lee. It took some doing but we finally got lucky when we got to Newark and we learned that Kessler opened a combination grocery store and bakery."

As soon as Frank Angelone finished taking a sip of spiked coffee, the veteran detective remarked, "Once you found Kessler and his daughter you found Mueller?"

"Correct," responded Andy who took two quick puffs on his cigar before he continued. "The day Willie spotted Mueller, we learned that he bought a delivery truck and moved into the building next door to his father-in-law's store. We also found the Wagner brothers and Max Hoffman, the three truck drivers who Willie said were Mueller's closest friends in the Bund next to Miller. In fact, of all the

Bund members on Miller's list, the Wagner brothers, Hoffman and Kessler know Mueller the longest. These guys go back to the early days of the Bund, when Miller and Mueller owned a butcher shop in Germantown, PA and they used to come up to New York for rallies."

After tapping the ash from his cigar into the ashtray on his desk, Andy went on to say, "Rather than have Willie conveniently run into Mueller, we had him run into the Wagner brothers in a bar in Hoboken where they hang out on Saturday night. The way we set it up they ran into Willie. Within twenty four hours, Willie was invited to have Sunday dinner with Mueller, his wife, his father-in law, the Wagner brothers and Max Hoffman to talk about the old days over a plate full of thick steaks."

While Andy paused to take another sip from his coffee mug, Johnny Mc Donald remarked, "If Mueller served a plate full of thick steaks for Sunday dinner he must be following in Miller's footsteps."

"It sure looks that way, Johnny," said Andy as he put his mug down.

Frank Angelone also spoke up and said, "That makes Mueller crooked butcher number two."

"Right again, Ange," responded Andy who continued by explaining in vivid detail how Willie played Mueller and the other former Bund members like a fiddle, especially when he criticized FDR and every politician under the sun for fighting the Germans when the Russians are our real enemies. Andy finished describing how this Sunday meeting went by saying, "Willie also fudged the truth about how he was wounded, when he told Mueller and the others that an inexperienced trigger happy British pilot mistook his Liberty Ship for an Italian merchant vessel."

"I can't wait to meet this guy," remarked Frank Angelone. "He sounds like a real piece'a work."

"He sure is," responded Andy.

"I'm glad he's on our side," added Johnny Mc Donald.

After hearing Jim say, "Go ahead, Andy," the veteran FBI Agent picked up where he left off. "Once they heard that Willie was planning to take a civilian job in the POE, Mueller asked Willie if he wanted to make some real dough selling black market meat. As soon as this offer was made, we had a man on the inside of Mueller's operation."

After draining the last drop of whiskey laced coffee from his mug, Andy went on to say, "The day Mueller took Willie around to meet his customers and take their orders, we were once notch closer to making a case against this group of black market operators. In fact, thanks to Willie, we know that Miller, Mueller, Kessler, the Wagner brothers and Max Hoffman intentionally got involved in the black market as a way to make money, while also doing their part as good Nazi sympathizers to hurt the American war effort. Even Mueller's wife is involved and handles the books for her husband. Once we heard this, we were twice as convinced that we had to make a case against Mueller in order to get him to cooperate."

As soon as Andy stood up with his coffee mug in hand, he continued while he walked over the Frank's desk and picked up the bottle of whiskey and poured a healthy shot of whiskey into his mug. "In order to catch these guys red handed, some of our agents along with Eddie Evans and two other OPA officials will be following the Wagner brothers when they make their return trip from out west with a truck load of illegal meat. Based on what we know, their truck is due back sometime tomorrow and we're invited to be part of the reception committee."

While Andy sat back down and took a sip from his mug, Jim Beauregard spoke up and said, "If Mueller and Miller were partners in a butcher shop in Manhattan before the war, it stands to reason that some of their best customers might have become some of Miller's black market customers once rationing was imposed. If Mueller can identify these customers and if we can put the squeeze on any of these characters, we might be able to learn more about Ivan Larson and Shorty Mc Ghee. If we get real lucky, we might also be able to find out who killed Miller."

"That's a lotta ifs, Major," remarked Al Parker.

After nodding his head ever so slightly, Jim responded and said, "You're right, Al. That's a lotta ifs."

After finishing his drink, Andy described what would happen next. "Once that truck load of black market beef arrives at Mueller's warehouse, crooked butcher number two should be well motivated to cooperate. Whether he knows anything that can help us find Ivan Larson is yet to be determined."

In keeping with his sarcastically irreverent sense of humor, Frank Angelone decided to lighten the moment by teasing Andy Dubrowsky. While Frank looked at his favorite FBI Agent, he raised his right index finger in the air as he spoke up and said, "Hey, Andy, I have a question."

As soon as Andy said, "Shoot," Frank Angelone did his best to sound like he was being serious. "We handed our Uncle Sam another case of the century, along with a ton of leads to follow and it took this long for the FBI to find a Kraut butcher from of all places but Germantown, PA, who runs a black market meat operation from a warehouse that's located next to his goosestepping father-in-law's Kraut bakery and grocery store in Newark, New Jersey where his Kraut wife works. To top all this off, Kraut Mueller employs three Kraut truck drivers who belonged to the same Nazi loving Kraut fan club as his recently deceased crooked Kraut partner Johann Miller? How come it took so long to put this mystery together? I thought you G Men could leap tall buildings in a single bound and were faster than a speeding bullet."

As soon as Andy Dubrowsky played along and remarked, "I'm sorry it took so long, Ange. It won't happen again," everyone at the table had a good laugh.

Once everyone settled down, Jim Beauregard asked Andy when they should be in position in Newark. Immediately after Andy finished taking a quick puff on his cigar, he looked at Jim and said, "The ASAIC wants to brief us at ten tomorrow morning. After the briefing two of us will be assigned to work with one of the Newark agents, while three of us keep Dan Phillips company in the building that overlooks Mueller's warehouse."

"That means we're off for the rest of the night," responded Jim who quickly added, "I don't know about you guys but I think I'm gonna hit the sack early tonight."

"A night off. I can't believe it," said Al.

Johnny Mc Donald agreed, then went on to say, "My eyes will be closed before my head hits the pillow."

As usual, Frank Angelone couldn't resist joking around and said, "Don't forget to say your prayers first, Johnny."

Once they arrived in Newark, New Jersey in two unmarked cars, Jim and his men met with the Assistant Special Agent in Charge of the local FBI Field Office. After they were given an update about the case, Jim, Andy and Al joined FBI Supervisor Dan Phillips inside the building that was being used by the FBI to observe Mueller's warehouse and his father-in-laws bakery. In order to increase the coverage of the two locations of interest, Frank Angelone, Johnny Mc Donald and FBI Agent Walter Merchant were positioned inside a corner bar that was located one block away from Mueller's warehouse.

As soon as Al Parker called out, "We have company," Rudy Mueller arrived at his warehouse at 7:23 PM with his father-in-law and the truck driver identified as Max Hoffman. The two teams of FBI Agents and New Jersey State Police Detectives that discretely followed Mueller and his associates to his warehouse broke off and surrounded the immediate area.

While Al Parker, Jim Beauregard and Andy Dubrowsky observed Mueller's warehouse from the building that was being used as a surveillance platform, Dan Phillips answered the phone on the first ring. As soon as Dan hung up the phone, he explained to the three representatives from the Army CID Task Force that the truck carrying the black market beef should be arriving in a few minutes.

Without wasting any time Dan Phillips picked up the phone and quickly dialed a local number. As soon as Agent Merchant answered the pay phone, Dan said, "The truck's on the way, Walt. Standby to move in."

After relaying the news to Detectives Aneglone and Mc Donald, FBI Agent Walter Merchant left the bar with the two New York City cops and got in their car. A few minutes later the truck carrying the black market beef turned the corner.

Once the large wooden garage doors to Mueller's warehouse were opened and the truck carrying the illegal beef drove inside, a small army of FBI Agents, OPA Enforcement Division officials, New Jersey State Police Detectives and representatives from the Army CID Task Force waited for the signal to move in. As soon as Willie saw that the truck was loaded with illegal beef, he excused himself so he could hit the head.

On the way back from the bathroom, Willie opened the front door to the warehouse office and spit on the sidewalk, before he walked back into the building to join the others by the back of the truck. A few seconds later, a dozen FBI Agents, New Jersey State Police Detectives and OPA officials moved in to execute their warrants. Accompanying these men where members of the CID Task Force.

While Dan Phillips, Andy Dubrowsky, Jim Beauregard and Al Parker stood in front of the warehouse, Rudolf Mueller and his associates were taken into custody and a truck load of illegally possessed beef was being officially seized by Eddie Evans and his fellow OPA officials. In order to maintain his cover for a little while longer, Willie Gunderson was also handcuffed and led away by a pair of FBI Agents.

From the moment Mueller and his associates were arrested, to the time they were transported to the FBI Field Office in Newark, the prisoners refused to speak English and only responded in German. Once it became clear that Mueller in particular was being a first class prick, Dan Phillips and the men from the CID Task Force decided to use a slightly different approach when they interrogated the belligerent prisoner.

When Dan Phillips introduced Rudolf Mueller to Major James Beauregard and the other members of the Army CID Task Force, the prisoner had the look of sheer contempt on his face when he spoke in German and refused to be interviewed in the presence of a "nigger" cop. None of the men in the room needed Al to translate to understand what Mueller just said. Instead, Detective Angelone leaned closer to Mueller and said, "Do you know who you just insulted?"

After seeing the look of surprise on Mueller's face, Frank Angelone twisted the prisoner's left ear and forcibly turned his head so he had no choice but to look up at Al Parker. While Frank continued to force the prisoner to look up at Al, he sounded dead serious when he remarked, "In addition to being our friend, Patrolman Parker is also our secret weapon. Now you show him some respect, Fritz, or we'll leave you two alone."

As soon as Frank let go of the prisoner's ear and stood up, Jim Beauregard turned to Al and said, "He's all yours, Al."

The last thing that Rudy Mueller expected was to have a U.S. Army Major from CID allow a Negro cop to conduct his interrogation. While towering over the prisoner to reinforce who was in charge, Al sounded like a full blooded Nazi storm trooper when he explained the severity of the charges against Mueller and his associates, all while speaking fluent German.

The second Al instructed the prisoner in German to start identifying the customers who patronized his butcher shop in Manhattan, Mueller looked as if he forgot that he was being interrogated by a Negro. When Mueller tried to explain that his wife was not involved in his black market operation, Al Parker sounded like he was with the Gestapo, when he waved his right hand in disgust and discounted what Mueller said as pure bullshit.

Al reinforced his point when he picked up the ledger book that was found in Mueller's warehouse office and he slammed it down on the table in front of the prisoner, as he continued yelling in German and said, "Your wife's not involved!

How 'bout I bet you a thousand German Marks that we can prove that this ledger book is filled with entries of illegal transactions that were made in your wife's handwriting!" Then, after pausing for a split second, Al remarked, "Gretchen is going to jail and so are you and your other goosestepping buddies. We're also going after everyone you did business with. That means that you and your pals won't be very popular once we start making your customer's lives miserable."

The one thing that impressed Mueller the most, was that the Negro cop who spoke fluent German wasn't stopping to translate their exchange to the white cops who were in the room. While the U.S. Army Major from CID, along with two FBI Agents and two police detectives stood nearby and remained silent, it became painfully clear to Rudolf Mueller that Patrolman Parker was in complete command of his interrogation. Even when Mueller said that he was willing to cooperate, if the authorities dropped the charges against his wife and his father in law, Al played his part to the hilt when he continued to address the prisoner in German and said, "Why should I do anything for you? You're a Nazi, your father in law is a Nazi, your truck drivers are all Nazis and your wife is a Nazi. Even that old man who works for you is a fucking Kraut!"

Everyone in the room knew that Mueller was ready to cooperate when he finally spoke in English and said, "At least let my wife go. Yes, my wife is German and my wife handled the books, but she's not a Nazi. If you let her go I'll answer your questions."

As soon as Al removed a pen from his suit jacket pocket and he handed it to Mueller, he pointed to the stack of paper on the table and said, "If you want us to consider dropping the charges against your wife, I suggest you start writing down everything you know about black market operations. We also want a list of your customers when you owned a butcher shop in New York with Johann Miller."

The moment Mueller accepted the pen, Al Parker figured he had nothing to lose and everything to gain by asking Mueller if he ever met a teenager by the name of Ivan Larson or heard that name? Without hesitating Mueller responded and said, "A kid by the name of Ivan picked up meat orders on a few occasions but he always dealt with my partner."

After hearing what Mueller had to say, Jim Beauregard stepped closer to where the prisoner was seated, just as Al Parker presented Mueller with copies of the original wanted posters. A second later Jim remarked, "You can start cooperating by taking a look at these wanted posters to see if you recognize anyone."

Again Mueller didn't hesitate when he pointed to the original composite sketch of Ivan Larson and said, "I remember reading about what this kid did in the papers. I also heard about what he did on the radio." Then, after a brief pause, Mueller looked up at his interrogators and remarked, "It's been a while but this looks like that kid Ivan."

As soon as Jim produced a copy of the most recent composite sketch of Ivan Larson, Mueller stated that even though there was a similarity between the two sketches, the original wanted poster looked more like the teenager known as Ivan. Mueller also stated that he never met anyone who looked like the sketch of Francis Shorty Mc Ghee.

When Jim asked Mueller if he remembered if Ivan Larson was picking up meat orders for anyone in particular, crooked butcher number two kept his response short and to the point. "I know he picked up a few orders from our store, but I never paid any attention to who he was doing it for."

As soon as their prisoner finished answering Jim's question, Frank Angelone asked Mueller if his former partner ever talked about his dealings with Ivan Larson or mentioned who purchased his black market meat.

Once again Mueller responded like a broken man who had no choice but to cooperate to save his young wife. "Even though Miller and I were partners and friends, he wasn't much of a talker. Once he introduced me to my supplier out west, we helped each other out on a few occasions but that's about it. All I know is that everyone of our old customers who owned a bar, a restaurant or a grocery store purchased black market beef from Miller. He even took care of some of our other customers who made smaller purchases. We're talking about a good twenty five customers from the old neighborhood. Miller also made some new customers, but he never talked about them other than to say that business was booming."

When Mueller didn't finish answering his question, Frank Angelone let the prisoner know that he wasn't completely happy with his response. "What you're telling us is great, but you left something out. What about Ivan?"

Cooperating with the police, the FBI and the U.S. Army was a new experience for Rudy Mueller, one that he didn't particularly care for. He proved that every time he answered a question. This time was no different. "The only time Miller ever talked about that kid was when we were on a trip out west to meet my supplier. He called him a real hustler and said Ivan and some big colored kid delivered whole sides of beef to two different Irish bars that were owned by one of our old customers."

As soon as Mueller stopped speaking, Andy Dubrowsky asked, "What's the name of these bars?"

"One of them is called The New Dublin Bar. Me and Miller used to eat dinner there once or twice a week," responded Mueller.

"And the name of the other bar," asked Jim.

Once again Mueller didn't seem all that happy about cooperating when he responded and said, "The Shamrock Bar."

Because Johnny Mc Donald's parents owned an Irish bar that also served food in the city, he was familiar with the other Irish bars and restaurants in the area. As soon as Johnny heard what Mueller had to say, the Irish American Police Detective turned to his colleagues and said, "I know the owner of those joints. He's a hot headed Irish SOB by the name of Mickey Flynn."

Frank Angelone was his usual colorful self when he looked at Jim Beauregard and said, "What Johnny's trying to say is that Mickey Flynn definitely gives Irishmen a bad name."

"That bad huh? remarked Jim.

Under the circumstances, Johnny limited what he said in front of the prisoner by suggesting that Jim speak to Joe Coppola and Jack Donovan to learn more about the Flynn brothers and some of their relatives.

As soon as Jim said, "I read you loud and clear," Johnny Mc Donald asked Mueller a followup question to make the prisoner go all the way as far as his cooperation was concerned. "Something tells me you're holding back on us, Laddy. If you and Miller knew Mickey Flynn, you had to know his brother and some of his other family members."

Even though Mueller continued to appear reluctant to cooperate, he managed to do so. "According to Miller, he used Eddie Flynn to make some late night meat deliveries in his fleet of taxi cabs. I also know that Miller was friends with Eddie Flynn's uncle but that's about it."

Once again Johnny spoke directly to Jim Beauregard. "Joe Coppola and Jack Donovan can also tell you everything you need to know about Eddie Flynn's famous Uncle Mike."

As far as Jim and his men were concerned, if everything else that Mueller said was the equivalent of a base hit, the comment he just made scored their first home run. After looking at his colleagues, Jim asked Mueller to identify the name of Eddie Flynn's cab company?

This time Mueller didn't hesitate when he answered a question. "The Westside Taxi Company."

In order to go over what the prisoner just said, Andy Dubrowsky asked Mueller two questions. "So what you're telling us, Mr. Mueller, is that to the best of your knowledge, Johann Miller sold black market beef to Mickey Flynn and Ivan Larson and one of his friends delivered the meat to The New Dublin Bar and The Shamrock Bar? You're also telling us that, as far as you know, Eddie Flynn delivered some of Miller's black market meat in his fleet of taxi cabs?"

As usual, Mueller didn't seem all that happy when he looked up at the FBI Agent and limited his response to a simple, "Yes."

Jim Beauregard knew that trying to get a guy like Mueller to fully cooperate was more like pulling teeth than milking a cow. As a result, Jim decided to change the subject and take the conversation in a slightly different but related direction. "Tell us, Mr. Mueller, did Miller ever introduce you to his contact for black market gasoline and cigarettes?"

For some reason Mueller seemed to have an easier time answering this particular question. "Even though I never met his supplier, Miller got me a few gallons of gasoline whenever I needed it. He also sold me a few cartons of cigarettes but that's about it."

After asking if he could smoke one of his cigarettes, Mueller continued after receiving a light from Jim Beauregard. "Even though Miller was the counter man and dealt with our customers, I still knew who they were. I'll give you the list you want, but I can't tell you anything more about that kid Ivan." Then, after pausing for a split second, Mueller added, "It might help me put this list together if you get me a Manhattan Classified Telephone Directory so I can take a look at some names and addresses."

As soon as Dan Phillips remarked, "I'll dig one up," Johnny Mc Donald asked Mueller if there was a reason why Miller dealt with their customers.

Once again the black market operator responded without thinking and said, "We decided it was better for Miller to do the talking because I have more of a German accent. Miller also recommended that we tell everyone that we're Dutch."

While Jim retrieved the wanted posters from the table in the interrogation room, Andy Dubrowsky asked Mueller if he had any of the old records from the butcher shop that he owned with Johann Miller. Once again Mueller sounded as if he was telling the truth when he responded and said, "Whatever wasn't tossed into the garbage was kept by Miller when we parted company. The only thing I took with me when I left New York were a few aprons and the tools of my trade."

Now that Mueller answered their battery of questions, Jim made eye contact with Frank Angelone and Johnny Mc Donald and nodded his head once. This prearranged signal let his two favorite New York City Police Detectives know that it was time to discuss Miller's murder with the prisoner.

The moment Frank Angelone broached the topic of Miller's death, Mueller took a drag on his cigarette before he responded. "I've been waiting all night for someone to ask me where I was on the night Miller was murdered."

"Now's your chance to tell us," remarked Frank Angelone.

This time Mueller seemed more cooperative when he responded. "I spent most of that day meeting with some of my customers. At 7 that night my wife and I had dinner in the Lamplighter Restaurant in Elizabeth. On the way home we stopped to visit Max Hoffman and his sick mother. We were home by nine. I didn't hear about Miller's death until Bruno Wagner called me in the morning when the story broke on the radio. The only reason I moved was because I didn't need a visit from the cops while I was selling black market meat."

After hearing what Mueller said, the more tactful Johnny Mc Donald asked, "Do you have any idea who would want to kill your old partner?"

Once again Mueller sounded like he was telling the truth, when he answered a question that involved the death of his former partner. "At the time I assumed he was probably robbed. Johann didn't believe in banks. He always carried a big wad of cash and liked to hide his money."

After hearing Mueller's response, Jim extended his hand as he faced Agent Phillips and said, "Thanks, Dan. You and your men have been a big help."

"It was our pleasure, Major," responded Dan who continued as he opened the door to the interrogation room. "As soon as Mister Mueller completes his list, I'll get a copy of my report to Andy. I'll also contact our search teams to see if they came up with anything that might help you in your investigation."

After being introduced to Willie Gunderson and thanking him for his assistance, Jim left the FBI Field Office and addressed his fellow task force members while they stood on the sidewalk next to their parked cars. While Jim looked at Al Parker he seemed to be in very good spirits when he said, "Good show, Al. You scared the swastika right off that guy's arm and got him to talk."

The moment Frank Angelone remarked, "You also scared the crap outta me when you started yelling at Kraut Mueller in German," the other members of the New York CID Task Force had a good laugh thanks to the funniest cop in the unit.

After pausing to light a cigarette, Jim continued and said, "When I was a rookie my father told me that good cops make their own luck. By pursuing the leads that were found in Miller's warehouse and in his apartment, we learned a lot about Ivan Larson and his involvement in black market activities. Even the credibility of certain witnesses in this case has been bolstered by what we learned so far."

As soon as Jim took a drag on his cigarette, he added, "If we continue to make our own luck, we should be able to learn more about the relationship between Ivan Larson and people like the Flynn brothers. In the process, we might also learn more about Francis Shorty Mc Ghee. If all else fails, we can canvass the neighborhood where Mueller and Miller had their butcher shop, to see if anyone else besides Mickey and Eddie Flynn had dealings with Larson and Mc Ghee. Regardless of what we do with the information on Mueller's list, I say we have something to celebrate."

When Johnny Mc Donald asked Jim what he had in mind, Jim continued to sound as if he was in exceptionally good spirits when he responded and said, "I'm sure you'll all agree that because the FBI will receive the lion's share of the publicity for shutting down another black market operation, our favorite FBI Agent should buy the first round of drinks at Mc Donald's Bar."

As soon as Andy Dubrowsky patted his pockets and joked, "But I left my wallet home," Frank Angelone opened the door to the FBI car and said. "Let's go G Man, you're buying the first round or we're filing a formal complaint with Mister Hoover."

While the other men got into their cars, Jim faced Al Parker and said, "Ange was right. You really are our secret weapon."

As Jim and Al faced each other and cracked smiles, "Frank Angelone honked his car horn and called out, "Let's go! Johnny's thirsty."

Once Jim and Al got into the FBI car with Andy, the representatives of the New York City based Army CID Task Force drove away from the FBI Field Office in Newark, New Jersey and headed straight for Mc Donald's Bar in Manhattan."

★ ★ ★

The high point of the press conference that was held in the morning, was when government officials allowed newspaper reporters, photographers and radio show personalities to examine the contents of Mueller's warehouse, that included a truck loaded with illegally possessed sides of beef. The fact that Rudolf Mueller, his three drivers, his father in law and John Johann Miller were former members of the German American Bund was the cherry on top of the cake that made this case receive nationwide publicity.

Once it became known that Willie Gunderson was working for the FBI, every defendant in this case, including Rudolf Mueller, decided to plead guilty.

After hearing the latest news report, Mike Connely began to think about the potential ramifications of Rudolf Mueller's arrest in New Jersey. Even though Mike always dealt with John Miller, he had no way of knowing what Mueller observed, overheard or knew. At the very least, Rudy Mueller knew that Mike Connely was a New York City businessman who owned several pieces of real estate, including the land where The Westside Taxi Company was located. If Mueller and Miller knew anything about Mike's colorful past, they never mentioned it to his face.

Mike was also concerned that Mueller might remember that Ivan picked up several orders at the M&M Butcher Shop. At the very least, Mueller would also be able to tell the feds who their biggest customers were when he ran the M&M Butcher Shop with Miller.

Even though Mike Connely hadn't had any contact with the police or the feds in years, the mere mention of his name would be enough to have the authorities focus their attention on everyone associated with him. That included the Flynn brothers. Mike also knew that Mueller and Miller used to frequent The New Dublin Bar. This was a major concern, especially if John Miller told his former partner that he sold black market meat to Mickey Flynn and that Eddie Flynn used his fleet of taxi cabs to make some of his late night deliveries. It would be even worse for all parties involved, if Mueller knew that Ivan and Amos delivered Miller's illegal meat to The New Dublin Bar and The Shamrock Bar.

It was also no government secret that Andy Gooding was cooperating with the police and the feds. This meant that the cops knew that Miller recommended Ivan to Andy Gooding. It was also no coincidence, that the same Army Task Force that was involved in the shootout at the Ft. Hamilton Diner, also raided Miller's warehouse, found his dead body and assisted in the investigation that resulted in Mueller's arrest.

The one thing that comforted Mike Connely was that his closest family members were incredibly loyal to him and Ivan. The proof that this was true was evident by the fact that none of his relatives, who were aware of certain aspects of Ivan's escape plan, ever contacted the police. Had any of them done so, the police would have been able to focus their attention on Mike Connely a long time ago.

Mike also knew that the authorities would apply unbridled amounts of pressure on anyone they thought could help further identify and locate Ivan and Shorty. For this reason Mike never had a conversation with his lawyer about Ivan, once he became wanted by the police.

To counter any pressure that the authorities might place on his family members, Mike became extremely generous and transferred ownership of the property where The Westside Taxi Company was located to his cousin Eddie Flynn. Mike also transferred ownership of the property where The New Dublin Bar was located to his cousin Mickey Flynn.

Since Mike already had Mickey fronting for him on the liquor license, Mickey Flynn was now the owner of an expensive piece of New York City real estate and a very profitable business. Eddie Flynn also had no reason to complain now he was the sole owner of a profitable taxi cab company. In addition, Mike promised to give the Flynn brothers the warehouse that he owns on Pearl Street. Mike also did what he could to help his closest relatives in Ireland to prosper and made sure that his widowed sister in Jersey City was well cared for.

Even after taking extra special care of his closest relatives, Mike still had other pieces of New York real estate that he asked his lawyer Murray Silverman to sell on his behalf. All Mike wanted in return, was the Flynn brothers to promise that they would deliver the cash that he asked them to hold to Ivan and Shorty, if and when they ever heard from them again.

Now that Mike knew that he only had a few months to live, he became more concerned about Ivan and Shorty than he was worried about himself. This meant that Mike had a limited amount of time before he became bed ridden and virtually incapacitated. This also meant that the cops had a limited amount of time to get to him and even if they did, Mike had no intention of helping them find Ivan or Shorty.

In order to continue to help Ivan and Shorty maintain their new identities, Mike decided to use whatever time he had left to send Danny Gannon and Gus O'Malley a steady stream of mail and packages from "home." These packages would include hand written letters, Jersey City, New Jersey newspapers, magazines and food parcels.

Mike also took the time to let his family members know that they might be visited by the feds and the police who were determined to find Ivan and Shorty. When he did so, Mike felt the weight of the world lifted from his shoulders when his sister Clara and the Flynn brothers assured him not to worry.

In the last meeting that Mike Connely had with his two cousins and Murray Silverman, he paid his lawyer for transferring the property where The Westside Taxi Company was located to Eddie Flynn and the property where The New Dublin Bar was located to Mickey Flynn. As soon as this meeting was over, Mike made one of his last trips to New Jersey to buy local newspapers and send off a trunk load of letters and packages to Ivan and Shorty.

CHAPTER 37

DOING WHAT COPS DO BEST

Thanks to the cooperation of a famous radio personality and a major broadcasting company, the first U.S. Army CID "Manhunt Report" Radio Show was aired live from a Manhattan studio one week ahead of schedule. Just as planned, the first broadcast included an interview of Major James Beauregard and FBI Special Agent Andy Dubrowsky, who provided a riveting account of the murder of Tommy Mulray and the blazing shootout that the government men had with Ivan Larson as he fled the scene of the crime.

Within an hour of the first radio broadcast being aired, a number of military police and CID units began receiving calls from U.S. Army personnel who thought they had information that could help identify one or both of the fugitives. The number of prospective witnesses increased even more, when the updated newspaper articles about the intensified search for the two fugitives began hitting the stands in different parts of the country. A steady stream of reports were also being received at CID Headquarters that relayed the number of incidents that were taking place overseas, when military police, CID Agents as well as local commanders investigated leads involving Ivan Larson and Francis Mc Ghee.

While sitting in the busy squad room. where investigators were answering one phone call after another, Detective Johnny Mc Donald turned to his partner and said, "The good news, Frankie, is that we stirred the pot with our radio program and the newspaper articles that feature the new wanted posters. The bad news is that we stirred the pot so much, we have more leads to follow than we can handle unless we get some help."

As soon as Frank Angelone finished filling out another witness statement, he tossed his pencil down and remarked, "All I want'a know is who's idea was it to offer a 30 day furlough as a reward in this case?"

While Johnny Mc Donald, Joe Coppola and Jack Donovan had a good laugh at Frank Angelone's expense, their break was cut short when the telephones on their desks started ringing again. One by one each of the men in the office answered their phone by saying, "CID Task Force can I help you."

Inside Lt Colonel Richmond's Office Jim Beauregard was receiving some bad news. While the Colonel continued briefing his second in command, he removed a pipe from the large ashtray on his desk. "I don't like this anymore than you, Jim, but I just got told that despite the significance of our fugitive investigation, the fighting of this war takes precedence over police work."

In all of his years as a cop Jim never had to deal with such a complex bureaucracy as the U.S. Army. While Jim sat in a comfortable chair across the desk from his commanding officer, he removed a pack of Lucky Strike cigarettes from his pant's pocket and said, "Tell me, Sir, what do I tell the men? That the U.S. Army wants to postpone the next episode of our radio broadcast, because the first show that went on the air generated too many leads for us to follow? After all, Sir, we're not looking for a pair of AWOL G.I.s who got drunk and stole a Jeep."

After pausing to light his pipe, Colonel Richmond responded to Jim's question in his usual trademark soft spoken tone of voice. "Unfortunately, the Army has its fair share of men who are orphans, who come from broken homes and who don't have much of a family life that match the general description of Ivan Larson and Francis Shorty Mc Ghee. The fact that some of these men have had all kinds of brushes with the law has made them targets of accusations and in some cases fights with other soldiers. Based on the reports that have been called in to our office, as well as to numerous CID and MP units in the states and overseas, there are enough men who have been called Shorty at one time or another to keep every man in this office busy conducting interviews for several months."

While Jim used his Zippo lighter to light his cigarette, his commanding officer continued with his briefing. "The sad part is that the success of our radio show, combined with the articles that we've been publishing, has stirred up a hornets nest of interest in this case. Unfortunately, this intense level of interest has become a distraction for MPs, CID Agents, squad leaders, platoon leaders and company commanders who are trying to support and fight this war. While experienced investigators like us look forward to having more leads to investigate, the U.S. Army sees the expanded interest in our case as being too much too soon."

After taking a few puffs on his pipe, Colonel Richmond continued as he looked at his exhausted second in command and said, "The other problem we have is that MPs and CID Agents who are stationed overseas are inundated with work. In addition to directing traffic, transporting and guarding incredibly large numbers of enemy POWs, manning check points, breaking up fights, checking passes, arresting men who are AWOL and protecting bases and field headquarters, our MPs and CID Agents also have to contend with one hell of a black-market problem overseas. Everything and I mean everything that we need to win this war is being stolen in massive quantities by our own men, by deserters and by local thieves in Allied occupied territory. Our agents also have their hands full investigating everything from rapes to robberies. This means that every time a G.I. hears about some guy in his unit who was called Shorty, was an orphan, comes from a broken home, rarely if ever gets mail or had a brush with the law in civilian life, MPs and CID Agents have to stop performing their duties that directly relate to winning this war, in order to conduct a collateral investigation for our office. The other problem we have, is that the United States Army is filled with 18 and 19 year old young men who are similar in size and stature as Ivan Larson and Francis Shorty Mc Ghee."

While Jim Beauregard sat back and did his best to accept the bad news, Colonel Richmond took a few quick puffs on his favorite Peterson pipe before he continued and said, "Like it or not, Jim, I've been told that from this moment on every lead that relates to our fugitive investigation will receive the lowest priority, unless we can generate a lead on our own that impresses CID Headquarters enough to get us the assistance that we need."

After placing his pipe in one of the ashtrays on his desk, Lt. Colonel Richmond went on to say, "I've also been told that MP and CID units assigned to the states will have more leeway in assisting us but will do so with one restriction. Effective immediately, the Provost Marshal General has ordered all military police and CID units assigned to Ports of Embarkation to continue to assist us in screening troops who are being shipped overseas. However, this assistance will not be provided if doing so does causes a delay in the movement of Army personnel to various theaters of operation. In other words, if there is any chance that a troop transport will be delayed in leaving a POE on schedule, Military Police and CID units, including the members of our task force, are under strict orders to stop searching for the two fugitives, if that's what it takes for Allied ships to leave on time. The same order applies to trains and aircraft that transport U.S. Army personnel."

While Jim sat in his chair without responding, Fred Richmond did his best to sound more like a fellow law enforcement officer than a commanding officer when he said, "The good news, Jim, is that we have a number of worthwhile leads to pursue after hearing what Mr. Mueller had to say." Then, after a split second pause, Fred Richmond added, "Meet with the men and put a game plan together. Once you're ready, we'll meet with Captain Murphy and execute the plan."

As soon as Jim said, "I'll brief the men, Sir," and he stood up, Colonel Richmond held up his right hand and remarked, "One more thing, Jim."

After letting his second-in-command know that their meeting wasn't over, Colonel Richmond continued as he stood up and handed Jim a file folder. "In this file you'll find letters of commendation to this task force from CID Headquarters, from FBI Headquarters and the OPA congratulating us for developing the leads that dismantled Andy Gooding's black market operation and the operation run a group of former German American Bund members. There's also a letter of commendation in that file from the FBI and CID Headquarters for Al Parker, a copy of which has already been sent to the Police Commissioner and Captain Murphy. If there's one cop who deserves to be promoted to the rank of Detective it's Al Parker. Hopefully, the contribution that Al is making to this task force will motivate his superiors to do the right thing and promote that man."

When Jim Beauregard walked into the squad room to tell his men what Colonel Richmond had to say, he found Frank Angelone, Johnny Mc Donald, Andy Dubrowsky, Joe Coppola and Jack Donovan huddled around a large map of New York City that was displayed on the back wall.

The moment Frank Angelone noticed Jim heading their way, the Italian American police detective called out, "You're just in time, Major."

When Jim asked what they were working on, Andy Dubrowsky handed him a file folder and said, "I just brought Mueller's list of customers over. If we thought we were onto something before, wait 'till you hear what Joe and Jack have to say."

While Jim examined the list, Andy Dubrowsky began to fill him in. "While you were meeting with the Colonel, Johnny suggested that we check the map to see where these customers are located. The biggest customers that Kraut Mueller and Johann Miller did business with were nine restaurants, six neighborhood bars, two grocery stores, a deli and two small hotels. The other customers on this list live in the general vicinity of the address where the M&M Butcher Shop was located."

Jim responded as he handed the list back to Andy. "I assume we still agree that we should focus our immediate attention on everyone associated with The New Dublin Bar, The Shamrock Bar and The Westside Taxi Company?"

"That's correct," responded Andy before he turned to Joe Coppola and Jack Donovan and said, "Why don't you and Jack take it from here since you're more familiar with the Flynn brothers and the other troublemakers in their family."

While Joe spoke in a matter of fact tone of voice, he pointed to three different locations on the map. "During the early days of Prohibition The New Dublin Bar, The Shamrock Bar and The Midtown Taxi Company which is now known as The Westside Taxi Company were under the control of a well known Irish gangster by the name of Mike Connely. To give you an idea how crazy this guy was, his nickname was Mad Mike."

As soon as Joe finished referring to the map, he continued as he turned and faced Jim. "In order to make everything look legit, Connely brought two of his cousins over from Ireland to front for him on the businesses licenses and run the day to day operations. A few years after Prohibition ended, Connely faded from the limelight and retired when his health started to fail."

After lighting a cigarette, Jim spoke up and said, "In your opinion what are the odds that The Westside Taxi Company is the hack outfit that Ivan Larson delivered drums of black market gasoline to in Andy Gooding's truck?"

Joe answered the question without hesitating. "Based on what we know now, the odds don't get any higher, Major."

The next to speak was Jack Donovan. "Those of us who worked this city in the old days know Mike Connely and his two nephews the Flynn brothers. There's not a legitimate bone in their bodies, Major. We also have no love for some of their employees or their lawyer. Mickey Flynn's brother in law is another piece of work that me and Joe had dealings with during Prohibition."

After agreeing with what Jack had to say, Joe Coppola proposed a way to determine if the Flynn brothers and their other infamous family members were worth investigating. "All we have to do to prove that these characters are associated in some way with Ivan Larson is to find out if Mike Connely or the Flynn brothers own a black 1937 Suburban and if their lawyer Murray Silverman drives an Oldsmobile. We'll really hit one out of the park if we find out that Murray's wife drives a Cadillac and his girlfriend drives a convertible Chevy."

Jim agreed and remarked, "That's an excellent idea, Joe."

While Joe Coppola continued, he removed a cigar from his shirt pocket. "There's something else you need to know, Major." Immediately after Jim produced his Zippo and gave the U.S. Customs Agent a light, Joe took a few quick puffs on his cigar before he continued and said, "The only thing Mike Connely ever did right in his entire life was serve in the Marines. After he lost a piece of his leg in the last war, he changed sides and became a crook. In the process he made a fortune wheeling and dealing in every way imaginable."

"Even though we have our work cut out for us, this is all good news," said Johnny Mc Donald.

"What, no bad news?" remarked Frank Angelone.

While facing his partner, Johnny Mc Donald explained the situation at hand in one sentence. "The bad news, Frankie, is that we're gonna have to work morning, noon and night while we continue to search Army camps, screen troops leaving the port and thoroughly check out every customer on Kraut Mueller's list, starting with Mike Connely, the Flynn brothers and their lawyer."

Once again, Frank Angelone lightened the mood and made his colleagues grin when he looked at his partner and said, "You know, Johnny, you're like my wife. You're always right."

As much as Jim liked the way his men joked around, he also appreciated the fact that the men assigned to the CID Task Force had the local knowledge to come to conclusions that made perfect sense. Jim also knew that it would place a tremendous strain on his men to take on a major surveillance operation, while they continued to conduct the search for the two fugitives.

"Johnny's right. There's not enough of us to go around," said Jim, who sounded even more frustrated when he continued. "In fact, I hate to tell you guys this, but Colonel Richmond just told me that until we develop some promising leads we're basically on our own and will not be receiving much if any help from the Army. Even the MPs and CID Agents assigned to the POEs are under orders to stop screening U.S. Army personnel, if doing so delays the departure of a troop transport, a plane or a train. The agencies that contributed men to this task force are also short handed and can't do much more to help us out."

The first to respond was Joe Coppola. "Don't worry, Major. We can sleep when the war's over."

Jim received a massive boost to his morale when everyone present to a man agreed with Joe Coppola and reacted as if they were more determined than ever to make this case with or without help from the U.S. Army or anyone else. After stamping his cigarette out in a nearby ashtray, Jim seemed invigorated when he told Johnny Mc Donald what he needed him to do. "Johnny, I want you and Eddie Evans to open case files on Mike Connely, the Flynn brothers and any of their holdings. We also need to find the black Suburban and the vehicles that are associated with the lawyer who purchased black market gasoline and cigarettes from Ivan Larson. Those of us who are assigned to search teams and screening duty will do what we can to give you and Eddie a hand after hours. If all else fails we can take Amos Washington for a car ride at night to see if we can jog his memory. I also want you to get a copy of this list to Captain Murphy."

As soon as Johnny Mc Donald acknowledged his orders, Jim turned to Jack Donovan and Joe Coppola and said, "Jack, I'd like you and Joe to see if any of Mueller's former customers are receiving mail from G.I.s. Pay close attention to The Westside Taxi Company and the Flynn brothers. We also need to find out where Mike Connely hangs his hat so we can keep an eye on his mail as well."

After hearing the two federal law enforcement officers enthusiastically acknowledge their orders, Jim faced Frank Angelone and said, "Ange, we need to get this information to the detectives handling the Miller homicide. As long as they continue to work with us, I want you to be our point of contact with the homicide dicks. I'd also like you to give Johnny and Eddie a hand whenever possible.

"You got it, Major," said Ange.

When Jim continued he sounded like a man who was reinvigorated by the discussion that he was having with some of his men. "As soon as the men covering the port get off duty, we'll go over how we plan to handle these new leads. I also have some commendations to tell you about."

"Excuse me, Major," said Joe Coppola, "but when do we start working on these new leads?"

As soon as Jim finished lighting another cigarette, he looked at Joe and the others and said, "We start tonight after we grab some chow."

★ ★ ★

Once the Chief of Detectives Office assumed direct operational control over the Johann Miller homicide investigation, Captain Patrick Murphy Sr. was able to remain more involved in the search for Ivan Larson and Francis Shorty Mc Ghee. This included helping members of the CID Task Force to investigate the relationship between Ivan Larson and the customers on Mueller's list, especially Mike Connely, The Westside Taxi Company, The New Dublin Bar, The Shamrock Bar, the Flynn brothers and their lawyer, Murray Silverman.

While Captain Murphy worked tirelessly to acquire the business licenses and real estate records for every business under investigation, U.S. Post Office Inspector Jack Donovan and U.S. Customs Agent Joe Coppola visited every postman in the area before they delivered mail to the customers on Mueller's list. By doing so, Jack Donovan and Joe Coppola were able to determine the type of correspondence that every business or individual on Mueller's list was receiving.

Now that Captain Murphy was handling the background checks on the businesses and individuals in question, Johnny Mc Donald and the men who were assisting him were able to intensify their surveillance activities in the field. As soon as the port closed, the men who worked screening duty met the day tour crew for supper in the back room at Mc Donald's Bar. After supper, every member of the CID Task Force, including Captain Murphy, Andy Dubrowsky and Jim Beauregard, spent several hours conducting surveillance activities. It was tedious and exhausting work but it had to be done.

After learning more about the customers on Mueller's list, Captain Murphy knew that it was time to expand their capabilities to monitor individuals and locations of interest. In order to accomplish this task, the CID Task Force would need more men, men who could be trusted and were familiar with the section of the city where they were operating.

★ ★ ★

While Jim poured himself a cup of early morning coffee, Captain Patrick Murphy Sr. sounded as if he was in exceptionally good spirits when he entered the conference room and said, "I've got some good news, Jim."

When Jim asked if the Captain would like to join him, Pat Murphy Sr. remarked, "If you're buying I'm drinking."

By the time Jim filled a second mug with some freshly brewed coffee, Captain Murphy began filling him in. "I managed to get us some help from an old friend. Captain Steve Reynolds and I came up through the ranks together. I asked Steve to give us a hand for several reasons, including because he worked the area on the west side where we're currently operating. The other good news is that some of the cops that Steve worked with in the past are still assigned to this precinct. Steve also remembers Mike Connely and the Flynn brothers. Both of us have also had a few runs ins with their lawyer over the years."

After hearing the good news Jim asked, "How long can we count on Captain Reynolds to help out?

"From now until the end of the year, but hopefully we won't need him that long," responded Captain Murphy.

Jim also had high hopes that this end of the investigation would produce positive results sooner than later and remarked, "With someone we can trust in charge we won't have to sneak around while we try to keep an eye on the subjects of our investigation."

After taking a sip of coffee Pat Murphy Sr. responded and said, "Far be it from me to question the integrity of a fellow officer, but under the circumstances we had to face the fact that even an honest cop with a big mouth could compromise our investigation. Unfortunately, ever since we started watching The New Dublin Bar and The Shamrock Bar, our men have spotted a number of cops from the local precinct patronizing these locations. Even the local precinct captain has been observed eating and drinking with Mickey Flynn in The New Dublin Bar. The fact that The Westside Taxi Company is located in the confines of a neighboring precinct, makes it possible for us to keep an eye on Eddie Flynn without any of the local cops giv'in a shit."

Captain Murphy continued after pausing long enough to take another sip from his coffee mug. "In order to get Captain Dennis "Boats" Baldwin out of the way, I made arrangements to have him temporarily transferred to the serve as our liaison officer with the 3rd Naval District. Fortunately for us, Captain Baldwin has spent more time on police boats than any other cop in the department. As a result, no one had to twist his arm to take this detail."

While Pat Murphy Sr. and Jim Beauregard sat facing each other in the conference room, the Captain explained himself further and said, "To make it possible for us operate with a free hand, the Chief of Detectives arranged to have Captain

Steve Reynolds take Baldwin's place. This means a police captain who doesn't associate with Mickey Flynn will be in command of the precinct where we're currently operating."

Jim proved that he was frustrated enough with the lack of progress that they were making when he remarked, "I know we're handling this case the right way, but there are times when I wonder if we should'a gone in like gang busters."

Because Pat Murphy Sr. liked Jim Beauregard a great deal, he made sure to respond in a fatherly tone of voice. "There are times when I feel the same way, but the simple truth is, we made the right call when we decided to keep an eye on the individuals that we have under investigation, while we screen their mail and obtain property and licensing records. We also knew from the beginning that the bars and restaurants that we needed to keep an eye on, would be frequented by cops from the local precinct. That's why it made no sense to let any of the cops in the local station house know why we're really operating in their area."

After pausing to take another sip from his coffee mug, the Captain added, "Now that Steve Reynolds is taking temporary command of this precinct, we'll have help from a hand picked group of cops who know the area and best of all can be trusted to keep their mouths shut."

Jim Beauregard had been in this business long enough to know the importance of working with cops you could trust. Up until now, his men were telling the local beat cops they encountered that they were looking for AWOL G.I.s.. Since the city was filled with soldiers on leave, this was a believable cover story to spread around, especially since the men who were conducting these surveillance activities were members of the New York based U.S. Army CID Task Force. Now that Captain Reynolds was in temporary command of the precinct where they were pursuing important leads, Jim and his men could operate more freely and with the right kind of local help.

"You're right, Pat. This is good news," remarked Jim, who continued as he removed a cigarette from the pack that he carried in his pant's pocket. "How do you recommend that we proceed?"

Once again Captain Murphy spoke in a confident tone of voice when he responded to the Jim's question. "I asked Steve to meet us for lunch. We'll put our plan together over a dish of spaghetti. If there was ever an Irishman who loves Italian food more than Johnny Mc Donald it's Steve Reynolds."

Long before the term "networking" became popular, policemen used the word "rabbi" to describe a person who was in a position to influence decisions and insure that certain favors would be granted. A cop with the right "rabbi" or connections could insure that every effort would be made to have their favor or request approved. In police work, cops relied on a "rabbi" or an influential contact to get promoted or transferred to a sought after detail or assignment. In addition to getting someone's friend or relative hired, a "rabbi" could also be used to fulfill a "contract" that would protect a cop from certain disciplinary action.

In addition to knowing where all of the political bodies were buried, Patrick Murphy Sr. and Steve Reynolds were old timers who helped build the city police force into a well respected law enforcement agency by "modern" 1944 standards. Steve Reynolds and Patrick Murphy Sr. were also best friends.

Immediately after Jim Beauregard was introduced to the acting captain of the local police precinct, Pat Murphy Sr. provided Steve Reynolds with a general overview of the fugitive investigation and the significance of receiving Rudy Mueller's list of customers. As soon as Captain Murphy handed Captain Reynolds a copy of Mueller's list, Steve proved that he was familiar with the subjects of their investigation when he pointed to two of the names and said, "Of all the people on this list, the Flynn brothers have gone from rags to riches and they didn't make this transformation because they have the luck of the Irish."

After hearing what Steve Reynolds had to say, Jim Beauregard spoke up and said, "It's also important to bear in mind, Captain, that when Andy Gooding decided to cooperate, our black market operator from Parkisde Avenue gave us some very interesting information. This information is a lot more useful to us now that Rudolf Mueller decided to cooperate. Even Amos Washington gave us information that matched what was said to some degree by Andy Gooding and Mueller."

While Captain Reynolds sipped his glass of wine and listened, Jim continued and said, "According to Andy Gooding, he agreed to do businesses with Ivan Larson because he was recommended to him by his black market meat supplier, a person Mr. Gooding knew as John Miller. Andy Gooding also told us that he let Ivan Larson use his truck to deliver fifty five gallon drums of black market gasoline to a cab company in the city but he never identified this company by name."

When Jim paused to light a cigarette, Pat Murphy Sr. leaned closer to their lunch guest and said, "Our reliable informant Andy Gooding also sold Ivan Larson over fifty cartons of premium brand black market cigarettes that were stolen from the Brooklyn Army Depot. According to Andy Gooding, Ivan Larson purchased these cigarettes on behalf of a lawyer that he knew. This same lawyer also purchased several fifty five gallon drums of black market gasoline. Ivan Larson also told Andy Gooding that this lawyer could be trusted because one of his clients purchased black market beef from John Miller for both of his restaurants. If Andy Gooding is telling the truth and we believe he is, Larson also said that he never had a problem when he delivered Miller's black market meat to these Gin Mills that serve food."

Both Steve Reynolds and Jim Beauregard could see that Pat Murphy Sr. was on a roll and had more to say. After hearing Pat remark, "That's not all," Captain Murphy took a quick sip of wine before he continued and said, "The recently arrested Mr. Mueller was even more specific when he stated that according to his old partner, Ivan Larson and a colored kid, who we believe is Amos Washington, delivered Miller's black market meat to The New Dublin Bar and The Shamrock Bar, two licensed premises that are represented by Murray Silverman. To top all this off, Mueller also stated that Eddie Flynn used his fleet of taxi cabs to make some late night meat deliveries for Miller."

Just as Pat Murphy Sr. expected, Steve Reynolds reacted to his last comment with a grin, as he put two and two together and said, "You're making my day, Patty, if you're telling me that the CID Task Force can even come close to proving that Ivan Larson sold black market gasoline and stolen black market cigarettes to Murray Silverman. I'll be equally ecstatic if the Flynn brothers can be prosecuted for being involved in black market activities."

After taking another sip of wine, Captain Murphy continued as he leaned closer to the table. "Even though Ivan Larson never mentioned this lawyer by name, he did identify the three cars that this attorney was buying black market gas for, including his gas guzzling Oldsmobile, his wife's gas guzzling Cadillac and his girlfriend's Chevrolet convertible. In order to confirm our suspicions, we had Frank Angelone drive by Murray Silverman's home and office. Sure enough, Frank confirmed that Murray drives an Oldsmobile, his wife drives a Cadillac and his secretary owns a Chevrolet convertible. Unfortunately, we haven't been able to find the black 1937 Suburban with a dented left rear fender that Ivan Larson drove when he delivered fifty cartons of stolen smokes to the unidentified lawyer that we believe is Murray Silverman."

Steve Reynolds was impressed and proved it when he looked at Pat Murphy Sr. and Jim Beauregard and said, "I can see you boys have been busy lately."

"You're 110% correct about the Flynn brothers," remarked Captain Murphy. "Their success had nothing to do with the luck of the Irish. We all agree that the man behind their success is none other than Mad Mike Connely. We also know that the legal brains behind this family of Irish crooks is none other than Murray Silverman, an officer of the court who purchased black market gasoline and cigarettes in violation of federal law in time of war."

After hearing what Pat had to say, Steve Reynolds remarked, "Now there's a man who went from rags to riches by hitching his wagon to an Irish gangster like Mike Connely."

Even though cops knew that lawyers had a responsibility to represent the best interests of their clients, they hated to see criminals get a break because they had a fast talking attorney who used whatever means necessary to beat the system. This included the fact that Murray Silverman was always able to go before certain judges to achieve what he wanted for a client. Murray was also a well known deal maker who managed to get more for his clients than he gave to the system.

Because they were both well aware of Murray's court room antics and influence peddling, Pat Murphy Sr. made Steve's day when he looked at his best friend and said, "We've waited a long time to screw with Murray and that day has finally come. I say we enjoy this for all it's worth and use what we know to squeeze Murray for every drop of information that can help us find Ivan Larson and Shorty Mc Ghee."

While they enjoyed a cup of coffee after a delicious meal, the next phase of the investigation was planned with the help of Captain Steve Reynolds. All it took was a meeting over lunch, in a well known Italian restaurant on 9th Avenue and 39th Street, for Steve Reynolds to assign two detectives, a uniformed sergeant and three cops that he trusted and worked with in the past to assist the CID Task Force and the Chief of Detectives Office. With Steve Reynolds and six cops from the local precinct assigned to work this case, the CID Task Force was in a much better position to proceed.

CHAPTER 38

BOTH ENDS AGAINST THE MIDDLE

While meeting with the Flynn brothers in the back room office at The New Dublin Bar, Murray Silverman was becoming more and more frustrated when he tried to explain that his clients needed to be prepared to be visited by the police and the feds. "I know how they operate," said Murray, who quickly added, "How do you guys think you stayed outta jail all these years."

Between the two brothers Mickey Flynn was the one who had the temper and ran the show. After picking up the newspaper and examining the headlines, Mickey proved that he was no where near as sharp as his Uncle Mike when he said, "It says right here, that Mueller ran a black market meat operation in fucking New Jersey. What the hell that does that have to do with us? We bought our meat from Miller and since he's dead he won't be talking to the feds about his black market customers."

Murray couldn't believe that Mickey Flynn was unable to make the connection between everything that was happening ever since Ivan got in trouble. After exhaling and doing his best to calm down, Murray leaned forward in his chair and said, "I'm gonna say this one more time. Ever since Ivan got in trouble and he vanished from sight, an entire unit of city cops, feds from different agencies and U.S. Army Investigators have been working day and night to find him and Shorty Mc Ghee. Once they raided Gooding's Garage and they got Andy Gooding to cooperate, they found Miller's body and enough evidence to help the FBI and the OPA make a case against Mueller and everyone associated with him. In between all that, this special Army unit made cases against Andy Gooding's suppliers at the Staten Island Fuel Depot and the Brooklyn Army Depot. The next thing that happens is the police department assigns Captain Baldwin to work with the U.S. Navy and who takes his place, a police captain who is best friends with the police captain whose son was killed by Ivan in that bank robbery in Brooklyn. I'm not even gonna speculate what the police and the feds learned when they interrogated that idiot Amos Washington."

Once again Mickey Flynn proved that he wasn't concerned when he said, "We know you're always looking out for us, Murray, and we appreciate it but you're getting worked up for nothing. The only people who can prove that we purchased black market gasoline, cigarettes and meat are our closest family members, a few friends and some trusted employees and they're not talking to the cops because they lived real well, while everyone else was forced to deal with rationing. Since Miller is dead and none of us ever dealt directly with Andy Gooding we have nothing to worry about. Even if Miller told his old partner who his black market customers were, it'll be our word against his. As far as Amos is concerned, what are you worried about? Even though he was a nice kid, Amos was a dumb son of a bitch who was only useful when we needed someone to pick up heavy shit like a side of fucking beef."

Even though his brother ran the show, Eddie Flynn was no fool and knew that Murray was making perfect sense. After putting his drink down, Eddie addressed his brother in his trademark soft tone of voice. "Murray might be right about this special Army unit. From everything you read in the papers and hear over the radio, they seem determined to find anyone who knew Ivan and Shorty."

"So what," said Mickey.

While Eddie picked up the newspaper, he continued as he pointed to the article about Mueller's arrest and said, "I'd agree with you, Mickey, if this special Army unit wasn't involved in this case or any of the others but they were. It's almost as if they're following a trail of breadcrumbs that were left by Andy Gooding, Amos Washington and the evidence that they found when they raided Miller's warehouse and apartment, all of which led to the Mueller's arrest. Worse yet, they might know other stuff as well."

"Let's say you're both right," remarked Mickey Flynn, "And this special Army unit shows up one day and threatens to prosecute us for buying black market gasoline, meat and cigarettes. We tell 'em, prove it, speak to our lawyer. That's what we pay Murray for."

Murray could not believe how stubborn Mickey Flynn was. After lighting a cigarette, Murray let out all of his frustrations when he raised his voice an octave and said, "If that unit of military and civilian cops show up, they won't care about getting a conviction on a black market case. They're hunting a cop killer and his accomplice and they'll screw with anyone who stands in their way. That includes trying a case in the press against anyone who did business on the black market in time of war, especially with a guy like Miller who turned out to be a Nazi loving member of the German American Bund. They can also try to make my life miserable and even if they fail to do so, you boys will be looking for another attorney."

As hot headed as he was, Mickey got enough of Murray's message to ask an appropriate question. "OK, Murray, let's say those Army cops were banging on our door right now. If and when they ask us about Ivan and Shorty, what are we supposed to tell 'em? I don't know about you but all I'm gonna say is I haven't seen them since last year. I have no idea where they are, case closed. If they want to make a bullshit case against us for buying some black market merchandise, I can't stop 'em."

Murray Silverman had been a successful defense attorney long enough to know that a good lawyer never asks a question unless he already knows the answer. There were also times when a good lawyer knew better than to ask a question when they didn't want to hear a certain response. Due to the severity of the situation at hand, Murray felt that he had no choice but to have a conversation with his clients that he was hoping he would never have.

While speaking in a very calm and soft spoken tone of voice, Murray sat back in his chair as he addressed his clients and said, "I really didn't want to bring this up but suppose this special Army investigative unit asks about your Uncle Mike? After all, two of the feds working with the Army to find Ivan and Shorty investigated the shit outta your uncle and everyone he was associated with during Prohibition, including the two of you. I'm telling you this to remind you, that as good as you boys were in covering your tracks, these two feds were still able to put Colin Devlin and a cab driver who worked for your uncle behind bars. In other words, don't underestimate them. They want Ivan and Shorty in the absolute worst way and they intend to rip this town apart and go anywhere in the world to find them, including in this neighborhood."

Once again, Mickey became defensive and said, "If and when they ask me about our Uncle Mike, I'll tell 'em he's dying of cancer and I don't know where he is. Maybe he took one last trip. I'll also tell 'em that if they can find Amos Washington, Andy Gooding, John Miller's dead body and Rudy Mueller, they should be able to find Mike Connely without help from the Flynn brothers."

Rather than give up, Murray continued with his line of questioning and said, "What are you gonna say when they ask you to provide your Uncle Mike's last known address and what am I supposed to say when they ask why my clients refuse to answer a simple question?"

As Mickey Flynn stood up behind his desk, he was glad his bar wasn't open for business yet, when he responded to his lawyer in an emotionally charged raised voice. "When my brother and I came to this country all we wanted to do was work hard and make a new life for ourselves. Our Uncle Mike gave us more than a living, he gave us dignity and a future. The police and the United States Army can go to hell if they think any of us will lift a finger to help them find our Uncle Mike, or that kid who was like a son to him. Besides, the way Mike set everything up, we'll only have contact with Ivan and Shorty if they survive the damn war. Even then, they'll have to reach out to us."

Murray couldn't believe what he just heard and proved it when he blurted out, "I can't believe you're telling me this. I don't want'a know anything about Ivan and his bank robbing buddy. In fact, don't ever mention their names to me again."

Rather than reveal everything that he knew about Mike's plan to help Ivan and Shorty, Mickey limited his response to saying, "Relax, Murray. The only reason Mike told us that Ivan and Shorty joined the Army, is because he needs someone he can trust to make sure the boys get the money that he wants them to have after he leaves this world. In fact, most of that money is coming from the sale of Mike's real estate holdings that you're handling for him."

Murray was now in the middle of a first class mess that had the potential of causing him and his clients a great deal of trouble. Clearly, the situation would get down right ugly, if the authorities ever learned that Murray and his clients had any knowledge of Ivan's escape plan and aided the two fugitives in any way.

After pausing to think about what to say next, Murray did his best to let his clients know that they had to cooperate enough to protect themselves in some way, shape or form. Just as Murray expected, Mickey was adamant when he responded and said, "You're wasting your time, Murray. We'll never say or do anything that will help the cops or the fucking Army find our Uncle Mike or Ivan. The same goes for Shorty."

Despite Mickey's attitude, Murray decided to try one last time to appeal to his clients before he did what he needed to do to protect himself. After stamping his cigarette out in the ashtray on Mickey's desk, Murray did his best to sound more like a friend than their lawyer when he said, "I've known you boys since you came to this country and I've known your Uncle Mike longer than that. We've all done well together. That said, whether you want to hear this or not, I'm obligated as your lawyer to tell you that you have a tough choice to make. I say that because next to being a traitor in time of war, Ivan committed one of the worst crimes possible when he killed a cop. The fact that Patrolman Patrick Murphy Jr. was a war hero who came from a cop family makes a bad situation worse."

While choosing his words carefully, Murray continued and said, "The legal facts of life are simple. Anyone who lifts a finger to help a cop killer will pay dearly for any involvement they have with that individual. As a result, I'm obligated to tell you that even though you have every reason to be loyal to your Uncle Mike, you boys are risking everything if you ever lift a finger to help Ivan Larson and Shorty Mc Ghee."

After everything that Murray said, Mickey Flynn remarked, "We know you're doing your job, Murray, but the less you know the better."

As soon as Murray stood up, he looked at the Flynn brothers and said, "I think the time has come to reconsider our arrangement. I suggest you boys retain the services of another attorney, to include having someone else sell your uncle's remaining property once he passes away." Then, after nodding his head, Murray said, "Goodbye boys," before he headed for the door to the office.

Eddie Flynn was the first to react and called out, "Come on, Murray." The second Murray heard Mickey remark, "Let him go. He's right. It's time we got another lawyer," he was consumed by a very uneasy feeling.

Once Murray left the bar, Eddie turned to his brother and said, "Did you have to tell him what Mike asked us to do? You and your temper, Mickey. Thank God you didn't tell him the rest. We'd really have something to worry about."

As usual, Mickey Flynn proved that he was a know it all when he remarked, "Relax, Eddie, talking to a lawyer is like telling your sins to a priest in a confessional. They can't repeat a word of what you said to anyone."

"I hope you're right," said Eddie.

While Mickey finished his drink, he considered what his brother just said.

As usual, Mickey gave the orders. "Just to be on the safe side we should have Colin keep an eye on Murray for a few days."

"You think that's necessary?" asked Eddie.

"It can't hurt," responded Mickey who quickly added, "I call Colin and have him meet me at The Shamrock before he heads up to the Bronx. I need to go there anyway to take care of some business."

★ ★ ★

After returning to his office, Murray removed the Colt Detective Special that he was licensed to carry from his desk drawer and strapped the holstered revolver to his pant's belt just as Sylvia Krause entered the room.

"Is that really necessary?" asked Sylvia.

At first Murray didn't know what to say. As far as secretaries and mistresses were concerned, Sylvia was a dream come true. Rather than have her worry, Murray did his best to limit his response by saying, "I figured I'd take it with me since I'll be carrying a lotta cash tonight."

Sylvia knew when Murray wasn't being completely truthful. More importantly, she knew when something was bothering him and proved it when she said, "You always carry a lotta cash and you don't always carry a gun. You want'a tell me what's go'in on?"

After pausing to light a cigarette, Murray stood up and faced his mistress/ secretary and said, "I just dropped the Flynn brothers and Mike Connely as clients. Don't send them a bill. I don't want you or me to have any contact with them ever again. In fact, we're leaving town first thing in the morning."

"Where too," asked Sylvia.

"Pack light and for warm weather because we're going to Florida," responded Murray, who took a quick drag in his cigarette before he added, "Call Jack Furman and tell him to run the office while we're gone. I'll meet you back here in the morning. Jack can drop us off at Penn Station and use my car while we're gone."

Even though Sylvia was curious to learn what Murray intended to tell his wife, she chose to do as she was told and let the man she loved worry about what she considered was a minor detail.

After kissing Murray tenderly on his lips, the woman who was seven years younger than him left the office to pack for their trip. As soon as Sylvia left his private office, Murray picked up the phone on his desk and called the one person who would be well motivated to help him.

Even though Murray requested that they meet alone, Captain Murphy decided to bring some backup with him when he met one of the most famous criminal defense attorney's at his office in the Bronx. While meeting with Fred Richmond and Captain Steve Reynolds at the CID Office, Pat Murphy Sr. remarked, "Murray's scared, I could hear it in his voice, especially when he said that he needed to see me because he had information about Ivan Larson and Shorty Mc Ghee."

"I'm glad you called us in on this, Patty," remarked Steve Reynolds, who quickly added, "You definitely shouldn't be meeting anyone who is associated with Mike Connely who has information about Larson and Mc Ghee without someone covering your back."

Fred Richmond was another veteran law enforcement officer who worked in New York City long enough to know Murray Silverman. While Colonel Richmond filled his pipe with a fresh bowl of tobacco, he joined the conversation and said, "Steve's right. In fact, if you don't mind, I'm going along tonight. I'm just as anxious as everyone else to hear what Murray has to say."

After checking his watch, Captain Reynolds said, "We have a few hours to go before you have to meet him. That gives us plenty of time to get into position on Fordham Road before you pay Murray a visit."

As soon as Lt. Colonel Fred Richmond finished lighting his pipe, he looked across his desk at Captain Murphy and said, "Is there anyone in particular you'd like to have backing you up tonight besides us?"

Without hesitating, Pat responded and said, "Why don't we take Jim, Al, Joe and Richy with us. That'll give us enough men in case Murray says something that we need to act on right away."

As soon as Fred Richmond picked up the phone on his desk, he called Richy Olsen who was serving as the duty agent and said, "Do me a favor, Richy, and get in touch with Major Beauregard at the command post in the port. Tell him something's come up and I'll need him, Al Parker and Joe Coppola to get back to the office in an hour. We'll also need you to join us as well."

After hearing Richy say, "Yes, Sir," the Colonel hung up the phone and said, "That gives us three two man teams. If we need more than that we'll call men in from home."

Before he sent his brother-in-law up to the Bronx, Mickey told Colin just enough to motivate him to do as he was told. As far as Colin was concerned, Murray Silverman was no longer part of their inner circle and was a potential threat. For starters, Murray knew enough to put Colin back in prison for his involvement in black market activities. Murray also knew that Colin was a lot more involved in smuggling activities, than the one time that he was caught in the act by Customs Agent Joe Coppola. As a result, Colin Devlin was well motivated to agree to eliminate Murray before he had an opportunity to make contact with the police.

When Mickey asked if Colin brought a gun along and the ex con pulled his jacket open to show that he was carrying a 1911, Mickey remarked, "I suggest you take this with you tonight, 'cause there's no missing with this thing." As Mickey continued, he opened the leather musical instrument case that was converted to transport a partially disassembled Model 1928 Thompson Submachine Gun and various accessories including, a removable wooden stock, loaded twenty round magazines, a loaded fifty round drum magazine and a pair of brown leather gloves.

After recommending that Colin wear the gloves and use the Thompson without installing the wooden stock, Mickey continued and said, "The other Tommy Gun that Mike bought back in the old days, was dumped in the Hudson River after Shorty used it during that bank robbery in Brooklyn. I suggest you do the same with this one, when you're on your way back to Wheehawken."

After handing Colin $1000 dollars in cash as a bonus for taking care of their combined problem, Mickey continued and said, "Before you head up to the Bronx get yourself a New York license plate to put on your car, but don't forget to put your Jersey plate back once it's safe to do so."

Mickey knew that he had the right man for the job when a confident sounding Colin Devlin remarked, "Relax, Mickey, I know what I'm doing and don't worry, I never liked Murray anyway."

"Just make sure our former attorney doesn't survive the night," said Mickey while his brother-in-law closed the gun case. Once Colin told Mickey that he would call him from the Bronx, he left the basement of The Shamrock Bar with the converted musical instrument case in hand.

While Mickey made his way upstairs, he admitted to himself that his brother Eddie was right. Fortunately, Mickey managed to refrain from telling their squeamish lawyer that they also knew how their Uncle Mike was remaining in contact with Ivan and Shorty, now that they were serving as soldiers in the U.S. Army.

★ ★ ★

As soon as Captain Murphy arrived at Murray's office he slipped his back up gun into his trench coat pocket before he stepped out of his unmarked car. After looking around, Pat Murphy Sr. walked into the law office that was illuminated by a single light in the back room.

After hearing Murray call out, "I'm in the back, Captain," Pat kept his right hand on his Colt Detective Special as he walked into Murray's private office.

As soon as Captain Murphy entered the room, he spotted the Colt revolver that Murray was licensed to carry resting on top of his desk next to a bottle of scotch. "Expecting trouble," asked Captain Murphy as he pointed to Murray's revolver with his left hand.

"Anything's possible after the meeting that I had today with the Flynn brothers," responded Murray who continued as he picked up the bottle and said, "Can I buy you a drink, Captain?"

As Pat Murphy Sr. sat in the chair in front of Murray's desk, he tipped his hat back on his head and said, "Make it a short one, Murray. Based on what you said on the phone, it sounds like we might have a long night ahead us."

After handing the police captain a glass that contained a healthy shot of whiskey, Murray held up his glass and said, "Cheers."

As soon as the toast was over, Murray sat down behind his desk and said, "I know I'm asking a lot but I hope what I have to say tonight can square things between us to some extent."

After hearing the Captain remark, "Stranger things have happened, Murray," the famous defense attorney began to explain the reason for their late night meeting. "I told you when I called earlier that I had information about Ivan Larson and Shorty Mc Ghee." As Murray continued, he leaned forward and passed a file folder to Pat Murphy Sr. "The reason I asked you to meet me after hours, was because I needed time to put this file together for you."

As Murray sat back down, he continued and said, "During the meeting that I had today with Mickey and Eddie Flynn, Mickey admitted that they knew that Ivan Larson and Shorty Mc Ghee joined the Army. Mickey Flynn really shocked the hell out of me when he said that if Larson and Mc Ghee survive the war, Mike Connely set up some way for them to contact him and his brother. While I have no idea how this contact will be made, once Ivan Larson contacts the Flynn brothers, one of them will make the necessary arrangements to deliver the cash from the sale of Mike Connely's properties to one or both of your fugitives."

"I'm curious, Murray, but why are you telling me this?" asked Captain Murphy.

"I'm done, Captain. I'm not representing those characters anymore. Knowing that they smuggled and sold booze during Prohibition, loaned money, ran a gambling house, and bought black market gasoline, cigarettes and meat is one thing, but helping a cop killer does it for me. Bear in mind, I can't prove that either one of the Flynn brothers have lifted a finger to help Ivan Larson and Shorty Mc Ghee but based on what they said earlier this morning, they're planning to do so. Worse yet, they also gave me the distinct impression that they know more than what they're willing to discuss."

After pausing to light a cigarette, Murray pointed to the file that Captain Murphy held in his left hand and said, "Most of what you need to know is in that file, to include information about the portion of the money that Mickey Flynn is expected to turn over to Ivan Larson and Shorty Mc Ghee if they survive the war. I say a portion of the money, because once I heard what they plan to do with this cash, I refused to sell anymore property for Mike Connely. Just to be fair, I gave Mickey and Eddie Flynn an opportunity to do the right thing but they chose to remain in step with their Uncle Mike. That's when I told them to get another lawyer and I walked out."

Once Pat Murphy Sr. had a chance to examine the contents of the file, he looked at Murray and said, "Two fugitives could live like kings overseas if they ever got their hands on all this dough."

"That doesn't include the money that Ivan and Shorty made from the bank robbery and their other criminal activities," added Murray.

"No it doesn't," responded Pat Murphy Sr.

After Murray took a drag on his Camel, he sounded as if he was anxious to provide Captain Murphy with some additional information when he said, "You should also know, Captain, that on the two occasions that I delivered payments from the sale of Mike Connely's properties to Mickey Flynn, he put the cash in a black leather satchel like the kind that doctors carry. The initials MC for Mike Connely were on the outside of the bag in gold letters. On both occasions Mickey Flynn secured the money in the office safe in The New Dublin Bar in my presence."

Before Murray continued he tapped the ash from his Camel into the ashtray on his desk. "There's one more thing you need to know. Mike Connely has cancer and doesn't have long to go. When I saw him a few weeks ago he had three maybe four months to live."

"I guess that means we better find him fast," remarked Captain Murphy.

Once again Murray took a drag on his cigarette before he continued and said, "There's something else I have to get off my chest. I never told you this because I knew what you thought of me but I'm sorry about what happened to your youngest son. Patrick was one hell of a cop. The first time I saw him testify in court, I realized how much he reminded me of you when you were a young cop. For whatever it's worth, if I have to take sides, it won't be to lift a finger to help a punk like Ivan Larson get away with murder."

After pausing to stamp his cigarette out in the ashtray on his desk, Murray went on to say, "When I heard what happened to your son, I thought about my boys who are in the service and how they're risking everything to do the right thing. That's when I started to see that I needed to change. I guess you can something inside of me clicked when I heard Mickey Flynn talk about his plans to help Larson and Mc Ghee."

"I knew you had sons but I didn't know they were in the service," said the Captain.

When Murray responded he sounded like a father who had good reason to be concerned about his sons. "My oldest son is a bombardier on a B25. I worry sick about him getting shot down and captured by the Germans and having them find out that he's Jewish when they check his dog tags. My youngest son also left college and is serving as a tank commander in Europe. He had two Shermans shot out from under him in one day while fighting in Normandy. His commanding officer calls him Kraut Killer because he's knocked off more Germans than anyone else in his unit."

Despite their differences, Pat Murphy Sr. sounded sincere when he said, "You have every reason to be proud of your sons, Murray."

"Thanks Pat," responded Murray.

"I'm glad you called," said Captain Murphy before he added, "There's always room for one more on our side."

As much as he appreciated the Captain's kind words, Murray had a lot more to say and proved it when he said, "I swear on my two sons who are fighting in this war just like your son Patrick did, Mike Connely stopped talking to me about Ivan Larson right after I heard about the shootout at that diner in Brooklyn. In fact, it was Mickey Flynn who told me not to mention Ivan to Mike, because the old man was pissed at himself for not doing a better job of raising that kid. Even when the radio and newspapers started reporting on the search for Ivan Larson and Francis Shorty Mc Ghee, Mike never sought my legal advice or mentioned anything to me about Ivan being in trouble. I also had no idea where Ivan and Shorty were hiding out, or that they planned to go in the Army once they became fugitives."

Captain Murphy sounded as if he was in exceptionally good spirits when he looked at the famous defense attorney and said, "I gotta tell you, Murray, I'm not used to you being one of the good guys."

"It's a new experience for me as well," responded Murray, who quickly added, "How am I doing?"

"You seem to be getting the hang of it," said the Captain, before he stood up and remarked, "As soon as we lock this place up, I'll introduce you to the men I brought with. Three of them you already know. Steve Reynolds, Fred Richmond and Joe Coppola. They're all parked nearby on Fordham Road."

"OK, Captain. I'm all yours," said Murray as he stood up and put his Colt revolver in the holster that was secured to his pants belt.

Once the attorney was ready to go, Captain Murphy remarked, "I hope for your sake, Murray, that I'm wrong, but I'd carry that thirty eight with you at all times until we deal with the Flynn brothers and we find Mike Connely.

As the two men left the office, Murray shut the light before he opened the front door and said, "It certainly is a nice night to change sides"

The moment Colin Devlin saw someone who looked like a cop walk into Murray's office, he was glad that he got into position when he did. Even if Murray talked to this cop, Devlin still had time to prevent his former attorney from making a bad situation worse. While talking to one cop was bad enough, once Murray was taken to meet a federal prosecutor or the district attorney, there would be no stopping the authorities from taking action against his former clients.

As soon as Devlin returned to his car, he got inside, put his gloves on and rolled down the passenger side window, before he removed the blanket that covered the Thompson Submachine Gun. Once he loaded the chamber, Colin drove toward Murray's office with the Tommy Gun on the front seat next to him.

As soon as they saw Pat Murphy Sr. and Murray Silverman leave the lawyer's office and walk over to the back of the Captain's unmarked police car, Jim said, "There they are, Al."

Once Al had the unmarked Army sedan in gear, he pulled out of his parking space and drove west on Fordham Road. Al didn't get very far when a black 1937 Chevrolet Suburban passed the CID sedan in the left lane then got in front of their car.

"That's a '37 Suburban, Major," remarked an excited Al Parker."

"And it's the right color," responded Jim as he instinctively drew his Colt 1911 pistol and held it in his right hand.

Further down the street, Joe Coppola and Richy Olsen just pulled out of their parking space when the U.S. Customs Agent got excited and remarked, "Richy look, a black Suburban is pulling up in front of Murray's office."

The moment Pat Murphy Sr. spotted Joe and Richy, followed by Steve Reynolds and Fred Richmond coming their way from the opposite direction, he turned to Murray and said, "Here comes the cavalry." A split later Murray spotted Colin Devlin drive up from the other direction and come to a stop, as he held a Thompson Submachine Gun out the open passenger side window.

"Lookout, Captain!" screamed Murray as he pushed Pat Murphy Sr. out of the line of fire, just as as a hail of .45 caliber bullets riddled the famous defense attorney's body. By the time, Murray collapsed on the sidewalk, Captain Murphy was up on his feet firing his Colt revolver at the Suburban as it fled the scene of the crime.

While Jim Beauregard said, "Stay with him, Al," he racked the slide to load the chamber on the Colt 1911 that he decided to carry, instead of the less effective .32 ACP Model 1903.

"Don't worry, Major. We're following this guy to the ends of the earth," remarked Al Parker as he kept up with the Suburban.

While Pat Murphy Sr. began administering first aid to Murray Silverman, Colin Devlin realized that he was being followed by two men in an unmarked car.

With Captain Reynolds and Fred Richmond following the unmarked U.S. Customs car, Joe Coppola said, "Hang on, Richy," as he made a sharp left turn and just missed hitting an on coming trolley car, before he crashed his Chevrolet into driver's side of the black Suburban. A split second later Al Parker brought the unmarked Army sedan to a screeching stop right behind the Suburban to block its escape. To further prevent the Suburban from trying to flee the scene, Captain Reynolds pulled his unmarked police car into the on coming lane of traffic at a slight angle.

As dazed as he was from being rammed and sandwiched in between three unmarked government cars, Colin Devlin had no intentions of going back to jail. After ignoring several commands to exit his vehicle with his hands in the air, Devlin responded by screaming, "Is that you, Coppola?"

"Give it up, Devlin. You haven't got a chance," responded the Customs Agent as he took cover behind his wrecked car while aiming his Colt revolver at the convicted felon.

While Devlin screamed, "We'll see about that!" he reloaded the Tommy Gun with another twenty round magazine and began firing burst after burst out of the open driver's window and the back window. As soon as Devlin did so, Joe Coppola, Richy Olsen, Al Parker, Jim Beauregard, Fred Richmond and Captain Steve Reynolds opened fire on the Suburban, just as several New York City Police cars arrived on scene.

Even though he was hit several times, Colin Devlin managed to crawl out of the open passenger side window with his Colt 1911 in hand and fall to the ground mortally wounded. While Jim reloaded his pistol and called out, "Watch it! He's on the ground but he's still armed," Richy Olsen, Fred Richmond and Steve Reynolds reloaded their handguns. At the same time, Al Parker held up his badge and identified himself to the responding police officers as he called out, "Patrolman Parker, Army Task Force, while he and Joe Coppola drew their back up guns and repositioned themselves to cover the gunman.

While Jim and Al stood by the passenger side of the Army sedan and kept Devlin covered, Joe Coppola stood behind the left front fender of Captain Reynolds unmarked police car and called out, "Last chance, Devlin. Drop the gun."

Rather than surrender, Devlin cracked a smile and slowly began to raise his pistol in the direction of the U.S. Customs Agent who arrested him for smuggling during Prohibition. As soon as he did so, Joe Coppola, Al Parker, Jim Beauregard and a uniformed police sergeant who responded to the scene opened fire and finished the gunman off.

Back on the sidewalk in front of Murray's Fordham Road office, a crowd of on
lookers was being held back by three uniformed patrolman who responded to
the sound of shots being fired. While Pat Murphy Sr. held Murray's head off
the ground, he tried to sound as supportive as possible when he said, "Hang on,
Murray. The ambulance is on the way."

Not since World War I had Pat Murphy Sr. witnessed such a badly wounded
man cling to life. While Murray coughed up blood and had trouble breathing, he
did his best to speak and said, "You OK?"

"I'm fine thanks to you," responded Captain Murphy.

Even though he was barely alive, Murray whispered, "Not sure, but Connely
could be in an old hideout downtown or in his first apartment." These were the
last words that Murray Silverman spoke before he passed out.

Once Murray was taken to the hospital and placed under heavy guard, the decision was made to use the release of information about the attempt on Murray's life
to suit the needs of the fugitive investigation. The fact that Murray was in critical
condition and wasn't expected to live, made it possible for the police to speculate
about what happened without having to outright lie to the press. It also helped
that the War Department was able to sensor what was published and disseminated
over the radio when it came to matters that impacted the fugitive investigation.

Under the circumstances, the death of Colin Devlin was a big relief for his brother-
in-law. After all, had Colin lived he might have been convinced to cooperate with
the police. Mickey Flynn was twice as happy when the police were quoted as saying
that Devlin was a disgruntled former client, who was believed to be upset that
his attorney didn't do a better job of keeping him out of federal prison. Mickey
Flynn was also elated to read that Murray Silverman was in critical condition with
multiple life threatening gunshot wounds.

Once Mickey read the latest edition of the evening newspaper, he felt as if he and
his family members had nothing to be concerned about, especially when another
article described how the Army CID Task Force was focusing all of its efforts on
screening troops who were heading overseas. After relaying a message to his Uncle
Mike, Mickey Flynn went back to running a pair of Irish bars in New York City, while
his brother Eddie focused his attention on managing The Westside Taxi Company.

By the time he finished his second cup of morning coffee, Jim Beauregard received a call from FBI Supervisor Dan Phillips who reported that Colin Devlin was employed as a dispatcher at the Weehawken Taxi Company and his wife was listed as the owner. As soon as Jim finished talking to Dan Phillips, he relayed the news to the members of the CID Task Force who were meeting in the conference room.

Once Joe Coppola finished briefing Jim Beauregard, Fred Richmond, Captain Murphy and Captain Reynolds about Colin Devlin's rum smuggling and illegal liquor distribution activities, Jack Donovan added that Murray Silverman was the attorney who represented Devlin and another Midtown Taxi Company hack driver during their Prohibition era arrests. The fact that Devlin was Mickey Flynn's brother in law, also explained a great deal about the relationship between the different subjects of the current investigation.

Joe Coppola also let everyone know that when Devlin was convicted and went to federal prison, his wife was working for her brother at The Shamrock Bar. Agent Coppola also found it interesting that according to the FBI, Mrs. Devlin opened the Weehawken Taxi Company the month her husband was released from federal prison in September of 1942. After pausing for a split second, Joe continued and said, "Even though we can't prove it, Jack and I believe that Colin Devlin took a fall for Mike Connely and the Flynn brothers and got paid off for keeping his mouth shut about their involvement in smuggling and illegal liquor distribution activities during Prohibition. How else did a guy right outta federal prison end up with enough dough to have his wife who worked as a waitress buy a hack outfit in Jersey."

"We should definitely interview Mrs. Devlin once we're ready to move on the Flynn brothers," said Jim who went on to say, "She probably won't say much but it never hurts to ask."

Pat Murphy Sr. was the next to speak and said, "The fact that the black Suburban was registered in New Jersey also explains why an army of New York City Policemen were never able to locate this vehicle."

As soon as Jim picked up one of the 8x10 black and white photographs that Richy Olsen took of Devlin's Suburban, he looked at the others and remarked, "Al was right when he said whoever tried to bang out the dent in this fender did a lousy job."

"Who knows, maybe Ivan Larson also switched license plates when he used the Suburban to pickup black market merchandise from Andy Gooding," said Captain

Reynolds, who went on to say, "Or Andy Gooding forgot that the Suburban was registered in New Jersey when he observed Larson using this vehicle."

Once again Joe Coppola expressed his opinion with conviction. "Either way, the odds that Ivan Larson used a different black 1937 Suburban with a dented left rear fender to deliver black market merchandise from Andy Gooding's garage to the Flynn brothers and Murray Silverman are at least a million to one."

Fred Richmond agreed and quickly added, "Locating this vehicle makes it a lot harder for the Flynn brothers to refute the statements that Andy Gooding made about his dealings with Ivan Larson and John Johann Miller."

After checking his watch, Jim stood up and said, "I better get back to the port. I'll see you guys later."

"We better go too, Joe. We have more mail to check," remarked Post Office Inspector Jack Donovan as he and Joe Coppola stood up in preparation of leaving.

After hearing Pat Murphy Sr. say, "Good hunting," the three men who were on their way back into the field waved as they left the office.

While Murray Silverman was still in a coma under heavy guard, the specially selected men from Captain Reynolds new command, along with the detectives assigned to the Miller homicide and the members of the CID Task Force were able to devote more manpower to their surveillance operation. This phase of the investigation included having Captain Reynolds most trusted men use funds provided by the FBI to patronize the bars and restaurants on Mueller's list. Simply put, these men became the extra eyes and ears of the investigation.

Unfortunately, even with the extra help, the men performing surveillance duty were unable to locate Mike Connely. After following the Flynn brothers for several weeks, Johnny Mc Donald decided to expand the search by following other members of the Flynn family, as well as some of their employees. When this tactic failed to achieve results, Johnny met with Jim Beauregard and Captain Murphy to discuss other ways to locate Mike Connely without raising suspicion.

Thanks to Captain Murphy, a hand picked member of the New York City Police Department's Hack Bureau was assigned to assist Johnny Mc Donald to monitor the activities of the cab drivers from The Westside Taxi Company. This was done because during Prohibition, Mike Connely used his cab drivers to deliver smuggled rum and Canadian Whiskey to speakeasies in the city. No one knew this more than the men in the CID Task Force who pursued Mike Connely and other gangsters and smugglers during Prohibition.

Since Eddie Flynn reportedly used his fleet of taxi cabs to deliver black market meat for John Johann Miller, the men from the CID Task Force had no choice but to start following hack drivers from The Westside Taxi Company to see if they were assisting Mike Connely in some way. Unfortunately, doing so was another time consuming endeavor.

Even with two additional U.S. Post Office Inspectors providing assistance, it also proved to be a labor intensive task to screen the mail that was being delivered to the businesses and subjects of this investigation. This was the case because the homes and businesses of Mueller's customers, including locations under the control of the Flynn brothers, periodically received mail from family members, friends and former employees who were serving in different branches of the service. Once this was done, every personnel file, for every serviceman who was identified by Jack Donovan and his team, had to be checked to see if their official photograph matched the description of the two fugitives.

After another long day of screening duty and surveillance work, Jim Beauregard and Captain Murphy sat in the back room of Mc Donald's Bar to discuss the case. While the Captain sipped his whiskey laced coffee, Jim wasted no time in expressing his frustrations about the fugitive investigation. "I thought for sure that screening the mail would produce better results by now."

Captain Murphy agreed then added, "Just because it hasn't produced the desired results doesn't mean that screening the mail was a bad idea. Unless things change, checking the mail could prove to be the only way for us to determine if Larson and Mc Ghee are corresponding with any of their old friends while using their new identities. After all, they certainly didn't go through the induction process using their real names."

Under the circumstances, Jim knew that their options were limited. They either worked this case by being as discrete as possible, or they went on the offensive and confronted every subject they had under investigation. Unfortunately, everyone working this case knew that there was no guarantee that taking a more direct approach would automatically insure the desired results. If that was true, the men participating in this investigation could have saved themselves a great deal of work by handling this case differently from the beginning.

After taking a sip of pre war Irish Whiskey from Mr. Mc Donald's private stock, Jim continued while he removed a cigarette from the pack that was on the table. "Unfortunately, like Johnny Mc Donald likes to say, the good news is we intercepted mail from a number of servicemen who needed to get checked out. The bad news is it takes time to do so."

Once again Captain Murphy agreed, "You're right and that's the price we have to pay for being thorough."

After pausing to use his Zippo to light a cigarette, Jim leaned closer to the table and said. "Andy's been in DC for weeks checking personnel files to see if any of the servicemen that Jack Donovan and his crew identify while screening the mail look like our fugitives. Every time the poor guy makes plans to come home, Jack Donovan calls and gives him another name to check out."

Once again the mild mannered Captain Murphy spoke up and said, "We're certainly covering all the bases."

"I just wish I knew where this was going," remarked Jim before he continued and said, "I'm also worried about the men. They're working day and night and have to be ordered to go home and take a few hours off."

As soon as Captain Murphy agreed, Jim took another drag on his cigarette then said, "I'm also worried about you, Pat. You're the first in the office in the morning and the last to leave. You need a break as much as the rest of us."

After taking another sip of his whiskey laced coffee, Captain Murphy volunteered to work on a schedule that would give the men more time off. The Captain then looked at the tired Army Officer and said, "As far as the way you're feeling is concerned, allow a fellow policeman who is also your friend to give you some advice. Maybe it's time to take a different approach and maybe it's not. Either way, know that you're a good cop who has excellent instincts. Trust those instincts and do what your gut tells you to do."

As soon as Pat Murphy Sr. finished speaking, Jim opened up and said, "I can't explain it, Pat, but something tells me we're close to getting a break in this case. I also know that if we start pulling people in for questioning and they clam up, we'll be put out'a business as far as these leads are concerned."

After pausing to take a drag on his Lucky Strike, Jim continued and said, "I know New York City is a big place but we have to find Mike Connely."

It's settled then," remarked Captain Murphy who quickly added, "We keep doing what we do best. I suggest we take it day by day and week by week. If we don't like the way things are going we can always switch gears. In the meantime, I'll get you that schedule. You and I can also take turns covering both operations so we can take a break as well."

While Jim tapped the ash from his cigarette into the closest ashtray, he looked directly at the police captain who was still coping with the loss of his youngest son and said, "Thanks, Pat. We couldn't do this without you."

While Dan Phillips stood by the gangway of the Liberty Ship that was getting ready to set sail, he handed Willie an envelope and said, "Our Uncle Sam wanted me to give you this before you left."

The moment Willie opened the envelop and he saw that it was filled with U.S. currency, he looked at the senior FBI Agent and said, "This isn't necessary, Dan. You know me. I didn't do it for the money. It was my pleasure to help you get those guys."

"You deserve it, Willie. Consider it a retirement gift from the Bureau for services rendered," responded Dan as he handed a second envelope to his favorite informant. "Here's your travel orders. Sorry I couldn't get you a ride back to Italy on a plane. At least you don't have to work on this trip."

When a young Merchant Marine Officer walked over and said, "We're ready to go, Mister Phillips," Dan smiled and extended his hand in friendship to the old man. "Good luck, Willie. Keep in touch."

While Willie Gunderson shook hands with his favorite FBI Agent, he remarked, "You know where to find me if you need me, Dan."

As soon as Willie started to walk away, he glanced back and called out, "And don't forget to let me know if you find those fugitives."

"You'll be one of the first to know," responded Dan.

After watching Willie board the ship, Dan faced the young Merchant Marine Officer and said, "Do me a favor and take good care of my friend. He served our country in more ways than you can imagine."

After nodding his head, the recently commissioned Merchant Marine Officer responded and said, "Don't worry, Sir, we'll take good care of Chief Gunderson," before he turned and walked up the gangway just as the mooring lines that connected the ship to the dock were cast off.

When Johnny Mc Donald returned to the CID Office from surveillance duty, he headed straight for the conference room where Captain Murphy set up shop. "As soon as Johnny entered the, he called out, "I have good news, Captain. Murray's awake and is asking for you."

The moment Captain Murphy looked up from the pile of case files that were spread out all over the table, he called out, "Thank God," as he stood up and asked, "Whose with him?"

While Johnny stood by the open door to the conference room he responded and said, "Kevin Kalb just relieved Steve Klein. We also have two patrolman on him as well. Even though they're supposed to be off duty for the rest of the night, Al and Frank headed up to the Lincoln Hospital once we heard that Murray was back from the dead."

After removing his hat and coat from the coat rack, Captain Murphy looked at Johnny and said, "I miss my son, Johnny. I still can't believe he's gone. One thing is certain, working this case is helping each and every one of us who knew and loved my son Patrick to get through this ordeal."

"I'll drink to that, Captain," said Johnny Mc Donald as he left the Army CID Office with the police captain who lost his youngest son during a bank robbery in 1943.

As soon as they arrived at the hospital, Al Parker told Captain Murphy and Johnny Mc Donald that Kevin Kalb and Frank Angelone took Murray's wife and her two sons who were back from overseas to get something to eat. When Al continued he relayed a message from one of the doctors, "The doctor wanted me to tell you, Captain, that Murray's speech is gonna be a bit slurred and not to stay too long."

"Thanks, Al," responded Captain Murphy who quickly added, "I want you boys to come in with me and be prepared to take notes while I talk to Murray."

"We're right behind you, Captain," remarked Johnny Mc Donald as he and Al removed notebooks and pens from suit jacket pockets as they followed Captain Murphy into the patient's room.

After sustaining multiple gunshot wounds at fairly close range, it was a miracle that Murray Silverman was still alive. As serious as the gunshot wounds to his abdomen and lungs were, the .45 caliber bullet that put a nasty gash in Murray's head proved to be considerably more life threatening. This was the case because this type of head wound caused tremendous swelling and made the patient go in and out of consciousness for almost a month. Murray also sustained a few less serious wounds that added to the overall trauma that his body endured, when he was shot several times at close range.

As Captain Murphy leaned closer to Murray, he spoke in a soft tone of voice and said, "How you doing, Murray?"

"How long have I been out?" responded the heavily bandaged patient who had one eye completely covered.

"You've been in an out of it for almost a month," responded Pat Murphy Sr.

As weak as he was, Murray was anxious to talk to the police captain that he knew ever since he was a uniformed patrolman. While Murray reached out and grabbed Pat Murphy Sr. by the arm, his speech was definitely slurred when he tried to say too much too fast. "Mike Connely instructed me to transfer ownership of the property where The Westside Taxi Company is located to Eddie Flynn and give the building where The New Dublin Bar is located to his cousin Mickey Flynn. If you ask me he's buying their loyalty so they'll help Larson and Mc Ghee. He also put the licenses under their names a long time ago to conceal the fact that Mike Connely was the real owner."

While the Captain patted the patient's good arm, he did his best to calm him down, "Easy, Murray, slow down. Take your time."

After asking Al to pour some water in a glass, Captain Murphy gave Murray a drink to quench his thirst before he continued. Even after all he went through, Murray showed that he still had a sense of humor when he whispered, "What, no gin?

While both men cracked smiles, a nurse entered the room to check on her patient. "I'm sorry, Captain, but your special visiting hours are over."

"Two minutes?" asked Captain Murphy.

"OK, Captain, two minutes," responded the nurse as she left the room.

Since their time was short, Murray spoke up and said, "Your men told me you haven't found Connely."

"Unfortunately, you were having a bad night when you were trying to tell me where you thought he might be," responded Captain Murphy.

Once again Murray did his best to relay information to Par Murphy Sr. "The location isn't in the case file that I gave you because that property can't be put up for sale until after he dies."

When Murray flinched after feeling a lightening bolt of searing pain shoot though his body, he grit his teeth for a second before he continued and said, "First floor apartment in the back, can't be seen from street, corner building 46th Street 9th Avenue. Connely instructed me not to sell this property for a few months. His mother lived there, so did Mike when he came home from the last war. Supposed to be vacant. I smelled cigar smoke when I entered the building to spend time with Sylvia in the top floor apartment. Talk to Sylvia, she'll remember. Also, check my old files for a warehouse on Pearl Street that Connely bought during the depression. It's an old hideout of his. If he still owns it, he might be there as well. He had another warehouse in the city that he wanted me to sell after he died but he never told me where it was."

Pat Murphy Sr. had been around enough hospitals in his career to know when a patient was unable to engage in anything close to a meaningful conversation. After seeing Murray in pain, Captain Murphy turned and said, "Get the doctor, Al."

As soon as Al returned with the doctor and the nurse, the doctor sounded like a man who knew his business when he said, "Don't worry, Captain. Being in pain means you're alive. If your friend made it this long, he'll make it the rest of the way." The doctor then addressed his patient as he administered an injection. "Isn't that right, Mr. Silverman?"

CHAPTER 39

EVERY DAMN DAY

By the time Lieutenant Colonel Mike Kirby returned from maneuvers outside of Orleans, France he could barely walk. As disturbed as he was that one of his glider engineering officers committed suicide, he knew that some men could only take so much before they cracked under the strain of being in combat or away from home for an extended period of time.

Despite outward appearances it was now quite obvious that Lt. Steve Perkins had some very serious psychological problems that made him snap when he received bad news from home. Although he kept his opinion to himself, Lt. Colonel Kirby believed that any man who would kill himself over a woman, especially when he was stationed in a place like France, had to be pretty screwed up.

At any other time Lt. Colonel Kirby would be cursing the day he met Gus O'Malley. After hearing reports that O'Malley was taking the death of Lt. Perkins very hard, Mike Kirby didn't have the heart to give his second best glider engineering officer a hard time because his ankle was never the same after the crash landing in Texas.

Despite his bad ankle Lt. Colonel Kirby refused to slack off and take it easy. Even though he was a hard ass by reputation, Mike Kirby loved his men and their mission. As a result, he drilled his men harder than any other glider unit in the theater. Because he led from the front, he was bound to pay a heavy price and suffer with a terminal bad ankle.

Like most gung ho types Mike Kirby avoided sick call and refused to see the flight surgeon for fear of getting grounded. Unlike other commanders who allowed themselves to be lulled into a false sense of security, Lt. Colonel Kirby refused to believe that the Germans were a war weary beaten adversary. While others were planning their return to civilian life, Mike Kirby was training his glider pilots for another crack at the enemy.

Today's exercise involved a trip to the firing range, followed by a lecture from an airborne officer and a mock battle to protect a fixed position from being overrun by the enemy. The good news was his men did well. Unfortunately, Mike Kirby twisted his ankle again when he ran across an open field, while observing a group of glider pilots repel a counter attack by a mock enemy force.

If anyone knew the importance of cross training glider pilots to be good combat soldiers it was Mike Kirby. While other pilots only saw the enemy up close when they got shot down, glider pilots were forced by the nature of their unique duties to land near or behind enemy lines and fight on the ground, if necessary, as airborne infantry, until it was safe to make their way to a collection point for evacuation to a rear area. This was done to limit their exposure to encounters with the enemy and make it possible to have every surviving glider pilot available to participate in future glider missions.

Ever since the D Day landings at Normandy, Allied glider pilots were receiving more and more training to prepare them to survive behind enemy lines. This training came in handy during the Allied Invasion of Holland, also known as Operation Market Garden in September of 1944, when British and American glider pilots distinguished themselves in some of the fiercest ground fighting by airborne troops of the war.

For good reason, the events of Operation Market Garden served to further motivate Mike Kirby to prepare his men for the Invasion of Germany. Mike Kirby pushed his glider pilots hard because he knew that every shot fired on the rifle range and every mock battle that was fought would save lives in combat. This was especially true for the men in his command who were untested in battle.

As painful as his injury was, Lt. Colonel Mike Kirby felt better knowing that he was doing everything possible to prepare his men for combat glider operations. After returning to the base, Flight Officer Clyde C. Nelson pulled up in front of his Commanding Officer's quarters and spoke as he down shifted the transmission in the Colonel's Jeep and came to a stop. "Excuse me for saying this, Sir, but that ankle of yours isn't getting any better by you running around on it all the time."

If any man in his unit could talk to Mike Kirby in this fashion, it was the glider pilot known as CC. Besides being decorated with the Purple Heart, an Air Medal and the Silver Star, C.C. Nelson had the honor of being Mike Kirby's first student back in the early days of the glider program.

No matter how many men he trained, Mike Kirby was always very impressed by the Wyoming rancher turned glider pilot who proved himself in action during the Invasion of Normandy on June 6, 1944, as well as during the Invasion of Holland.

In fact, during Operation Market Garden, Flight Officer C.C. Nelson was one of the famous 300 brave glider pilots who participated in ground combat operations, while supporting the 101ˢᵗ Airborne Division's 505ᵗʰ Parachute Infantry Regiment outside of the hamlet of Mook along the tree line of the Reicshwald Forest.[12]

As Major Kirby gently lifted his swollen ankle back into the jeep, he grimaced in pain as he turned to Flight Officer Nelson and said, "OK, C.C. You win. Run me over to the flight surgeon."

Before Captain Billy Davis took off to deliver a load of ammunition and rations to the RAF controlled base in Brussels, he stopped by the base hospital to visit Lt. Colonel Mike Kirby. Mike Kirby was proving to be a terrible patient when the attractive nurse removed the thermometer from his mouth in the presence of his smiling friend and he said, "Would you mind telling me, Lieutenant why you take my damn temperature every damn day, when there isn't a damn thing wrong with me except my damn ankle is badly swollen?"

While Nurse Wallace rolled her eyes and ignored the Colonel's comments, BillyDavis spoke up and said, "Is he like this every day?"

Since she had plenty of work to do the petite blonde from Waco, Texas checked the grumpy senior officer's pulse and made a quick notation on his chart, before she brushed past Billy Davis on her way out the door and remarked, "Every damn day."

The minute Lt. Wallace left the private room Mike Kirby grinned and said, "Feisty, isn't she?"

The moment Billy Davis nodded his head in agreement, he remembered something important and remarked, "I almost forgot," as he removed a half a dozen Hershey bars from his leather flight jacket and placed them on the small table that was positioned next to the Colonel's bed.

After giving up cigars, Mike Kirby developed a viscous sweet tooth that made him crave anything with chocolate in it, especially Hershey Bars. The mere sight of a handful of America's favorite chocolate bars was enough to make the Colonel's mouth water as he remarked, "Thanks for the sweets, Billy."

While Killer Kirby removed enough of the wrapper to expose the first section of chocolate, Billy Davis looked at the Colonel's swollen ankle and made a face when he spotted what had to be a very painful injury and asked, "I'm afraid to ask but how's the ankle?"

While reacting as if he was annoyed at the mere mention of his bad ankle, Mike Kirby stopped what he was doing, looked up at his visitor and said, "It hurts like hell." As Billy Davis ignored the Colonel's grumpy disposition, he zipped up his flight jacket as he said, "I better get going."

When Lt. Colonel Kirby asked his favorite C47 pilot what he was hauling, Billy Davis slipped a piece of chewing gum into his mouth before he responded and said, "Rations and ammo but I have to stop at the 439th on the way back to drop off some spare parts that we have plenty of, that they need."

Whether he was flying a mission or commanding a contingent of glider pilots, Mike Kirby had a great deal of respect for the troop carrier pilots who delivered paratroopers, gliders and supplies to forward areas often under very hazardous conditions. Rather than hold his friend up any longer, Mike Kirby pointed his right index finger at his favorite C47 pilot when he spoke in a friendly fashion and said, "Watch your ass and that's an order."

As soon as Billy tossed the Colonel a friendly salute and he headed for the door, Mike Kirby called out and said, "By the way, if you see Gus O'Malley over at the 439th you can tell him for me that every time I take a step and it hurts, I think of him."

After reacting as if he was surprised to hear that his buddy Gus was stationed on another air base in France, Billy Davis remarked, "The 439th?" Billy then paused for a split second and added, "Don't tell me you transferred Gus just because you're crazy enough to run around on a bad ankle that you originally busted when you were fighting on Sicily?"

While Major Kirby adjusted his position in bed, he responded to Billy's last remark in a down to earth tone of voice. "Even though there are times when I'd like to get rid of that pain in my ass I can't. He's too damn good at what he does. Besides, now that Lt. Perkins is gone, Gus O'Malley is the best glider engineering officer in the whole damn group, but don't tell him I said that. I don't want him getting a swelled shaved head."

Since Captain Davis and Mike Kirby were good friends Billy felt comfortable asking, "Then why send him to the 439th? You might never get him back once Colonel Gately gets a look at his work."

"I'm getting to that," said Mike Kirby who paused long enough to slip another piece of chocolate into his mouth before he continued. "I had no choice. Gately has an inspection coming up and half of his engineering staff is sick as a dog. I sent O'Malley to the 439th to give Colonel Gately's engineering section a hand. I sweetened the deal by agreeing to send Danny Gannon to the 439th to keep O'Malley company and give Gately an extra pilot to cover for some of his men who are on leave. They'll both be back after the New Year."

Then, after pausing long enough to slip another piece of chocolate into his mouth, the Colonel remarked, "By the way, you don't think I'm helping Gately outta the goodness of my heart do you? He's donating two cases of champagne, a case of French wine and a bottle of scotch to our Christmas Party. He's only renting O'Malley, he's not buying him. The same goes for Danny Gannon."

As Billy Davis grinned, he opened the door just as an orderly arrived pushing a juice cart into the room. Having a quick witted sense of humor, the Captain pointed to the patient and said, "Make him a double and put it on my tab."

Because he was used to the antics of the well known Billy Davis, the orderly smiled as he delivered the cart to the Colonel's side and said, "One double coming up, Captain."

Even though he was pressed for time, Billy Davis couldn't resist and stretched his neck as he watched the orderly pour a glass of orange juice as he remarked in a joking tone of voice. "Why that's orange juice. What kind of a bar is this?"

As Mike Kirby accepted the glass of juice and yelled, "Get outta here before I call the MPs," Billy Davis tossed the Colonel another friendly salute as he left the room and headed to the flight line.

In addition to confirming what Murray said about the aroma of cigar smoke in the West 46 Street apartment building, Sylvia Krause located the file that referred to the first piece of property that Mike Connely purchased during the depression. Just like Murray said, the warehouse was located on Pearl Street in Manhattan. After thanking Sylvia for all of her help, Pat left the office that was still being guarded by a uniformed patrolman from the 46 Precinct.

As soon as he returned to the CID Office, Captain Murphy met with Fred Richmond and Jim Beauregard to go over what they knew so far. After grabbing a cup of coffee, Pat sat with the two Army officers and began to discuss the case at hand. "After checking Mike Connely's arrest record, I had Frank Aneglone and the two detectives working Miller's homicide visit the address that he used at the time. Needless to say, he wasn't there. I also have men sitting on the warehouse on Pearl Street but so far no one has been seen entering or leaving the building."

When Pat asked how the other surveillance was going, Jim Beauregard finished lighting a Lucky Strike before he responded and said, "According to Johnny Mc Donald, someone is definitely in the first floor apartment that faces the alley behind the building on West 46th Street."

After taking a sip from his coffee mug, Captain Murphy continued and said, "Between the signed statements from our various witnesses and the other evidence that we've gathered to date, we have more than enough to get a stack of search warrants when we're ready to make our next move. If all goes well, we'll find Mike Connely, the money that the Flynn brothers intend to give to the two fugitives and some evidence that can help us locate Larson and Mc Ghee."

When newspaper and radio reports announced that Murray Silverman was conscious and talking to the police, Mickey Flynn had a decision to make. In addition to being responsible to get his uncle's money to Ivan and Shorty, Mickey Flynn was also asked to act as Mike Connely's conduit with his sister Clara.

According to his instructions, if for any reason the day ever came when Mike needed to stop corresponding with Ivan and Shorty, Mickey Flynn was asked to relay a simple coded message to his aunt. It was necessary to go through his Aunt Clara, because Mike Connely decided not to tell Mickey or Eddie Flynn where he intended to hideout until he died.

As per his uncle's instructions, Mickey Flynn used a pay phone to call his aunt's house. The second the old lady answered the phone, Mickey used the prearranged signal and asked to speak to Mad Mike. As soon as the old lady said, "There's no Mad Mike here," she hung up the phone.

Just as Clara was instructed to do if she ever received this call, she destroyed the two letters that Mike just sent to her to forward to Danny Gannon and Gus O'Malley. After burning the letters and flushing the ashes down the toilet, Clara went shopping in Jersey City. While doing so, she stopped at a pay phone and called Mike. As the only person who was able to get in touch with her brother, Clara knew that Mike recently moved from the warehouse on Pearl Street to his old apartment on West 46 Street.

Even though she hated being the bearer of bad news, Clara made the call because Mike needed to know what was going on. As soon as Mike answered the phone, Clara said, "Someone just called for Mad Mike but I told them you weren't here."

After hearing what his sister had to say, Mike knew that no more mail would be sent to Ivan and Shorty. When Mike asked his sister if everything else was OK, the old lady remarked, "Everything's fine, you have nothing to worry about."

As someone who learned how to speak in code when her late husband worked with Mike during Prohibition, Clara Connely Mac Carthy knew that she just told Mike that any correspondence that she still had in her possession was destroyed. Even if the police or the feds showed up to ask her any questions, all she had to do was act like a forgetful old lady.

Since Clara recently read two letters from the Ivan and Shorty to Mike over the phone, she had no reason to believe that any mail from Europe was in route to Jersey City. Now that she destroyed Mike's letters, Clara knew that Ivan and Shorty would stop writing to their Uncle Mike when no mail was received on their end. The only other correspondence that could possibly come to their "home address," was a telegram from the War Department that reported that one or both of the boys was injured, killed, missing in action or taken prisoner by the enemy.

As a result of the new leads that were developed, Lt. Colonel Fred Richmond was able to convince CID Headquarters and the War Department to authorize the release of the next CID Manhunt Report radio show over the Armed Forces Radio Network. This episode featured Al Parker giving a riveting performance, as he described the robbery of the Lincoln Savings Bank and the subsequent arrest of Amos Washington. This episode included statements by Major James Beauregard, FBI Agent Andy Dubrowsky and Captain Patrick Murphy Sr., the father of the slain policeman.

As soon as Johnny Mc Donald determined that someone was in the first floor apartment on West 46th Street and 9th Avenue, the decision was made to have members of the CID Task Force, along with two detectives from Captain Reynolds precinct, observe Mike Connely's apartment building on a 24 hour basis. While this surveillance operation was being conducted, U.S. Customs Agent Joe Coppola and Post Office Inspector Jack Donovan began screening every piece of mail that went into and out of Connely's apartment building before it was delivered. In order to cover all of the bases, a smaller team from the Chief of Detectives Office remained on the Pearl Street location as well.

Now that Murray Silverman was on the mend and it was possible to spend more time debriefing him, Captain Murphy was interested if Mike Connely had any other relatives who might be helping him in any way. While Murray had no idea if she was still alive, he knew that Mike Connely had an older sister who lived in New Jersey. Murray was aware of Clara Connely Mac Carthy because her late husband worked for her brother Mike for many years.

Once Murray told Captain Murphy as much as he knew about Clara Connely Mac Carthy and her late husband, FBI Supervisor Dan Phillips was asked to locate this woman in New Jersey. By close of business that day, teams of FBI Agents had the old ladies house under round the clock surveillance. In addition, a U.S. Post Office Inspector was assigned to screen the mail going into and out of Clara Connely Mac Carthy's home in Jersey City.

Due to the volume of mail from military personnel that was handled by the local post office, the elderly postman who delivered mail to Clara Mac Carthy's residence wasn't able to remember much in the way of details. While being questioned by a Post Office Inspector and an FBI Agent, the only information that the mailman could remember, was that the old lady occasionally received mail from two different soldiers, from army bases and air bases in the United States, as well as from England and more recently from France. The mail carrier also reported that when he asked Mrs. Mac Carthy how her relatives in the service were doing, the old lady said that her nephews were alive and well.

CHAPTER 40

PEACHES

When Ivan Larson wasn't flying a CG-4A Waco glider he volunteered to serve as a co pilot on a C47 to satisfy his love for flying and because all pilots needed to log in a minimum of four hours a month in order to qualify for flight pay. Another reason had to do with the fact that the last glider mission was flown in September of 1944. With no winter offensive planned, U.S. Army glider pilots had nothing to do except train, go on leave, perform administrative duties and fly in other aircraft while they waited for the next glider mission.

When the U.S. Army Air Forces was not mounting major airborne operations all available troop carrier aircraft were used to transport cargo to the forward areas and fly wounded, sick and injured troops to hospitals in rear areas. While making these deliveries, C47s flew into every kind of strip imaginable, including controlled and uncontrolled fields.

Just like other red blooded American males in uniform, Ivan Larson aka Danny Gannon had vibrating trousers and was always interested in women. So far, all of his liaisons since joining the service were with prostitutes and very loose women who enjoyed a night out with a generous American G.I. More recently, his attentions were focused on a cute little brunette from Georgia who he affectionately called Peaches.

From the moment they met Ivan felt like he was on a roller coaster ride in Coney Island. Just seeing her was enough to put his stomach in knots. Even though he was a murderer and a thief, Ivan found himself speechless the first time they met. Lt. Gloria Rutherford would also later admit that it was love at first sight.

Due to the locations where they were currently stationed, the best way for Ivan to share any time with the nurse he called Peaches, was when he served as a co pilot on board a C47 that delivered supplies to her aid station and transported injured, sick and wounded troops to a rear area hospital. After eagerly volunteering to fly another run to forward areas, Ivan boarded the C47 that was piloted by Lt. James Donnelli.

As soon as Ivan landed the C47 in a tree lined open field, he smiled wide as he caught the love of his life waving to him from the side of a Dodge ambulance that was loaded with two litter cases. Even though things along the front were unusually quiet, there were still a few instances when U.S. Army troops came in contact with the enemy. Soldiers also got injured and became sick just like civilians did, especially when they lived in fox holes, tents, man made bunkers and abandoned buildings.

Once the C47 came to a stop, Lt. Donnelli could tell by the look on his co pilot's face that Flight Officer Danny Gannon was biting at the bit to get off the plane and into his girlfriend's arms. As Lt. Donnelli motioned to the back of the aircraft with his right thumb, the Pilot in Command smiled and said, "Go ahead, Danny, I'll shut her down."

The second he received the green light to leave the co pilot's seat, Ivan grinned from ear to ear and remarked, "Thanks, Jimmy," as he left the cockpit and made a bee line for the large door located in the cargo bay of the aircraft.

The moment Ivan jumped out of the open cargo door she was in his arms. Even the two injured G.I.s propped themselves up on their stretchers and began howling and whistling at the sight of two people in love displaying their affections for each other in a forward area. After realizing that they were making a scene, the young couple walked off to the side and took cover behind an empty ambulance.

While Ivan smiled and gently brushed her hair, Gloria looked into his eyes and spoke with a slight southern accent and said. "I must look terrible." "You look great," remarked Ivan as he pulled her closer and kissed her tenderly on the lips.

Halfway through another passionate kiss the sound of a man clearing his throat brought the couple to pull apart. "I'm sorry to break this up kids, but there's a war on," remarked the Captain in charge of the aid station.

As the couple stood at a relaxed attention, Ivan saluted the surgeon and said, "Sorry, Sir." When the medical officer asked what Ivan and his crew brought along on this trip besides gasoline and medical supplies, Ivan Larson aka Danny Gannon removed the musette bag that he carried over his shoulder and handed it to the Army doctor as he remarked, "Just a little something to make this place bearable, Sir."

As soon as the Army doctor opened the shoulder bag and removed a bottle of Johnny Walker Scotch, he nodded his head in approval before he started to walk away and said, "Carry on you two."

While the medical officer in charge of the field hospital returned to a nearby tent, he had no idea that Flight Officer Danny Gannon was anything other than a red blooded American serving his country with distinction. So far, Ivan and Shorty managed to elude the New York City Police, the FBI, Army CID and the MPs for over a year. In the process of doing so, the fugitive who was now known as Flight Officer Danny Gannon managed to fall in love, while he served in the European Theater as a U.S. Army aviator.

Lt. Gloria Rutherford had all of two minutes to spend with the love of her life, while the crew chief and the radio operator unloaded cans of fuel and supplies from the cargo plane. As soon as they were finished, the two injured soldiers were carefully placed onboard the C47. With their mission complete it was time to leave. In order to drag out their time together, Ivan helped Gloria climb into the C47 so she could check on her patients one last time before they were transported to a rear area hospital.

When Lt. Donnelli looked into the cargo bay and called out, "We're ready to go, Danny," Ivan responded and said, "OK, Jimmy." Once Ivan and his girlfriend walked up to the cockpit, Gloria gave Jimmy Donnelli a hug and a kiss on the side of his face.

As the C47 pilot looked up and said, "Take care, doll," Ivan removed the musette bag that was hanging on the side of the co pilot's seat. While Ivan handed the shoulder bag to Gloria, he hated to leave her in such a dismal place but the choice wasn't his to make. After telling her that he put a few extra things in the bag for the rest of the staff, Ivan gently grabbed Gloria's right hand and said, "You better go."

After giving Ivan a goodbye kiss, Gloria turned and entered the cargo bay where she said goodbye to the crew and its passengers before being helped out of the aircraft by the crew chief. While Ivan sat in the co pilot's seat and prepared to perform his duties, Lt. Donnelli stuck his head out the pilot's side window and yelled, "Clear." By the time the starboard engine came to life, Gloria was standing by an ambulance admiring the contents of the shoulder bag that contained two cans of condensed milk, several packs of Camel cigarettes, a bottle of French cognac and a bottle of French perfume. A few seconds later the port engine was started.

As soon as he received the thumbs up signal from the crew chief, Ivan turned to Jimmy and said, "We're ready to go." As soon as Lt. Donnelli applied the right amount of power, the C47 slowly moved away from the aid station in preparation of taking off. While Ivan performed his duties as a co pilot with perfection, he turned to Jimmy Donnelli and spoke in a slightly raised voice and said, "I hate leaving her in a place like this."

Even though he was just as worried about the nurses and the other medical personnel who were stationed fairly close to the front line, Lt. Donnelli did his best to reassure his co pilot that he had no reason to be concerned about his girlfriend. "Relax, rumor has it the war will be over soon. The Krauts are finished. One big push and they'll surrender. Even the guys in intelligence are saying the Germans are down to drafting old men and boys."

While it was true that with the exception of a few minor incidents every sector along the eighty mile front was dead quiet, something told Ivan Larson that the German Army had no intentions of capitulating. Ivan felt this way because the Nazi high command had committed too many atrocities to voluntarily surrender when they still had the means to wage war on the Allies. Even if they wanted to surrender, the world had gone through too much hell to let the Nazis off the hook with a political slap on the wrist. Ivan also suspected that once the war was over, the world would learn even more about the atrocities that were committed by the SS and the Gestapo. As a result, Ivan believed that the war would go on until the Germans were beaten into submission or wiped off the face of the earth. The same applied to the fanatical Japanese.

As Lt. Donnelli pointed out the pilot's side window and said, "You better say goodbye while you can," Ivan leaned to his left to get a look at Gloria smiling and jumping up and down while she held the bottle of perfume in her outstretched hand. After cracking a smile, Ivan waved one last time before he sat back and read the check list out loud, while the aircraft commander went through a quick run up procedure and prepared for take off on the unimproved field. Once the crew chief checked on their two injured passengers, he made his way to the cockpit just as Ivan and Lt. Donnelli applied full power to the controls.

As the C47 picked up speed Ivan took one last look at the only woman he ever truly loved. Even in those instances when girls were attracted to him because of his gangster image, no one back home ever made a mark on his heart like Gloria Rutherford did.

In many ways Ivan Larson was living the dream of his alter ego; the dashing Army pilot who goes off to war and meets the woman of his dreams in a mud soaked field hospital, falls in love and lives happily ever after. While Ivan Larson the gangster would only bed down whores and girls of questionable reputation, Flight Officer Danny Gannon was in love with an Army nurse from a wealthy southern family.

As soon as Lt. Donnelli rotated the twin engine transport plane into the air, Ivan called out, "Gear up," as he repeated the command and retracted the landing gear. Once the cargo plane leveled off and headed back to France, Ivan wondered what the Germans were doing just a few miles away on their side of the line.

Under the circumstances it felt good to think like a soldier instead of a man on the run. When Ivan concocted his escape plan he had no idea that he would actually like the person that he would become in his secret life as a soldier. As a result, the thought of intentionally giving it all up by going AWOL or becoming a Prisoner of War was something that did not sit right with him. In fact, the day Ivan flew the Holland mission he decided that he would never go AWOL, unless doing so was the only way to avoid being arrested. Unfortunately, it was proving to be a lot harder to live life as a fugitive than Ivan ever expected.

Even a tough kid like Ivan Larson felt his stomach churn, when he heard the voice of the colored cop who came close to capturing him during the bank robbery, being interviewed on an Armed Forces Radio program. Shorty Mc Ghee was even more perplexed when he listened to the radio program that provided a detailed description of their criminal activities, as well as the efforts that were being made to capture them. Their situation was made worse when Army CID publicized the fact that several witnesses, including Patrolman Al Parker and Sister O'Rourke were inspecting Army bases with CID Agents and MPs in an effort to locate the two fugitives.

As Ivan stared out the co pilot's side window, he thought about the day he put a cocked .45 caliber pistol in the hand of Lt. Perkins, while the Glider Engineering Officer sat slumped over in a drunken stupor and he fired one shot into the side of the young man's head. Ivan then remembered the crowd of soldiers who showed up to see who fired the shot that disturbed their otherwise quiet leave in Orleans, France and how he and Shorty told everyone present that Lt. Perkins was distraught after receiving a Dear John letter. While Ivan continued to take a stroll down memory lane, he recalled how everyone who responded to the scene, including two MPs shook their heads in amazement when they accepted what Ivan and Shorty had to say about the Lieutenant's unfortunate death.

Ivan was also very proud of Shorty Mc Ghee for the way he performed when he was interviewed by the military police. If there was ever a time when it paid for Shorty Mc Ghee to act like a nervous wreck, it was when he provided a statement to U.S. Army officials, after experiencing the sudden loss of a close friend and a fellow glider engineering officer.

While Lt. Donnelli flew the C47 back to base, Ivan wondered what his life would be like if he joined the Army before he killed Tommy Mulray, Tony Giordino and Patrolman Pat Murphy Jr. Despite the thickness of the psychological armor that protected him from real and perceived threats, Ivan Larson was a human being who was susceptible to becoming paranoid. Deep down inside Ivan was also just as concerned about being captured by the police as Shorty was. Fortunately, Ivan was more confident than he was worried.

As far as Ivan was concerned, it didn't matter whether they escaped detection because it was too difficult for the police, the FBI and CID to find them in such a massively large organization like the U.S. Army, or because they were just plain lucky. Unfortunately, being a fugitive was like living on a seesaw ride in a park. One minute you were up and the next you were down.

While the good news was that Ivan and Shorty had eluded the police since the winter of 1943, the bad news was that the authorities were still hunting them with a vengeance. This meant that Ivan and Shorty lived a life of extremes, where they enjoyed their freedom until they were reminded by a radio program, a newsreel, a newspaper article or by the display of a wanted poster, that they were still being pursued by a group of law enforcement officers who were determined to take them into custody.

Just like the German Army, Ivan Larson and his partner in crime had no intentions of surrendering. As a result, their plan was the same in 1944 as it was in 1943; to survive the war and live as free men in Europe. In order to accomplish this, Ivan and Shorty had to remain one step ahead of the authorities and be prepared to make a run for it at a moments notice.

Needless to say, there was no room in Ivan's escape plan for a law abiding U.S. Army nurse. In fact, Ivan knew that he was fooling himself to believe that he had a future with a young woman like Gloria Rutherford. After all, a well bred southern girl who came from a prominent family would never have a murderer and a thief for a husband no matter how much she might love him. Even if Ivan never confided in her about his past, there was also little or no chance that Gloria would remain in Europe and never return home when the war was over. So, for various reasons, Ivan knew it wasn't fair to lead Gloria on, any more than it was smart to tell her the truth and hope for the best.

After wrestling with an array of thoughts, Ivan was glad for the chance to fly when he heard Jimmy Donnelli ask, "You want'a take it for a while?"

"Sure," responded Ivan as he gently took the controls and said, "I got it." As Lt. Donnelli let go of the controls, he noticed that Ivan seemed to be in a very pensive mood as he flew the C47 called "Full House" on a straight and level course back to base. After offering his co pilot a Camel cigarette and a light, Lt. Donnelli spoke up and said, "Are you all right?"

As soon as Ivan took a long drag on his cigarette, he looked at the aircraft commander who was not that much older than he was and said, "You know, Jimmy, whenever I get airborne I don't have a care in the world."

Lt. Jimmy Donnelli knew exactly what Flight Officer Danny Gannon meant. As the C47 pilot from Oregon who flew combat missions during the Normandy Invasion, as well as in Operation Market Garden, sat back in the pilot's seat he nodded his head in agreement and said, "I know what you mean. Life only sucks on the ground."

While Ivan glanced back into the cargo bay, he felt good about being in a position to transport two injured soldiers to a rear area hospital. What Ivan had no way of knowing at the time, was that he and the other members of Lt. Donnelli's C47 crew just saved two men from certain death.

CHAPTER 41

ANOTHER RAID

While Jim Beauregard addressed the men who would take part in the raid the different locations that were associated with Mike Connely, he looked around the squad room and said, "I think we all agree, if Mike Connely was corresponding with Ivan Larson and or Shorty Mc Ghee under assumed names, he started doing so once they were inducted into the Army. If this is true, this explains why we've never been able to find two soldiers who look like our fugitives and never receive mail, because they have no family members to write to them."

After pausing long enough to light a cigarette, Jim remained standing while he continued and said, "As you all know, according to Murray Silverman, Mike Connely is dying and is spending his last days in one of two locations. Location number one is the first floor rear apartment in the building on the corner of West 46th Street and 9th Avenue. While some of us have been sitting on this apartment house, Jack Donovan and Joe Coppola have been screening every piece of mail that goes into and out of this building. We've also been checking the trash from this building. In addition, we have men sitting on the warehouse that Mike Connely still owns on Pearl Street. This location is important because according to Mr. Silverman, Mike Connely used this location as a hideout in the past."

As soon as Jim took a drag on his cigarette, he went on to say, "From the moment we started watching the West 46st location, we confirmed that someone is living in the first floor apartment that faces the alley. We also confirmed that a Mrs. Mc Namara and her twenty one year old son live on the second floor and are the only other permanent occupants of this building. The apartment on the top floor was periodically used by Murray Silverman. As far as mail is concerned, not much seems to be going into or out of this location. We certainly haven't found any mail coming from or going to any military personnel. The same goes for his sister Clara's house in Jersey City. In addition, we know that there hasn't been a mail delivery at Mike Connely's warehouse on Pearl Street for some time."

Once again Jim paused to take a drag on his cigarette. He continued after he tapped the ash from his Lucky Strike in a nearby ashtray. "Now that we know how close Mike Connely is with Ivan Larson and that he made arrangements to get a sizable amount of money to Larson and Mc Ghee once the war is over, we secured search warrants for the apartment building on West 46th Street, his warehouse on Pearl Street, The Westside Taxi Company, The New Dublin Bar, The Shamrock Bar, Mike Connely's sister's house in Jersey City, as well as the apartments where the Flynn brothers live. In order to cover all the bases, we will also be searching The Weehawken Taxi Company, as well as the home of the late Colin Devlin."

After pausing for a split second, Jim looked around the room before he added, "We'll be assisted in this series of raids by a dozen FBI Agents from the New York and Newark Field Offices, two New Jersey State Police Detectives, a dozen New York City Police Detectives and three additional Post Office Inspectors." Once again Jim paused before he added, "I'm sure you'll all agree. We need a break in this case and we need it now."

"Then it's settled," remarked Andy Dubrowsky, "We'll raid every location simultaneously and hope we get lucky."

As soon as Jim agreed with Andy, he stamped his cigarette out in a nearby ashtray and asked Al Parker, Frank Angelone, Johnny Mc Donald and the two detectives handling the Miller homicide to standby to go with him to raid the apartment on West 46th Street.

Once again, Frank Angelone lightened everyone's spirits, when he removed a leather bound blackjack from his back pocket and he slapped the open palm of his left hand as he remarked, "Major, you just made my day."

Jim then told the men in his raiding party that they would leave as soon as he asked Captain Reynolds to provide some local backup.

Once the assignments were handed out, Andy Dubrowsky was placed in charge of the raid on the Pearl Street location. Joe Coppola led the team that included Eddie Evans on the raid of The New Dublin Bar, Jack Donnovan was asked to handle The Shamrock Bar, Richy Olsen led the team that would hit Mickey Flynn's apartment, Steve Klein had the team assigned to Eddie Flynn's apartment and Sal Jacobi was asked to coordinate the raid on The Westside Taxi Company. While Lt. Don Lorenz from CID was on his way to Jersey City to represent the Army Task Force when the warrant was served on Clara Mac Carthy's residence, Lt. Scott from

Naval Intelligence was assigned to accompany the New Jersey based FBI Agents during the search of The Weehawken Taxi Company and the Devlin residence..

As soon as Jim and the members of his raiding party arrived on the corner of West 46th Street and 9th Avenue, the men who worked all night to watch the apartment house were relieved, while Captain Steve Reynolds had a sergeant and three uniformed patrolmen cover the front and rear exits. Once the perimeter was secured, Captain Reynolds entered the building with the raiding party.

Because this case involved the murder of one of their own patrolman, Jim decided to have detectives from the New York City Police Department go in first. With Al Parker, Jim Beauregard, Captain Reynolds and the two homicide detectives providing backup, Frank Angelone and Johnny Mc Donald prepared to lead the way. Once Al Parker kicked the door open, Frank Angelone and Johnny Mc Donald identified themselves as they entered the apartment with guns drawn. After quickly clearing one room after another, Frank Angelone and Johnny Mc Donald, followed by the rest of the raiding party, headed for the back bedroom.

Normally, Mike destroyed the mail that he received from Danny Gannon and Gus O'Malley the day it was received. He did so to insure that he never had any trace of their existence in his possession for any length of time. Now that Mike knew that his days were numbered, he allowed himself the luxury of holding onto one of Ivan's letters and a photo of Ivan dressed for war. This particular photograph was special, because it showed Ivan standing next to the aircraft that he flew during the Holland mission; a glider that had the name Mad Mike written on its fuselage in white chalk. Clearly, one of the hardest things that Mike Connely ever did was destroy this particular letter and this particular photograph. In addition to destroying Ivan's letter and his photograph before the raiding party arrived, Mike also destroyed his personal telephone directory and a few other scraps of paper.

All along Mike knew that it was only a question of time before the police stumbled onto him as a way to get to "his" boy. After doing everything humanly possible to help Ivan and Shorty make their escape and avoid detection, Mike Connely felt as if his purpose in life was now complete.

With his cancer ridden body barely keeping him alive, Mike Connely decided to die in a shootout with the police, rather than endure a grueling interrogation and confinement in a prison hospital. As Mike sat up in bed, he picked up the Colt pistol that he kept nearby and prepared to open fire. The moment the raiding party got within a few feet of the back bedroom, Mike Connely raised his Colt Model 1908 Pistol and fired three shots in rapid succession into the hallway that led to his bedroom.

Rather than expose the other members of the raiding party to danger, Detective Angelone held out his left hand and blocked the entrance to the doorway, as the small but deadly .380 caliber bullets struck the wall where he was standing. In an effort to prevent the old gangster from firing another volley of shots in their direction, Frank stepped into the back bedroom and fired four rounds from his Colt Official Police Model revolver into Mike Connely's chest.

As Mike Connely fell back in bed barely alive, he had enough fight left in him to raise his Colt pistol one more time in preparation of firing. The second the pistol discharged and destroyed a nearby lamp, Detective Angelone fired two more shots from his service revolver, just as Johnny Mc Donald entered the room and opened fire as well. After being hit eight times at fairly close range, the last bit of life was drained from Ivan Larson's mentor.

As the other members of the raiding party filed into the room, Detective Mc Donald inspected the destroyed lamp where his partner was standing and said, "Jesus, Mary and Joseph. That was a close one, Frankie."

After Detective Angelone thanked his partner for backing him up, he looked at Mike Connely's lifeless body and said, "He's not gonna tell us anything now."

While speaking with a soft Irish brogue, Detective Mc Donald remarked, "Remember, Frankie, they didn't call him Mad Mike Connely for nothing."

As unfortunate as it was that Mike Connely was dead, Jim Beauregard knew that Frank Angelone and Johnny Mc Donald had to defend themselves, while also protecting the other members of the raiding party. After using his handkerchief to pick the partially loaded 380 caliber pistol, Jim turned to the others and said, "Let's do what we came here to do."

While acting as if there was no dead body present, the raiding party began to methodically search the apartment. After leaning over Mike Connely's body, Captain Reynolds put his handkerchief around the Irish Shillelagh that was in the bed next to the deceased.

When Captain Reynolds handed the walking stick to Detective Teddy Henderson he said, "Captain Murphy has a hunch that Mike Connely might'a been the one who killed Johann Miller. If he did, he might'a used this Shillelagh to bash in the back of his head. I doubt the lab boys can find anything of interest on this walking stick after all this time but have it checked out anyway."

Immediately after Teddy Henderson acknowledged the order, Captain Reynolds addressed the two homicide detectives again and said, "Why don't you boys take the living room and the kitchen, while we take the rest." This time Detective Matthew Duffy responded and said, "You got it, Captain," before he left to search the rest of the apartment with his partner.

Even though he felt no remorse for doing his job, Detective Angelone stood over the dead body of one of the most notorious retired gangsters in New York City and second guessed himself. As soon as Detective Angelone remarked that maybe he should have backed off instead of returning fire, the others looked at each other just as Frank came to the conclusion that he played right into the old man's hands. After carefully putting the handkerchief wrapped pistol on safe, Jim Beauregard walked over to Frank Angelone and said, "We got this, Ange. Why don't you get some air."

Even when Captain Reynolds walked up behind Detective Angelone and remarked, "It's not your fault, Ange. He didn't give you and Johnny much choice."

While Frank seemed to be in a trace as he continued to look at Connely's body, Jim Beauregard turned to Al Parker and said, "Hey, Al, why don't you take Ange across the street to the deli and grab some coffee."

Without hesitating, Al stopped searching a dresser drawer and said, "Sure thing, Major." While Al escorted Frank Angelone out of the apartment, he gently patted the colorful Italian American police detective on the back and said, "How 'bout a little coffee sport, Ange?"

While the two city cops stood inside the corner delicatessen and sipped hot coffee that was laced with Irish whiskey, Al turned to Frank Angelone and said, "Hey Ange, why don't we talk to that old lady on the second floor to see what she has to say about Mike Connely?"

After saying, "Good idea," Frank continued as he pointed across the street, "We should also check the trash before it gets picked up."

As a hard charging detective who was no stranger to dropping the hammer in the line of duty, Frank Angelone recovered quickly from the way things went down inside Mike Connely's apartment. After enjoying a cup of Irish Whiskey laced coffee, Frank Angelone sounded as if he was ready to get back to work when he said, "That coffee hit the spot, Al. I'm ready when you are."

As soon as they walked across the street, Detective Angelone removed the tops of a few garbage cans and remarked, "There's not much in here." After quickly going through the trash, Frank remarked, "I don't see anything we can use."

After checking the contents of another garbage can, Al agreed with Frank and said, "Once we interview the old lady and her son on the second floor, we can check the basement, especially the incinerator."

"The incinerator! How could I forget?" remarked a reinvigorated Frank Angelone who quickly added, "Come on, Al," as he vaulted up the steps to the entrance of the apartment house. As soon as Frank entered the vestibule, he asked the uniformed police sergeant to let Major Beauregard and Captain Reynolds know that he and Patrolman Parker would handle canvassing the rest of the building, including the basement.

When Jim Beauregard heard that Al Parker and Frank Angelone were checking the rest of the building, Jim thanked Captain Reynolds and his men for their help. With a precinct to run, Captain Reynolds wished Jim and his men good luck, before he directed a patrolman to remain with the body, while he returned to the station house with the rest of his men.

After calling downstairs into the basement, Jim Beauregard let Al Parker and Frank Angelone know that they were heading over to the warehouse on Pearl Street. As soon as Jim heard Frank call out that they would meet back at the office, he left the building with Johnny Mc Donald and the two homicide detectives.

The moment Al Parker and Frank Angelone returned to the office with a shoe box in hand, Major Beauregard left his corner office just as Al called out, "We got something, Major." By the time Al placed the shoe box on his desk, Johnny Mc Donald, Andy Dubrowsky and Jim Beauregard were heading his way.

As soon as Al removed the lid from the shoe box, Frank Angelone remarked, "Easy does it, Al," before he addressed the other members of the CID Task Force who were huddled around Al's desk. "After we checked the garbage cans and came up empty, Al suggested that we canvass the rest of the building, including the incinerator."

While Al used the larger blade on his bone handled pocket knife to carefully retrieve small shreds of partially burned paper, Frank Angelone continued to brief the others. "When we spoke to the old lady on the second floor, she told us that as sick as he was, old man Connely insisted on burning some of his trash in the incinerator in the basement. Even when she offered to have her son take care of this chore for him, Connely refused and said that he could handle it. According to Mrs. Mc Namara, Mike Connely returned from the basement early this morning just as the old lady was bringing him his breakfast."

After pausing for a split second, Frank sounded excited when he continued describing what happened next. "Once we made a bee line for the basement, we began to carefully sift through mounds of ash looking for any evidence that might further our investigation. After several minutes of searching, me and Al removed a number of pieces of paper that were partially burned but still legible." Then, after pausing for a split second, Frank cracked a devilish grin then said, "Wait 'till you see what we fond."

As Al Parker and Frank Angelone placed each shred of evidence down on the front cover of a case file, it looked as if they were assembling the hand written pieces of a puzzle. While Frank used the tip of his pocket knife to arranged the pieces in order, Al Parker continued to use his bone handled pocket knife to carefully retrieve another piece of partially burned paper from the shoebox. Once the small shreds of paper were laid out on the top of Al's desk, Johnny Mc Donald, Andy Dubrowsky and Jim Beauregard began to make out different words and partial sentences.

As soon as Al removed the last sliver of partially burned paper from the box, he looked up at Jim Beauregard and said, "That's it, Major."

While Jim stood over Al's right shoulder and Detective Angelone leaned over his left, the Major admired the excellent piece of police work and said, "Outstanding work, men, outstanding."

After hearing Frank Angelone remark, "Check it out, Major," Jim continued to lean over Al's shoulder, while he read the remains of a handwritten letter that contained ten whole and partially legible words out loud. "flew Hollan sion air ase Fran wi Shor. fav nephew.

Just as Jim Beauregard stood up straight and said, "We'll get these guys yet," Colonel Richmond entered the squad room and walked over to join the men who were huddled around Al Parker's desk. As soon as Jim spotted the Colonel walking his way, he spoke up and said, "We have some good news, Sir. Al Parker and Frank Angelone found the remains of a hand written letter in the basement incinerator of Mike Connely's apartment. According to the words that are legible, Ivan Larson is an Army aviator of some kind who flew an aircraft during the Holland mission and is stationed with Shorty Mc Ghee on an air base in France. Ivan Larson also identifies himself in this fragment of a letter as Mike Connely's favorite nephew. This piece of information alone could prove very worthwhile, because it establishes a piece of the fictional cover story that Larson is using to prevent other soldiers from identifying him as an orphan. In fact, for all we know Shorty Mc Ghee might be part of the same cover story."

While facing the men under his command, Colonel Richmond addressed the group and said, "Unless we come up with some reason to believe that someone like the Flynn brothers or their Aunt Clara was corresponding with our fugitives, Mike Connely might have been the only person sending letters and packages to Larson and Mc Ghee. If that's the case our fugitives will not be receiving any more mail now that Mad Mike is no longer with us. That means the subjects of our investigation should be easier to single out during mail call."

As Colonel Richmond packed his pipe with a fresh bowl of tobacco, he looked at the faces of the men under his command and said, "As I see it we have an important decision to make. So far we managed to keep the story about Mike Connely being shot and killed while resisting arrest in the local papers. We now have to decide if we should publish information about his demise and how Mad Mike Connely was affiliated with the two fugitives when we release details of this incident to Army personnel."

After pausing to light his pipe, Colonel Richmond turned to Major Beauregard and said, "Let me know what you and your men decide, Jim, and I'll back you all the way." The Colonel then congratulated Al Parker and Frank Angelone for a job well done before he remarked, "Carry on, men," and he returned to his office.

As Jim looked at the partially charred remains of the recovered letter that were laid out on Al's desk, he asked Frank Angelone and Al Parker to secure the evidence and get a photographer to take photos. The Major then looked at his watch and said, "All we have to do now is wait to hear from the other raiding parties."

The morale of the men from the CID Task Force received another giant boost when Joe Coppola and Eddie Evans returned to the office after searching The New Dublin Bar with a leather satchel like the type that doctors carried. Inside this bag was $31,275 dollars in cold hard cash.

As soon as Jim Beauregard filled Joe in on the demise of Mike Connely, the U.S. Customs Agent emptied the contents of the leather satchel on his desk and explained how he and Eddie Evans located the bag full of cash. "Just like Murray said, we found this bag inside the office safe in The New Dublin Bar. It was locked but not hard to open. When Mickey Flynn tried to tell us that we had no right to take his uncle's property, we told him to have his uncle come down to the CID Office, so we could talk to him about what he planned to do with his money. That was before we knew that Mike Connely was dead."

When Jim asked Eddie if he came up with anything interesting, the retired detective who was serving with the OPA Enforcement Division responded as he pointed to the stack of business records that he seized from Mickey Flynn. If there's nothing in here that we can use, we might want to turn these records over to the IRS." During the search of The Shamrock Bar, Jack Donovan found another set of business records that would be used by the OPA and the IRS to investigate Mickey Flynn.

Even though no incriminating evidence was found during the search of Clara Connely Mac Carthy's home, Lt. Don Lorenz and FBI Supervisor Dan Phillips located two neighbors who remembered seeing her brother and two young men staying in her house back in 1943. When Mike Connely's sister was questioned about the identity of these young men, she claimed that they were nice boys who worked for her brother and were on leave from the Army. She also claimed that her brother used her address to receive mail when he took business trips. She also claimed that she never opened or read his mail and didn't remember the names of the two young men who stayed with her for a brief period of time."

Mickey Flynn couldn't believe his eyes when The New Dublin Bar was raided twice in the same day. The second Captain Steve Reynolds pointed at one of the bartenders and yelled, "Pull the plug on that or go to jail," the crowded bar went dead silent the moment the music stopped.

While being backed up by Captain Pat Murphy Sr., two uniformed patrolman, a uniformed sergeant and every member of the Army CID Task Force, Captain Reynolds continued and said, "By order of the State Liquor Authority this bar is closed pursuant to Chapter 478 of the Alcoholic Beverage Control Law. The license for The Shamrock Bar has also be suspended."

As the customers began to leave the bar, Mickey Flynn reacted like a man who had sheer contempt for the police when he faced the raiding party and screamed, "I hope you're real proud of yourselves for killing an old man who was trying to enjoy whatever time he had left on this earth."

Pat Murphy Sr. was waiting for Mickey Flynn to say something stupid. The moment he did so, Captain Murphy ignored the fact that people were still walking by to leave the bar when he remarked, "For your information you hot headed Mic, your Uncle Mike decided to go down fighting and opened fire on the officers who were executing a search warrant on his apartment."

Once again Mickey Flynn became defensive and twice as nasty when he said, "I have a right to know why my liquor licenses are being suspended?"

Pat Murphy Sr. was never more composed in his life when he paused to light a cigar before he looked at Mickey Flynn and said, "You can thank Andy Gooding, Amos Washington, the late John Johann Miller, Rudy Mueller and your former attorney Murray Silverman for enabling us to convince the State Liquor Authority to suspend both of your licenses, licenses that you obtained in an effort to conceal the true identity of the real owner who happens to be a well known gangster and a convicted felon. The State Liquor Authority also took a very dim view of your involvement in black market activities. They were especially unhappy to hear that you purchased large quantities of black market beef for this joint and your other gin mill."

After taking a few quick puffs on his cigar, Captain Murphy went on to say, "The good news is, you'll be given the opportunity to challenge both suspensions at a formal hearing. The bad news is, my colleagues and I have been assured that whatever you say will fall on deaf ears and the two liquor licenses that were issued in your name will be revoked."

While Pat Murphy Sr. twirled the freshly lit cigar in his mouth, he looked at Jim Beauregard to signal the Major from Army CID to take a verbal crack at Mickey Flynn. As soon as Jim identified himself, he addressed Mickey Flynn is a dead serious tone of voice. "My men and I came here tonight to tell you to your face that you're finished, done, outta business." While Jim continued, he pointed to Eddie Evans and said, "In addition to making sure that you never own a bar again, our friend Mr. Evans from the Office of Price Administration will be taking you and your brother over the coals for violating rationing regulations in time of war. An IRS Agent will also be paying you and your brother a visit."

Once Jim said what he had to say, Captain Murphy waited until the last employee left the bar before he stepped closer to Mickey Flynn and said, "Don't think for one minute that we don't know what really happened, as far as the attempt that was made on Murray Silverman's life. As Agent Coppola so eloquently put it, Colin Devlin never had an original thought in his life. As a result, we find impossible to believe that after being outta federal prison for over two years, your idiot for a brother-in-law decided to kill his former attorney, on the same day that Murray Silverman refused to represent you and your brother, because he wanted no part of your plan to help Ivan Larson and Shorty Mc Ghee."

Once again Mickey Flynn proved that he was a first class prick when he looked directly at Pat Murphy Sr. and said, "Are you finished, Captain?"

After jabbing his right index finger in Mickey Flynn's chest, Captain Murphy remarked, "Get outta here before I throw you out."

As pissed off as he was, Mickey Flynn knew that if he didn't move fast enough, he would be removed from the premises the hard way. With no other options at his disposal, Mickey Flynn left The New Dublin Bar without his hat and coat. He would never return.

Now that Mickey Flynn and all of his customers and employees were gone, Captain Murphy removed a money clip from his pocket and tossed some cash on the bar as he called out, "Secure that door, Al. I'm buying the first round. After that the drinks are on Mike Connely and the Flynn brothers!"

As soon as Johnny Mc Donald and Captain Murphy walked behind the bar, they poured a drink for everyone present, including Captain Reynolds and his contingent of uniformed cops. Once everyone had a drink in hand, Captain Murphy proposed a toast.

"To police work. It's what we do best."

In December of 1944 the U.S. Army Air Forces or AAF was a massive organization that had a large number of air bases in the European Theater of Operation. Even though they now had a lead that allowed them to focus their search on air bases in France, the men of the New York CID Task Force had to plan their moves very carefully. If they failed to do so, they risked having the two fugitives go AWOL before they could be apprehended.

As a result of the new leads that were developed in this case, CID Headquarters authorized Jim Beauregard and his men to record another broadcast of the CID Radio Show. CID Headquarters also authorized the CID Office in Paris to begin assisting the New York CID Task Force by following leads in this case. To begin this process a copy of the case file was sent to the CID Office in Paris, France. CID Headquarters also notified the CID Office in Paris that Major James Beauregard would be traveling to France to coordinate the search for the two fugitives with CID personnel stationed in the ETO.

CHAPTER 42

THE BATTLE OF THE BULGE BEGINS

O n the morning of December 16, 1944 at exactly O530 hours a massive barrage of German artillery shells began falling on positions held by the U.S. 28th, 99th and 106th Infantry Divisions, the 14th Armored Cavalry Regiment, the 609th and 705th Tank Destroyer Battalions, the 969th and the 333rd Field Artillery. The American troops caught in this barrage included front line fighting troops as well as support personnel. After this bombardment, the forward elements of a 200,000 man German Army advanced and engaged some 80,000 plus American troops who were protecting a sparsely defended front line that ran for 85 miles from north to south.[13]

All along the front-line several American units displayed tremendous courage as they held their positions under the strain of repeated attacks by the enemy. While many American soldiers stood their ground and put up one hell of a fight, others retreated, were killed, wounded or taken prisoner. In fact, it was due to the effective way that some American soldiers fought, that prevented German units from achieving some of the critical objectives of their offensive.

In December of 1944 the U.S. Army Ground Forces in Europe realized that there was a serious shortage of trigger pullers available to counter the German offensive. The shortage of trained infantrymen caused the American Army to ask for volunteers and utilize support personnel as combat troops. The situation was so dire that the decision was also made to allow Negro troops to volunteer and to serve on the front line in infantry units that were previously comprised of all white troops. Even though many of the men who were rushed to the front were not properly trained as infantrymen, the bulk of the men who were pressed into service from rear area and support units performed as expected.[14]

This included asking walking wounded who could carry a rifle to move into position to hold the line at all cost. When more riflemen were needed to repel the German advance, cooks and anti aircraft gunners were converted into infantrymen.[15] This was also done on a more limited basis earlier in the war after the

Normandy Invasion, when regular soldiers were converted into tank drivers and sent into combat with minimal on the job training.[16]

When the smoke from the opening salvo cleared, the American generals committed their only reserve, the 82nd and 101st Airborne Divisions, to the fight. Despite the fact that the 82nd and the 101st Airborne Divisions were in need of rest, refitting and replacements, these divisions would have to hold the line as best as possible until reinforcements could arrive.

One problem that plagued the U.S. Army Ground Forces involved the number of casualties that were sustained from injuries, combat wounds, accidents, friendly fire, sickness and battle fatigue. Some U.S. Army Divisions were so badly decimated after the Normandy Invasion, they sustained massive casualties to include killed and wounded.[17]

Just as perplexing was the fact that up until the winter of 1944, the Americans seemed to have everything that was necessary to wage war and plenty of it, except in the Ardennes. Between a shortage of riflemen in the infantry, especially men with combat experience, the American lines in the Ardennes were thinly defended islands of resistance, manned in many cases by men who recently arrived in the ETO. The under strength 101st Airborne Division actually went into combat with a shortage of ammunition and other equipment.[18] Other American units had so much ammunition that some of it had to be destroyed to prevent it from falling into German hands when the Americans were forced to pull back.

CHAPTER 43

FIGHTING A WAR AND FIGHTING CRIME

U nder normal circumstances CID Agents and MPs stationed in Europe would initiate an immediate search of air bases for Army Air Forces personnel who looked anything like the composite sketch of Ivan Larson and Francis Shorty Mc Ghee. Unfortunately, once the German offensive began on December 16, 1944, U.S. Army CID Agents and military policemen in the ETO were working overtime to protect general officers and perform other critical duties as required. These duties included, directing traffic, protecting the routes taken by truck convoys, manning checkpoints and rounding up troops who were needed for front line service.

As a result of the impact that the German Offensive was having on U.S. Army Military Police and CID units, Lt Colonel Fred Richmond requested that CID Headquarters authorize Major James Beauregard to travel to air bases in France with FBI Special Agent Andy Dubrowsky, Detective Johnny Mc Donald, Detective Frank Angelone and Patrolman Al Parker from the New York City Police Department to spearhead the search for the two fugitives. Lt. Colonel Richmond stressed the need to include Patrolman Parker in this search team because he was a key witness in this case who could identify the fugitive known as Ivan Larson.

Initially, the Army's position was crystal clear. Civilian law enforcement officers would not be allowed to travel to the ETO to conduct a criminal investigation, especially if additional leads were developed that required investigators to travel anywhere near a forward area. However, if military authorities located and arrested the fugitives in the ETO, FBI Special Agent Andy Dubrowsky would be authorized to travel to England on priority travel orders to assist in the transportation of the prisoners back to New York.

Lt. Colonel Richmond was also informed that under no circumstances would the Army allow a civilian Negro policeman to operate in and around white troops, especially in a forward area where combat operations were taking place.

Unfortunately, even the severity of the crimes that were committed by the two fugitives was not enough to put racial issues aside.

Major Beauregard's argument about civilian war correspondents being allowed to travel with U.S. military personnel, including in forward areas, also fell on deaf ears, despite the fact that Article 4 sub section 4 of the Geneva Convention authorized non military personnel to travel with the armed forces in time of war. In order for a civilian to be accorded the protection of the Geneva Convention as a Prisoner of War, they must be officially authorized to travel with military personnel and they must possess identification that specifies their status as non combatants.

Even though this section of the Geneva Convention could easily be applied to civilian law enforcement personnel, U.S. Army lawyers were concerned that any civilian who was armed while operating in or around a forward area, could find themselves in danger if they were captured by enemy troops. Army lawyers were especially concerned, that armed civilian police officials who were compelled to engage the enemy and were captured would likely be viewed as acting in violation of the Convention. The War Department was also well aware of the fact that certain German soldiers had already committed war crimes and executed Allied troops who should have been granted the protection of the Geneva Convention.

After receiving this legal opinion, the U.S. Army was also not willing to allow "unarmed" civilian police officials to travel overseas, especially to a forward area. The basis for this decision involved the fact that Ivan Larson and Francis Shorty Mc Ghee had access to many of the same weapons that were carried by paratroopers and infantrymen. Even if unarmed civilian law enforcement officers traveled with armed military personnel, the Army would be unable to guarantee their safety, if they were present when it was necessary to challenge and capture an armed fugitive. In addition, the Army was concerned that well intentioned civilian police officials would be tempted to arm themselves while operating under potentially hazardous circumstances.

As much as Jim hated to admit it, the Army lawyers made a valid point. Even Lt. Colonel Richmond knew that any civilian police officer or federal agent who was allowed to travel to the ETO would find a way to arm themselves, if they were "officially" ordered to leave their firearms in New York before they were transported overseas.

After everyone in the unit was informed about the War Department's position, Al Parker approached Lt. Colonel Richmond and Major Beauregard in the presence of Captain Patrick Murphy Sr. and asked to be inducted into the U.S. Army and assigned to CID so he could continue to provide assistance on the fugitive investigation. Under the circumstances Jim was waiting for Al to make this request. The moment he did so, Jim removed a letter from his desk and handed it to Al to read.

This letter, which was signed by Lt. Colonel Richmond and co signed by Major Beauregard, requested that Patrolman Alvin Parker, a decorated World War I veteran, be immediately inducted into the U.S. Army and assigned to CID to work under the command of Major James Beauregard for the duration of the current fugitive investigation.

As soon as Al finished reading the official request, Captain Murphy spoke up and said, "Since I know you won't rest until you help close this case, I asked the Police Commissioner to endorse this request and grant you emergency military leave to assist in the search for the two fugitives, who fraudulently joined the U.S. Army to evade capture. This letter has already been provided to Colonel Richmond and Major Beauregard."

As soon as Al handed the letter back to Major Beauregard, he thanked everyone present for doing everything possible to allow him to remain actively involved in this investigation.

"All we can do now is wait to hear from the Army brass and the War Department." remarked Fred Richmond who went on to say, "But please understand, Al, that this is a bad time for us to be asking the War Department to make such a concession now that the Army is struggling to deal with the German breakthrough in the Ardennes."

Immediately after Major Beauregard placed the official correspondence in his attache case, he looked at Captain Murphy then over to Al Parker and said, "I leave for Washington on the morning train to brief CID Headquarters and the War Department on this case before they send me overseas. During this briefing I intend to present them with this request. As the Colonel and I discussed, if they don't say no on the spot it could take a day or so to receive a response." Then, after pausing for a split second, Jim looked at Al Parker then over to Captain Pat Murphy Sr. and said, "I suggest we start praying because I'm afraid it will take an act of God for us to get what we want."

The end of Book I
To be continued

NOTES

1   New York New York - "America's Gateway to Victory" by E. Rod Redman - *Sea Classics Magazine* - December 2000

2   *V For Victory* by Stan Cohen

3   *V For Victory* by Stan Cohen

4   *V For Victory* by Stan Cohen

5   *G.I. The American Soldier In World War II* by Lee Kennett-Univ. Oklahoma Press

6   *G.I. The American Soldier In World War II* by Lee Kennett

7   *G.I. The American Soldier in World War II* by Lee Kennett

8   *Green Light By: Martin Wolfe & Silent Wings* by Gerard M. Devlin

9   *Green Light By: Martin Wolfe & Silent Wings* by Gerard M. Devlin

10   *G.I.* by Lee Kennett

11   *Silent Wings* by Gerard M. Devlin

12   *Silent Wings* by Gerard M. Devlin

13   *A Time For Trumpets* by Charles B. Mc Donald

14   *Citizen Soldier* by Stephen E. Ambrose and *Strength For The Fight* by Bernard C. Nalty

15   *Citizen Soldier* by Stephen E. Ambrose

16   Lt. Belton Cooper, 3rd Armored Division

17   *Citizen Soldier* by Stephen E. Ambrose

18   *Seven Roads to Hell* by Donald R. Burgett

HIGHLIGHTED REFERENCE SOURCES AND FOOTNOTES

1. Green Light – A Troop Carrier Squadron's War From Normandy to the Rhine by Martin Wolfe

2. Into The Valley – The Untold Story of USAAF Troop Carrier In World War II by Colonel Charles H. Young. (An excellent general reference source.)

3. NYPD A City And Its Police by James Lardner and Thomas Repetto is a well written and easy to read book that gave me an additional insight into the history of the New York City Police Department. This included information about the employment of African American police officers in the early days of the 20th Century. (An excellent general reference source.)

4. Brothers In Arms by Kareem Abdul–Jabbar and Anthony Walton is an excellent book to read if you are interested in the history of the 761st Tank Battalion, an armored unit comprised of African American enlisted personnel, six white officers and thirty African American commissioned officers. Brothers In Arms proved to be an excellent general reference source that described the problems of racism that African American U.S. Army personnel faced during World War II. Despite being subjected to treatment that no white soldier would tolerate or be subjected too, African American troops like the men who served with the 761st Tank Battalion served in numerous combat actions with tremendous distinction. I included the 761st Tank Battalion in The Frontline Fugitives because one of the fictional characters in this series is a "Negro" military policeman assigned to this armored unit.

5. Article 4 sub section 4 of the Geneva Convention states that individuals who are not military personnel can travel with members of the armed forces, providing that their travel is officially authorized and they are issued the appropriate identification that confirms the specific reason why they are operating during a conflict.

6. G.I. The American Soldier In World War II by Lee Kennett. This book is listed in the footnotes and is an excellent reference source about World War II.

7. The Forgotten Heroes-The Heroic Story Of The United States Merchant Marine by Brian Herbert proved to be an excellent general reference source about the Merchant Marine during World War II.

Made in the USA
Middletown, DE
08 November 2022

14395207R00245